Acknowledgments

Original cover design courtesy of Stories to Tell
www.storiestotellbooks.com

Original publication acknowledgements:

"After the Empire", Summer 2008 issue of *The Armchair Aesthete*
"11", Fall 2008 (Vol. 7/34) issue of *Allegory*
"Icon", January 2009 issue of *Midnight Times*
"Creep", Spring 2009 issue of *The Storyteller*
** "Creep", 2010 Pushcart Prize nominee
"Return", Fall 2009 issue of *Lullwater Review*
"Flowers for Colleen", April 2010 issue of *Absent Willow Review*
"Memento", web publication, 2010 issue of *Reed Magazine*
"The Great Hunter", September 2010 issue of *Foliate Oak*
"Apogee", Fall 2010 issue of *Rose & Thorn Journal*
"The City of Never", October 2011 issue of *Aphelion*
** recipient, *Aphelion* Editors' 'Best of 2011'
"Conquest's End", issues 477-481 of *Bewildering Stories*
** recipient, 'Editor's Choice', *Bewildering Stories*, Q2 2012
** recipient, 'Mariner Award', *Bewildering Stories*, Annual Review 2012
"Turn the Wheel", 'Garden Nettles' issue of *Midwest Literary Magazine*, 2012
"Beheld", Summer 2012, *Raphael's Village*

Table of Contents

After the Empire

The soldier sat on the dry turf of a hill to overlook a city. It wasn't any city; it was the city of his youth, the city whose sky he beheld with his first breath. In that time the city had bustled with vibrant life, but it had changed in his long absence. Yes, *changed* was the word he sought as he stared at the now haunted ruins beneath the setting light of a chilly day. The watch fires along the city walls sat unlit and neglected. The gates were left open. The temple chimes, once melodious in the summer evening breeze, sang no more. Crows broke the still silence with their harsh, intermittent squawks, reinforcing the unmistakable odor of death rising from the once crowded streets, where the aromas of a dozen exotic imported spices had drifted from many cooking fires.

The gnawing hollow of his belly mocked those memories. The comrades that had marched with him were gone, spent away like the last days of summer into the cold emptiness of the approaching winter. The storms of change were coming, and he believed they would ride a tide of fury upon the city. He, like so many others, had tempted the wrath of the gods with boasts of immortal glory and enduring empire. Yet, in the beginning, no one was to know the outcome. Oracles blessed the effort, elders failed to counsel a different path, planners and officials expressed every confidence that their efforts would carry the day. All those well-regarded people were gone, silenced, as if their very existence was nothing but a whisper in the wind, a jest of the gods to once again deceive proud men and mock them in their ruin.

He coughed and spat on the ground. Such thoughts were a fool's charade, he told himself. Where was the space for regret, and would it matter? He knew what was following his return to the city. Despite the decrepit sight before him, he knew the worst of his fears was yet to manifest. He knew what was to come and the awful reality of its implication.

He stood with a grunt. He was saddle sore, even though his mount had collapsed and died the day before. His feet ached in his worn boots. His dented armor hung from his half starved body; his dull sword dangled from his belt. A blue cape, so caked with dirt it was almost brown, wrapped his huddled form. He took his water sack from his belt and raised it high to drain the last drops before tossing it aside.

He shuffled down the hill, into the delirious delusion of a dead city.

***

He woke, coughing, and found himself sitting against a pillar along the old parade grounds. Between the looming clouds in the night sky he could discern a few scattered stars, their pale light seeming lost and lonesome in the vast emptiness around him. It seemed another life when he stood there with thousands of others before the king and the decorous arms and armor of the nobles who extolled the city's conviction that right lies with might. It would be swift, came the promise. The people of the outer lands were savages—pathetic, disorganized, and primitively armed. They needed to be conquered, saved from themselves, shown the light of the city and its ways, and the might those ways had bestowed upon the city.

It wouldn't be as the promise foretold. The further they marched and the more tribes they defeated served only to summon ever larger, ever more furious forces. It made him shake his head, remembering that last awful battle, the waves of screaming savages darkening the very horizon to finally silence the nobles and their delirious cries to fight and continue the effort. It was then when he made his escape; turning his horse and driving it without relent until the screams and dreadful clamor were behind him. Even though the horror of the slaughter tingled along his spine as he rode, it wasn't the greater part of what had shattered his will and left him a ghost of a man. It was the bitter memory of his own hand, his own voice, condemning others who had deserted the effort in its early darkening days.

In those moments of flight he would've given anything—anything—to have even one of those fellows by his side; to have anyone at his side. Nevertheless, he didn't see himself as a hypocrite, despite the barren depths of that horrible irony. He still saw himself as a rational, loyal soldier of the city. The effort was lost. As a leader he was trained that it was his responsibility not to waste the resources and men of the city. He was a man of responsibility, and the responsibility, in the end, was to protect the city, above all else. Protect the city. He had called off attacks that he knew would be foolish, and was complimented by his superiors. He had protected his men. He loved his men.

Yet, on that last horrible day, he rode off. He knew his men were dead. He had buried the last of them several days before. He was a leader of none but himself. The effort was lost. Had he really deserted anything by riding off that day? Was there any sense to give up his life on that field of stupid futility?

It wasn't desertion. It was his responsibility, and it was all that remained to him. He was a rational, loyal soldier. The effort was lost, so he would protect the city.

Alone, and with a dull sword. He closed his eyes and rested his head back.

***

He coughed. He rubbed his face, opening his eyes to peer between his fingers.

He whipped out his sword.

The woman before him fell back a step. She put out her hand, the other clutching her shawl against the chill of the night. "Sir—"

"Do you have a horse?" he said, his voice ragged.

She studied him for a moment and looked to either side before speaking. "I think you need water. I have water. Is there anyone with you, any of your men with you?"

He rose to his feet and sheathed his sword. "The water?"

Her eyes swelled on him. "Where are your men?"

He ground his teeth. "Water."

They stared at each other. She stepped away, but kept her eyes on him as she led him off. They walked between several ransacked houses, large ones in the once prestigious area beside the parade grounds, until she slipped into a dark doorway. "This way," she hissed.

He hesitated, his eyes narrowing as he peered into the darkness.

"There's a well. There's a well here, in this lord's house. I'm his servant. I've been watching it, keeping it safe, waiting for his return. He's a leader of many men. Many men," she said, raising a hand in respect.

"And this lord's family?"

She stared at him with a wide gaze. Her lips settled to a small straight line before she gave a quick, short sweep of her hand to the ground. Then she took a step toward him, one that made him lean back, wary of her intrusion. Her eyes darted about. "They were hording," she whispered, as if it was still a secret. "People came. Took them. Ate them." She nodded and pointed to his sword. "It's only me now. I have things. I, I could share things. I could share them with you. I could share many things with you. I, I would give myself to you, if you would just give me a soldier's oath to watch me, just as I have watched this water for you, and for my lord's, return."

He swallowed in horror at her words, calloused as he was after everything he witnessed before returning to the city. The stickiness of his throat only reminded him of his thirst. "The water," he said. "I ask nothing else of you, nor your honor."

"Honor?" She blew out a breath. Her large dark eyes held on him in an unblinking stare. She smiled when he coughed. "Follow," she said and stepped inside.

Desperate, he followed her through the doorway. Once inside his eyes adjusted so that he could make out a comfortable home, one with its own courtyard and well. The soft tinkle of the water was enough to drive all sense from him, his feet hurrying him forward until he plunged his face and hands into the well. He drank deeply before lifting his face to look at her.

"Thank you," he said, forcing out his voice between breaths. She nodded, but he looked away, his gaze roaming the little courtyard. He could almost imagine how it must have been in better days. Under the stark starlight, though, it was nothing more than empty shadows. By one doorway he noted a bow and a quiver of arrows. He looked back to the woman. "You have weapons here?"

"It was the huntsmen's bow. He was killed when the family was taken."

His eyebrows sank as he considered the bitter irony of that fate, but then he coughed and remembered himself. "Can you use the bow?"

Her face went blank. "He was my husband."

He looked down and nodded.

She let her breath go. "There's nothing else here for you."

He turned to her. "I need a horse." Before she could answer, he began coughing again, hunching over with the spasms in his chest.

She cupped her shawl over her mouth. "You have the sickness, the sickness from the plains. I've seen it. I've seen it too many times. The king, his family, they had it, like all the others who staggered back here in the last weeks. They all died. You ... you're—"

He clenched a fist and pounded it on the rim of the well to silence her. He forced himself up and caught his breath. "The horsemasters across the river; do they still have their stables?"

She shook her head. "Nobody goes to the other side of the city."

"Do they have their stables?"

Her eyes widened. "You'll find nothing there but madness. The few who remain there, they ride out, ride out into the rest of the city and feed on those they find."

He shook his head. "So they have horses?"

"They will have you if you go there," she said, but eased when he turned to leave. "Wait, sir, please! The rest of your men, are they coming to help us? You must know it, you must if you came here, that the city is surrounded. The savages are everywhere, preying upon anyone who has tried to work the fields under the city's banner. Ruin without, and madness within, this is all that's left to us. There's no one left to man the walls, no one left to close the gates, to protect our city. The rest of your men—my lord and his men—they are coming, are they not?"

He stared at her, silent to the delusion he saw beneath her questions. Her power of denial, though, he found no less seductive than his own denial in those last days of fighting. Regardless, he tried not to remember that he was still in the embrace of his own delusion, despite his fatalism. He coughed and took a step.

She grabbed his arm. "Wait, please, I beg you! My lord's stable—"

He glared at her, his patience fading. "Where?"

She blinked.

He clenched his teeth. "Where?"

She lifted her hand from his arm, but then grabbed his wrist and led him down a labyrinthine series of walkways. He assumed familiarity guided her as it was so dark he couldn't see her before him. At last she pushed open a door and the heavy odor of hay and excrement assaulted him. When he stepped through the door he stared in disbelief before turning a caustic gaze on her. His temper was at once dispelled, though, as he discerned what hung on the wall behind her—one of the city's blue and white checked banners. He put his hand on her shoulder and gave her a gentle but decided push so that he could gaze at the pristine condition of the banner. He stepped forward and ran his trembling fingers along its length before turning back to her.

"Forgive me," she whispered. "I know he's little more than a sickly pony."

He looked back to the banner. "I'm going to take this. And your pony," he added, glancing at her.

She studied him as he took the banner from the wall, rolling it with care as he went. She faded into the shadow of the doorway. "There are no other men," she said, understanding. "And still you ride?"

He turned to her with the folded banner in his hands. He coughed. "Yes. One last time."

Her gaze bored into him. "Then the cough is not all that has infected you."

His eyes narrowed on her.

***

Astride the little pony, he peered out the city's main gate to the plains and loosed the banner to let it drape along his side. In the still air it hung from the pole he had slid between the straps of his breastplate to secure it to his back. It was still dark, but the first hint of daylight showed in a faint pink line on the most distant hills. It was enough to reveal the rising dust cloud nearing the city. The sight of it made his heart buck. He coughed.

She came up beside him. "Why do this?"

"Protect the city," he said under his breath.

She looked to him. "What city? All that it was is lost. Now we need them," she said, pointing to the dust cloud. "We need them to save us from ourselves."

He held his silence, trying to ignore her. He drew his sword.

"Sir, please, don't do this," she said, craning her neck to catch his eye.

He looked to her. He coughed, grimacing against the increasing tightness of the spasms. Closing his eyes, he caught his breath, and then looked back to the plains. "I was raised in this city," he said, his voice hoarse. "It meant something to me. It's why I chose to be a soldier. What we had, it had never been seen before us. And now that it's gone, where am I to go without it? There's no place left in the world for me, for I will always know that I'm part of something that was lost. But I won't let it go silently. It must not go silently, because if it's forgotten it can never live again and find its rightful way, rather than the folly we brought upon it. So, I will ride. Maybe they'll remember it and wonder why it was I did such a thing. In their curiosity, the city may live again." He coughed, doubling over before he could regain himself. He held that way for several slow, rasping breaths before looking back to her. "I ride for the dream that was," he whispered. "It's all I have."

She stared at him, holding his gaze. "Then you never had anything."

He sat up straight, defiant, and looked down at her. "I shall ride again. You'll see."

He spurred the pony. The little mount sauntered off on the plains.

Clear of the city, a breeze caught him, his gaze rolling to his side to see the banner waver and snap to. Then he gasped, the sword falling from his hand. He looked down to see a bloody arrow tip protruding from his chest. He trembled, but looked over his shoulder to see the huntsman's wife standing beside the city gate, drawing another arrow to her bow.

He closed his eyes.

He grunted at the impact, but felt nothing until the ground seemed to rise up and slap against his side. A ragged, shallow breath teased his lungs. Tendrils of vapor rose from his warm blood where it ran down the two arrowheads poking from his chest.

The sky was gray.

The earth shook beneath him, shook to the thunder of many, many horses. He closed his eyes.

All but a memory now, a whisper in the wind.

The breeze died.

The banner sank in the air until it settled over him.

And there he lay, in the dust, unheeded, as the mounted horde charged past him.

Behold my life: it's not the white walls that imprison me.

He who writes this, he lives in fear. He can feel it when he breathes, he can feel it when he eats, he can even feel it when he sleeps, although the fear hinders any full respite of consciousness. The fear crawls over his skin, presses into his pores; sometimes he thinks it's tingling in his ears, like little unseen insects crawling inside his head to drive him insane. But for all its illusions and delusions, there's one thing that has always remained, and that is the fear.

It's not a shapeless fear, nor an aimless one. Carl knows it must have a name, but he prefers not to know it, because to name it would be to humanize it, and it's human enough. The fear is a man, and this man stalks him, stalks him without relent. For what reason, Carl has no idea, but he accepts it, this embodiment of dread, because the fear is innate.

He felt the presence in his earliest memories. It was there in his neighborhood while he grew up, perhaps around the block, or on the next street. It came to infect his nature. All his life it seemed this human incarnation of his fear was just out of sight, just off to the side, just out of hearing range, but nevertheless always—somehow—*there*. When he was little he'd cringe in bed at night, dreading the next day, wondering when he'd feel the cold tingle up his spine that told him he was being watched. He considered telling his parents about his suspicions. When he considered the questions they would ask, and his empty answers, he knew the inevitable response. What were they to do about someone whose name he didn't know, whose face he couldn't describe, whose only existence was verified by his swearing that he was being followed, stalked, hunted?

Such was Carl's childhood. There was little help for him because in that time such things as he suffered didn't receive serious consideration. Bullying, and being bullied, was part of growing up. Not only was it tolerated, it was considered to build character in its victims. In that climate, how was he to explain his dilemma, or hope to get relief, or understanding? For it wasn't bullying, it was *predation*, something yet to register in the realm of social conscience. Yes, it was predation, because even then Carl deduced one thing with certainty: it was *fear* that *he* thrived on, the fear of the hunted, just as the lion's heart swells before it springs. It was a perpetual moment of suspense, one that could never end.

Nestled in that futile conclusion Carl found what he thought was his salvation, for he realized an ironic truth. If the goal was nothing but the pursuit, then there could be no culmination—it was potential in a vacuum. The fear evaporated. For the first time in his young life Carl felt free. Even his perception of that nameless *him* was shed in a blissful epiphany. It was one wonderful day; one that he thought would change his life. He believed he'd know days without nervous trepidation, nights without nightmares and restless trembling. Or so he thought, but he found he was to be proven wrong, that he'd be taught a bitter lesson and levied with a grotesque punishment.

The horror of it was there when he woke the next morning. He went outside to feed his dog but he heard the shouts from the front yard. The neighbors had found what was left of his dog. Her head had been crushed while she slept. The police came. They looked, but they didn't seem too interested. In the end, it didn't matter, because the message was clear.

Carl was on his own.

He grew up in fear, always suspecting that some night might be his last—that he'd be killed, just like his dog. On the rare occasions that he slept, he often woke trembling with nightmares. He couldn't pay attention in school, so his grades plummeted. His parents lost patience with him, perhaps assuming he was going through some kind of 'phase', because other than meaningless reprimands, they did nothing. What few social associations he had, he lost. His world imploded. He missed all the shiny happy things people get to remember from high school. He hid in his house, in his room, staring at the walls for hours wondering when it would come, when *he* would come after him, because Carl figured that sooner or later the thrill of the predation would lose its hold and *he'd* have to act out once more.

It was intolerable. Carl's parents thought he was listless, lazy, but they had no idea how much energy he burned up in fear and worry. He became emaciated as the fear consumed his body along with his mind. The inevitable breakdown came one summer night after he graduated high school. He raided his father's liquor cabinet, drank himself delirious, stood in the backyard, and screamed out a challenge: if *you* want me, come and do it. Just do it already!

The neighbors shouted for him to quiet down. His father hauled him into the house by the collar, complaining that the police would come to the house on a domestic disturbance complaint. Carl cared little for the embarrassment. "Let them come, then they'll see," he protested in his drunkenness. His father threw him in bed. Maybe it was the alcohol, maybe it was his mental break, but he fell fast asleep.

It was the best sleep he had since the night his dog was killed.

He woke up on the curb among flashing lights and chaos. Firemen scurried about while the neighbors stood around in shock. *He* had heard the challenge, and had once again lashed out with vicious retribution, burning down the house with everyone inside.

Carl's parents were dead. Looking at the faces around that scene on such a dark night, he curled up in a ball because he knew one thing, knew it with a dread that froze his blood in his veins and stilled his heart in his chest.

Somewhere, somewhere in the crowd, he was being by watched by laughing eyes.

***

Carl moved around after that, living off the insurance money while it lasted. It wouldn't have been fair to call him a drifter, even though he appeared to be living as one. He moved often because he had no choice. He was on the run. He had to run, as somehow, some way, *he* always managed to return. Sometimes it took a few weeks, sometimes months, but one thing seemed certain: the more content and settled Carl was in his current situation, the sooner *he* arrived, and with more vengeance. Complacency, it seemed, was the greatest offense. *He* of course came unannounced, but the presence was unmistakable and undeniable. Carl could feel it, could feel that malevolent gaze watching him. Whenever *he* was close, the fear would once again boil over and consume Carl.

His efforts to resist it, to deny it, only brought more destruction. He adopted a little stray dog one time, but no sooner did she come into his life than he woke up to find her strangled outside his door. He grew friendly with a waitress in a diner where he had a job washing dishes, but she was killed with equal disregard. Her house burned down, too.

Carl eventually found something that he thought would insulate him. He took a job as a night janitor in a low-rent building for students at an art college. They were a tight-knit little group, so if anyone new came around, he would—should—hear some talk about a stranger and might be able to elude the threat before it struck. He worked at night so he didn't have to deal with too many people. It suited him well. He knew he had lost the ability to relate with people.

Doing so seemed like condemning them to death.

Nevertheless, he hated his job, despising it for its filth. It was demeaning and unfulfilling, mindless and monotonous, reminding him with mounting bitterness that he was not, by any measure, a stupid man. Every night when Carl picked up his mop, or fixed a toilet, it served as a reminder how that faceless stalker had taken his life away, how that monster had demeaned him and ruined him. In those moments Carl discovered a new realization, a new sense, that the fear was no longer alone, that something else grew with it, festering within him, and that thing was anger.

Yet, for all the things he hated about his job, he began to think that maybe it was the very demeaning nature of the job itself that kept *him* away, that it may amuse *him* enough not to inflict new miseries of torture or violence. Among the bohemian denizens he had to tolerate in that building, there were some who added to the misery of his life, rubbing his face in his sub-mediocrity in their own arrogant little art-house way.

There was one resident in particular that turned Carl's stomach and boiled his blood. His name was Michael Gibbs, or "Gibby", as the others called him. He was the son of a wealthy family, in appearance a fledgling impressionist painter, but in actuality he was a flagrant womanizer, a misogynist. A steady stream of women cycled through Gibby's apartment. Gibby wasn't rude or condescending; rather, it was Gibby's apathy that disgusted Carl. Even so, Gibby both amazed and demoralized Carl. There was a man dissolute, arrogant, conceited, and disrespectful of women, yet he had somehow managed to ingratiate himself to the point that he was given a cozy nickname. Gibby was, in fact, popular among the residents of the building, at least in the sense of casual social acquaintances.

It was this seeming hypocrisy that led Carl to hate all the building's residents. Was he not polite to them, did he not tend to their needs, did he not answer their calls when toilets ran and sinks clogged? Then again, did they not ignore him while cleaning up after their biological waste, after tending to their own human detritus clogging their building, dismissing him with as much forgetfulness as the feces they neglected to flush away? Oh, how he grew to hate them, how the anger festered within him, mounting with counting days as he came across a new realization, a bitter irony that impaled him with his own cruel fate. He was, in fact, important to only one person. Just one. Only that person was the specter of his nightmares, the embodiment of his fears, the one who had always been there, that person was … *him.*

Sometimes, though, Carl took pause, for there was one person that part of his twisted self was compelled to exclude from his toxic emotions. She was the pretty girl, the pianist, Marina Yotomo, who practiced every morning. She lived right over him. He often listened to the muffled chords of her piano while he sat staring at his walls before succumbing to his restless sleep.

As much as he found an inclination within himself to regard her with a certain interest, he was haunted by the memory of that unfortunate waitress he had once fancied. It disgusted him because he often amused himself with little flights of fancy involving Marina. Nevertheless, she was the only redemption in that job, in that building.

She always said hello.

She was always nice.

She was also friendly with Gibby, though, and Carl couldn't overlook that offense.

***

Winter break came. The building was emptying for the end of the semester. There was a big party at Marina's, and it carried on through the night. Carl could hear Gibby talking to her. It offended him. He thought of turning off the power to the building, turning off the heat, and a dozen other malicious things to ruin their party. In the end he did nothing, instead sitting inept and alone in his little apartment in the basement, tortured by the merriment above him. He fought to ignore it, tried to think of something else, tried to watch his little television with the grainy picture, but he just sat.

Until, that is, there was a knock on his door. Startled from his bitter lethargy, he realized that the party had ended. The building was quiet. He rubbed his face and staggered to the door, hesitating before pulling it open. When he did, he found Marina waiting for him, aglow with alcohol, the blush of her cheeks matching her red dress and the elf's cap on her head, its fuzzy white ball jingling with two little bells she had sown into the material.

He was dumbstruck. No words came from his open mouth.

"Ho-ho," she said, greeting him with cheer, but she had to force a smile in the discomfort of his detached silence. "I baked these for you. I hope you enjoy them." She offered him a paper plate covered with aluminum foil. When he took it from her, not having uttered a word, a nervous shrug pulled at her shoulders. "Okay, well, ah, goodnight then, I guess," she said and turned away.

He closed the door. He walked to his bed and turned off his little television before lifting the foil to peer beneath its cover. She had baked him brownies. He stared at them. He was so bewildered by the very notion of his existence having entered her thoughts that he considered not eating them, just so he could keep them. But he did eat them, for the very reason that she made them for him. He believed he encapsulated that sentiment within him as he digested the brownies, assimilating the energy she invested in their making. He gathered up the crumbs with due diligence, put them in a small zip bag to keep them fresh, and put them inside his pillowcase.

She knows I think of her. How?

He sat for some time in contemplation. He shook his head, "Clever girl," he said to himself and crawled into bed. He pulled the covers up. He breathed. The building would be empty. Only Marina and Gibby were staying for winter break. He would almost have her to himself. He knew what he would do, knew it with a welcome rush of anxiety. He would approach her with old-fashioned respect and ask her out for dinner. He thought of her smile. It was going to be perfect.

For the first time in a very long time he forgot himself and drifted off to sleep with a smile on his face.

***

He woke to the scream of his alarm clock, dressed, and looked out his little window to a pitch black, moonless night. He sighed, opened his door, and went upstairs. Finding a phone on the hallway floor, he picked it up. The moment he had it in his hand it came to life, startling him. Hesitating, he put it to his ear and said hello.

There was a long pause, and then he heard *it*, and when it came his blood ran cold, his heart froze in his chest, and his skin tingled with a cold electric spasm of terror. He couldn't breathe, he couldn't think, he couldn't drop the phone, he couldn't believe what he knew with insane certainty—it was *him*, it was *his* voice, rasping over the phone.

"Time to change the game."

Carl's hand recoiled from the phone. It tumbled in the air. In a heartbeat he reconsidered, some decrepit part of him craving the contact, craving the moment in which he could substantiate the reality of *his* existence from delusions of fear to the tactile reality of a living, breathing entity. Carl's hand shot out and snatched the phone before it crashed to the floor. He stood there, holding it, his skin crawling as if he held some venomous serpent in his grasp and not the plastic body of the phone. His inhibitions, born of his fear, threatened to toss it down and run, but the urge to confront his tormentor after so many years won out. He was overwhelmed by a sense of perversion when he put the phone to his ear and felt its plastic body against his cheek. In the tumultuous ebb and flow of his emotions his voice was lost. His throat knotted.

"Keep the phone close. When I call, do what I tell you," the voice in the phone ordered. "Do you understand?"

Carl's teeth clicked together. His gaze darted about. He sank to the floor, curling in a ball against the wall as he clutched the phone to his ear and wrapped his other arm over his head. His instincts distilled to one point. He had to hide, but how could he hide from a phone? He was raw, he was naked, defenseless and on the curb again outside the smoldering remains of his house. A trinity of fear, anger, bitterness, it all mocked him, leaving him a trembling mass before the one question that had always haunted him.

"Why?"

"Because I can."

The call ended. He scurried back to his room, locked the door, and hid in his bed, pulling the sheets over his head. He lay there, trembling, until he remembered the bag of crumbs in his pillowcase. He held them tight, and fled from his terror to his dreams.

***

"Wake up."

His eyes popped open to a cold, gray day. The phone was already at his ear. He cringed, wincing at his hopelessness. His voice seeped from his lips as a thin rasp. "Leave me alone."

"I don't like it when you sleep," the voice said. "Tell me what you were dreaming."

His heart raced. Was he to have nothing, not even the freedom of his sleeping delusions? His anger woke, snapping some resistance into him. "Leave me alone."

"Tell me what you were dreaming and I'll hang up."

He hesitated, debating with himself. He had never considered the prospect of a compromise.

"I bet I can guess what it was," the voice said with cruel confidence. "I've seen enough. How were the brownies?"

He blinked before bolting up in his bed. "How … how did you know about that?"

"I know everything. The dream?"

He looked to his window. *Oh God, he knows!* "I, I was with her."

"The piano girl."

He squeezed his eyes shut. "I had her here, with me, in my room."

"Never going to happen," the voice said, dismissing the notion with a mocking tone.

His jaw clenched. "No, listen! I, I took her. I took her … grabbed her … brought her down here, and I … I made her mine. You couldn't stop me. I kept her here and she learned to love me and I kept her safe from you. Now go away."

There was a long pause and then, like an impaling barb, there came a short laugh.

He squeezed the phone in his hand. "To hell with you."

The voice returned, laced with calm lethality. "What do you think you're doing?"

He sank under his sheets, retreating into himself. "I—"

"Who are you to dream about having her? You're a loser. Besides, you're a little old for her. But I have to tell you, she is a pretty little thing."

He sat up. His heart raced. "Stop!"

Laughter mocked him once more. "A real man would know what to do with her."

"Who are you to insult her? Who are *you* to talk like that?"

"Hey, it's your dream."

"I ...." He froze. He didn't know what to say.

"Answer me. You want her, don't you?"

"Yes," he admitted.

"Oh well," the voice said with a sigh of resignation. "Now I have to kill her."

"What? You son of a bitch—"

"Watch your mouth. Shut up or she'll be dead tomorrow. I'll rip her head off."

"Stop it!"

"Make me."

He sobbed in desperation. "Stop it, leave her alone, please?" He put a hand over his eyes. "Please, I'll do anything, just don't hurt her, okay? I'll do whatever you want, just don't hurt her."

"Fine. I'll make you a deal, but first I want to tell you something. Are you listening?"

"Yes, yes."

"Listen!"

"Okay, okay, I'm listening."

A deep breath sounded over the phone. "I want to tell you what kind of life I have. Did you know I'm married? That's right, I'm married. She's real nice. We have two kids. I'm an executive. I travel a lot—that's how I've kept up with you all these years. I have a nice house, nothing too fancy, but nice enough, certainly nicer than anything you have. In fact, that's what it's all about. All this—my life, you know— it should be yours, but it's all mine. People think I'm a nice guy. They look at you and see a creepy loser. In my world, I have respect, I have confidence and, I have power. I want you to know that I took all that away from you, that I've been taking it away from you since we were little, just because you're stupid, weak, and pathetic. But I've decided to make you stronger, because you're so pathetic you really don't entertain me anymore. Torturing you doesn't satisfy me like it used to. Understand, I invest a lot of time into making your life miserable, time I could spend at home with the wife and kids, time I have to account for, so the least you could do is make it worth my effort. I'm going to be generous and give you some tough love. Are you still listening?"

He sat in disbelief. "Yes, yes, I'm listening, still listening—"

"Stop that mumble-mouth shit," the voice said with disdain. "As much as it pains me, I won't kill her yet, if you do what I tell you. Are you going to do what I tell you?"

He ground his teeth. He wanted to die, he wanted to disappear, but he knew there was no escape. There was only the fear, *him*, and a chance to control and contain them both. "Yes, yes, I'll do what you tell me."

"Good. You know I've been watching that building you're in, watching those bratty little art students go in and out. Some of them really annoy me. Since you've made me sit through that, you owe me. This is how you're going to pay me back. Next time I call, you do exactly what I tell you. Do you hear me? Exactly. Say, 'I'll do exactly what I'm told to do.'"

"I'll do exactly what I'm told to do."

"Good. Now go to sleep."

Hours passed.

He woke in darkness.

His hand shook with the phone. He put it to his ear. Perhaps, if he said nothing, it would end.

"I can hear you breathe, stupid," the voice whispered.

He ground his teeth.

"Do you know what my favorite number is?"

Carl held his silence, but his eyebrows sank in thought.

"Get something to write with."

He groped about his end table before slipping his hand under the sheets with a pen. He stared at his hand, damning himself for listening, for having curiosity, for having any interest in any taste of *his*.

"Write the number eleven."

He wrote it in his palm for lack of any other place to write.

"Good. Look at it. Do you see what it is, two ones; one behind the other? Split them up and add them together and you get two, but slide them next to each other, one behind the other, and you get eleven. Eleven is a lot more than two. The first one is just one until the second one pushes it over to be a ten, and then it still has its back. One makes the other far more than what it was. It even protects it, watches over it. Do you understand?"

He looked at his hand. Despite himself, he was intrigued. "I, I think so."

"Enough talk. Get out of bed. Make sure you have on those rubber winter boots. Get your heavy plumber's wrench. Then go to the top floor and knock on the door."

He got out of bed. He put his boots on. He took the wrench in hand and went upstairs, to the top floor, to stand before a door. He knocked. Music played inside. His hand trembled with the phone. He put it to his ear.

"You know what to do when Gibby opens the door?"

He shrugged, not having considered what would come next. "No."

"Take that wrench and smash his head."

He retreated from the door, shocked. "What?"

"Kill him. He's put in a lot of time with her. You know what that means."

He slumped against the wall and shook his head. "What—"

"Think about it, and then smash him."

His gaze fell to the wrench. His hand jerked back to let the wrench thud to the floor. "No, I can't, I can't ... that's wrong."

"I saw them, you know. But, maybe ..."

Carl pressed his fingers to his eyes as he paced the hall. *Marina and Gibby? No!* He wanted to vomit; he wanted to pound his head against the wall. He clenched his fist, still pressing the phone to his ear. A visceral, crime-scene curiosity budded within him, demanding to know the details. "What did he do to her?"

"I don't think you want to know."

"Hey, this time you answer the question. This time you answer!" He jabbed his finger before him. "Listen, you know I have to know. Now tell me."

There was a pause before he got his answer. The specific words failed to register, but he visualized that apocalyptic, pornographic scene in all its disgusting and degrading detail, fulfilling every worst nightmare of Marina's corruption beneath Gibby. His blood boiled. "Son of a bitch. That son of a bitch."

"Then what are you waiting for?"

He dropped the phone in his pocket and snatched up the wrench before pounding his fist on the door.

After several moments the door opened. Gibby stood there, half asleep, rubbing his eyes. "What gives, man? Dude, like, you know what time it is?"

He stared at Gibby. It wasn't a moment of hesitation; it was the moment he needed to refresh the vile image in his head to summon his boiling rage until it exploded. He swung the wrench. It crashed into Gibby's forehead with a wet crack, spraying blood across the ceiling. Gibby dropped straight back to the floor. Carl was on Gibby in a heartbeat, taking the wrench in both hands and raising it high to smash in Gibby's face with a vicious blow. Blood spattered in all directions as if Carl had stomped a bag of ketchup. He held there for a moment and then jerked on the wrench, its heavy end coming loose with a wet sucking sound from the shattered pulp of Gibby's cranium.

Perhaps it was the sound, perhaps it was the sight of all those blood stains on the white walls and oak floor or the sound of his heavy breathing, but he fell back several steps, retreating from the mess in a trail of red boot prints. The wrench clattered to the floor, his hand numb. The phone vibrated in his pocket. He put it to his ear. He didn't know what to say.

The voice came to him. It was full of glee. "Did you see how his head split open?"

Carl vomited on the floor as realization collided with him. He braced himself against the wall with his bloody hands. "Wait, what did I … what did I do?"

"Tick, tick. Get the wrench and get moving."

He put the phone back to his ear, his head shaking. "Get moving? Where?"

"Move."

He walked down the hall, paced down the stairs, and stopped at the bottom. His hand trembled with the phone, and even though he turned it on, he didn't answer, instead waiting before putting it to his ear. "What?"

"You're at the bottom of the stairs, aren't you?"

He sat down. "Yes. Hey, how do you know all these things?" He looked about the stairwell. "How do you know my every move?"

"I know everything about you."

"What? How? Is it cameras? I know about surveillance, you know. I've read all about that. Cameras, everywhere. The government, they can probably listen in on these phone calls. They're probably recording them right now."

He jumped to his feet and dropped the wrench. "I could call the police. That's it. Why didn't I think of that before?"

Silence.

"Oh, I've got you now."

"Point at the phone all you want, you don't *have* me."

"What, watching me through cameras again?"

"Whatever you say, sure, watching you through the cameras, fine. Let them record the phone calls. Nobody would believe I'd be involved in this mess. Remember, I'm the nice guy with the wife and kids, not the creepy drifter with a trail of death behind him. No, they'll never find me, but they'll find you."

Defeated, he sank back to the stairs. "Why are you doing this to me?" He sucked in a breath as realization collided with his awareness. "Oh, oh no, I killed someone. I killed a man. Shit!" He clapped a hand to his forehead. "Why can't you leave me alone?"

"Because you're stupid and weak. Who lives on this floor?"

He closed his eyes, trying to forget the wrench on the stair tread next to him.

"Come on, you know. I wonder if she even liked Gibby."

He rose to his feet.

"Yeah, I bet she did. Accept it. Next to him, you're nothing to her."

"No, that's not true. She's nice to me. She *likes* me. She talks to me, she—"

"Really? She tolerates you because you take out her garbage. She's too busy rolling in the gutter with Gibby to care about you. He didn't respect her like you do. You wouldn't treat her the way he did."

"That's, that's right. I love her. I'd never … I wouldn't." He snatched the wrench, cursing under his breath. "You saw him in your cameras, didn't you, saw him with her?"

"As you say. Do what you have to do. Now it's her turn."

"What? I, I don't understand, I-I can't hurt her."

"She turned you into a murderer and you can't hurt her?"

"No, no … you made me do that!"

"If you didn't give a rat's ass about her, you still would've killed Gibby?"

He started to pace. "Yes … no … stop. You're turning everything around."

"Look what she's done to you. You're standing there in the middle of the night with brains and blood splattered over you. It makes me proud, but is that what you want, to please me?"

He squeezed the phone in his hand.

"Hey? Are you listening? Say no and she's dead. Do it, and you get a crack at me."

"A crack at you?" His face flushed. "You're dead, dead, I'll crush you, smash you—"

"That's it. Now move."

He kicked the wall. He cursed and growled, but knew he had no choice. He had to obey, because it had to end, and he'd end it, end it that night.

He raced down the next flight of stairs. He slipped with his blood-soaked boots and tumbled down the last set of steps to land in a pile on the floor. The phone slid from his hand and clattered across the floor outside the stairwell. He scrambled after it, flopping forward to slap his hand over the phone. He sighed with relief, but then froze as he caught the sight of slippers from the corner of his eye.

He looked over and found Marina standing in the hall, staring at him in surprise.

"Are you okay?" She crossed her arms over her thick blue night coat, her dark eyes wide with concern. "I heard some noise."

He stared at her.

She pointed at the phone. "Hey, is that my voice recorder? I've been looking all over for that."

He drew the phone into his hand. "No, that's mine."

"Are you sure?" She paused, her lips parting when she looked at his hand. "Is that blood? Did you hurt yourself when you fell?"

"Are you hearing this?" he whispered to the phone as he stared at her.

Her gaze fell to the gore-soaked wrench.

"Marina—"

She glared at him and fell back a step, then two. "What's going on?" She retreated another step, her gaze darting to the unseen floors above. "Gibby? Hey!"

"Him, you're calling him?" His eyes narrowed to menacing slits. "Gibby's gone."

She gasped.

He ground his teeth before calling out to her.

She broke into a run, screaming for help.

He pounded a fist on the floor. "You ungrateful bitch. Do you know what I've done for you?"

He charged after her. He slid around the corner leading to her door only to see her slam it in his face. He drew back and threw himself at the door, his shoulder pounding it open before she could secure the locks. Knocked from her feet, she stumbled back and tripped over her shoes to flop on the floor, stunned as her head smacked down on the old oak slats. He kicked the door shut behind him with his heel, keeping his gaze on her as she propped herself up on her elbows, her eyes wide with fear.

Her coat fell open. He could see the little lavender chemise that covered her bare body.

He began to tremble.

She inched away from him on her elbows. "Please, don't hurt me?"

He blinked. "Why, why Gibby? I wouldn't treat you like some cheap whore."

She winced at his outburst, raising a hand before her.

He shook his fists. "Get up. Let's go, get up."

She cringed beneath him.

He stepped back. He glanced at her piano before returning to her and pointing to her piano bench. "Play." He opened his hands. "Come on, play."

She rolled over and scurried to the piano, her eyes fixed on him as she moved. She watched as he looked to his hand, his hand then snapping up to his ear. Settling on the bench, she lifted the cover from the keys, clenching her fists when she saw how her hands shook. She looked back to him, fighting to find her voice. "What, what should I play?"

He stared at her. "What should I tell her to play?"

"What are you doing?" said the voice from the phone.

"I want her to play."

"No."

"I want her to play."

"Music soothes the savage beast. She'll play and you'll go weepy and lame. There's no turning back now. You're a murderer. You broke into her apartment. You think she wants anything to do with you? Look at her."

He shook his head, but he knew the disgusting truth. Everything he did to have her made her unattainable. His mind was torn in many directions at once. He was terrorizing her. It was insane.

His face bunched up. "Close the piano."

"I thought you wanted me to play?"

"Close the piano!"

"That's it," he heard from the phone.

She shrank against the keys, whimpering among her tears. "Just tell me what you want me to do, okay? Please, don't hurt me, please—"

"Listen to her," he heard from the phone. "Who does she sound like now, what pathetic loser does she sound like?"

"What?" she said. "I can't hear you, you're mumbling—"

Carl waved her off. "Shut up."

The voice skewered his ear. "I told you I was going to set you free. Look at you. She turned you into a worm eating her dirt. If it wasn't for her, you'd still be in your bed. Get it? She's the one that made you kill. She's to blame."

She cowered, pleading her innocence between her sobs.

"She has to die."

"Please, don't kill me, I didn't do anything."

"Kill her and you get a crack at me. Come on, I'm right here."

"I—"

"Do it!"

"I, I can't, she's been so nice to me, and all these years you've tortured me—"

"Here I come, I'm here, time to face up. Kill her!"

Her gaze darted about as she cringed on her piano bench. She tensed, her focus locked past him. She pointed behind him and a piercing shriek burst from her lips. "He's right behind you, he's right behind you!"

He spun. He froze. The phone fell from his hand. He lowered his head and launched himself.

She put her hands over her face as his head smashed into the mirror on the back of her steel security door. He stood there for a moment, leaning on the door as pieces of the broken mirror came loose and fell. Blood dripped down the door past his chin. His gaze sank to the kaleidoscopic reflection staring back at him.

Clever girl.

20

It was his last thought. His senses dissolved, and he slumped to the floor.

***

They tell me I'm getting better, because I no longer deny my crimes.
They don't know the half of it.
Sometimes, at night, I wake and look at the number in my hand. It's because of that number that I still live in nervous anticipation, because I know one thing as sure as I know the sun will rise and night will come: he's still out there, and he won't stay idle. I know this, more than anyone else, because I know now what we're capable of. He'll find me—even in this place—he'll find a way to come, a way to get me out of here, because there's one thing I've learned over the years that no one can deny, that no statement can refute, that Marina couldn't understand, that I didn't understand until that night in her apartment. It's something that makes my heart pound and seethe with fury, but, at the same time, makes me feel more alive, more powerful, than I ever did before.
I crave my madness.
I may fear him, but he needs me. Eleven. We can't escape each other.

Icon

The critic hovered through the city's sprawling neon night like a dragonfly over a moonlit pond, unseen except for the shimmers he obscured with his outline. It was his way to move in such a fashion, to be in the midst of the desperate and disparate energy of that place and remain untouched, for the insulation of his apathy was both the most treasured and most despised aspect of his personality.

Nevertheless, the critic was well respected. In fact, he knew well enough his unspoken power in that place. He had the ability to lift the chosen few who sparked his curiosity, elevating them from obscurity with viable opportunities of success and acclaim. It was his way to redeem his own artistic failure with praise for those he adored, embodying them with a vicarious carte blanche of creative license. It was an old formula, he believed, an old relationship between critics and the criticized; a very special bond. It was one he preferred. He could relish it without having to risk opening his emotional barriers and abandon the reservations he felt restrained the less balanced aspects lurking within his nature.

Such was his mindset when scouting his chosen environment, a tidal pool of maladjusted emotions from the cast-offs of society. Some would call them derelicts; others might call them hedonists, bohemians, or simply, the artistic fringe. He cared little for the label, or the derision for their locale. To him it was no more than the old corner of the city, run down, low-rent, allowing underground bars and clubs to survive and serve as an incubator for whatever creative movement was breeding among the lost, confused, misguided, yet occasionally brilliant youths scratching out their meager existence.

The critic came one particular night on the tip of an acquaintance—he wasn't one to have friends—an acquaintance that was a local, a man who could have aspired to something greater if his lesser habits hadn't ruined him. The critic walked the streets until he found one of the more grungy clubs that let unknowns take the stage. Known as the critic, he was allowed in and his usual table in the back of the club cleared. He looked at the bar stool behind the table before he settled down, then crossed his arms on his chest and looked to the stage.

Some seedy looking people were milling about in front of the stage, obscuring the critic's view until they seemed to part at the unspoken impatience of his distemper. When they did, his eyes narrowed as he studied the stage, and then something struck him, struck him like an icy javelin through his heart. He looked, and found *her*, and the moment her eyes caught the light between a break in her dark disheveled hair he was entranced. He saw a hurt there he had never quite seen. His ears perked up at the sound of her voice, a voice rising from deep within her, afloat on emotional wreckage so bare and broken he found it hard to believe what he was witnessing.

It was a selfless, humiliating act of emotional disembowelment on that dark little stage in that dingy little club. It struck him the more he listened, as the dregs playing behind her were barely competent with their instruments and her voice wasn't one he would call rich in talent by any means; rather, it was the cumulative effect of the discordant music, the irregular percussion and the static-laden, muddy guitars that droned into one low, tidal moan beneath her voice as it rasped, cracked, and undulated in an unearthly dirge.

He found himself motionless as he listened that night. He sat through the rest of the set, which was something unusual with unknowns, and he wasn't to be disappointed. At the last song the lights on the stage went out except for one small, pale bulb before the drum riser. There was a glint, a reflective sheen of glass as she hoisted a bottle and began to drink from something so clear he could only guess it was vodka. One of the guitars came in, but it was different now, issuing intermittent, irregular notes, and then the bass drum, a slow thud that reverberated through the guitar's quiet moments. The bottle glistened several more times as it was hoisted and he wondered if she'd pass out, but then she settled her hands on the microphone and stood before the light to reveal nothing but the black shape of her body.

"Gutted," she said, slurring the title of the song, and then her voice came again and the critic leaned his elbows on the table, leaned forward as if he could float over the people in the club to get to the stage and study her as she strained to push her voice through a mumbled mess of words he struggled to decipher, even as they bludgeoned his heart.

And then it was over. The lights went out. She didn't wait for applause, instead vanishing before the lights came back. The band retreated from the stage, waving off the ragged yelps and calls from the club. The critic wouldn't let go, though, pursuing her as only he could. The layout of the club, like so many others, was branded into his subconscious. He found her back by the bathrooms, lurking in the dim lighting of a corridor littered with graffiti, her eyes smoldering over the glowing tip of her cigarette. She was smaller than he thought, almost delicate. After what he witnessed on stage, the word seemed both fitting and alienating as a description. She looked at him with a typical street-tough, get-lost stare but, when he introduced himself, she blinked and flicked her cigarette to send the ashes cascading to the floor.

"What do you want?"

He shook his head. He was accustomed to a stammering welcome after dropping his name. It took a moment to find his voice. "Your set was impressive."

She shrugged it off. "So?"

He blinked. "I'm going to write about you in my next column," he said, further confused by her dismissive attitude as he could see it wasn't an arrogant charade. It deepened his fascination. He could see she didn't care who he was, or what he could do for her, or what a single positive comment from him could do for any aspiring act. "My word carries weight. I only have to give the word and all this could change. You could be playing in front of thousands instead of a few dozen." He opened his hands. "I can break you."

Her eyes narrowed. "Yeah, right," she said with a sigh.

He stared at her, possessed with the sudden belief that their lives had snapped together. It left him speechless.

She tipped her head back, staring at him over her cigarette as she slid across the wall into the bathroom.

***

He wrote his article despite her flippancy. He went to see her every night he heard she was going to perform, and she succeeded in avoiding him after every show. It seemed a tease, even as his column fulfilled his prediction. Within a month crowds filled the club, and her band was handed up the chain to bigger clubs. Other columnists took note, but the critic ignored them, for they failed to see her as he did. He watched the full range of her act, watched when she set the stage on fire one night and was taken away by the police amid the chaos of firemen and large red trucks. When he bailed her out of jail she refused to see him. He continued to watch her, amused when she banged her head on the stage until her forehead was a ragged mess during a volcanic drum solo, then to stand and finish her set with her eyes burning through her blood smeared face.

It wasn't her first brush with violence. One night a young man in the crowd screamed out a proposition in the crudest possible language. She took her microphone stand and slammed its base into his head, shattering his face and sparking a massive brawl. The critic was shocked another night when she drank so much she vomited a gut full of alcohol beside her microphone. He laughed when she tossed a match on the vodka soaked mess and set it on fire. Amid the horrible stench, she went into "Gutted," the closer of the night.

It was the song he felt was the strongest of her material, so hypnotic that he froze with the anticipation of its performance. It took several shows before he noticed that she only sang her own material. This, as well, he wrote into his columns and concert reviews until one of the independent record labels took note and signed her for an album. He waited, desperate and eager. He tried ever harder to speak with her, to get an interview, but she earned a reputation of being "difficult" in her first waking moments of fame. She refused interviews and, on the rare occasion she consented, she was drunk, vicious with her bottle of vodka in hand, railing with sullen rage against the interviewer to the awkward embarrassment of her band.

It became a show in its own, and the interviews became hit and run affairs in the night, other critics sniping at her when she'd depart the stage, delirious from exhaustion and drink to goad her into confrontations. They portrayed her as the next hellion, the next wanton child, the next upstart punk, but failed to see what the critic saw. She was surrounded by sorrow, her impenetrable mask of aggression so like the critic's own mask of apathy and, like his, so transparent, failing in its one goal to hide the demons within.

Her album was released. It came with rumors of nightmarish recording sessions, violent fights with producers, and conflicts with even the loose tolerance of an independent label. But, when it came out, *Agony and Adversaries* was like a bolt of white lightning, and the critic felt the vindication of her success even as she continued to act out in more destructive ways. Fights with roadies, an arrest for throwing a toilet seat out of a tour bus, two drunk driving charges and three car wrecks later it seemed the lid had popped off her bottle of lightning. Yet the critic always found a way to help her, whether it was securing legal representation or paying her bail. He never minded the thankless job of cleaning up after her because he knew it would afford another opportunity to see her, to watch her perform, to let his innards melt, congeal, and spasm as he listened to her wailing torment.

After a brawl with a bouncer that left her lacerated from being thrown through a plate glass window, his inevitable bail payment at last earned a reply. It wasn't what the critic expected, but he savored it nonetheless. One of the couriers for the magazine he wrote for brought it to him, a plain looking white envelope with his name scribbled on it—a child's writing, he thought. It contained a piece of toilet paper, the cheap kind found in ratty bathrooms, with a short message scrawled in mascara: *Leave me the fuck alone!* It stunned him, but he knew in that moment with searing certainty that the sun was setting on them both and that they were indeed bound.

The album continued to soar. She was threatening to break into the mainstream. A threat it was, as her reputation for anarchic behavior swelled in the rumor mill to mythic proportion. The critic saw the genius of it, hiding in plain sight, the evasion of her hurt before the bright lights.

He continued to write about her and her music, defending her as one of those rare personalities that erupts onto the scene, a meteoric talent that defied quantification and classification to be that rarest of rare finds—the *icon*.

When this profound claim of his hit print she was again in jail, this time waiting to get released on a public profanity complaint after throwing a bag of manure at an abortion protester and cursing out the police who came to break up the ensuing brawl. "Abort me. It's not too late," she had screamed as blue uniformed bodies had stuffed her writhing form into the back of a patrol car. No sooner was she out than he got his second reply from her. It was a ragged sketch on paper towel, an unflattering self-portrait that she made in her cell. A large dark 'X' obscured the face; he only needed a faint whiff to realize what she had used to cross it out.

That's my girl. He grinned and stored the picture in a zip-lock bag.

Despite his efforts, despite his praise, he couldn't defend her from everything. Six months after the album's release there was talk about the second album's prospect. She appeared on a late night talk show, not to perform, not even invited, but she had somehow wound up with a ticket and lounged in a front row seat drinking from a long brown bag until the host called her up to the stage. With clear reluctance she shuffled from her seat and dumped herself next to him. When he asked about her newfound celebrity and the source of her energy and inspiration and where it might go for a second album, she frowned and shook her head.

"I never wanted any of this," she said. "I just want to die in peace."

***

Over those months the critic's life changed as well. His growing insistence on writing about her, and only her, led to escalating letters from his editors who reminded him, with growing impatience, that he was to cover the entire underground music scene, not just her. The requests rolled off the critic like so much rain off his umbrella as he stood outside a courthouse waiting to see her again, knowing she wouldn't speak to him. The reason was no longer important, because he knew every relationship had its ground rules, and if that had to be their ground rule, he'd accept it. She came out to the flash of bulbs from the trash magazines that stalked her and glanced at him.

She stuck her arm up high, her middle finger raised, before disappearing into a limousine.

The second album seemed to erupt from nowhere since he heard little buzz regarding studio sessions. It was a mish-mash of songs stitched together during the previous tour and came out under the title, *Details of*

My Entrails. He praised it, of course, because he was incapable of anything else at that point and he had no care that he had lost his objective view of anything she recorded. In the past he often took perverse delight in skewering the oft-failed attempts of once 'hot' acts to maintain their momentum on a second album. His editors reminded him that the album was being panned as a simple rehash of songs from the first album. Reviewers claimed the album showed no growth, creative expansion, or change in influence. Other columnists made a particular point of revising their praise of the first album, claiming that it was aimless, noisy, urban punk trash.

They had no understanding, the critic knew, but the effect was the same. The tour for the second album was hyped by the record label but lacked the steam of the first tour. Sure enough the other columnists swooped down like vultures smelling the fresh kill, another flash-in-the-pan celebrity to crucify with her own arrogance and indulgence. Troubling rumors began to circulate once more, managing to penetrate the critic's surreal perception of the world. There were whispers of her growing excess and self-destructive behavior. It was hard to hide with the increasing paleness of her skin and her steady loss of weight.

Perhaps in sympathy, perhaps by will, but nevertheless with sullen inevitability, the critic found himself slipping into his own state of decay. He stopped taking his medications and withdrew from his therapist. This sent out an alarm among those who appeared to have at least a passing interest in his welfare, which only fueled his sense of paranoid isolation. His editors added to the fire with their caustic phone calls, confusing him as to the source of their derision until he remembered the angry letters he shot out when they had urged him to write of something other than her. Some of his peers at the magazine came to his little apartment to check on him; he rebuffed them the moment he noted the dismayed look in their eyes. He ranted and raved at them, standing unwashed and unshaven in his bathrobe. He tried to explain to them what he was doing, how important it was to pry into her expression and untangle the mystical mysteries of her suffering.

That was when they laid it out for him, the ugly, simple, and all too common truth he had so long ignored and discredited. They were gentle with him, knowing his past instability and eccentricity, but they were rough on her, or so he felt, sparing no salvo from their bitter personal attacks. All of it was personal, her recordings not even entering the conversation. He paced before them as they talked, slapping his hands on his head as he tried not to listen. They told him of her disastrous childhood, the alcoholic father who abused and abandoned her, the trailer-trash mother who had no qualms about quenching her addictions and paying for them by prostituting herself while her daughter sat in the next room. They told the critic how she had run away and lived as a street urchin. She had been stabbed by a man who tried to pimp her and everyone in her short life had exploited, abused, humiliated, and dehumanized her. Their conclusion was mixed with concession as they admitted her life was tragic, not mysterious. Nevertheless, she was a wreck, a hopeless wreck.

They ended by using the preferred, cold expression to define any performer's professional and mortal decline: she was circling the drain.

The critic turned on them. "But that's just it! Don't you see? She's the genuine thing. You complain her music didn't *grow* on her second album? You're all fools. Can't you see her drive is pure—to change it would be to corrupt and contaminate her. Is the brightest light not white? I know her heart," he said, trying to assure them with his confidence. "I know it as no one else knows it, maybe even more than she knows it, and if I could just help her, if I could just hold it in my hands ..." His voice trailed off, his fists clenching over his chest before he glared at his colleagues. "She has suffered, and her suffering has spurred her to transform her pain and express something that can't be duplicated. This is art you savages, true art, the art that endures, because it consumes and won't be corrupted by the artist's inevitable waning through old age."

They left. They didn't return.

He wrote in fits. He found it difficult to sleep and wrestled with his thoughts to keep some semblance of order in his head. It was the lack of medication, he knew, but he refused to return to that regimen and the emotional dissociation it inflicted. Instead of sleep he sat in the dark and listened to her albums, living the nocturnal life to which she claimed to be banished because of her nervous nightmares. When the moon rose he'd wonder where she was, what she was doing, and if she was alone. Despite the best efforts of the trash magazines to embarrass her with various allegations of her sexual nature, she showed nothing but apathy toward sensuality. Her life was devoid of intimacy. He thought of that as he sat in the dark, listening until the hurt in her voice grew to a physical pain within him. Sometimes the knots in his chest and gut were so tight he couldn't eat and he paced without relent.

His own nightmares returned to rob him of what little peaceful sleep was left to him, the chaotic fragments of his deranged youth whispering to him when her voice didn't drown them out. Somewhere in that delirium he saw their ethereal link, deducing that she was his kindred spirit. She was trapped in her life, in her hellish life, to sing out not only her pain but his pain as well. It drove his obsession to a new height, to a new compulsion within him to hold her, to protect her, to somehow set her free from what he did to her. He knew if he'd never penned a word about her, had never brought attention to her, her one avenue to vent her torment wouldn't have overwhelmed her to end up being larger than her, freezing her in the very things she sought to escape. It haunted him so that he wept as he sat in the dark; wept for her as the victim that she was, that he couldn't save her from being, that he yet needed her to be so that she could sing for him again.

He wrote a column that the magazine accepted—only for its surprising cohesion, given his muddled condition. He wrote of her childhood, of her torment, and asked people to forgive her, for she knew not what she did and did it not for acclaim or record sales, but only because she must. It was all she had. He reminisced about the story of her start and how she walked up to an open mike one night in a seedy club and stepped into a magical fairy tale of music legend. Her band congealed around her on that very stage, and she never looked back.

He kept following her, though. He kept up on her by calling his various contacts. He left his apartment less and less. Once the hellion, then the upstart punk, she devolved to a pathetic one-hit wonder cliché, her second tour having fallen apart as her band disintegrated around her. Her last show she clung to the microphone stand during the opening of "Gutted", but when it came time to sing, she leaned her forehead on the microphone and wept. She stood there, frail and pale, desolate and disconsolate, wearing a baggy, black, long-sleeved shirt. White block letters across her chest spelled out a stark phrase: KILL ME. Her band played on, looking at each other in confusion until she slumped to the floor, unconscious. The lights went out. Her guitarist dragged her off stage, kicked her head in frustration, and was never heard from again.

The record label dropped her. It made little news.

But then she did an interview, or more it was one of those things that just happened, the critic decided. One of the street reporters for a cable music station found her sitting outside a little coffee shop in the deep of night. She was wearing her black KILL ME shirt, her long sleeves dangling past her wrists on a hot, humid night. The reporter, obnoxious in that young urban way, asked her some barbed questions to try to bring out the old fire of her infamy, but received only a hollow, sad gaze into the camera lens. The critic watched the interview without tire, mesmerized. Although she ignored most of the questions and responded to others with dismissive shrugs, at the end she scratched her forehead with her cigarette hand and looked back at the camera.

"You know, I never asked to be famous, I didn't sing to be famous," she said in a detached monotone. "I just … I've got these things in me, and that's the way they come out. And, you know, I hate it when people eat it up. I just want those things out of me. I hate those things and you people, you can't get enough of them. You want that shit, and that's screwed up, because I know where they come from, and if you knew, you'd friggin' run, but hell, you think those things are me and they're not. I was trying to escape, and all you people did was trap me."

She shook her head and ran her hands along her arms. "You know, it's like, what the hell is that?" She reached under the table to pick up a long brown bag, pouring some vodka into her coffee while the reporter asked her what she thought of newer acts that imitated her. She shook her head and gulped some of her coffee. "What do those assholes know?" she said, her voice slurred. She shrugged. "They want my life? Shit. You know what? They can fucking have it.

"If I can't live in peace, at least let me die in peace."

***

She wouldn't go quietly, though. The compulsion within her was still too strong. With what clout remained to her she managed to piece together a third album and released it under a tiny, upstart label. *They Stole My Soul* received little review or mention and produced no more than a faint glimmer on the sales charts. It was difficult to find in stores. The critic, of course, secured his copy the day the album came out and listened to it without tire. The anger was gone from her voice, leaving only the hurt and desolation. The time was coming, he knew. It was obvious from her picture on the back of the CD case, her little body cadaver pale and lost in the baggy folds of her now characteristic, long-sleeved KILL ME shirt.

He responded to her effort by convincing his editors to let him print a column about her, one last review of her latest album. To the puzzlement of his editors, and perhaps the only reason they published it, was the fact that he panned the album, saying her drive was wrung out. She was spent and it showed in the highlight of the album, the closing track, with the apt title of "Consumed."

The review ran in one of the magazine's small pulp sister publications, as his old column space had been handed over to one of his former colleagues. His reputation, his own clout, had evaporated. His name had become as inconsequential as hers and so many others he himself had banished in caustic reviews. He cared little for the irony. It was no longer important to him.

He hoped and waited, and it wasn't in vain. He woke one afternoon to find an envelope left on the floor outside his door. It only took him a moment to notice it had no stamp, no addresses. She had been outside his door to deliver the message. He opened the envelope to find a copy of his column, crumpled and torn from a magazine before it had been folded and stuffed into the envelope. Before he read the message scrawled along the margin beside his review, he ran his thumbs over the creases in the pulpy paper, imagining her fingers as they touched and tortured the print. He took a breath, smoothed it out, and turned it to read her spidery, child-like writing: *So you get it after all you creepy fuck!*

He closed his door and retreated into his apartment. He stared at the message for some time before he had the nerve to pick up his phone and call through his old contacts to find her. Nobody knew where she was. The only fact he dredged up was that she'd been thrown out of her apartment under complaints of back-rent from her landlord. She was homeless, out somewhere on the street. It was over, he knew.

He slept the rest of the next day and woke in the late evening. He opened a window and left a light on as the darkness of night approached. He repeated this through the week. One night, at some inhuman hour, he heard a thump in the hall. Trembling, he opened the door and there she was, sitting on the floor across from his door, her knees pulled up to her chest to leave her as a tiny, dirty rag doll in the darkness. Her head rolled back to thud against the wall, her sunken eyes glaring at him.

He helped her in and closed the door. She swayed in the middle of the apartment, her head rolling from one side to the other before she sat Indian style on the floor. "Live alone, huh?"

He sat on a couch to stare at her. He nodded.

"Yeah, I figured." She sighed before letting out a wet cough. She wiped her nose on the back of her hand, snorting the congestion in her sinuses. She fidgeted through her pockets to take out a cigarette and light it.

Instinct got the better of him. "I don't smoke."

She shrugged, ignoring him. "You know why I'm here, right?" Her eyes narrowed on him through her disheveled hair. The cigarette dangled from her mouth.

He frowned. His hands knotted together to stop his trembling. He nodded once more.

She took the cigarette in her hand. She stared at him for some time before she spoke. "Got a candle?"

He got her a candle.

"Got a spoon?"

He got her a spoon.

She shrugged off the ratty army-surplus jacket she wore, her gaze locked on his. "If things had just been different, you know, maybe I could've been a real artist. I always knew something in me was different from everybody else, but I didn't think this is where it would go. But hell, what the fuck, right?" She sniffed, her eyes glistening as they bored into his. She held for a moment before rolling up the sleeve of her black KILL ME shirt.

His face bunched up.

She only looked down once, when she needed, and when she was done she took a deep drag on the cigarette before extinguishing it on her pant leg. Her eyelids drooped. She tipped her head back to keep her gaze on him. "Hey, you remember the last thing you said to me ... that first night?"

His throat closed in shame. He couldn't talk, so he nodded and drew in a tight breath.

"Yeah, me, too," she said. "Me, too."

She sat there, staring at him from the drooping slits of her eyes until she slumped over. Her body, unstrung, tipped with gravity to dump her on her back.

He sat there, quaking, and watched. She twitched a few times before a wet gurgle rattled in her throat and then she went still, a last long breath emptying from her lungs.

He sobbed, balling his fists and pounding them on his temples. He rocked back and forth where he sat before he ran to the bathroom and vomited in the toilet. Then he washed his face and paced about his apartment, his arms wrapped about his chest. He shed his bathrobe for some clothes and did something he hadn't done in a long time, having survived on doorstep food deliveries—he left his apartment. Dawn was yet to come, so he walked down to the twenty-four hour mega-mart and bought some women's shampoo, body wash, a roll of white gauze, and a bolt cutter.

He returned to his apartment, lifted her little body and carried her to his bathroom. He removed her dingy clothes, stuffed them in a black garbage bag, and put her in the tub. He ran the water until it was warm, filled the tub, and washed her. Her body was a map of her memories. There was the ugly scar on her side where she'd been stabbed, the uneven lines on her forehead where she shredded her skin banging her head on stage, the bumps and lines across one cheek and down her neck from when she was thrown through the plate glass window, and a series of small round cigarette burns on her lower back that he tried not to consider.

He scrubbed her nails clean, washed her hair, and scrubbed the caked filth from her feet until they were pink. He kept at it until she was pristine clean from head to foot, then took her from the tub, laid her on the floor, and dried her. He wrapped the gauze about her arms to cover them. He couldn't stand the sight of what she did to herself. He walked over to his kitchen table, swept the piled papers and garbage to the floor and extended the table before putting down a clean white sheet. Then he picked her up and laid her out, arms at her sides, before folding the sheet over her. Last, he brushed her hair back so he could look her full in the face.

He sat beside her the rest of the day, unable to move or think. He was devastated, distraught, and hopeless. As much as he wanted to weep like a madman, hold her, and stab at the demons haunting her, he couldn't help but see the remaining torment under the apparent peace of her closed eyes. It set him to pacing during the late afternoon and, by evening, he couldn't stand it any more. The pain that lingered within her scraped across his nerves like casket nails on glass.

He beat his fists against his temples. *Forgive me, I should've left you alone, I never should've written about you, I never should've looked at you. But don't you see that I couldn't help myself? Don't you see we suffer the same affliction? I tried to help once I understood, you have to know that, but still I can't take your pain away, I can't take away the pain in your little heart.*

He stepped back from the table and froze. He looked over his shoulder. He winced and hid his face in his hands, but he wept, knowing there was no other way, that he could find no other way, that he must have known all along there was no other way. He drew the sheet aside with care, exposing her before kissing her forehead with a single, tender brush of his lips. He went to his bathroom, tore through his medicine cabinet, then went to his kitchen and tore through other drawers to find what he wanted. It was a blur, but then he found himself beside her with a pair of pliers, a large steak knife, and the bolt cutter.

With all the care he could muster, he cut out her heart.

He sat beside the table, holding the dripping lump in his trembling hands.

He looked at her before he ate it, weeping as he set her free. Her face faded to an angelic white mask while his stomach bucked with her demons, the lot of them trapped and consumed in its acid. He wiped his eyes and mouth clean before leaning over to kiss her forehead one last time.

With her free, he knew it was time for his freedom as well. He swallowed a bottle's worth of sleeping pills, settled back in his chair, and smiled.

He was happy, because he knew he'd see her soon.

***

The macabre incident made the news. From the depths of disinterest there rose many people with decided opinions about the two of them, but more was left unanswered than anyone cared to question.

Her old record label picked up *They Stole My Soul* and released it as her final recording. Sales peaked somewhat, but then petered out.

The years passed, and then something changed.

Perhaps it was the tragic end of her life, perhaps it was her material, but the critic would've felt vindicated nonetheless. At long last the music community judged her an icon, just as he had argued with such conviction during her life. Her influence on a spectrum of new performers was unmistakable, her sound groped for but never quite duplicated. Her albums were reinterpreted as singular works of human disillusionment and selfless expression. She was seen as a tragic, misunderstood figure that shined too bright before succumbing to her demons and her grisly demise with the one man who had championed her, her obsessed critic.

He would've been further satisfied to know that she didn't fade in full to the realm of memories and sentiment. The cable music channels played on, and they needed to fill their programming hours. She remained a spectacle to behold on stage, even in the grainy edits that remained of her concert footage. So, every now and then, late in the quiet peace of night, one can still see her, and listen to her sing.

Creep

1:36 a.m.

The bedroom is dark, except by the bed, where there's the soft, faint light of a clock, its red numbers glowing on the bed's disheveled white sheets. The shape of a small body huddles beneath the covers. An opening, like a tunnel into a cave, leads under the sheets to where the red glow illuminates the single wide, staring eye of a boy.

He blinks as he stares out at the clock. He's familiar with the situation. A quiet night, the lonesome darkness, nothing but him and the lurking, shapeless shadows of his imagination run wild. His eye holds on the clock as a silent debate rages within him: could he be brave enough to emerge from his refuge for some water? His mouth is dry and sticky from anxious breaths that pulse between his lips as he stares at the clock, anticipating the far off dawn.

He knows that at some point he must rise. The anxiety within shifts and it's no longer the trepidation of emerging from his refuge. Instead, it's the challenge of making his foray across his sleeping home without making a sound. He knows the way, he tells himself. When no one watches, when no one can notice during the day, he tests the floor, probes it with his weight on the ball of a foot to see which slats in the oak floor will creak, which will be silent, which have minute bow, and moan if he puts his weight in the middle of their length.

But first he must make it from the bed, and that's the greater challenge because of all the darkness in the house, there's no darkness like that under his bed, the darkness where the lower depths of his imagination hide. He never sleeps with a hand or foot dangling over the edge. He'd hate to tempt whatever waits in those shadows, whatever monstrosity wakes under the bed as he sleeps.

With due patience he gathers the sheets as he rolls them down from his head to the small of his back. It's an awkward process, but something he's practiced over many nights and soon enough he's ready. He rolls them down no further. Instead, with hands planted under his chest as he lay on his belly, he swings one foot out wide, as far as he can, and lowers it until he feels the cold floor on his toes. Then, using his hands and his foot as his base, he slips his other leg free before pushing up with his hands.

Standing at last, he pauses. He scans the floor. He's a good arm's length from the edge of the bed, too far for any claw or tentacle to snag him. Forcing a swallow, he begins the precarious journey to the bathroom. His eyes adjust to the dark but, even without sight, he knows where to step, which parts of the floor to avoid, where he left his toys as unseen obstacles.

There. He congratulates himself as he halts just outside the doorway of his room. His gaze darts to either side. To the left his parents sleep, their door parted a mere crack. To the right his older brother sleeps with the door wide open. It's the most difficult part of the journey because the floor takes a lot of traffic every day and only the areas of the floor right along the wall can take his delicate footfalls without making a sound. He trembles, his heart bucks, thunders—it has to be done in three precise steps to make it without a sound.

Diagonal left, sidestep left, diagonal right—made it!

He halts opposite the door to the bathroom to let the pounding of his racing heart recede. He looks about. He's alone. Nobody knows where he is, that he has escaped from bed and that he stands in the hallway in his pajamas. It's no longer his home in all its familiarity; it's something far different, far stranger. It's his little world, his private little world, as long as he remains silent. If someone woke and found him, what would he say? Sneaking about the hall in the dark; how to explain that? During the day everything was different. Sneak a drink when no one looks, no problem. Sneak a peek when no one knows, no problem. Caught doing those things, easy enough to explain, even if they could land him in trouble. But sneaking in the hall at night? It would scream guilt in a profound, disturbing way. What could he say to that?

I could tell the truth. It's a stark, simplistic thought, but his heart resumes its pounding terror at the thought of that scene. *Tell the things in my head? That would never work. They should never know. This is mine, all this.*

He blinks. He sees himself at school the next day. His guts knot when he thinks of that sunny world. Cold and hostile, he finds no comfort in it, nothing in it but repulsion and revulsion. The teacher drones on. He doodles on his papers instead of paying attention. He implodes to his own world, his shadow world, far away, fantastic and frightening, but nonetheless his. If he had to admit that all the monsters he draws are real to him, and worse, what he imagines they do and could do in his silent refuge, they'd lock him up and throw away the key. *Sure they would.*

He's young, but he's clever enough to understand. The night, the dark, the shadows, they're the realms of his imagination, the spheres of his freedom, but they're traps as well. Someday the fragile boundary between those spheres could pop, and things he knows shouldn't see the light of day could take their hold on him. Maybe, he wonders, that's the reason he fears the monsters under his bed. Once they get him, he'll see they're not monsters, they're just things and thoughts he put there and, if they're monstrous, that would make him....

His mouth goes so dry he finds it hard to swallow. Steadying himself, he makes it into the bathroom—*diagonal right to the edge of the doorframe, two small sidesteps in, feet to either side of the sink.* He braces a hand on the bathroom counter and extends his other hand until he finds the faucet. He must turn it just so. Too low and the trickle will make loud plops; a little further and the water will foam, emitting a low whistle as it comes out of the faucet's aerator screen. No, it has to be done just right, in one quick, small motion to give a silent, steady stream into the bowl of the sink. He clenches his teeth, gives the valve a turn, and gets it right.

Relieved, he holds for a moment before leaning forward to sip the water. It's an odd stretch for his height, awkward and off balance, but he manages. *Why is everyone so much bigger than me? I'm so small. I fit better in my world.*

He turns off the water and holds in the silence. No one moves. There's no sound. Nobody heard him. For a moment he feels an unsettling power burn inside him and the monsters vent their urge within him, their chorus channeling straight through his head. His gaze darts toward the bedrooms. *I could do anything in my world. I could do anything to them. From my world, I could do anything to anybody.*

His eyes squeeze shut in fear at those thoughts. There's no denying their presence, though, until the inevitable questions form in his mind.

Where do they come from?

Why do they come?

They come all the time.

He forces his eyes open and shivers in the chill of the night. He looks back in the direction of his bedroom and knows he must go. The darkness presses about him. He follows his way back with haste. He can feel the shadows, can feel them right on him, pouring out of his back and threatening to drown him with icy tingles if he doesn't make it under his sheets soon enough.

Quick, they're coming.

He pads across his room only to halt before his bed, his gaze sweeping along the edge of the impenetrable darkness spilling from under his mattress. *Hurry.* In his carelessness he overlooks the part of his bed where in nights past he isolated a creaky spring. It lets out a ratcheting groan as he settles in, but he doesn't stop to check if someone heard. Instead, he rolls the sheets up over his head and reforms the tunnel to view his clock. It's done the very moment before he's certain the shadows might be aware of his exposure, but if they gaze down now, there's nothing to see but a crumpled sheet.

His breath drains with relief. *Made it. I made it.*

He looks at the clock. 2:02

For a moment, he's just a frightened boy, a boy lost in thoughts that are maybe too big for him, too wild for him, too subtle for him to see through, but his nonetheless, and he trembles at the echo of their passage through his restless mind. He pleads for forgiveness, constricting against his pillow in fear. He wishes he could sneak back through the moments, creep back in time to take those thoughts and strangle them, but he knows it's too late. It's just his imagination, yet his imagination comes from him. He knows enough to be sure he can't deny it, can't separate it, from himself. The monsters may be everywhere, but they come from him.

They watch him, of that, he's sure. They watch, and wait.

He fears to breathe, that even the little rise of the sheets with his breath will give him away and leave him at their mercy. He fights to hold still, and stuffs his thumb in his mouth to keep his teeth from chattering.

Hold it tight, that's it. I need the sun to rise. Come on!

His wide eye locks outward.

2:04

Something, something's coming, coming for me.

The moments, they just don't stop. The race begins anew. His mouth dries from anxiety and fear.

Return

"Dreaming again?"

Lucas stirred, his eyes sliding open to reveal the white ceiling over his head. For some reason he remembered having painted it not too long ago, but it seemed to have turned a dull gray. The sound of rain came to his ears. In the trace of its patter he realized his lips were moving, that his voice was mumbling an incoherent train of thoughts. The moment he became aware of his mumbling, though, it stopped.

His head rolled on the pillow to look to his side.

A woman sat in the big, dark leather chair by his window, her face pale in the rainy morning. "Dreaming again?" she repeated.

He stared at her for several moments before he blinked and his memory returned, his subconscious stunning him with a simultaneous flash that filled the many blanks of his mind. He blinked once more to sort it into something he could understand, into something that made sense of the world for him. "Oh, ah, good morning, Eva," he said, his voice rasping from his dry throat. He struggled to sit up in bed. He winced at he stiffness of his limbs.

He nodded. "Yes, dreaming again, I guess," he whispered.

"Do you want to talk about it?"

He opened his eyes and looked down. Both his forearms were wrapped in bandages. His left hand was covered in tape and an intravenous line trailed away to the stand beside his bed. Under the sheets he knew his left ankle was wrapped and that drove him to lift his right hand to feel the bandages on his head.

He dropped his hand and looked to Eva. She was his home nurse. She could've passed as his wife's sister.

His heart began to pound. He remembered his dream, and it came back in a rush. It was the same moment again, that same awful moment, relived and dissected in his mind to find some option, some other choice that could alter his present. *I should've heard the car coming. Why didn't I hear it coming sooner? Was it the second bottle of wine we had with dinner? She asked me to stop, but it was good wine, and if I'd skipped it, I wouldn't have insisted we walk after we ate, and if we hadn't been walking....*

He closed his eyes. He saw it all again. Laughing with her as they walked, holding hands. Then a crash and they turn, too late, too late. The car is already over the curb and hurtling toward them. He yanks on her hand but then he feels it, that terrible, irresistible weight pulling her hand from his. *Hold on, hold on, hold on!* It feels as if the weight of the planet itself is pulling at her. His grasp gives out, overwhelming him with that last awful feeling of her fingertips sliding across his palm, down his fingers, and then nothing, emptiness, the titan ripping them apart in its destructive rush.

It wasn't a dream; it was a nightmare. Worse, it wasn't a nightmare; it was reality.

His eyes popped open. He stared down at his left hand, outstretched before him.

Eva glanced at him. "Are you sure you don't want to talk about it?"

"Yes," he said and, cradling his hand to his chest, turned away in shame. He fought for several moments to calm down. "Where's my brother? I remember something, somebody, telling me I would see him. Is that right?"

"He's off to work."

"Before you got here?"

She hesitated. "Yes."

"He couldn't wait?" He looked to her. "Is there a problem between you two?"

She shook her head. "We get along," she said with a shrug. "How do you feel today?"

His eyes slid shut. "How could they send me home like this?" He blew out his breath in frustration. "I don't belong here."

"You're well enough. This was your choice. Do you remember?"

He frowned. He remembered the bright light of the exam room blinding him with its white glare. It was the one clear memory he had before waking in his bed at home. "It was too bright," he said. "I don't want to be where it's so bright. I don't want to be in the light at all. I belong in the dark."

"It's a natural reaction," she said with an even, soothing tone. "You can talk about it when you're ready."

He grunted. He looked over his bedroom, taking in the details. It was a spacious room. On a clear day it was full of light from the tall windows to either side of his bed. To his side there was a dressing area, the leather chair, and the doorway to the bathroom. Across from him, beyond the footboard of his bed, were two doors: his closet on the left, his wife's on the right. For a reason he couldn't identify, he stared at those doors until a rumble of thunder startled him.

Eva looked to the window.

"When can I see her … my wife?"

Eva turned to him. "Are you ready to see her?" She waited before looking to the clouds. "I'm not so sure you are."

He opened his mouth, but then closed it.

Eva looked to him. "You're wondering if she would want to see you," she said, drawing a glare from him before his gaze sank away. "Only you can answer that for yourself."

He watched her as her gaze returned to her hands. She was knitting something small and white. He tipped his chin to her lap where her hands were busy with their work. "What is that?"

"A sweater." She paused, a small grin drawing across her lips. "A baby's sweater."

"Yours?"

"No," she said, her eyebrows rising in apparent wonder at that idea. "Someone else I look after. It's going to be a gift."

"I thought, for now, you were my guardian angel," he said, but felt guilty at once for even that weak attempt at some humor.

She gave him a small smile, but kept her eyes on her knitting. "Well, I have been assigned to you. But that will change at some point, and I have to be ready." She took a breath before letting it go in a long sigh. "Oh yes, always have to be ready for the change."

He looked away and once again found himself staring at the doors beyond his bed. He hesitated at some imperceptible thought that nagged him, that urged him to get out of bed and open one of those doors, but trepidation from the pain in his ankle stilled him.

He sank back on his pillow and slipped off to sleep.

***

Some time later he rolled on his back and opened his eyes. The ceiling still looked gray like the amorphous clouds he imagined outside. The patter of rain came to his ears again. He rubbed his face before laying his hands on his chest and looking to the big leather chair. He blinked in surprise.

His brother had one leg crossed over the other and a cup of tea in his hands as he stared out the window. Sensing a gaze upon him, he looked toward the bed. "Hello, Lucas."

"Robbie? Are you home early?" He looked about trying to get a fix on the time.

"Robert," his brother said and tipped his head. "I'm grown up now, you know. And no, I didn't get here early. You slept late."

"Eva went home?"

"Yes. I saw her off."

He looked to Robert. "You don't like her, do you?"

Robert set his tea down and stared at him. Thunder rumbled outside. "Eva and I have a certain history," he said, but held up a hand to stop the obvious assumption. "Acquaintance only. She's been very kind to me. We didn't meet under the best of circumstances. Whenever I see her I can't forget those circumstances. I admire her, though. I guess that's why I'm following in her footsteps — my job, that is. I'm not the accountant like you are, but we both balance the books, so to speak." Robert took a sip of his tea and looked out the window. "Do you feel comfortable with her? I know the resemblance—"

"I'm fine," Lucas said and looked away. His gaze fell on the closet doors across from him. In a matter of moments he began to fidget and looked back to his brother. He was struck by the oddness of it, this calm conversation with his brother. Surreal as it felt, it disarmed his reservations to let the burning question within him gain voice. "Where were you all these years? I never heard from you."

Robert's face fell. "I've been busy."

"Robbie—"

Robert held up a finger. "I'm not little anymore. That's why it's Robert, not Robbie. I grew up here," he said, tipping his chin to the world outside the window.

"And we never bumped into each other?"

"We were more distant than you think."

"But you'd think sooner or later, I mean, we're twins. I always wondered about that connection you hear about between twins, how they're always drawn back to each other, and why it never happened with us. But even without that, you'd think somewhere along the line, somehow, it would've come up because someone would've confused us." He opened his hands in thought before laying them on his chest. "Which reminds me, now that I think about it, how'd you find me?"

Robert's eyebrows rose. "I was found. They called me. The hospital, that is. You know Mom and Dad, how they are."

He looked with curiosity at Robert. "They're both dead. You know that." He shook his head. "They must have found you by our last name."

Robert opened his hands. "I suppose. They have their ways, people like Eva. They're quite resourceful."

"Eva found you?" He blinked in confusion. "I thought you found her."

Robert shrugged. "Different sides of the same coin. Does it matter? You're here, I'm here, and you're cared for. What else is there?"

Lucas opened his hands at the obvious. "I want my wife back."

Robert frowned and looked out the window.

Lucas clenched his fists. "I want my life back. I don't want to lose another piece of it." He hesitated as he considered his thoughts, but then they started to spill from him and, as they did, he found himself powerless to stop his confession. "You know, there's this hole, this blank, from my childhood. I remember us together, when we were little, walking to school, holding hands as we walked on Main Street before taking that long hilly path to the school. I remember all that clearly. And then there's this *skip*, and I'm still little, but you're gone. Dad's gone, too, but when he comes by, good God, if it wasn't the mortuary-like tension, it was the screaming." He fell silent, his forehead knotting as he perceived a glaring inconsistency in a new light. "Where were you all those years?"

Robert's face was blank. "I told you."

"You know what I mean."

Robert took a deep breath before letting it out. "I stayed on with Dad. He couldn't let go of the past. That's why he and Mom argued like they did. Aimless blame and resentment. But I lived on with him."

"You know, I did a terrible thing," Lucas whispered.

Robert stared at him.

"I, I forgot you," he said, laying his hands on his face to hide from Robbie. "I didn't forget I had a twin, but the emptiness of you not being there. You know, I asked Dad a few times if I could visit you; why we couldn't see each other. He just said it was complicated and then Mom would get into it with him and they'd have a huge argument. I stopped asking." He looked back to Robert. "I never should've done that."

Robert took a long breath before he spoke. "I understand."

"No. I don't want to repeat that mistake," Lucas said with determination, perceiving the source of his confession. "I loved my wife, I loved her so much, and I don't think I want to be here without her. I knew it from the first time I saw her. It was like she filled in the blank of some question I didn't even know I was asking, and now I've lost her. All I had to do was hold on, and I failed her."

Robert shrugged. "You did what you could."

"It wasn't enough." Lucas rubbed his forehead, his emotions knotting within him. "I let go once with you, and now I did it again. I wanted to hold on, that's all I had to do, one simple thing." He dropped his hands in his lap and stared at his feet beneath the blanket. Then his gaze rose to fix on the closet doors, holding on them until his heart pounded with the effort it took to look away. *What's the fascination there? Is it more guilt, our lives stored so neatly in two little areas with all this mess outside? What's happening to me? I've been condemned; condemned to a nightmare I can never wake from.*

"Forgive me," Robert said and shifted.

Lucas looked to his brother, surprised. "What?"

Robert cleared his throat. "I'm sorry." He shook his head as he rose from the chair. "I shouldn't have brought you here. Eva was right."

"What do you mean?"

Robert held up a hand as he left the room. "Get your rest, brother." And with that, the door clicked shut.

***

Lucas woke some time later, somewhat disturbed by the fact that he didn't remember falling asleep. Nevertheless, he found himself staring up at the gray cast of the ceiling, depression and frustration creeping through him like partners in a silent conspiracy. He blinked, possessed with the bad feeling that he'd never be his old self again. It wasn't for his wife, even though that pain seemed a distant oddity at the moment, but more a brooding suspicion that he'd been displaced from the natural course of his life.

It made a certain sense, he decided. He wasn't a bad man, and he didn't lead a bad life. By all accounts of his friends, acquaintances, and coworkers he was an amicable fellow, respected, respectful, and thoughtful, if perhaps not a little selfish in the degree of his introspection. Considering the turbulence of his childhood, he carried no hidden grudge for his separation from his brother and had maintained a workable relationship between his parents and the animosity between them. With all that being true, he thought he had earned, in his accountant's sensibility, some cosmic right, some weight in the balance of greater existence, to have more than a brief moment of happiness.

He sat up and let his feet slide out from the blankets to settle on the padded carpet. Thunder rumbled outside. *Go ahead, growl away.* He glared at the window. His sorrow steamed within him. *This is exactly why I had so much trouble entertaining any notion of You. I put up with so much all those years that any idea of God just didn't add up for me, but I'll admit that when I met her, I was so thankful. You—if You are what everyone claims You to be—You've seen that in my heart, how I loved her, and still I lost her. Wasn't I thankful enough? Was I guilty of complacency? I was thankful for her every day and still I lost her.*

He balled his fists and pounded them on his knees.

"I wasn't ready for this," he said to himself as he looked to the ceiling. "I wasn't ready. I want my life back. Somebody took it away, and I want it back. This isn't right."

The door to the house closed with a thud.

He grabbed his IV pole and went to his bedroom door, opening it a crack to peer down the hallway toward the living room. He saw Eva there, sitting in a chair, and then his brother, pacing across the mouth of the hallway. Robert was shaking his head and waving his hands, but his voice was hushed. Eva listened in silence as she opened her knitting box and went to work on her little white sweater. When she spoke, she didn't whisper. Instead, her voice came even and forceful, as if to refute and rebuke some position Robert had argued.

"I told you this might happen," she said, "and I told you he wasn't ready. This was wrong."

Lucas closed the door. His heart raced. Suspicious paranoia seized him, only to be reinforced when he realized he walked to the door without an ache or limp. His gaze fell to his ankle, his jaw clenching. With a trembling hand he followed the IV tubing under its bandages to find that it ended in a sealed tube. He closed his eyes to gather his wits but, failing that, he rushed to his bathroom, knocking over the IV pole in his haste. He sucked in a breath, turned on the bathroom light, and tore loose his bandages.

There wasn't a scratch on him

He spun, but recoiled when he found Eva standing in the doorway of the bathroom. His voice faltered with hysteria as words bubbled from his mouth. "What is this? I want to see my wife."

"Easy now," Eva said. "Just look at me and relax." She reached toward him. "Why don't you lie down, and we'll sort this out."

"Don't touch me!"

She held her hand up to calm him. "Everything's going to be okay. Just look at me, look at my face, and let yourself remember."

Despite her assurance, his anger won. "I don't care if you look like her. I want to know what you people did to me, I, I want to see my wife. Now." He grabbed the wrist of her outstretched hand. "Now!"

His voice died in his throat.

He froze, his stare locked on her face.

She said nothing. Only her unblinking stare met him.

He trembled, his lips quivering in confusion. His mind sparked in a chaotic storm. Images emerged within him, things long buried, long lost things he had suppressed and locked away so deep he forgot their very existence.

"You," he hissed. "I, I know you."

Her gaze softened as she smiled on him.

He continued to stare at her through the storm of his memories until he gasped, perceiving the sense of it that yet defied logical sense. "You, you don't look like her, she … she looks like you."

"The answer to your unspoken question, isn't that what you thought?"

"Wait, wait … I saw you once, long ago," he said in disbelief, her words gaining little purchase on him. "But that's impossible, that was just a dream. You look exactly the same, you haven't aged at all, but I was a little boy."

"Easy," she said. "Just remember."

He continued to stare at her, but the confusing kaleidoscope of images in his head sorted and produced an image he never before deciphered. He jerked his hand away from her to clutch the side of his head. The nightmare returned to him with the intensity of a hammer blow to the back of his skull. He staggered from the bathroom, cradling his head in his hands as his heart pounded in his chest.

He saw himself walking hand in hand, but not with his wife, with Robbie, all those years ago, walking to school. *But it's not all that different, is it?* The vision that came to him was jarring in its familiarity. A car hurtled over the curb toward him and Robbie. Everything stopped in a spasm of time, a spasm of his perception in time, and it seemed he was afloat in a dream. Somewhere in that dream he and Robbie pulled at each other's hands, each trying to get the other clear of the car. The only thing Lucas could see in the milky expanse of headlight glare was his clutch of Robbie's hand, but then things changed, and he perceived something else.

It was another set of hands. He looked up to see a woman standing between them, smiling down on them, and he was dumbstruck by the beauty lurking in her peaceful gaze. In that moment she was the bridge between him and Robbie. Her lips moved, but Lucas couldn't hear her.

Eva.

Robbie heard. There were tears in his eyes. Then he let go, but not from Eva.

The memory erupted in an overload of noise. The ground slammed into Lucas' side as he hit the ground. Robbie had pushed him clear, but Robbie was lost, obliterated in a wail of screeching tires and a horrible thump.

Lucas' eyes popped open. The seismic pound of his heart shook him, leaving him hunched by his bed. He looked between his fingers to see Eva standing by the bathroom door. He tried to swallow over his dry throat. "What, what is this? Where am I?"

"Keeping the books," she said. "You know what it is. You had the thoughts yourself,the cosmic right, the balance in a greater view of existence."

He looked away from her to stare at the floor. "Robbie, he, he died that day?"

Eva lowered her head somewhat, but her eyes widened on him. "Robert made his choice, and so did you. It was already in his nature to understand what I was, and he wanted to be with me, to be as me, and so he came with me. Your will was different, so your choice was different."

His gaze rose, full of accusation. "You took him away?"

"No," she said. "It's mine to give the choice, but not mine to make the choice."

"I tried to make that choice for you, now," Robert said. "I'm sorry."

He spun to find Robert standing behind him. "What?"

Robert frowned and lowered his gaze. "I missed you all those years. I heard your will to visit me. It rings in my ears like it was yesterday. But you need to know everything's in order now. I see Mom and Dad all the time. The fighting's over between them. It's like we remembered, before."

Lucas shook his head.

"You were hiding from yourself and that never works," Eva said. "Your past and your present have dovetailed in a most curious way, and whether that was to balance things or just blind circumstance isn't ours to decide. It simply is, but now you have a new choice."

He glared at her.

Eva smiled. "Love her for who she is, not because you see her as me."

Thunder rumbled outside. Robert nodded. "Time to choose."

Stunned, senseless, Lucas couldn't frame a single thought in the muddled mess of his mind. Memories skipped about. He saw through the illusions and half-truths his denial had created to comfort him in a perilous disconnect from reality. He never accepted Robbie's death. In Lucas' denial Robbie lived with his father. His parents argued because his father refused to accept Robbie's death and coddled the illusion that Robbie was living elsewhere, while his mother was frozen in the abyss of her grief. All those years the image of Eva was a shadow in Lucas' dreams, one that seized him when he first saw the woman that would be his wife, the woman that he came to love. Of all things, it was the one thing of which he was still certain, the one thing that was free of the delusions he created to hide from his past.

The idea that it took his current dream to wake him from the dream he'd been living was too dizzying to comprehend. He shook his head to clear his thoughts, only to hear Eva whispering in his mind.

Reality is a shapeless thing one creates by the decisions one makes in the twists and turns of life, but one constant is that the past can't be denied, the past will always return, and until the past is settled, it will corrupt and meddle with any choices yet to be made.

He turned on his feet to look at the closet doors. He staggered toward them and stared at the doorknobs. He looked to one, but then looked to the other and rested his hand on the knob.

He closed his eyes, opened the door, and knew no more.

***

He woke to a disturbing series of beeps and pings. His gaze darted about. He was a mess of bandages, tubes, and pain. Every breath felt like ground glass going through his chest. He heard a voice. It was muffled through the pain and medication and seemed far away.

He looked to his side and gasped. Eva was there, sitting with him.

His mind bucked and raced. His memory returned. It was almost too much to comprehend. He saw the car and made his decision, made a decision that stirred and erupted in a heartbeat from his past. He had whipped his wife across his body to throw her clear, only to be hit by the car himself. He clung to her as long as he could until the titan ripped them apart. In his last conscious moment he felt her fingertips as they slipped from him, trailing across his palm before he was gone. He found it hard to believe he had the strength to clear her like that, but then he knew that he hadn't been alone, that another had pulled with him.

He looked to his side again, studying the face of the woman beside him.

No, not Eva.

He let out a breath, and understood his choice.

He clutched his wife's hand as their fingers meshed.

Flowers for Colleen

It was the first Saturday morning of the month, and Darryl went to get flowers for Colleen, as was his routine. He stood in the florist shop, waiting behind a rather impatient man, while the young woman behind the counter prepared the man's bouquet. The customer stood there, his impatience evident in the nervous tap of his foot and his repeated sighs of frustration, as the woman held her smile and tried to calm him with harmless small talk. She was a perky little creature, adorable with the little sprigs of baby's breath tucked into the loose bun of her brown hair. Her large eyes held a welcome innocence for the world's intentions.

She wrapped the man's bouquet and turned. "Is there anything else, sir?"

He shook his head and took out his wallet. "No. Just ring it up already."

Darryl tipped his chin, an almost imperceptible movement, his eyes narrowing on the back of the man's head. He frowned as he gazed through the glass doors of the shop's refrigerator. He turned to the woman. "Excuse me, but do you have any roses? I was looking for six red roses."

The bright curve of her smile fell, but her eyes glowed with empathy. "Oh, no, I'm so sorry, we're getting some in later. I just opened a few minutes ago and these were the last we had from yesterday," she said, opening a hand to the bouquet she just made.

The man in front of Darryl took the bouquet. He turned and patted Darryl's shoulder. "Early bird gets the worm, buddy."

Darryl's face fell. He looked at his shoulder. He watched the man go. He turned to the woman, raising a hand in goodbye, before following the man out of the store. They walked across the parking lot, beneath a heavy gray sky. Darryl slid his hand into his coat pocket, and his fingers settled around a small handgun. It was going to be so easy it almost lost the thrill of anticipation, but his mind was made. The man didn't even look back, so self-assured in the delusion of his security, so arrogant in the notion of his personal safety. He got into his car. Darryl gave a quick glance over his shoulders to make sure no one was watching.

He walked up to the man's car and tapped a knuckle on the window as the man set the bouquet on the passenger seat. The man turned in surprise, but his expression soured at Darryl's presence.

Darryl opened his mouth, but the man flipped up his hand, his middle finger extended.

Darryl shifted, angling the gun in his pocket before squeezing the trigger. He felt a slight tug as the bullet ripped through his coat, followed by a collection of sounds only his imagination could dissect: the muffled pop of the silenced gun, the crystalline crack of the window, the dull plunk of the bullet punching into the man's temple. The glass went white with fracture lines, the few specks of blood that spattered from the man's temple caught on the inner glass. The man's head rolled to the side, his hand dropping in his lap. Darryl knocked in the glass with his elbow and grabbed the man's shoulder to hold him upright in his seat, but it was too late. The small round from Darryl's gun had remained in the man's head, spinning around the inside of his skull, rupturing the inner canal of his ear. A thick red discharge dribbled from his ear onto the roses, ruining them.

Darryl frowned and looked over his shoulder. It was early. It was a Saturday morning. No one saw him. He lowered his head and walked away. The woman in the floral shop, well, he had already decided she'd live, and he never second-guessed himself.

***

The gun and silencer, which he had fabricated in his apartment from industrial plastics, he tossed into his apartment building's incinerator to melt away. He went upstairs, sat in his little kitchen, and sewed up the hole in his coat. The television droned in the background, the morning news saying something about a dismembered body found in the woods outside the city, another apparent victim of the so-called "Lumberjack killer." He glanced over his shoulder to watch the report before finishing with his coat. It was the second hole he had to repair; one more, and he'd replace the coat, sending this one to the incinerator. He made a cup of black coffee and listened to the rain as he stared out his one window to the gray urban emptiness ten floors below. The day was still young. He was yet to find flowers for Colleen.

He went to his closet, reached past the janitor's overalls he wore for his night job at the plastics factory and popped loose a panel he had fashioned in the wall. He slid another one of his silenced guns, with its single shot loaded, into his pocket.

He pulled up his hood, locked his door, and walked away.

***

An hour later he sat at a red light, watching his wipers as they squeaked across the windshield. He was driving about the city, not quite in an aimless way, but more a deliberate randomness as he sought another florist. Not any shop would do; no, the shop needed a certain appeal through the presentations in the window, the sign, the location—

an incomprehensible culmination of minutia to attract him. He thought about the shop he visited in the morning, frowning as he considered whether or not the woman would remember him if she was questioned. Perhaps she would understand how close she came to her end, how her life had rested in his hands, how she had been judged and been deemed worthy and in return, feign ignorance regarding Darryl. It was a thought that comforted him, that elevated his judgment of her, but not to the point where he'd be satisfied to call her Colleen. No, that tireless search would have to continue.

The light turned green. He drove off at a leisurely pace, sipping his black coffee, his gaze dissecting the world before him.

***

It was early afternoon, and he found himself driving along an empty stretch of the city's loop parkway where the road ran through a state park. He enjoyed that stretch, even in the current dismal downpour, as it left the gray urban monotony a fleeting memory before the rolling hills of towering evergreens and blue spruces.

His mind wandered. He thought again of the woman in the floral shop, but his thoughts moved with their usual senile elusiveness to other contemplations, all of them revolving around the odd pursuit of his life. He had killed sixteen people over the years without any trace of guilt. To him, those acts weren't crimes; they were nothing more than exercises of inevitability. People were flawed creatures, he knew, but some were flawed in rather malignant ways and when he came across them, if opportunity would lend its grace, he'd act. Malignant flaws led to one end and, understanding that finality, he saw himself as a blameless catalyst. He didn't deceive himself with notions of superiority or moral imperative. He knew full well his ability to elude law enforcement rested on his own benign flaws. Unlike the Lumberjack, he left no discernable trail, garnered no media attention, and held to no modus operandi. He was a nobody, forgettable, average to the point of inconsequence; yet, he was patient, he had a purpose, and a reason.

He remembered his *first*. Some of the 'guys' from work had convinced him to join them at a nightclub for somebody's birthday. It wasn't his preference, but he went anyway, knowing that if he refused it would draw attention. So he went, only to hover on the periphery of the merriment. The louder the music, the more disaffected he felt until he could hardly hear the tones, only feeling the resonant thud in his chest from the deafening volume of repetitive dance beats. His gaze floated on waves of sensory overload, the flash of strobe lights like crests of rising water, dark tides of aimless promiscuity buoying an undulating mass of empty-eyed cadavers.

A woman had bumped into him as he waited for a beer at the bar. She was drunk, she was delirious, and leaned against him, laughing before draping an arm over his shoulder and tugging him away from the bar. She soon separated from him, but he followed her, his jaw clenched. She was defenseless, but worse, she had *made* herself defenseless, and her security—that elusive charm of feminine vulnerability he found so intriguing—she had left it dangling like a hunk of raw meat. Did she not know, did she not care, had she no idea about Colleen, and the horrible things that could happen to a woman's innocence?

He followed her to the bathroom. He waited, lurking in the shadows, counting until he was certain she was alone. Then he went in. He took her hand, touched her cheek and led her to a stall. She never stopped; she never worried. Instead, she giggled. He closed the stall door and only then did it hit him, the odd existence of the moment colliding with his conscious senses to leave him forged in the fire of self-realization. The moment it came to him, the rest flowed with such ease that reality slipped to the dreamy world of the surreal. All he knew was the awful, relentless pressure of his hands, and the increasing divergence of his pounding heart and her fading pulse.

His thoughts wandered back to the woman in the floral shop. The notion of letting her live, he saw it as something other than a gift. It was a moment of incongruence, a moment of total inconsequence in her conscious perception; yet, unknown to her, it may have been the most important moment of her life, the moment when her life was allowed to continue. To her, such an incredible, life-altering moment was just a forgettable moment. Such complacency, it was the greatest malignancy to him, forgivable only when held in child-like ignorance, such as she possessed. When held in contempt, though, it was unforgivable. Every moment could be a singular existence, unique, incredible, irreplaceable, precious as the red rose, and its delicate beauty possessed with innocence.

He blinked. A set of red lights pulsed in the distance, off on the shoulder ahead of him. He slowed, his eyes narrowing, the memory of his *first* still tingling within his fingers. He neared the stopped car. There was a woman there—he could tell by the way her long coat was tailored to her frame—and she stood by the passenger side rear wheel.

After a quick debate he pulled over on the shoulder behind her, glancing in his rearview mirror to check that no one was behind him. He flipped up the hood of his coat, checked his pocket for the gun, and stepped from the car. "Can I help you?"

The woman turned to him, studying him as he stood by his old, beaten car.

He closed his door and stepped before his headlights. "Flat tire? I'll change it."

She had dark hair; it hung about her face in a wet, black mass. She fell back a step as she shook her head. "No, no, I'm okay."

He looked to the tire. It was indeed flat. He stepped to the trunk of her car, which was opened enough for him to see she had hit the release. "It'll only take a minute. You shouldn't be out here alone like this. It's not safe."

He put his hand on the trunk lid.

He could see her move in the corner of his eye.

He flipped the lid up. Two severed legs rested on a sheet of plastic in her trunk.

Instinct drove him down, just as the tire iron whistled over his head. He had no time to contemplate how his killer's instinct just served to save his life; rather, he moved on her, grabbing the iron in one head and whipping his handgun free with the other.

Her eyes locked on the simple plastic cylinder of his gun. The open trunk, with the severed limbs, lingered in his peripheral vision. They stared at each other, both befuddled in the realization that dawned between them.

She forced herself to swallow as rain dripped from her hair.

He tipped his head. "You should cauterize the stumps. Blade patterns. They won't be able to identify them."

Their eyes narrowed as they stood in the rain, frozen there, the tire iron humming between their opposing holds, his gun hand steady with the barrel pointed at her forehead. As the moments mounted they began to relent, the tire iron sinking between them as their arms relaxed.

"How'd you …." they said in unison.

He took a breath. "Police website. I check it at the library. No trace."

She nodded. "I know." Her gaze darted to the barrel of his fabricated gun. "You have a pattern. I can see it. I don't think they do."

"They call you the Lumberjack," he replied. "The limb stumps."

She shrugged. "So, here we are. Kind of an odd moment, don't you think?" She motioned with her eyes to the tire iron.

He hesitated, but consented.

They rebounded from each other with a quick step. Safety in distance.

She gestured with the tire iron at the severed legs. "I didn't pick that stupid Lumberjack name. Gallows humor among the cops, I guess. My real name is Morgana. How about you?"

His jaw clenched, but then he found his voice. "Darryl."

She tossed the tire iron in her trunk, her eyes steady on him. She raised an eyebrow, the spinning of her mind's gears almost audible. "Well, Darryl, I think, maybe we need to talk, you know?"

He lowered his gun. "That would be odd."

She stared at him until her lips curved in a smile, her eyes widening with a sudden, childlike excitement. "I know. We'll have coffee. That's ordinary. What do you say?"

There were two severed limbs in her trunk. She was a killer, but then so was he. For some reason his suspicious nature was silent, his apprehension mute, his guarding instinct restful. He eased, his shoulders loosening. "Let me take care of your flat."

***

He changed the tire, huddled beside her car in the rain. She watched him after she fetched an umbrella and stood, hovering in the periphery of his vision, toward the front fender. It was a truce of sorts, he concluded, a basic framework of trust. What might necessitate such a trust, or the strange impossibility of their paths crossing, failed to penetrate his thoughts. Once he had the spare tire on, it came to him. Perhaps it was the fact that he had to move the two severed legs to get to the spare, or more so that moving two severed legs on the side of the road in the rain didn't strike him as strange. Nevertheless, tightening up the lug nuts gave him time to do some thinking. It was a lonesome existence, the path of a predator, but they had found each other, against all improbability, in a moment that seemed to possess a singular property of inconsequence.

He stopped short, his gaze resting on the wheel.

She turned to him, her attention darting from her vigil on the road. "Something wrong?"

He looked to her. "No. Everything is just right."

She smiled. "Okay. Coffee?"

"Start the car. When the muffler gets hot we'll use it to cauterize the stumps and ditch the legs." He stood and wiped his hands clean before tossing the tire iron in the trunk. He looked at the legs. One was slender, with pink toenails, the other somewhat beefy, with hair. The engine started. He waited until she got out of the car. "You've been busy."

She came up beside him and shrugged before looking at him. "Opportunity presented. The targets were right. You know how it goes."

He nodded. "Creatures like us, we're more complicated than anyone knows."

She grinned at his thought. "That's what makes us special." She waved the exhaust fumes from her face and glanced over her shoulder. "So. Barbecue time?"

He couldn't help but join her grin.

***

He followed her along the road until she got off at an exit by the university. They passed a few lights and turned into a little plaza to park. The rain poured, so they hurried to a coffee shop that sat near the middle of the plaza. Huddled in the foyer, they waited until a young college student set a table for them. The shop was narrow, but deep, and Morgana asked for a table in the rear where they would be alone. When the student looked at them, Morgana slipped her hand through the crook of Darryl's arm and smiled. It took effort for Darryl to maintain his composure. It reminded him why he was entertaining this madness, as the reality of his life's pursuit had compelled him to a monastic existence. They sat in the back of the shop, in a booth with high walls and a dim, hooded lamp that hung low over the table. The table itself was narrow, leaving them somewhat close, so there was no dodging the probing stare of Morgana's large, brown eyes, glistening like two pools of oil.

She ordered a basket of scones and a cup of tea, her grin revealing itself once again when he ordered his plain black coffee. When he looked at her, she opened her hands. "You seem like the black coffee kind of guy, Darryl." She shrugged off her coat. "I'm going to dry my hair a bit with some paper towels. I'll only be a minute."

He had to lean back when she got up, the table so narrow that they almost bumped heads when she rocked forward to slide out from the booth. The scones came; they were piping hot in a basket, kept warm beneath a napkin. They were served with some cold, hard butter, lightly salted. The smell was delicious, but he kept to his coffee, taking a few sips until she returned.

Her hair was pushed back, still damp, but he could see she preferred to part it on the side. She patted her hands on the table before taking a sip of tea and letting out a deep sigh. "Oh, that feels good," she said, bobbing her head side to side. Her eyes widened as she poked a finger under the napkin to get a peek at the scones. "Still too hot, I think. You have to try them. They're outrageous. The kids who work here, they're from the university's culinary program. You come in here later, say around seven or so, and it's standing room only."

He nodded. "I don't eat out much." Realizing he had chilled the conversation, he shifted and pointed to his coffee. "Like you said, I'm a black coffee kind of guy."

"Whatever suits you." She poked in a bowl for a packet of raw sugar and dumped its large brown granules into her tea. She gave it a stir before tapping her spoon on the rim of the cup. Fingers meshed on the table before her, she sat up straight, fixed her gaze on him, and smiled. "So, Darryl. Let's get to it. We both follow a, well, shall we say, a profession of exceedingly select membership. Of those rare few, we have achieved mastery in our skills, evidenced by the fact that we sit here and not in some dark concrete hole. So, by default, there's a pretext of fellowship between us; we're not adversaries. And if we're anything alike in our skills, which I think we are, we have similar sensitivities, otherwise this moment would be impossible, correct?"

He studied her, hypnotized by her unblinking gaze. "Yes, yes, impossible."

"And even though our profession is, shall we say, a consuming pursuit, it's a lonely one, right?"

He took a deep breath, his eyebrows rising as he let it go. "By it's nature, yes."

She took a scone and set a wedge of butter with her knife. She waited a moment as it softened on the hot scone. She took a quick bite, smiling at him as she chewed. "You're a little shy—guarded, I should say," she said, dabbing her mouth with her napkin. "It may not seem like it, but I'm shy … guarded, too." She shrugged. "In fact, I don't really talk to anybody. I guess you know that, because when you talk to people, you get a feel for them, right? And sometimes after you get that feel, you get that odd anxiety, that anxious excitement, and then, it's time."

He sipped his coffee. It took some effort to find his voice, to acknowledge this part of himself that had formed the focus of his life. "Yes, yes, that's it, exactly."

She leaned forward. Her foot bumped against his knee as she crossed her legs. Her eyes widened, glittering beneath the dim light as she pointed at him. "I bet you're very smart, that you possess a really developed mind, don't you?"

He frowned. "I did well when I was young, but I never got to follow through."

She leaned closer to him as she rested a hand on his wrist. "I don't mean to brag, but I'm really smart. Quantitatively brilliant. I have a one-sixty IQ. I have a doctorate in astrophysics and I'm working on quantum theory as well." She put her scone down and lowered her hand so that her fingers rested across both his wrists. "People like us, Darryl, we're a different breed. Not better, no, that would be arrogant, but *different*."

His face felt warm. He was afraid he blushed, but the moment that embarrassing thought came to him he knew that he had, certain of it when she smiled. It wasn't a mocking smile. He knew that contempt well enough, could sense it in people without them forming any expression at all, in fact. Her sentiment was genuine. He could see it in her eyes, heard it in her intonations and insinuations of empathy, felt it in the warm steady clasp of her delicate fingers. "It's such a lonely life," he said with effort.

She tipped her head, her eyes devouring him. "How do you see it ending?"

He blinked. Such a thought had never occurred to him. "I, I don't."

She squeezed his wrists before settling back in her seat. "Me neither," she said, smiling again, adorable with her face framed between the wavy length of her drying hair. She gave her tea a stir and took a sip before looking back to him. "What got you started?"

Before he realized it, he set his elbows on the table and leaned forward. He raised a finger. "You tell me, first. I did change your tire, don't forget."

She bowed her head. "Fair enough. Well, like I said, I'm brilliant, so I graduated school early and went to college. The pressure was insane. There were so many expectations. My parents, they don't lack in intellectual capacity, but they're simple people, blue-collar types—good, honest people. They never understood me and once I was in college, that gulf just became impassable. In the meantime, there I was, younger than anyone around me, this freak in a training bra that could think circles around everybody but couldn't get a driver's license. Even the professors, I was their trophy instead of their peer. They'd throw problems at me they couldn't solve, and when I'd solve them, they'd be excited, but they'd resent me, too. I was totally alone, adrift among hypocrites and fools who all treated me like I was a space alien."

She took a breath, her smile fading. "I had a nervous breakdown, a total meltdown."

His face fell. "I, I know that breakdown."

She froze, her gaze locked on him.

"I had that breakdown," he continued, "had it when I was eighteen. It seems so long ago, now." He looked to her. "I was on the same path you're talking about. The future, life, it all seemed so bright for me, preordained, perfect." He waited as his thoughts coalesced. "I had a sister. She wasn't like me. I was full of thoughts nobody understood, but she was innocent. All the world was good in her eyes, and I used to think I'd trade all the intelligence, all the thoughts in my head, just to see the world once as she did. She was like an angel." He cleared his throat, squeezing his eyes shut before he could continue. "Some thugs, they raped her and drowned her. I was sixteen. My father couldn't take it, so he took off. My mother drank herself numb. She said she'd wait until I was a legal adult. I didn't know what that meant, and maybe I didn't want to know. It's hard to say now. The day I turned eighteen she hung herself. Everything was lost. It was just me. It's been just me since then."

She fell silent, fidgeting a moment before she leaned toward him. "Do you know what a neutron star is?" she said, but, when he shook his head, she only seemed all the more eager to talk. "You have stars out there in space, right? Well, they only last so long, and if they're big enough, they go out with a supernova. Then they collapse under gravitational stress, crushing themselves down. Now, depending on how big they were to start with, decides on how much they'll crush down. Not too big and they become a cold dwarf. Real big and they implode all the way down to a black hole.

"But if they're just right," she said, raising her index fingers, "they become a neutron star. It's an amazing balancing act, the last stop before complete surrender to gravity and implosion to a black hole. Instead, gravity crushes in on all those atoms, crushes them to the point that basic atomic particles, electrons and protons, fuse together and become neutrons. Think about that. Base elements, base opposites, crushed, fused to neutrality, holding that line against the will to devour themselves, superseding anything they were before. One ambivalent, disaffected, ultra-dense, ultra-pure existence."

He listened, his heart stilled, his mind devouring her every word.

"That's what happened to me the night I broke down," she said, her voice a whisper. "All these things, all this around us, it revealed itself for the madness it is and I broke from it, broke from it to the point where I almost broke from myself, but not quite, no, not quite. Still here, but free—emancipated, I would say. All the opposites in my nature, they were fused, nullified, to one truth, no doubt, no second guess, leaving me small and unseen. But I radiate, I radiate an invisible energy about me and it guides me, protects me, *talks* to me, tells me who, tells me when, tells me where, and the *why*, the why is a singular mystery in itself, encrypted in the action, at once blameless and congratulatory." She took his hands, squeezing them as if she clung to a rope. "Tell me you understand, Darryl. Please?"

He squeezed her fingers in turn before raising a hand to caress her cheek. Her face was very warm. "I understand," he whispered back to her. "The compulsion has a voice all its own."

"No condemnation."

"Blameless."

"Do you believe this moment was random?"

He lowered his hand and shook his head. "Consequence and circumstance have their own subtlety."

They could feel their pulse pounding in their hands. It wasn't the quickening when the compulsion called to them, but something else, strong and steady, undeniable. They were so close their noses almost touched, their eyes lost in shadow beneath the dim light.

She tipped her head, her eyes gleaming with mischief as her smile returned. "My place, my apartment, it's not five minutes from here."

He fought to breathe against the sudden tightness in his chest. He welcomed the madness of it, the odd delirium of that surreal prospect, glorious in all the pregnant malignancy of its ramifications, and found himself powerless to entertain any of his careful, calculating considerations except one, the one he couldn't deny, the one compelling his pursuit, his search, his tireless search.

"Do you like roses?"

Memento

Dawn came with the stark light of winter, a low slice of weak yellow under the heavy gray sky. The countryside was shrouded in the muted brown of its hibernation, secluded from the fantasy of spring and its long awaited thaw. Nevertheless, it held the rumor of its potential, of sweet fragrant flowers, tall sturdy trees with shady canopies for refuge from a hot sun, and rolling green fields and a soft warm breeze. But that was far off and perhaps would never be again, those good memories lost in time.

So it seemed within the distant thoughts of one man as he drove a rugged army truck along an old farm road. Henry's gaze fell to the door mirror, dark with the night far behind him until it was pierced with the strobes of artillery shells, too distant to be heard over the steady growl of the truck's motor. Somewhere beneath those distant flashes lay the desolation of the current front. He had served his time in that maelstrom and met the duty that had bound him. He found it hard to remember that life as his.

With a brief frown he ran his hand over his face, blowing a warming breath into his palm before returning his hand to the glove nestled under his thigh. He settled his hand on the steering wheel and removed his other hand to bury its glove under his thigh. He stuffed his frost-numbed fingers into the warmth of his armpit while he looked across the fields to either side, their brown turf still dappled in spots with frosted snow. As the warmth returned to his fingers his eyes caught the outlines of some old farmhouses, their skeletal walls charred and broken. The small groves of trees that used to shelter them were shattered and bare, the few remaining branches reaching out like twisted claws.

He slowed as he approached a column of men marching toward the front. The men parted to either side of the narrow road to let him through. It was cold in the truck with its broken heater, but he knew well enough the wretched cold of marching exposed with only a heavy overcoat for shelter. The men in the column looked to him, but then looked away when they realized the cargo his truck bore. It registered little with him, just as he failed to discern any difference in color between the brown coats of the column and the frozen landscape.

With a grunt he silenced the thought and looked off to his right where one of the fields had been leveled and dotted with the perfect geometric grids of small white crosses, linear no matter the angle they were viewed. It was the cemetery for his army, for men like him, yet different from him. He was appalled by the vastness of those rows of crosses, not for their number, or how they came to rest in that field, but for all the energy of those who had lived and were lost to a singular vast silence, a deafening silence—so many thoughts, both the low and petty, the noble and elaborate, but once alive, all stomped to silence.

Like him, but not like him.

At the end of the cemetery a road opened on his left. He turned onto that road, a narrow bulldozed track through a fallow field. He grimaced when he slipped his hand from his armpit to downshift, forgetting his glove before grabbing the cold knob. He stuffed his hand into his glove and followed the gully-torn road as it crested a hill and sank into an immense pit. Other trucks were there, bulldozers as well, but he waited until a miserable looking man waved to a spot over to the left. He turned the truck and drove across the grade of the pit before slowing and turning to point the nose of the truck to the rim of the pit. Then he put the truck in reverse, glanced at his side mirror, and let his foot off the brake. The truck crept back, but then picked up speed. After three lengths of the truck he slammed on both the clutch and brake pedals and looked away from the mirror.

The truck bumped to a halt and then rumbled as its burden spilled out the open back to roll down into the pit. After several moments he stepped on the parking brake until it clicked secure before slipping from the truck's cab. With a heave he pulled himself up the side of the truck and hopped into its bed. He kept his gaze down as he pulled out the heavy shovel he kept wedged in the slats and walked to the end of the bed where the last of the truck's burden remained. His nose wrinkled against the stench that assailed him, but he set the shovel's blade and pushed.

The last of the bodies tumbled out of the bed and into the pit, rolling down its slope to land on a wide pile of corpses. A bulldozer crept by, packing the bodies down with its weight as it covered them with a fresh layer of dirt. Scattered tendrils of vapor from rotting flesh rose through the packed earth.

They were the defeated of the enemy, those bodies. There would be no dignity of small white crosses for them, there would never be any sympathetic acknowledgement of lives lived and lost, of dreams dispelled, of passions hollowed to unheard echoes. It mattered not whether it was the pit or a small white cross, for the vast majority of those who went into the ground were just bystanders drowned by war. For the living, though, there was a distinct difference, a distinct meaning, something to embrace in the growing span of time's wearying forgetfulness.

To the victor went not only small white crosses, but justification.

For the vanquished, there was only disillusionment.

Like him, but not like him, Henry decided again.

He made his way back into the truck cab and drove away, passing several more trucks bumping along the rough road toward the pit. He looked ahead to the main road and across to the neat lanes of white crosses.

To the just go the spoils. He turned the truck and drove away.

***

Lost in emptiness, he found himself driving some other country road. His thoughts, formerly riotous guests within his mind, were silent. Perhaps it was the dreadful melancholy of his current duty, but he understood how he came to this disposition. Misfit, unfit; the labels were meaningless.

He trembled with the cold. The sky was a heavy featureless gray, the country about him brown and barren. He realized he was stopped, pulled over on the side of the road. He blinked, his eyes focusing on the bodies strewn before him. Their coats were still loose. The bloat of rot was yet to set in. The cold served a purpose, too.

With a rub of his gloved hands he slipped from the truck. Beyond the ruined trees, in the dark haze, the horizon flashed with artillery and explosions too distant to hear. By the time he paced over to the bodies he recognized them as nominees for the quaint cemetery, and not the waste pit. They were most likely victims of a stray shell, evidenced by the shallow crater in the middle of the road. He frowned, shaking his head at the insanity of it, the harsh reality of the death of these men on a quiet back road beyond any discernable, causal connection to the mass violence far away at the front. It made little sense to him by way of logic, even though it felt quite fitting.

He came to a stark conclusion. *When existence ends, this is how it will look. All living things will be stripped of their vitality; all will be a shadow of what was. All matter will be shorn of its spirit to leave the world hollow and cold and its remaining cursed inhabitants lone, starving wanderers in the void.*

He stood transfixed in the wake of that thought, bleak even for him. The truck's engine idled behind him. He watched the chaotic flashes along the horizon. Then he did something, something he would've thought impossible for him to do, even in the wake of his former life.

Hands in his pockets, he put his back to his truck, and walked away.

Not along the road, for he recalled the general area and one particular part he had taken pains to avoid. It was to that place he now felt himself drawn, propelling him across the rolling brown fields. He walked until the sky dimmed with evening, and only then sought shelter in a bombed out grain depot, a solitary stone structure left among the flattened ruins of an old farm.

With evening slipping away to night and its threat of freezing air, he gathered some hay and wood that wasn't charred. He retreated to an inner corner where the light of a fire wouldn't be seen. From his breast pocket he produced a lighter. He didn't smoke, having considered the habit to be unhealthy, despite the denial of men he once knew. Those men were all gone now, not from their habit, but from the war. It made his resisting the practice feel somewhat silly.

What concern for health, in that place, in that time?

Shaking his head, he lit some hay and worked the wood until he had a small but warming fire glowing before him. The crackling embers startled him, their little pops seeming like thunder in the perfect quiet of the night. Soon enough he adjusted, the way he knew people could always adjust, one way or another, to their surroundings.

The thought forced his gaze to the lighter in his gloved hand. The metal case was engraved. He rubbed it clean with his thumb. He didn't understand the words—they were in the local tongue—but he knew well enough it listed names, a date, and a town. After several moments he frowned, reaching inside his coat to pull out two worn pictures, both folded in half. In his typical fashion he ran a finger around the folded edges of the pictures, familiarity discerning one from the other. One picture he returned to his pocket; the other he opened to reveal a man and a woman in simple wedding attire before a small house. Handwritten at the bottom were a date and a town, matching the date and town on the lighter. It was a simple rural wedding, three years ago, to the day. He stared at the picture until he couldn't stand its sight, returning both lighter and picture to his pocket.

He pulled off his gloves and put his face in his hands. He thought of his canteen, wishing it held something more potent than cold water, kept from freezing only by the heat it leeched from his body. Wrapping his arms about his chest, he ignored the rumbling of his hunger and slumped against the rough wall behind him, stretching his feet toward the fire and using the thickness of his knit hat as a pillow. The stars peered down at him, remote and dim, from a rare break in the overcast night sky.

His eyelids drooped as sleep neared. Instead of slumber he found himself in the stupor of his memories, cursed from sleep by both the painful memory of the warm star-filled nights he once knew and the barren darkness he came to occupy. It was the source of the cancerous lethargy that had subverted him, reducing him from a promising, vibrant junior officer to an undead relic discarded as a body reclamation driver.

So much waste. He thought of his past, not in a personal sense, so as to insulate himself, but rather as a simple story. He had possessed good humor, was even told he was witty, and had enjoyed the workings of a quick, clear mind, complimenting, rather than conflicting, with the wild sways of his young passions. His life was free of turmoil; *charmed* was the word he often heard. From childhood it settled deep within him that the world was his plaything, warm and welcoming, and willing to excuse any blunder. The ideals behind the war appealed to his high-minded zeal, ignorant with its innocence. Nevertheless, he managed to sway his childhood friends to join him in the gathering recruitment calls. Their subsequent deaths he now counted among his worst sins.

Yet, in the beginning, he didn't fear the violence, nor was he stunned by the shock of war. Instead, he seemed to feed on it, to swell from the bloat of all human excesses and experiences around him, until his own inevitable implosion. For the disastrous spark that had burned his emotional self to a charred husk came from a source he never expected, had never considered in his blind arrogance and reckless confidence. Death, pervasive and insidious, caring little for borders, waited; waited with maddening patience to pounce on any unsuspecting fool.

And he had been such a fool, a fool of fools.

Nevertheless, it was over, and he became what he considered an echo of his former self, a hollow, mocking reverberation of the source. What hadn't been consumed of him in the funerary pyre of his emotions lingered, only to be obliterated by the unseen whiplash at the tail end of his contempt. Where he only knew exuberance, exhilaration and optimism, he was leveled with lethargy, indifference and pessimism.

The deeper his collapse grew, the greater his withdrawal from the convenient, tinted and tainted world of his perceptions. Where he was once popular and well received, he became one to avoid, one ostracized. The men of his command came to hate him, and fellow and superior officers, at first critical of his behavior, soon grew disgusted with him. He didn't resent it; on the contrary, it was accepted and understood. He was no longer part of their world, or part of his old world, for death and despair clung to him. Even though he walked and breathed and, on rare occasions, uttered a word or two, he belonged more to his new world, the world of waste and ruin.

In that world he found it a bitter work of irony that the particular lighter he came to possess would set a fire to save him from freezing to death on the night of his desertion.

Clouds came. The stars winked out one by one.

***

He rose in the twilight, stomping out his little fire before the smoke could be seen, only to pursue his course from the previous afternoon. In short time he paced over several rolling hills until he came to another road, less used, but torn with deep gullies from the last thaw's frigid rains. The sky above remained a heavy leaden gray that spoke of certain snow. Keeping his focus forward, he followed the road, passing a decrepit town marker. He knew the town's name; it matched that on the lighter and picture.

Traversing a low rise in the land he followed a turn to reveal a loose cluster of farmhouses about a narrow, winding creek. If it was once tranquil and picturesque, it was now dismal and foreboding. The farmhouses were all in various states of disrepair: the fields were pockmarked with shell craters, the winding creek was a frozen spillway of dark mud, and the little stone walls separating some of the fields were toppled.

As he trudged along the road he peered between his misting breaths to survey the houses, having little trouble discerning the one that was in the background of the picture. What he saw of that house was much different. The bloom of spring was inconceivable, and the heavy frigid silence of the air ridiculed any idea of warmth. Nevertheless, he pressed toward the house, his gaze darting to either side to catch the furtive glances of the remaining town dwellers. He felt no fear, even as an unarmed foreign soldier in their midst, forgetting his memories of similar towns where he had treated the local people with contempt for their simple life, where he gave little thought to appropriation of supplies and dwellings as an occupying force. His army's occupation of a town—liberation, as he had been taught to think—always earned a short-lived welcome.

Those were old sins, though, of a different life, and he was a different person. He was a footsore, frozen straggler. Not him, and yet still him.

He halted at the door of the house, fighting to unravel his arms from their constrictive wrap of his chest to knock on the heavy wooden door. The windows were shuttered against the cold and no doubt the glass was long broken, stolen, or bartered. A thin wisp of smoke rose from the chimney at one end of the small house. He could imagine what anyone inside would think of him. He was gaunt, unshaven, caked with field filth, his empty gaze burning in his eye sockets. His lone, unarmed presence confirmed the obvious suspicion that he was a deserter.

After some hesitation the door opened a crack. He was met by the drawn face and silvery beard of a balding, old man. The elder's eyes narrowed on him, studying him, the elder shifting to make clear the length of an old rifle held in the crook of the elder's arm. There was a single tip of the man's chin and the message was clear enough: *Go away.*

As a deserter from a foreign army, there was no reason to expect sympathy, nor hospitality. But Henry was humbled by his reality and conveyed it the only way he could figure, given that in his former complacency he never bothered to learn the local tongue. He put a hand on his chest and gathered his voice to mutter his name. Then he reached into his coat with trembling hands to produce the old wedding picture. He pointed to the bride.

The elder, perhaps her father, studied the picture, his bushy brows settling over his dark gaze before he glared at Henry. The elder looked over his shoulder and said something.

Another voice replied. It was a woman's voice.

She emerged from the shadows, her face poking out beside the elder's shoulder. Henry at once recognized her as the bride from the picture. She was thinner, and the glow of her eyes, which he had so often studied, had faded. She looked to the picture, and her rapid blink spoke of some expectation Henry was certain he was soon to disappoint. He extended his arm, but she snatched the picture, unfolding it and devouring it with her eyes before pressing it to her chest. She looked up to him and blurted several quick questions, to which Henry could only shake his head. She spoke with some urgency to the old man. The elder, scratching at his silvery beard, and with clear reluctance, opened the door for Henry to enter.

The house was cramped and tiny, but the details of a subsistent existence were lost in the dancing shadows of a meager fire. With a quick nod to her and the elder he sank to his knees before the fireplace, closing his eyes before opening his hands to receive the thawing warmth of the flames. After several moments he peered over his shoulder to find her watching him, keeping her back to a rough wood table. A small basket with bundled blankets sat atop the table. The elder, his gaze fixed on Henry, settled on a stool, his hand still on the rifle as he rested its length across his lap. The woman glanced at the basket before shifting to hide it with her body.

Henry shook his head and held his open hands before his chest. The palpable prospect of his being a thief, given his wretched state, and the past behavior of the army from which he had deserted, seemed to ease somewhat between the meek look of his eyes and the slow tap of the elder's leathery finger on the trigger guard of the rifle. The elder turned to the woman and gave a small nod. She took a second stool and set it before Henry.

Only then did he lower his hands, nodding his gratitude. Grunting against the stiffness of his legs he sat on the stool; he was surprised as she stood across the hearth from him. She began to speak, but he shook his head, understanding none of what she said. She relented, but then pointed to a small pot set on a rack over the fire before gesturing the spooning of soup. He nodded, but his guilt swelled as he watched her spoon out a watery brown mess into a simple bowl. She offered it to him. His hunger took over, and he forced the soup down despite its burning heat.

After several sips from the bowl he realized she was watching him, and his guilt rose higher. He felt himself a contemptible thief. Then he felt a temptation, one seductive and vile: the call to fill the emptiness of the house, to supplant the elder and rediscover his own youthful vitality. It would be a humble existence, but Henry was a humbled man, and it wouldn't be the first time servile humility had served as redemption. But, he clung to the last shred of humanity he possessed, the dignity held in a tattered semblance of honesty.

He stood and made to put his bowl on the table. He froze when she bolted and the elder slapped his hands on the rifle. Henry turned to look at her wide-eyed gaze on him, but then he looked back to the table, to the basket, only to see an infant's peaceful sleeping face nestled in the blankets.

The bowl fell from his hand to clatter on the stone floor.

The elder held a steady gaze on Henry, but his bony hands eased on the rifle.

The baby stirred. The woman stepped to the table to pick up her child and cradle it to her chest. Henry pushed his stool over to her side of the hearth and she smiled before sitting. He watched her rock on the stool and cupped his hand over his mouth as he sank to his knees. He felt his eyes well up and fought hard not to crumble, but there was no hiding the devastation in his eyes. She looked to the elder, and then to Henry, her eyebrows falling in curiosity until he reached into his pocket to produce the other picture. Her eyes filled with pity. She studied him for a long time after he put the picture away.

She nudged his boot with her foot, drawing his attention. The baby was fast asleep again. She shifted her stool closer and leaned toward him so he could look upon her child. He gazed at the little face, and the pain that seared him was at once so welcome and so bitter he gasped. He squeezed his eyes shut to hold back his tears.

Without looking at her he reached into his coat. Hands trembling, eyes downcast in the filth of his shame, he produced the lighter and offered it to her in his open hands.

It was quiet for several moments. When he opened his eyes he saw her outstretched hand frozen before her, her lips quivering. She took the lighter, clutching its silvery body as her gaze settled on him.

The elder stood when he realized what she held, his hands constricting on the rifle.

Her voice returned, tight and low as she forced out several words. Henry didn't need to understand her question, and the horror restrained just beneath. Was the picture given to him as some message? Had her groom parted with the lighter, a gift of exceptional value, given the simplicity of their pastoral life? Or, had Henry, this ragged deserter before her, found these two things or worse, had he taken them? Had she just offered him warmth, sympathy, the comfort of her child, when he was the one who had threatened the very existence of those things?

He dropped his hands. With his head still bowed, he let his silence answer her. He knew there was nothing for him to say, and no confession bold enough to excuse him in her eyes.

Her answers, as he imagined them, her disavowals, were the final hammer blows of that slow, invisible hand of eternal justice he felt he'd summoned upon himself. One night, in the dark confusion of battle, he shot this woman's husband as the man tried to surrender. The first hammer blow came several mornings later while he stared at the wedding picture and played with the lighter, only to learn the undoing of his own existence. The heartless, cruel leveling of life's frailty struck him not on the field of battle where he knew death was ever-present. Instead, it impaled him in the fold of his greatest vulnerability and his only refuge from the madness around him. His wife, his child—the infant he knew only as a picture—were consumed as his house had burned down in the far away night of home. Lightning had struck during a storm, he was told, a bolt that tore through time, space, and circumstance to skewer both him and the unknown man he had killed.

There was no sense to it, only waste. He wept with the madness of it, and his tears burned like hot acid.

Cold tendrils of air crept around him. He opened his eyes to see her peering from behind the open door, her child nestled to her shoulder, her shoulder turned away from him. The elder stood over him. Despite the level of the rifle barrel to Henry's head, the elder's face was full of sorrow, the sorrow only wisdom could afford. Henry nodded, understanding that he must go. He reached into the collar of his frayed coat, yanked loose the necklace with his dog tags, and tossed them in the fire. Then he set his jaw, nodding once more before struggling to gain his feet. To his surprise the elder grabbed his collar and hoisted him to a full stance with effortless strength. When Henry looked to the man's eyes, though, the elder only frowned, and the helping hand turned into an abrupt shove.

Henry shuffled to the door. When he looked to the woman, he met an opaque gaze of wide-eyed outrage. He lowered his head and stepped out. The door slammed behind him.

He lingered. He heard the door open. He closed his eyes, expecting the elder to shoot him. The moments mounted, but the shot never came. He looked over his shoulder. The elder stood in the doorway, rifle pointed, his rigid finger held away from the trigger. The elder lowered the rifle then, the balance of wisdom stilling him. He held steady before waving the rifle for Henry to leave.

The door closed.

Henry looked up. The sky was loosing its burden, the gray wash of clouds seeping to the ground in a torrent of snow. They would soon blanket the land, a blanket that would cover the waste and ruin.

Henry decided it would be a fitting shroud. He blinked and wrapped his arms about his chest as the cold pierced him. He moved through the falling snow toward the rolling hills. He knew it would be his last walk. He chose anonymity in that gray expanse, and would find his rest far from dark pits and little crosses.

The Great Hunter

It was a delightful morning in May when Nature seemed ready to burst in full from winter's hibernation. Clouds were clearing to reveal a blue sky, and the air was warm and fresh. It was a day that begged to have its open space filled with adventure, rather than have its precious time wasted indoors. For all the possibilities of such a day, it left any time of confinement aimless and shapeless, washing away any interest in the world beyond one's eyes.

Maybe it was a bit of a grandiose thought, a pompous thought, but it rang true in the mind of the boy who toyed with the thought. He was slumped at his desk, eyes lost in the depths of the blue sky outside the classroom window, while his teacher droned on about something for which he had no care. He hated such moments. They were little tortures, reminders that there was a whole big world out there, a world where interesting things were happening and there he was, stuck in the rut of school, learning dead things done by dead people in times dead and gone.

Who cares about this stuff? I want to live. There's got to be something more interesting. I know I can think of something more interesting.

He blinked and glanced at the doodles in his binder spread over the ruled lines that were meant to hold his notes. There were monsters, little tanks and army men, medieval warriors, and fanciful spaceships locked in spectacular exchanges of fearsome weaponry. Rather than serving as his usual refuge, they drew a frown upon his face, only serving to remind him of his current situation. He knew he had to get away.

Right. So, if I could go, where would I go?

It was enough of an invitation to set his imagination loose. He pondered some of the things in his drawings, but nothing caught his fancy in that moment. Maybe, he decided, it was due to the itch in his nose. His sinuses had been running all morning, annoying him without end. As much as he loved the prospect of spring, the season always seemed to set loose the molds hiding in every corner of the building. They released a storm of spores that spurred his allergies into a meltdown of mucous. It was disgusting and tiring, leaving him wheezing from one nostril, then the other, as if his sinuses were taking turns, like two lazy men in a rowboat arguing over who should take the oars. Besides the wheezing, whistling, and wet pops as he tried to sniff it all up into his head, there was the constant tickle in his nose. It was, perhaps, the worst. All that goop that came down his head into his nose congealed, making thick strands that would flutter against the hairs in his nostrils and send him into sneezing fits.

It was there again, that menacing tickle, like some elusive beast in the wild. If only he could stop it, beat it to the pass. He rubbed his knuckles against the side of his nose, but it was to no avail. In fact, it seemed to make it worse. It had to go. He had to do something. He had to do the unthinkable. His gaze darted about as he raised an eyebrow in mischief.

Have to be careful, have to be quick. Have to be like the hunter, ever so careful in pursuit of his prey.

His finger poked inside the rim of his nostril. *No, not just yet. The hunter, that's it, the hunter, the Great Hunter, he has come for his prey! And what is this foul beast that he pursues? Is it the lion, the boar, the crocodile and its vicious rows of teeth? No! It is none other than —*

He frowned.

Than what? The slime beast? The green man-eater? The giant African slug monster?

I can do better than that. The Great Hunter has to have a worthy opponent.

His fingertip ran along the rim of his nostril. When he felt it, he knew at once.

Part of it's starting to dry.

Yes … yes, the Great Hunter has come to save us, to face the lurking beast that none has dared to snare. It's none other than the claw-toothed, slime crusted, tunnel worm — the infamous Green Goober!

But the Hunter was brave, and he wouldn't turn away. No, he stalked his prey, stalked it among the dew-laden tunnel grasses that are the Green Goober's natural habitat. It prefers dark, slimy places, slithering along its slick belly between the blades, sticking to them until it grows large enough to let its jaws dry to a claw-toothed end, hovering to snare its prey. It isn't smart, but it is stubborn, and entwines itself with its slime in the tunnel so that none can dislodge it from its den to destroy it.

None but the Great Hunter.

See him stalk the beast, circling around to come down upon it unsuspecting, to snare it with his hook.

Grimacing against the stretch of his nostril, he pulled back with his fingernail, snagging the mess in his nose.

The Hunter has it. He has done what couldn't be done. He'll be celebrated the world over.

Waves of elation flowed through him. *Now, to remove the disgusting beast from its lair.*

He pulled back with his finger.

Aha, success. The Hunter has won. See the beast die beneath the light of the sun. The Hunter has saved us again, so all praise —

The teacher's shout hit him like a peal of thunder. "Excuse me!"

He froze. Instinct folded his finger into the depth of his palm, but it was too late. The other boys and girls were already laughing at him. He glared at the teacher with hidden rage, but the game was over. He wanted to be a million miles away, but that wish had already landed him in his current mess. His face turned twenty shades of red humiliation.

The teacher stared at him in disbelief. "And just what, just what— *what* is it that you think you're doing?"

He frowned. His eyes fell to his doodles. No one would understand.

Defeated, there was only one option for him. He cleared his throat. "Oh, uh, nothing," he said, his chin sinking to his chest.

The teacher shook her head and turned to the blackboard to resume her lesson with a droning monotone. The laughter around him died away. His eyes lingered on her back, though, his eyebrows settling low over his gaze.

And, with the Green Goober slain, the Hunter turns to his next prey.

Apogee

It was late and freezing rain fell through the darkness, glistening before a pair of headlights. The world seemed like a crystalline dream, an ice coated fantasy that rolled past William's car. He drove up a narrow mountain road, his hands clenched on the steering wheel as he prayed his balding tires would hold traction. He began to tremble, his gaze darting to the folder on the seat next to him. Anxious to reach his destination, and despite his better judgment, he pushed a little harder on the gas pedal.

He turned onto a dirt drive and aimed his old car between the bowed, silvery arches of evergreen trees, their branches slumping beneath the weight of the thickening ice. Soon enough the trees parted, retreating into the darkness to reveal a spacious log cabin beside a large, gravel driveway. He parked, the motor bucking and gasping before going quiet as his gaze rested on the elegant lines of a Euro-luxury sedan parked before the house. In the distance, poking above the trees, he could make out the shadowed dome of a private observatory, its shutters closed against the elements.

He grabbed the folder, pulled up his hood, and hurried to the door of the cabin, the frozen gravel crunching like broken glass beneath his boots. His breath misted as he stood before the door, his hand halting the moment before he knocked. Should he disturb the professor so late at night … on this particular night? But then, it was such momentous news he carried in the folder, data they had waited so very long to collect, that held a revelation dwarfing all expectations. He looked over his shoulder to the lone sedan, knowing a second sedan was covered and stored in the cabin's garage The absence of the other sedan seemed a matter of little consequence in relation to the wonder burning within the folder.

He drew in a breath and knocked on the door. It opened after a short wait. "Professor—"

Oleg Ilyanko narrowed his eyes for a moment. "Ah, William. What is it that you are doing here on such a night?"

William opened his mouth, but held up the folder instead. "I'm sorry, but I had to."

The professor debated with himself for a moment, took a breath, but then bobbed his head and opened the door for William. He watched his graduate student pass before him to stomp his boots clean in the foyer, the folder clutched under his arm. Oleg noticed that William's usual nervous energy possessed something of a different nature, something other than the jitters of the horrid energy drinks he consumed while laboring so many nights in the university's astrophysics lab. Oleg took his coat, an awkward exercise as William tried to maintain his protective grasp of the folder. Oleg opened his hand to the living room, with its crackling fireplace and large, comfortable chairs.

William nodded, his gaze rolling over the room. It was such a quiet, peaceful place; *serene* was the word his girlfriend used, after Oleg had invited William and Hannah to the cabin for the Ilyankos' fortieth wedding anniversary. It was the last anniversary the couple would celebrate, for cancer devoured Oleg's wife in the weeks that followed. William felt somewhat awkward intruding so soon after her passing, but he took it in stride, finding a lyrical—if somewhat callous—observation in the way events had juxtaposed.

Oleg sat in his chair, waiting with his usual patience, and perhaps with a little more, distracted by the grief secluded in the Siberian solitude of his emotions. He scratched at his close-cropped beard, the silvery hair in greater abundance than anything left upon the bare dome of his head. His glasses shone with the warm glow of the fireplace. "So, William," he said, his voice coarse but low, "you bring me some data from our Odysseus probe, yes?"

William's lips parted, but then he remembered the color-coded folder and nodded. His hands began to shake.

Oleg's face fell. "Have we lost the probe?"

William's eyes widened. "What? Oh, God, no, not at all. Odysseus is fine."

Oleg tipped his head as William sat in silence. "I am waiting, I should tell you," Oleg said, trying to jar William.

William jerked upright in his seat, his hands opening from the folder, only to tremble once more as they hovered over its contents. "It, I ..." William started, but then clenched his teeth. He closed his eyes, drew a calming breath, and settled his hands on the folder before looking to Oleg. "Forgive me, it's just that it's hard to get my head around this. And, before I tell you, I want to say a few things."

Oleg opened a hand. "I grew up on Tolstoy, you should remember. Take your time."

William licked his lips. "You've supervised the Odysseus program since before I was born. The probe was passing Jupiter before I could walk, and its destination in the Kuiper belt was something I didn't even understand until I was in high school. All that time—all this time— Odysseus has been out there, in the dark and cold, sending us images and data, flying faster than anything humanity has ever put in space. Your program, your research papers, they led me to pursue astrophysics. You always tell me how imaginative I am, how creative I can be when it comes to thinking outside of the box, but I want you to understand something, and, even though this is going to sound impossibly conceited,

I say it with the utmost respect and humility. When I was little I read some of the simple summaries about your papers. They opened such a depth of possibilities to me, this wonder of the universe and all its mysteries, that I felt there was something, something finally big enough to match the size of my imagination, something to check and dispel the petty notions of self-centeredness that seem to plague so many people, including me.

"I can't tell you how many nights I've laid in bed, staring at the ceiling, almost nauseous with the grandeur of it all, the sheer size of it, the endlessness of it. There's a question in me, a question that unravels all my very human inclinations to delineate existence, and that's to ponder infinity, to wonder what the universe is expanding into, what it means to expand endlessly, to be there when the known spills into the unknown." William shook his head, his eyes glazing before he blinked to regain his focus. "For some reason I always thought of the Odysseus probe, reaching so far out from us to the Kuiper belt, into that distant haven of comets and orbiting debris on the very edge of the tiny locale we call our solar system. Maybe it could answer some of that question, maybe witness a moment of the known breaching the unknown—a moment, a rapture of discovery, a birth of some new facet of knowledge that might change everything."

Oleg folded his hands in his lap. "I think that perhaps you have had too many of your energy drinks, eh? Tell me, when is it that you last slept?"

William shook his head. "I can't sleep," he said at once. "I don't think I'll ever sleep again." He took the folder and handed it to Oleg. "We thought the triumph of Odysseus was landing a sensor package on an asteroid in the Kuiper belt, the most distant navigated rendezvous of a man-made and a natural object. That's nothing compared to this."

Oleg took the folder. Rather than opening it, he held his gaze on William. "And what, might I ask, is this?"

"It's the first spectral analysis from the sensor package."

Oleg drummed his fingers on the folder. "William," he said softly, "what did you find?"

William leaned forward, resting his elbows on his knees as he opened his hands. "If it wasn't so preposterous, I might be inclined to doubt it." He grinned. "I know how that sounds, but the known has spilled into the unknown, and I was there. Right now, I'm the only one, the only person on this planet, who knows, and I've brought it to you. I haven't even showed Hannah yet. I drove here, instead of doubling back to our dorm, so I could tell you." He drew in a deep breath. "The analysis, the analysis data I worked on, it says the object we landed on was covered by a thin layer of dust. That dust is among the oldest carbon material yet found in the solar system."

Oleg opened the folder and pulled out the papers within. "And beneath the dust?"

William waited while Oleg looked over the papers, the professor's gaze coming to a decided halt on the last page. William held up a hand. "I checked it three times."

Oleg scratched his beard and set the papers in his lap. He looked to the fire and shrugged.

William's face fell. "Professor?"

Oleg took a breath, but said nothing.

William tipped his head. He found Oleg's lack of response baffling. A million thoughts stormed through his mind, too many for any one to escape his mouth. So he sat in silence, his eyes narrowing in utter confusion to the mute ambivalence of his mentor, the great man he had followed in his professional pursuit, the man he had stood with shoulder to shoulder as a lost wife's casket sank into the ground one week ago. After all that, the great man, the great mind, had nothing to say, no pearl of wisdom, no elegant thought to encapsulate what William brought to him.

After what seemed a very long wait, Oleg looked from the fire to the papers, a breath seeping from his lungs. He slid the papers in the folder and set the folder on the table beside him. There was a glass of red wine there, one that William had failed to notice until Oleg took it in hand. He didn't drink. Instead, he held the glass in his lap, swirling the wine and watching it lap across the smooth crystal.

William's head hung, his gaze darting about the floor before he looked back to Oleg. He wasn't angered, he wasn't annoyed, he wasn't even disappointed; rather, he felt a profound sense of emptiness, a vast, wretched emptiness that consumed the very air in Oleg's house. The sense of serenity in the living room, which Hannah had so enjoyed, transformed to something different, yet related. It was serenity's distant cousin, solemnity.

His mouth was dry. He found it hard to summon his voice. "Professor?"

Oleg blinked, looking up as if he just remembered that William sat before him. "You are so intelligent, my dear William," Oleg said, his voice sounding slow and tired. "This is a momentous discovery you have made. Truly momentous. But I would ask you this, and tonight I will ask you only this, and before I ask you, you will promise not to interpret it as the question of a lonely old man mourning his wife, humbled by the very old confrontation that the greater wonders he sought were in fact before him all along." He sipped his wine, pausing a moment before looking up from his glass. "William, why do you bring this great discovery to a broken old man, and not to your Hannah, to the woman you love?"

"What?" William blinked. "She's sleeping."

Oleg looked to the ceiling. "And why is it that you did not wake her?"

William shook his head. He rose, and stepped to the fireplace to lean on the mantle. It was a reflective pose, but he was a man of reflection, of inner distractions. He knew this, because he had stood that way, the day of the Ilyankos' last anniversary, when he decided he would save his money and, when ready, ask Hannah to marry him. Hannah found the pose endearing, claiming it created a certain allusion to his nature: a solitary soul, resident of a quiet moment to be treasured, a mysterious moment when all the vast wonder that could spill into the unknown gathered its mounting tide behind the reflective pools of one's eyes.

She had a flair for poetic notions, he reminded himself.

Oleg's voice came to him. "This moment, the moment of this discovery, it will never happen again in the ages of humanity. It will last forever, William. And few things, so very few things, last at all."

William tipped his head back and closed his eyes. His time under Oleg had fostered a paternal affection from the old man, and it was a treasured notion, but William was jarred in that moment by the whispers of other opportunities gone by, opportunities he had sacrificed to continue his work with the prestigious Professor Ilyanko. There were jobs, offers of greater reward than the subsistent existence he eked out from the university. He could've gone off on his own, could have published on his own, but he stayed loyal. Despite the fact that he first met Hannah through Oleg's wife, and that he owed so much to Oleg, standing there in the old man's living room he found it hard to imagine feeling any more alienated from his aspirations and his mentor. He had brought the discovery of a generation, perhaps a discovery more profound than anything yet discovered, and all Oleg could give him was recrimination and guilt.

He was ready to unload on his mentor in a tumult of anxiety and sleep deprivation, but as his breath gathered in his lungs for the sacrificial eruption, his gaze fell on a small picture resting on the mantle. His heart froze. It was a picture of Oleg, not as William knew him, but much younger, perched by a telescope, back in his days with the Moscow university. Beside him was his wife, lifting a cup of coffee to him as he gestured to the ocular, his wide eyes upon her. It was an old picture, its black and white contrast faded to ghostly tones of gray.

William clenched his teeth. His breath seeped from his body.

He held for a moment, but then turned from Oleg. He put on his coat. He walked out the door, past the Oleg's luxury sedan. He sank into his old car. The motor rumbled to life and he drove off, his gaze wandering over the boughs of evergreen trees, his ears absorbing the faint tinkle of ice against the windshield. All the facets of the world erupted around him as a universe of minutia to envelope his senses, and the coming moment—so short, so delicate—became everything to him, and he swore never to forget it, and all that it meant.

I drove home to the dorm and woke her. She was groggy; the way people are when you wake them from a deep sleep. Ah, such deep sleep. Part of us will never sleep again, will never sleep the same way again. I took her hand and I remember how I blushed. It all seemed so surreal. I was five years old again, looking through a telescope for the first time, looking at the surface of the moon, and the wonder of it warmed and comforted me.

I felt very comfortable sitting on our bed just then, and that's when I told her. For a moment, in all the world, in all of what anyone knew, there was only the two of us, and we were bound in that moment, and that bond will defy any human measure of time.

Far away, so far away, out in the darkness, on a small chunk of what we thought was rock, a sensor package sent us some data. There was dust, old as the oldest things ever found, and beneath the dust was metal, older than the sun itself. But it wasn't just metal. No, it was something far different, something greater, something that defied any human measure of time, something binding.

It was a weld.

The City of Never

An excerpt from the Coda Urbani:
THE CITY, by nature, is an amalgam of the natural and the man-made. Such a statement, obvious as it is, is not to be dismissed as pedestrian in nature, as it holds the pretense of so-called 'urban' design. That is, the creation of a human dwelling among that which is already created, Nature. One is not to preclude the other, for each is created in its own wisdom, and must find peace together in the tired eternity of shifting balances so casually referred to as yin and yang. For it must be remembered, remembered at all times and all costs during development, that nothing can or does exist in a vacuum; all things exist with at least a taste of their complimentary opposite.

***

I remember the freckles on the soft curve of her cheek under the golden light of dawn, like the photonegative image of morning dew glistening on Satan's apple.

***

Gregor gasped inside the stifling, claustrophobic confinement of the immense erector, heedless of the several square kilometers of havoc he left behind him. The erector, a massive, octopus-like machine known as the Saanos-7, clicked, hummed, and hissed around him. His gaze darted about. He was weak, bleeding from a stab wound in his belly. The sensor cap fastened to his scalp felt like an obscene nest of warm tentacles reaching into his mind, but it was through those neural connections that he wielded the might of the Saanos-7 and propelled its megaton metal mass with his thoughts alone.

He blinked, his arms easing to let his hands dangle from the auxiliary control yoke before him. Nests of analog gauges were clustered before his face, surrounding a small display screen the size of his hand. A delicate wood flute was taped in crude fashion to the top of the display; a thin silver necklace with a small, imperfect emerald dangled along one side. An old-fashioned spiral bound notebook was rolled up and wedged between some of the gauges to the immediate right of the screen.

His eyelids fluttered. It was stifling hot inside the Saanos-7, but then this wasn't the intended way for its use. No, those plans were long gone, long lost.

Sweat beaded and ran down his temples. He closed his eyes and surrendered to the machine. The world about him snapped into view, bleached under the scores of blinding searchlights that dotted the hull. The leviathan lurched like a wounded animal, but then brought two massive articulated arms to bear, each wielding claw buckets big enough to swallow luxury homes, and sent the buckets hurtling downward.

The ground trembled, torn and shattered under the assault.

***

"See that?" Maggie said, her whisper almost lost among the distant birdcalls echoing in the early dawn light. She turned and looked back, beckoning with the hand of her extended arm as she crouched behind a large bush. Dew-laden foliage surrounded her small frame. Her hands opened before her as her eyes widened with excitement. "This is the place I wanted to show you. There's no other place like this on any surveyed, inhabited world. It must be preserved. I'll give it to you, Gregor. I want you to have it, if you make me one promise."

"What?"

"Never to touch it," she said, her eyebrows rising over her large hazel eyes. "Just look, look between those trees, down into the valley. It's like looking into heaven. It must never suffer the hand or blight of man. Of all things that should never happen, this is the one I would stake my life on, that I give my life for."

"I don't understand."

She crossed her hands over her chest. "It's mine to decide, and I've decided," she whispered. She looked into his eyes and didn't blink. "The valley, as my life, I give to you."

***

AUDIO LOG 1, SESSION 2:

"Good morning class, and welcome to this semester's supplemental study course, *Modern Minds and Their Societal Impact.* I am Professor Lucas Latham. Our curriculum will commence with a study of Saanos Development. Without further ado, we shall now start.

"I'm sure at this point in your studies you've gathered at least cursory familiarity with Saanos Development. Going back ten decades—Saanos prefers this measurement of time—you will see the introduction of the great Saanos innovation, the modern miracle combining nanotechnology and recombinant genetics, the so-called constructors. The Saanos *constructor* is essentially living concrete, self-replicating into preprogrammed forms that generate structures at amazing speed. The resulting Saanos erector models—Saanos One, through the latest behemoth, Seven—utilize dispersal and programming of Saanos constructors to build Saanos environments. We call them cities, and Saanos builds them overnight in comparison to traditional construction techniques. Saanos Development has been responsible over the last three decades alone for the resettling of millions of people into newly built Saanos environments. This, of course, has reaped immense wealth for Saanos Development.

"This brings us to the focus of our discussion, the owner of Saanos Development."

***

Gregor hid behind an oak column watching as Karl Saanos settled himself in a rather fanciful wood chair. The old man gazed into the evening light streaming through the arched entrances of his retreat to the distant valley, site of his latest ambition. He reached beside his chair to a small round table and the glass of red wine awaiting him before tipping his chin back and letting his gaze roll over the dozen or so local reporters seated before him, beneath the immaculate timber construction of his domed receiving room. Karl looked up to regard the intricate carving of the dome's beams.

One thousand dowels.

He looked down at the reporters, only then realizing they were shifting in their seats with their growing impatience. After all, they were summoned by his invitation, his request, and under such conditions, he wouldn't suffer their intrusion any more than necessary. No, they would wait until he spoke, until he made his statement, and that would be that.

He licked his lips and set his wine glass down before settling his hands in his lap and gazing at the reporters. "Thank you for accepting my invitation," he said with a soft voice. "This won't take much of your time. By now you are well aware of the valley and rights I have purchased here. Such things are not noteworthy in themselves. However, I wished to gather your select group here to disperse in your local media outlets this simple announcement: I have chosen to build my next environment here, on your lovely world. This, too, is not a passing of note, as I have been responsible for the development of many environments on many worlds. This project, however, will be unique.

"It will be unique because it will not only be the greatest, but it will be the last, and then humanity will not hear of Saanos Development again."

***

An excerpt from the Coda Urbani:

THE CITY, by design, should not exceed a population of one hundred thousand. This is by no means an arbitrary number; rather it is the result of intricate mathematical flow models. Cities of the past have come to be complicated failures due to the one lingering curse of urban existence: over-development, that is, excessive population density. For it is the inescapable supply and demand of human presence that must be controlled within the city, as the city, a living thing composed of individuals as its cells and tissues, must not diminish and demean the resident by depriving the resident of humanity and individuality. One should be able to traverse the city by foot with reasonable ease to save on transit costs; the city must provide proper pedestrian conduits at public places to avoid the scourge of overcrowding; lastly, the city, of all things else, must be remembered for what it is—a mirror of its residents. Let it grow ugly, chaotic, decayed, and it will spawn within its resident population disrespect, apathy, and inhumanity. And then it will not be a city, it will be a crowded tomb of lifeless creatures, nevertheless unaware that they are stillborn, aborted by the very environment that was meant to nurture their lives.

***

Gregor coughed, cringing at the pains the spasm inflicted. He slumped onto the auxiliary control yoke. Sweat ran down his temples to drip from the ball of his nose. He was tired, so very tired.

He closed his eyes. At once the Saanos-7 filled his awareness with a panoramic view of his surroundings. The first twilight of dawn beckoned, but he cared little for that. Teams of much smaller, but faster, Saanos-1 and 2 erectors scrambled around the bulk of his Saanos-7, spraying clouds of nanobot constructors preprogrammed with the visions dancing through the back of Gregor's mind. The Seven, wonder that it was, converted his visions in real time to three-dimensional models mapped with GPS coordinates and relayed to the surrounding, lesser Saanos-1 and 2 erectors.

The city's firmament was taking shape. It was less than twelve hours since he started.

***

AUDIO LOG 5, SESSION 4:

"Ah, Professor Latham, and to what do I owe this harassment?"

"This is quite a show, Karl. Did you think I would miss it?"

"Miss what, my good Professor? The unveiling of my soon to be implemented Saanos-7, or the opportunity to pester me?"

"You forget who you're talking to, Karl. You've had me document your deeds for too long now. But I thought I sensed an opportune moment to add some more intimate material to my archives."

"Have you started writing that book about me yet, Professor Latham?"

"No, not yet. I'm still compiling my recordings. I don't quite have the proper handle on your personality yet."

"Then you better hurry, Lucas."

"Going somewhere?"

"I have far surpassed my life expectancy, Lucas, even with the good graces of the best care money can buy. As usual, I will be forthcoming for your benefit, to remind you of the privilege I have given you as my biographer. I will make it official for your records. I have secured the services of a certain fledgling bioengineering firm, which, for my sake, shall remain nameless. I have invested heavily in them and, in return, over the years they have furnished me with two heart replacements, an eye replacement, three knee replacements, and two hip replacements, all grown from my native tissues. I have planned far ahead of the Saanos-7's debut to the day of our mutual retirement. On the day I put the Saanos-7 to work on its final environment, I will achieve the ripe old age of one hundred and fifty years."

"And what can we expect then?"

"Ah, now that is a loaded question."

"Care to unload it?"

"You are a sly one, Lucas. In all of history there is no other machine like the Saanos-7 erector. It is unmatched in size, complexity, durability and versatility. It can perform the work of five Saanos-6 models, and it is fully capable of directing up to twenty Saanos-1 and 2 models autonomously. Further, it can be operated by remote, where my design team can consult on progress."

"So then, who will pilot the wondrous machine?"

"Now Lucas, you know better than that. I employ many architects, sculptors, engineers, various artisans, and any of them may have a turn at the helm depending on the stage of the project."

"But all under your name, right? In effect, you'll take credit for everything."

"I am responsible, don't forget."

"Well, it sounds as if this machine can't be topped, even by you."

"So they say."

"I know that smile, Karl. Will you humor me?"

"Of course. I'll tell you what you must tell no one else until you draft your book on me, hopefully after I have passed from this world. I'm considering a Saanos-10, to continue my good work after I have passed."

"Ten? What of Eight and Nine? Did you skip them?"

"No. I will simply say this, that Saanos-8 and Saanos-9 are already operational."

"Where?"

"Ah, but that's the beauty of those two models. They will never be known, but what they'll create, what they'll leave behind, will be the last thing, the greatest thing of Saanos Development."

"Is that so? It's hard to imagine anything more impressive than your Saanos-7."

"That's due to your very lack of imagination, Professor. Now, if you please, I have a waiting populace to awe."

***

Gregor looked about the newly constructed dome of the retreat, with Karl waiting by his shoulder. "Do you like it?" Gregor said, somewhat hesitant.

Karl looked about the wooden dome, admiring the crafting of the struts. At the peak of the dome a glass cap had been inserted to show the starlit night sky above them. "You've designed a thousand cities for me, Gregor. How is that you could disappoint me in the design of a mere dome?"

Gregor grew excited as he pointed to the beams. "There are one thousand dowels holding it together."

"One thousand dowels?" Karl grinned before looking from the dome to Gregor. "I see, one for each environment you've done for me. Do you think anyone will ever know?"

Gregor lowered his head and shrugged. "I'll know. It's for us, for what we've accomplished, or I should say, what you have allowed me to accomplish as my guardian, benefactor, and patron."

"You are too humble, Gregor." Karl patted him on the back. "So, tell me, have you seen the valley?"

Gregor's gaze darted about. "Yes," he whispered.

"And?"

Gregor turned to him. "It's too beautiful. I shudder at the thought of touching it, that I will never do it justice. I have some reservations."

"And so it should be with any great endeavor. But here, tonight, I'll disclose our intention to some of these local mongrel reporters. You have never failed me, Gregor, and I know that you'll not fail me now. But I want you to know something, something important. For too long you've labored under the shadow of my name. On this city you shall remain nameless as well, but I want you to do it for yourself. It is to be yours, and yours alone, Gregor. I am going to help you achieve your masterpiece."

Gregor stepped away with a nervous shake of his head. "Sir, I, I—"

"I won't leave you naked to the wolves," Karl said with a soothing tone. He opened his hand. "Now, listen."

Gregor looked about the dome. The chairs for the local reporters were set out before the fanciful chair that would hold his patron. Beside that chair sat a small table with a glass of red wine. Trimmed, lush plantings surrounded the diameter of the dome where it met the stone floor, its trusses framing the many arched gateways that led out to the warm night. Then, as if guided by some invisible brick road, Gregor stepped forward, raising a hand to his ear. He heard it then, almost lost among the gentle bongs of the wind chimes outside the dome.

It was the soft, lilting tone of a wood flute.

Karl grinned when Gregor glanced back at him. "Well then, I see you remember our master ecologist, Miss Maggie LaFey."

***

An excerpt from the Coda Urbani:

THE CITY, it must not be forgotten, is a work of art. One may differ and say that in the inherent need for functionality the city is precluded as a true work of art, as such an opinion would hold that only a thing which exists for nothing but itself is a piece of art. Yet, a city is a creation, it must be remembered, and all things that are created are pulled, culled, from the ether of imagination, that shapeless nether-space from which our thoughts descend to us. And if all things we create are likewise uncreated before our intervention, then all creation exists but for our thoughts, and they exist for reasons we have yet to fathom. It is such grandiose abstraction that must be plumbed to set the mind free to create not just this little word, *city*, but to create a living thing, a thing where the people within are at peace with what is around them, a thing that represents more than anything else the state of our civilization. For an asynchronous existence is one bereft of stability, and it will never know the solitude and serenity of existing for nothing but itself.

***

"What did you do with her? Tell me!"

"I sent her away, back to that place from whence she came, the whispers of my dreams."

Gregor's eyes popped open. Savage curses erupted from his mouth as he pounded a fist on the analog gauges of the Saanos-7. *You bastard.* His eyes fell on the little notebook rolled up and stuffed between the gauges.

All my memories, never mine to control.

He shook his head in frustration and wiped the tears from his eyes in embarrassment, even though no one could see him in the bowels of the Seven. He cringed against the pain in his belly, but then let it fly with his resentment.

The Saanos-7 responded by tearing into the hillside of the valley in which it sat.

***

"Such a machine, it's just beyond belief," Maggie said with a sigh as she stood with her hands on her hips, her gaze lifted to the sky. Sub-orbital transports were sinking on their gravity cushions to bring in the sub-assemblies of the Saanos-7, settling them in precise locations over the hill from the valley. She turned to Gregor as he stood behind her, studying the folded plans he held in one hand while his other hand held a radio headset to his ear to monitor the communication bands of the transports. "Gregor?"

He looked to her at once. "Oh, yes, it's an amazing machine," he said, guessing at her question.

She shook her head and crossed her arms on her chest, her face settling as she shifted about. It seemed an effort for her to meet his gaze. "There's something I need to tell you."

Gregor smiled. "You can tell me anything."

She took a breath. "Karl signed over the construction rights of the valley to me."

"He what?" Gregor blinked. "I, I don't understand."

Her eyes settled with a plaintive cast. "Neither do I, but he gave me specific instructions."

He glanced over his shoulder to the domed retreat before looking back to her. "Maggie, I—"

She stepped to him to lay a finger over his lips. "Please," she hissed. "You know him, sometimes his reasons are so hard to fathom." She hesitated, opening her hands before her. "It may be your design, Gregor, but it's to be my choice, and forgive me, please forgive me, but don't do this thing, don't build this city."

He studied her, taking her hand in his own to lower her finger from his lips. His face fell in confusion. "But I'm going to do this for you. It will be the greatest thing I'll ever do. It won't be about me, or you, or us, but what lies between us, which I can't name. My mind, you know, I don't remember things as others do. There are moments, scattered, broken, but the one thing that links them, that gives them any meaning, is you, Maggie. I long for you, even when you're right beside me."

She stared at him. Her lips parted, but she said nothing, her breath escaping her as a breeze rustled the short curls of her hair. The evening sun cast a glow on her face.

He found himself feeling very much at peace then, looking at her in that moment, even with all the work that lay before him. He dropped the headset and let it dangle from the wire connecting it to the receiver on his belt so that he could lay his hand on her cheek. "I want to show you later what I prepared for Karl's birthday. It's an emerald set on a fine silver chain, perfectly cut, but flawed with a small carbon inclusion. I remembered what you told me one time, about the perfect imperfection of organic life, and how it always resides in the imperfect perfection we create. It seemed proper."

***

An excerpt from the Coda Urbani:

THE CITY, as a creation, must be nothing less than a masterpiece of its setting. It must be so, as anything less will bring naught but disappointment and decay to its citizens. And, as such, the design process must not only be a labor, but a labor of love, a labor of inspiration, the sort of inspiration that keeps men restless at night with the prodding anxiety to conjure its reality. For the greatest works of art come from such fits. Genius is not an easy path, and the best of inspirational emotions always carry their tragic overtures, with that very looming tragedy driving the inspiration to greater heights of realization. It is not enough for van Gogh to love; he must cut off his ear—he must *suffer*. And then it is not enough for him to paint; he must be immortal in his work as an artist. So, too, the city, for long after the mind that conceived it has passed, the city will remain.

***

"And what is this?"

Gregor looked up at the adoptive father he knew as Karl Saanos. A small, old-fashioned spiral bound notebook lay open beside the lit candle on his desk, the empty first page of the notebook staring back at him. "It's a journal. Am I in trouble?"

Karl grinned and patted Gregor on the shoulder. "Of course not," he said with good humor. "Unless, of course, you mail any secrets of my brand new Saanos-6 before I get to unveil it."

Gregor's eyes widened. "I would never ...." he said, but bit his lip when Karl's eyebrows rose. He looked down at the notebook. The candle set shadows dancing about the wall against his desk, his room dark in the late night. It reminded him why he had asked one of Karl's security agents to acquire the little notebook. He cleared his throat, and though his gaze darted about the desk, he found it impossible to look up. "My memories," he said, but then fell silent. He shifted in his chair. "My memories, they're often confused, broken up, their temporal order jumbled. My objective memory—the mathematical side of my mind—that seems photographic and limitless. But my subjective memories, people, places, things I feel, I find it very difficult to keep them ordered in my head." He swallowed over a dry throat and looked up to Karl. "Why am I like this?"

"We can't help the way we're made, Gregor. I would have liked to be taller," Karl said and shrugged. He said nothing more. Instead, his gaze fell to the notebook, his eyes narrowing as he stared at the blank page. Then he reached out and flipped the page, the troubled look on his face at once passing to one of deep satisfaction. He looked to Gregor and patted him on the shoulder even as Gregor fidgeted and blushed. He gave Gregor a reassuring nod. "Everything will work out in the end," he said and left.

Gregor looked down. The open page showed the portrait he had sketched of the young woman he met earlier that day, a woman that captivated him the moment he saw her. He picked up his pencil and spelled out her name.

Maggie LaFey.

***

AUDIO LOG 6, SESSION 8:

"Ah, Professor Latham, we meet again."

"Congratulations, Karl. Your Saanos-7 seems to be a big success."

"Would I accept anything less?"

"No, but surely, Karl, you must know that your latest marvel here hasn't met universal acclaim. In fact, there has been a fair share of criticism concerning the first work completed by your Saanos-7."

"They criticize what they see, not realizing it as a great deed. All great deeds in human history have brought criticism because they represent change and threaten the status quo, that prickly comfort zone of the human psyche. Criticism is what criticism has always been, Lucas. Criticism of great deeds is nothing but the jealousy of the uninspired and the envy of the incompetent."

"There's a quote that'll go over well. Can I use it?"

"Sarcasm aside, Lucas, you know you can use all my quotes, after I've passed from this life. That was our deal, and I will keep it."

"Well, in that case, Karl, I'd be interested in what you have to say about the criticism you've received from your fellow urban and civil engineers concerning your private little publication, the *Coda Urbani*. They say it only showcases your vanity, that it reminds the rest of us how most of your cities have wound up being resorts and playgrounds for the wealthy. They're dismissing your book as a bunch of metaphysical nonsense that, they claim, displays the fact you're not the great engineering genius you claim yourself to be."

"Every genius is pelted with the stones of fools in his lifetime, Lucas. As far as my little publication goes, the *Coda Urbani* wasn't meant to be a textbook, it was meant to help the students of urban design comprehend a more conceptual and subjective approach to their work rather than the cold framing of calculations. I make no apology for what is contained in my little book because it's not from my heart, and not my mind, but somewhere else in between. And it's what resides in that place that makes me so unique."

"Yes, so unique, and still you remain the most eligible bachelor in known space. Have none of the corporate families sought a tie with you?"

"Ah, if I had the time for all the overtures, but no, such is not the way for me. I'll tell you something now, something to add to your archives. Do you see this splendid city before you? Its creation came from the work of many minds, but the over-riding inspiration, the *vision*, is my vision, long planned out, and what my artisans achieve together is all from me, from what I had the capacity to imagine and initiate. So I ask you, how could I be the integral part of things so grandiose, only to step down to something as small as a commitment to some single person? Look at this city before you, and more so, consider what went into summoning its existence. It is to such things that I am wed, and have no time to spare on paltry substitutes."

"You know, I think I finally understand your personality."

"Do you?"

"You're a monster, Karl."

***

Gregor sat with his legs folded before him, his back straight as he looked up to the stars, his little notebook open in his lap. Maggie emerged from the depths of a broad-leafed bush, her gaze on her fingers. "I put the repellor stakes down," she said as she walked by him to get a water bottle by their sleeping bags. She poured out some water and rubbed her hands on a small towel she pulled from her pocket. "That'll keep the bugs away for the night." She tiptoed beside him before settling down and stealing a glance at his notebook. "Still keeping the journal?"

He nodded. "Every day, even if it's only a word or two, but just enough so that I can look back and keep everything straight." He opened his hands. "It's conceptual, not factual. Impressionism, if you would classify it." He blinked and looked down at the valley. The river that snaked through its length glistened under the full moonlight, the little waterfalls along its length sparkling with silver and white foam. A long breath slid from his lungs as he turned and looked to her. "I can't thank you enough for taking me out to see this, to see it the way you see it. It made my decision easier, even though I'm nervous about Karl's reaction when I tell him. I'll never build a city here, Maggie, because I learned something else."

She stared at him, her lips parting. She looked to the valley for several moments before glancing down, her lips pressing shut. Then she took a deep breath and turned back to him. "Gregor, I—"

He did something he never did before, with anyone. He turned back the blank page in his notebook and laid it in her lap for her to read. She glanced at him, but he kept his eyes on the valley. She took his hand, worked her fingers between his, and took the notebook in her other hand so she could read what he wrote.

Before her eyes could focus in the scant light of their little battery lantern he recited the words for her: "She said, 'The valley, as my life, I give to you.' The city, as it is intended here, will never be built, because today I realized what I might have known all along. All these years, it was never about building cities, or inflating Karl's ego, or my humble servitude in the greater pursuit of human dwellings, or serving anonymously under Karl's name so that he could protect my seclusion. No, the root of it, the passion, has always been the same, and now I know why she is never mentioned here, except for one sketch. I never pin down my memories of her. Undefined, unbound, she is always with me, and there are no spaces between."

He turned to her, but she kept her eyes on the notebook. Then she swallowed and closed the notebook, pressing it to her chest before she laid it in his lap. For several moments neither of them moved, but then she rested her head on his shoulder and squeezed his hand.

A slow blink passed over his eyes, and when they opened, he saw the starlit night above. "A shooting star," he whispered.

They watched the silvery streak before it vanished.

***

"Wake up, Gregor."

Gregor sat up in his bunk, stunned, his eyes focusing on the portal of his cabin to see the stars drifting by the interplanetary transport. He blinked and rubbed his face, only to turn and find Karl standing by, wrapped in a night coat. He held a small box in his hands, which was odd, as Gregor knew how Karl detested lifting or carrying of any kind. "Sir," Gregor said, turning to face him.

Karl slid a hand from under the box to still Gregor before setting the box on Gregor's desk. "It's late, local time where we'll be landing. I've been debating with myself and I've come to the conclusion, this being the last planet and the last city we will develop, that you should have these to flesh out the memories that you keep in your journals. They're audio recordings of various sources. Some of them from my offices, but most of them are copies of interviews done by my biographer, Professor Lucas Latham."

Gregor stared at the box, unsure what to think.

Karl took a deep breath before letting it go. "Ah, Gregor, the end comes at us with haste, my friend. Our work will culminate in the city you will build in this valley I have chosen. Time, then, to close all the loops." He stared at the box for a moment, and then left without another word.

Gregor's gaze held on the box. He had no idea what Karl meant, but, in his innocent curiosity, his hands moved to the box.

***

AUDIO LOG 3, SESSION 2:

"Ah, my sweet Miss LaFey, I'm so glad to see you."

"Hello, Karl. I saw some of the preliminary plans for the Saanos-7. Impressive. And please, it sounds so silly when you call me Miss LaFey. Call me Maggie."

"And so I will, but even informal meetings should begin with some formal recognition. And this meeting will be very informal because I must discuss a certain intimate, very personal matter that has come to my attention. I shall be brutally and tastelessly blunt, so please excuse the brevity of my courtesies. We need to discuss your relations with Gregor."

Silence.

"I see. You must understand, Maggie, that Gregor is a very special man, as special as you. I have invested great wealth in developing him to his full potential. And I know, because it is so very obvious, that much of his drive springs from his attachment to you. And I know as well, because my life has not always been exclusively centered on my developments, that there has been no consummation between you two. I implore you, in the strongest way I can, not to do such a thing with him, or I will have to bar you from ever seeing him again."

"Karl—"

"Let me finish. His creative genius is founded on his desire for you. The greatest wellspring of passion is desire unfulfilled. Gregor is an emotional simpleton, but pure, and with his crippled temporal memories, his unfulfilled desire will not spoil as it so often does in most people. His creativity burns as he is, even though he does not understand why, and I will not suffer anything to change that, and if you change that, I will most certainly hold you responsible. Your relationship is to be platonic, and nothing more."

"Why are you punishing me? I haven't done anything."

"I have fostered you much the way I have fostered Gregor. I will not have that wasted."

"Wait, Karl, you don't understand, it's not what you think. Don't you think I've tried to feel differently, that I haven't tried to contain it in the time we're apart? You think I'm blind to how different Gregor is? How can you, of all people, ask me to contain my feelings, my love? Don't you think I've tried to find a replacement, a substitute? That I haven't been sensitive to how things could spoil between us? There's no conscious choice in this. For all your talk of creation and fostering passion and living life from its energy, you ask me this?"

"You and Gregor, I look at you two as my children, the children I never had. This request is only to protect you. For the sake of that, and only that, I ask that you honor my request."

More silence. "Why?"

"For things yet to come, my dear Maggie. It's for the greater interest. In time, all shall be as you wish it to be. You must trust me in this."

***

Gregor woke, the memory of the audio file whispering in his subconscious. The dawn light came across the valley to hit him in the eyes. He blinked and pushed himself up on his elbow. Maggie was still asleep beside him, her back to his chest. The little battery lantern's light was lost in the long early rays of the sun. He looked down, appreciating her in profile, her face quite peaceful as she slept. He studied her, cementing his memories of her with the reality of having her next to him. His gaze dwelled, memorizing the freckles on the soft curve of her cheek under the golden light of dawn.

There would be no city, he knew. And with no city, his work was done. And with his work done ….

"It's all over," he thought aloud. "Yes, it's all changed."

He shifted, moving his arm to brace himself as he leaned over her. She stirred at the sound of his voice, turning onto her back to look up at him. He swallowed, his jaw clenching for a moment. For years he never risked letting his imagination run to this place, but then it was happening, and he let himself sink down, closing his eyes as his lips brushed against hers. He backed off to look down at her, her gaze full on him. "Gregor—"

His heart raced and then he heard his voice whispering the one thing he yearned to say for so long. "Maggie, I love you."

He kissed her again as she held him to her. He had little thought for cities, or Saanos, or what was to come of them in the days to follow.

***

Gregor could hear himself sob as he trembled in the knotted center of the Saanos-7. Despite his grief, it was anger and resentment that formed the brunt of his emotional turmoil. He screamed, deafening himself in the little control pit as he closed his eyes and threw the massive bulk of the Saanos-7 into the hillside he had torn open.

The valley shuddered. The many trailing articulated arms of the Seven flailed in the air as its weight sent it sliding into the bowl he dug. It came to a halt with a boom that resounded across the landscape, masking the racket of the many Saanos-1's and 2's spraying frantic constructor streams to foster the nascent city's burgeoning foundations.

***

It was evening when Gregor returned to the retreat, his face a stolid mask. Maggie returned earlier in the day to pack her things while Gregor followed the now superficial pursuit of overseeing the final assembly of the Saanos-7 and the so-called firing of its power plant. The leviathan was ready to work, but there would be no work.

There were no security personnel in the retreat, and Gregor walked its ornate halls with growing suspicion at this oddity, so unlike Karl's obsession for notions of safety and privacy. He emerged in the wooden dome to find Karl alone, seated before a large planning table. A holographic display of the valley glowed above the table. Karl looked through it to glare at Gregor before summoning him to the table with a wave. "I want to show you something," Karl said and pointed to the hologram. "Our engineering corps finalized the subterranean infrastructure plans. They're being uploaded to the Saanos-1's and 2's so they can start tomorrow. I see you have the Seven set to go. You'll have a busy day tomorrow. Have you deduced your vision?"

Gregor stopped beside the table, across the hologram from Karl. As decided as he was, he felt a deep, sudden remorse. He detested the notion of hurting this old man that had been so good to him, that had done so much for him, and asked so little in return. But then Gregor thought of the whispers of the audio files and rallied himself for the confrontation. "No," he said. "I have no vision."

Karl shrugged. "No matter. You have several days before you'll have to address the urban over-structure. And with days come nights, and with nights, well, you know how it is. In the dark, creativity always runs wild through the consciousness of the creative mind."

"I have no vision for this city," Gregor repeated.

"Yes, I heard you."

"And I never will, because I'm not going to build it."

Karl glared at him. He crossed his arms on his chest. He looked away, and picked up a steak knife to slice off a piece of smoked meat from a plate resting on his side of the table. He chewed, seeming to ignore Gregor, but waved the point of the steak knife to a location of the hologram. Gregor looked down to find a green color-coded pipe—a sewage pipe—that trailed up the side of the valley and over its edge, straight through the spot where he had lain with Maggie.

Gregor's eyes widened. He looked up to find Karl staring at him.

"Did you think I wouldn't know?" Karl said with deceptive calm. "It called for a slight adjustment. You didn't respond to the audio files quite as I expected."

Gregor failed to find his voice. He stared in mute shock.

"Maggie knew the rules, but she wasn't strong enough. She decided not to wait to understand what I was trying to do here, what I had planned for so long and with such care. She is your inspiration. I know this. Your love, never recognized, that was to be the driving force, the tragedy behind your genius. It was why I brought her here for you to see again, to drive that nail a little deeper into your heart. I gave you the opportunity to create a final masterpiece, but no, you two thought you knew better. So now you have forced me to reintroduce the tragedy by less subtle means. Perhaps you will be better, creating through anguish, rather than through joy."

Gregor retreated a step from the table. "What did you do?"

Karl tipped his head, but he looked away and sliced off another piece of meat.

Gregor ran from the room. His footfalls echoed in the empty halls of the retreat. The place, he realized, was abandoned. It was just him, and Karl.

He grabbed onto Maggie's open doorway to stop his charge down the hall. His fears solidified when he looked into her room. Her things were scattered about, drawers were left half open, a light was still on, but what caught his attention was her flute, the precious wood flute she had made, left out on the floor. He forced himself forward, his quaking hand reaching down to the flute.

He winced and clutched it to his chest. "No, no!"

He ran from her room back to the dome to find Karl sitting by the hologram table, still eating his smoked meat. He seemed quite satisfied in his air of apathy. He paused to sip his red wine before looking over to Gregor. "Ah, so you see."

Gregor gasped. "Where is she? What did you do?"

Karl shrugged. "You don't understand, Gregor. It's time to play this out."

Gregor clenched his fists. "What did you do with her? Tell me."

"I sent her away, back to that place from whence she came, the whispers of my dreams," Karl said with a whimsical tone, waving his knife by his head. He smiled. "Enough. I want to tell you a story. The first time I had my heart replaced, I recognized that mortality would not overlook me. Being that my DNA was sequenced in full as part of the process to grow my new heart, I made a proposition, a courtesy in return for a large investment of capital. I knew I wasn't one to marry and, as such, not one to have legal heirs. I ordered the production of an heir, one very much to my requests. A boy, my little Saanos-8. But being that this boy had certain flaws—in particular, certain areas of his memory—I requested the crafting of a second child. I asked the technicians to be creative. They came back to me with a young woman, her mind imprinted with vague memories of a generalized childhood. That project was Saanos-9, but I decided to name her Margaret LaFey—my dear, sweet, Maggie. And the boy, yes, the boy, well, I decided to name him Gregor."

Gregor felt dizzy. "You, you *made* me?"

Karl sighed.

"And then, you, you *made* Maggie?" Gregor swayed on his feet, the awful realization hitting him. He looked down to the flute. Nausea swept over him. He wanted to scream, he wanted to cry, to tear his eyes out. He wanted to see her again, hold her and tell her he loved her and kill the disgusting secret truth, kill it by—

Karl glanced at him. "I know. It's repulsive, your consummation with her. That's why it was *not* supposed to happen. She's your sister, but more than that, she's your complimentary opposite, because each of you is almost all of me." He sliced another wedge of meat, his eyebrows arching in thought. "The two of you together, well, it is so very incestuous, if you consider the philosophical aspects of such a thing. Then again, perhaps I should have seen its inevitability, the yearning of two lesser halves to reunite to their greater whole." He looked up to Gregor as he chewed the meat before offering a shrug. "You understand this, yes?"

Gregor's heart froze in his chest.

"You'll never see her again," Karl said. "Ever. I'm dying, and there's nothing more that can be done for me. This city was to be our eternal achievement. It was to be your masterpiece, but artistic triumph is unfortunately realized only through tragedy. You see, Gregor, the heart must bleed. It must bleed."

Gregor fell back a step, his hands dropping to his sides before his knees gave out and he slumped to the floor. He felt disemboweled, he felt disowned, betrayed in every possible way he could conceive, and, worse, worse than anything, was the dawning realization, the agonizing realization, that Karl had planned this for so very long, all that time smiling upon him even as Karl plotted his agony and ruin.

Gregor sprang to his feet in rage. The emotion was something so new, so alien to him, he was powerless to resist or control its madness. He charged around the table and slapped his hands around Karl's throat. His momentum was too much, toppling Karl from his stool to send them both to the floor. Karl's head whipped down on the stone tiles, smashing against them with an awful crack as Gregor fell on top of him with a shriek. He rolled over, the steak knife buried in his belly, only to see Karl's vacant eyes fixed on the dome.

Gregor clenched his teeth and pulled the knife out with a quick jerk of his hands, clasping his side as his blood spilled. He laid there, his body losing tension as his mind sank into the delirium of what Karl told him.

Maggie, I ruined you, I destroyed you! All I wanted to do was love you.

He gasped her name and rolled onto his back. He squeezed his eyes shut in a failed effort to hold back his tears. "No," he hissed. "No, *Maggie.*" Blood from the wound seeped between his fingers as he screamed. Ignoring his weeping, he forced himself up on his knees and looked down on Karl. His gaze locked on the emerald he and Maggie gave as a gift. With a curse he ripped the chain from Karl's neck before shuffling to the table to retrieve Maggie's flute. Then he made his way to his room, grabbed his notebook, and went back to the dome. He paused in an archway, looking out to the night to discern the outline of the Saanos-7 where it rose above the trees.

He took several labored breaths, his gaze locked on the Seven. He heard the soft bong of wind chimes in the lazy breeze. He looked down at the flute and staggered toward the Seven, his mind sinking to the murky depths of delirium.

***

An excerpt from the Coda Urbani:

THE CITY, as a monument, is meant to outlive its creator, the one who envisioned its form and accompanying function. But the design, the design remains, and, if it is done right, if the mood of the creation is captured and pure, the emotion that drove it will live on and the city will be its witness and monument, for the created is always connected to the creator by inspiration and these three prime elements, like the sides of a triangle, can not exist apart.

***

Gregor slumped over the auxiliary control yoke. He coughed, his hand dropping from his side to let his blood spill from his belly. It was impossible to continue. Despite his failing body, his thoughts raced unchecked. In those last moments of anguished clarity that remained in his life his vision achieved its full form and became the final instructions of the Saanos-7.

The mighty machine, possessed by its mindless urge to follow the vision, didn't stop itself. It drew pipes from a deep bin near its base, clutching them in its metallic tentacles before impaling itself, driving the thick pipes through its metal innards until they emerged from the hillside. The machine sputtered, billowed smoke, but finished its orders.

The ground trembled, cracked, and fell upon the alloy hull of the Seven, burying it in the side of the valley as the Saanos-1's and 2's scurried about to finish their labor. When their work was done, they, too, fulfilled their orders by plunging their masses into the senile depths of a nearby lake.

***

An excerpt from the prologue of 'Paradise Crumbled: The Enigma of Karl Saanos':

What is one to think, looking at this, this empty thing one can barely call a city? It sits in a valley, its buildings set in strange geometric patterns that analysts say can only be appreciated from space. The structures, scattered about the glistening river of the valley, are small and simple, like so many little mausoleums, and come in several discernable types. The units of each type form the points of triangles, with the triangles merging into larger matrices that certain intrigued mathematicians have mapped to produce repeating sets of prime numbers. Each set culminates with the number seventeen. What significance that number carries no one has been able to say, and it remains part of the city's mystery.

Yet the haunting beauty of the place is not to be denied, even if it lacks any possibility of being occupied as a city. There is no infrastructure to speak of—no electricity, no plumbing, nothing. In fact, the utter lack of such things suggests that perhaps this city, for whatever reason, was never meant to have residents, and so it earned its odd name, the City of Never.

In the twenty years since its completion not one of these mysteries has been solved, even by interrogating the former employees of the now defunct Saanos Development. With the unsolved murder of Karl Saanos the company unraveled and all in its employ—even me, Karl's biographer—have been left with no recourse. As to the cities Saanos left behind, it seems there was a fatal flaw in the constructors that formed the cities. This has led to the exponential decomposition of the constructor material and the inevitable collapse of many buildings to piles of dust. All but the City of Never, which by luck of circumstance, or by some hidden agenda, will not suffer the same fate. The soil used by the constructors in the city's founding is unique to the valley in which it sits. With the secrets of the constructors lost, it's now impossible to tell.

All that as it is, people still come to this valley to look upon the empty city, the city that will never be lived in, the paradox of a city built as a ghost town. Even as tourists and students alike come to study the place and often mumble as to the waste of its construction, their eyes are inevitably drawn to the now densely vegetated hillside that contains the wreckage of the Saanos-7. They stare at the gleaming pipe ends poking from the ground, not understanding until the late evening winds come to the valley. Channeled through whatever maze of piping exists unseen to the eye, a new sound comes to the valley.

It's not the clank and roar of the once mighty Saanos-7, but something that only adds to the mystery, yet completes the experience, and leaves many who come here speechless. And, although I have spent many days here trying to figure how this place fits into the unsolved death of the greater mystery that was Karl Saanos, I, too, wonder what it means.

For it is music, music like that of a wood flute, whispering a sad melody through the valley under the starlit night.

-L. Latham

Conquest's End

Where to begin, now that the end of ends has come, that the march of ten years, ten years of blood fury and cold metal and razing fire, has come to the doorstep of that very place that has been sworn by wrathful parties not to be won or lost without sorrowful penalty, penalty to pale even all that has already passed with so much grief and lament?

Steady they march, the great columns of men in their red and black armor, trampling the green turf to dust as their Lord watches from a hill on high before the waning westerly sun. Long have they marched across the Three Kingdoms of the world, leaving only the choice of capitulation or carnage in their wake. They have marched until there was no prize left on which to march, and so their Lord led them across the Endless River, against the ceaseless gusting of the Tundra's Tongues' dry winds, to cross the Meadows of Morrow and the gray Sea of Senility, to disembark for this last march.

Glint of blades and glint of eyes, both hard and cold and eager for the piercing of the distant prey, they hunger for the end. And the end, it lies before them, a windswept city of lofty stone walls like none they've seen, for it is the bastion of the one whom they all whisper has fueled this war of wars, She of the Thousand Fold Gossamer Veils, who bewitched their mighty Lord and drove him to squash the world between them.

There he sits, his expression hidden behind the hard folds of metal and leather that form his helm, the cast of his gaze lost in the shadow of the sun behind him. Before him, above the winding, marching multitude of his devastating war machine, stretch on high those very walls of stone to encircle the impenetrable fortress of *She* for whom he has come.

He listens to the low moan of the evening air, but still he sits motionless. "Form the camp, Kyto," he orders to his Second. "The sun fades and will not rise in full on this pale land. We begin at dawn's twilight. It is the best light we will have in this place."

Kyto hesitates and, risking wrath, nudges his mount beside that of his Lord. "None have passed her gates in all the ages before us," he cautions one last time.

"And in all the ages before us, none have brought a host such as the one I possess," his Lord corrects. The Lord turns, and there is no pity in his eyes. "Now go Kyto, before I forget you are my friend."

***

And what is it that one sees from that hill where the Lord stood mounted those nights before, that naked outcrop of rock, to look upon the fury unleashed upon the bastion of She for whom he has come, She of the Thousand Fold Gossamer Veils, ethereal and eternal, elusive to the eye yet everlasting to the dreams of men, hidden still behind her walls, walls assaulted without parallel, beaten and blasted black by a relentless torrent of flaming projectiles, vomited from the very catapults of hell and earth that have been arrayed against her heights?

The days gain count, and worse the nights, yet no purchase is gained. The fields before her bastion are scorched lifeless, the trees are felled, a deathly rancor fills the air from flaming pitch for the Lord's projectiles, and scurrying through the heavy roiling black clouds that cling to the ground are the men of the mighty host, like some underworld fugitives gliding on the mists of their own heathen breaths.

Bodies fall under silvery arrows that rain down during the moon's light and, more threatening and more deadly for their disarming and befuddling beauty, the Espers of She of the Veils descend from the walls, screaming on the night air from the folds of their gleaming white robes to stab at the host with long vicious blades, piercing metal, flesh and bone alike as if they were so many layers of rice paper.

Resolute remains the Lord, and in such desperate hours of the Espers' fury he charges the bare hill with dutiful Kyto at his side to work powers of his own. Clouds he gathers, black storm clouds belching bolts of violet lightning to challenge the gleam of the Espers. With the moon's enchanted light obscured behind the clouds the Espers flee the battle to return to the bastion and its heights, heeding their lady's call as their strength wanes in the absence of their silvery moon sister.

The Lord, he stands in his stirrups, evoking the words of tongues perhaps only he and She of the Veils know among those who walk the world of the Three Kingdoms that he has conquered. He calls to spirits forgotten from elder generations and sculpts the clouds as he sees fit, yet in his rage holds them not back, but lets them drench the horror of the battle, and with a thousand fold drenching of sorrow lets the futility of stones and swords wash from the earth.

"She will not yield," Kyto cries to his Lord, his arm extending to the Espers as they gather upon the bastion's heights to loose their torrent of arrows.

"Let them sting, let them strike," the Lord says beneath his breath. With a sudden turn of his hands he summons a wind to scatter the piercing flurry like so many leaves to the rolling Sea of Senility beyond the battle. "Only one wound shall end this, and it is the one that cannot kill, that cannot heal, that has yet to be inflicted."

To this Kyto relents. He has no answer, for he perceives that which he has not perceived before, in all the tiring years of march and war, the aim of his Lord has little to do with conquest.

***

What is it that one could say, that one could even think, when confronted with such beauty, the beauty of an Esper, stilled for a moment by her will from destroying all about her in a rage of purity that borders and pales the boundaries of chastity? Mark the sheer elegance of her frame, so graceful, so proud in the power of her master, She of the Thousand Fold Gossamer Veils, emboldened by that patronage in the halo of translucent silvery and white veils that waver about her. Indeed, what is it that one could say to such a being?

For there is no mortal woman like an Esper, none regaled with such finery as an Esper. Behold her presence! The intricate weavings of her linen and leather armor, so light, so pliable, hypnotic in the embroidery of the Four Winds upon her breast to match the runes hammered into the slender length of her polished sword, brandished to rest on her shoulder, blending so with the pure silver length of her hair, trailing from the aquiline lines of the silver helm that frames the otherworldly beauty of her face.

Such is the sight of an Esper, and yet among them there is one above them, second only to her master, She of the Thousand Fold Gossamer Veils. She is marked by the piercing intensity of her eyes, blue as the bluest sky man has beheld—she is Captain of the Espers, Lady Luna, silver haired moon sister of the star laden night.

Kyto falls to his knee before the Captain of the Espers, disemboweled by her presence, awed and shamed by her beauty, the purity of her spirit burning within her blazing sapphire eyes, and struggles to find his voice.

The Lord is not so daunted, though, and meets Luna eye for eye, and yields not a blink of space to her. He sweeps his hand to his side and dispels the otherworldly tides of air that set her veils in motion about her, leaving them stilled. At that, Kyto is stilled as well.

"I have no words for you, my dear Luna," the Lord states, abrupt and audacious as he addresses her without title. "Your lady knows why I have come, and why I cannot leave, and why I have no joy in this world, and this world no joy beneath me. Only she can end this, and only she will understand. I have no terms to offer, nor terms that I can accept."

Mysterious Luna tips her chin, her wide, graceful forehead settling over the almond taper of her eyes. "Such is not what my lady wishes I discuss with you," she answers, and her voice is like the whisper of many breezes through the cherry trees Kyto remembers from his childhood, made more magical for the fact that her lips do not part as she speaks.

The Lord opens a hand to his side, gesturing from his hill to the camp of his war machine gathered before the walls of her bastion. "Ancient oaths have brought this. Your lady cannot deny this, my lovely Luna. Go, relay this, and this as well: She cannot hide from that which has bound us. She must come, or I shall never leave this place, and all that the world holds dear shall perish."

Luna holds her stance, but it is not her place, for all her power, for all the wisdom of her unearthly spirit, to speak for her lady in matters of mortals and their world. "So be it," she replies in her voiceless voice of cherry blossom breezes. She looks to Kyto, her eyes narrowing as he trembles on his knee, stealing furtive glances of her. "And what would you have?" she asks of Kyto.

His lips part. What is there to say? To hold one moment of such beauty in his heart, keep it there unblemished forever from the time-wearying waste of the world? That she has turned his hardened soldier's heart into a lovesick ghost?

But to Luna there are no secrets in the hearts and minds of mortals, and, in pity of what she sees in Kyto, offers him a token to preserve face before his Lord. She lowers her hand, extending the glistening edge of her blade until its tip rests before him. He offers up his hands, takes the tip in his palms, and presses his lips to the runes upon the blade.

And then she is gone from him, and all he knows is the sorrowful craving of a dream too beautiful to comprehend, too beautiful to hold, for he opens his eyes and looks up, only to see her fly like a comet of shifting veils through the night sky to her lady's bastion. He gasps, forgetting that his Lord stands behind him.

Yet his Lord offers no rebuke as he, too, watches Luna go. "And that, my dear friend Kyto," he says in a low voice, "is how mortals are made to be fools in the face of greater things." He lays a hand on Kyto's shoulder, but then walks off. "We must rally the camps," he calls over his shoulder. "The siege will continue."

But Kyto is left immobile, as if a man struck dead, dead with yearning for something he fears he will never know again. As he weeps, his falling tears crystallize in the air, only to hiss and steam upon meeting the ground.

***

What is it then, this notion that stills the hearts of men, that befuddles and entrances them when they behold that which mystifies them, which belittles their greater ambitions and leaves them as lost leaves in the storm, remembering the life they had known, but knowing it no longer, for they have beheld something, something they cannot explain, yet something they now yearn for beyond any pale of reason or misplaced nobility?

They only know that they must have it, that it makes a mockery of all else they have while at once giving them belief in something new, something greater — what would it be for mortal man to stand beside that which transcends the meaning of his own existence?

For three days, such is the manner of Kyto's thoughts. The siege continues without relent and he remains as a man struck dumb, for he has been possessed by a listlessness that defies the exhortations of his captains. For though he is Kyto, sacker of a thousand cities, he who possesses the daughters of forty deposed kings as his wives, whose mere countenance has given lesser kings reason alone to bow in servitude, who is Second to his Lord who has conquered the Three Kingdoms of the world, he sits as one dejected, whose soul has been dissected from him to leave him a mannequin of flesh among the world of mortal men.

He will not loose his sword, and he utters no order. He watches the ceaseless battering of her bastion not for its progress, but to await with trembling hands the emergence of her Espers and their captain, mysterious Lady Luna, silver haired moon sister of the star laden night. And, until he sees her, until he can return to her presence, he knows that he cannot live, that he cannot die, that he cannot find comfort in food or victory, for he is a man lost, lost from the battle, lost from the world, lost from himself.

"He has been bewitched," the Lord's captains utter behind Kyto's back, but they have no presence to challenge him directly, for the Lord takes no action against Kyto, but leaves him be: until the fourth night since Kyto beheld the presence of Lady Luna.

The Lord comes to him then, lays a hand on Kyto's shoulder in a most paternal way, and speaks words he has spoken to no one in all of the Lord's countless years upon the world. "You are not of her kind, my good friend," the Lord advises. "So Lady Luna has done to you, so she in her bastion did to me in the Time Before Time, and the restlessness has not left in all the ages of my time. Take heart, for you are of this world, and so will return to it, and be freed from this suffering."

Kyto says nothing, for he knows not what to say.

The Lord speaks, but his voice lowers, and a terrifying passion surges through his words. "But I am not of the world as you are, and can know no peace until she comes forth. She will not come forth while her Espers delight in their fury upon us. Tomorrow, Kyto, you will be freed from their madness. Tomorrow I will destroy them, for they forget in their pride the depth of my wisdom."

Kyto makes no reply, for he is far away, far away in the recesses of his memories. He is a boy again, running with arms spread between the flowering cherry trees beside his family's village. As he runs the sun and breeze are on his face, and he pretends he is flying, and the flurrying cherry blossoms about him are clouds. He knows no sorrow, but only joy, for he realizes only now that even then it was her voice calling to him in the undulating whisper of the breeze, that there is more to the world than mortals and their petty desires, and that such a notion is more than the innocent dream of a wanting child.

***

What then is there to say when the moment comes, that moment when allusions and the mortal world collide and, like so many winged Espers, they must come crashing to the ground, for is it not the fate of mortals in their sorely limited breadth upon the world that they must seek to quench all around them, even as they must be quenched themselves, for they will not suffer the presence of those who, unlike their works of undying stone for their own memories, unwittingly remind them of that which they fear most, their inevitable death and decay?

Such is the way of things on the next night, as Kyto sits on his mount, his life stilled in his heart, as his Lord rallies the captains of the great host. To him the Lord summons foremost the captains of the Orders of the Mantis and the Jackal, two companies of the host dreaded for their pitiless cunning and savage war craft. With the twilight of day fading and the Espers marshalling upon the heights of their lady's bastion, the time has come, the time when the Lord will work the venom of his tangled soul against the children of She of the Veils, to draw her to him in her sorrow and rage.

But for Kyto the words are nothing, they are lost to him, they are mindless chatter on the smoke laden breeze washing about the camp and its endless barrage of flaming projectiles. Yet, at some unknown, unheard call his gaze lifts and there, upon the crenellated stone works of the lady's bastion, the Espers appear in the gleaming lengths of their shifting veils. At their center he finds her for whom he longs, Lady Luna, silver haired moon sister of the star laden night.

And he, Kyto, sacker of a thousand cities, stirs to that which he has not known in his life. It is the sudden thunder of his heart, not for the joy of victory, but for the dread of agony soon to come, and for fear of something lost that no conquest of a thousand worlds can replace. It is the very thing that in its absence has given him such terrible force in battle—it is pity, it is sympathy, it is lament for those who would be his foes, and these three rise as one to rage within him, just as the winds rise and rage along the inhospitable crags of a stony cliff beneath the warming sun.

"You cannot stop this thing that will happen," the Lord says from behind Kyto's shoulder, surprising him.

Kyto turns wide eyes on his master, but says nothing.

The Lord urges his mount forward to take his place beside Kyto, tipping his chin toward the lady's bastion. "You cannot hide from me what you feel, for I am not like mortal men that walk and are bound to the world. I am more like she that awaits me, and this you have known in some part of your soul, known it as long as I have known you. I am older than time, Kyto, old as she is old, born in the Time Before Time, when the world moved in ways that are impenetrable mysteries to the men that walk in these times."

Kyto studies his Lord, for he knows of what his Lord speaks, having heard the tales and myths passed from the ancients to the elders.

"The elders know nothing," the Lord counters, laying a knowing, penetrating gaze upon Kyto. "The tales of the ancients are lies. They would let men believe that creatures such as the Espers, such as She of the Thousand Fold Gossamer Veils, such as myself, walk this world to make fools of men and the things men would have: power, fame, and love."

Only then does Kyto begin to understand, and his heart sinks, for he feels the march of their many campaigns as a delirious weight upon his shoulders. At the same moment he understands something else, the curious will of his Lord to have him present for the parley with Lady Luna. "You have come to join She of the Veils," he whispers in disbelief.

"You have seen all that she and I once made in the Time Before Time, for you have conquered it at my behest. And now that the conquest has ended, this, too, must end in the only way I know to end it. You see, Kyto, as you know from Lady Luna, so you know between She that waits and me. I offer her the world, but the more I offer, the more I distance her, and yet the more I distance her, the more she will resist me, for she cannot do other than that which will harden my heart. Such was the decree levied on us by our Master, for we defied the rules upon us, and created the world as ours to enjoy. For our blasphemy we have been doomed to destroy that which we love, and all that we love that we created, until we destroy each other. Only then can the world be free of our sorrow."

Kyto listens, but his heart has stopped. His gaze darts to Lady Luna, and then to his Lord. "Such things, we must not let them pass."

But the Lord, he has no reply. He gives Kyto a solemn stare, and nothing more, before he turns away.

Kyto, the sacker of a thousand cities, sits as the boy who once looked out his door, powerless and distraught, as the men of his village felled the grove of cherry trees that were the refuge of his dreams. Only then does he understand in full what is to come. The Espers take their place about their Lady Luna, ascending the bastion, and the Orders of Jackal and Mantis set to their beastly task, and their eyes gleam frigid and pitiless like the blades of so many sharpened axes.

Now upon the crenellated stone works the Espers gather, as is their wont, and from their ivory bows loose a storm of silvery shafts like vengeful moonbeams to impale the tender innards of the host. And when their gleaming sapphire eyes can no longer hold back the battle fury brewing within their spirits, the Espers take to their flight to descend from the bastion in the gleaming comet trails of their shifting veils. Down, down upon the host they come in the confidence of their lady's power within them, their blades whistling in the air on the channels of the Four Winds they command.

Yet it is not to be as it has been on so many nights before, no, for as they descend for their strike upon the host, the host parts to reveal the Orders of the Mantis and the Jackal, and it is they who seize the moment and loose a torrent of their own.

For at the command of the Lord they have woven sturdy nets of silk, and having secured the nets with stakes, they in turn crafted combine crossbows of devious complexity to shoot the nets aloft. They loose this trap upon the unknowing Espers and, in surprise, Lady Luna shouts as the nets open and seek to ensnare the moon-sister sprits of the air. But the nets are many, and although the Espers are quick and keen-eyed, the Mantis and Jackal hordes are persistent and ruthless.

The moment comes when one of the Espers is doubly enmeshed, and, try as she might she cannot cut free, and the men of the Mantis pull upon the trailing lines to deny the buoying Four Winds to send her crashing to the Earth. There she writhes, struggling for her sword on the ground outside her reach. She calls in anguish to her sisters, to her Lady Luna, but to all the Espers her hope is denied in a storm of nets unleashed as the Mantis ranks close upon her.

From the midst of those men a great foreboding figure appears. He is their captain, and in rage he hefts over his head a wicked double-bladed battleaxe and, with a roar, buries it in the chest of the bound and defenseless Esper. But she does not scream long, nor does she bleed, for she is made of things not of this world, and her corporeal form is not as the bodies of worldly life. She shatters in a blaze of light, a comet fallen to the ground and broken in a shower of fading embers.

The host howls in its victory, and it is not alone, for their assault is tireless, and three more Espers have already fallen, even though Lady Luna and her sisters struggle to cut the lines and slash the nets. And Kyto watches as a man dumb with horror, for in the wake of the death-light of the first Esper his sight has changed, and he sees the host not as he had before, but now as he knows the Espers see them, and he learns in a heartbeat their disgust for this seething multitude before the bastion.

For Kyto no longer sees the men he knows, but instead within their helmed heads he espies snarling countenances twisted and grotesque, as their reckless rape of the world has made them. They are monsters, and he is adrift among them, and he sees his Lord as a thing to both fear and loathe, the diametric of the Espers in their grace and beauty.

As he ponders these things his eyes widen, for in his gaze he beholds that which freezes his blood within his very heart and sends it as crystalline shards tearing through every vessel of his body in anguish. Ethereal Lady Luna is snared in one net, then two, and then two more, far from the help of her Esper sisters. Men of the Jackal and Mantis pull as one to the shouts of their captains, and she, despite all her otherworldly power, is shorn from the sky to plummet downward with a cry of sorrow, for she knows what awaits her among the dirt and swirling black clouds of clinging ash.

But it is too much for Kyto, and he can no longer sit idle. It is not enough to spur himself forward, no, he erupts forward, bolting his steed down from the height of his Lord's hill toward the nearing fall of Lady Luna. The host parts before and around him, not yet understanding his aim, but believing that he, sacker of a thousand cities, wishes to claim the head of this most cherished prize, or perhaps despoil her in a more despicable way, and add her defiling to his titles of lore.

As fair Lady Luna crashes to the cold earth and the captains of the Mantis and Jackal emerge to kill her, Kyto breaks from the host and, in a flash of his blade too fast for any to comprehend, sends both their heads tumbling to the ground. Amid the shower of their blood he dismounts and cuts Lady Luna free, and the sapphire light of her eyes rekindles and, without pause, she launches skyward as a comet reborn.

But she has not left noble Kyto alone, for the wake of her gleaming trail casts him as a nest of swirling shadows, so that he appears not as one man but a company of his own brothers, with him reborn at their center. In fear the host falls back, but they are not to be fooled for long, for as their captains fall to the ground, the host falls upon this most unexpected treachery of the sacker of a thousand cities.

They are unwise, though, in their hasty wrath, for they fail to measure Kyto's fury in full. For though Kyto has always fought as a warrior without equal, he now fights as a man without equal, and none can stand before him. The vengeance he wreaks upon the foul host is swift and terrible, all the more demoralizing as Lady Luna returns to aid him with a company of Espers about her. In the confusion and carnage the carefully ordered work of the Jackal and Mantis dissolves and the rest of the Espers dart upon the host, the air their own once more, and their wrath is an eruption without compare.

So the battle rages, and the Lord heeds such things little, but spurs the rest of the host, and the endless reign of their projectiles slacks not, but under the Espers and despite the slaughter they inflict, the assault upon the bastion doubles itself. It is too much, and, for all the skill crafted in the stone works they succumb, and the bastion begins to crumble in places. The smooth stone façade gives way, the crenellated heights are battered down, and the stout stones beneath crack and yield with an awful wrenching groan. The host draws back, but it is too late, for without warning the bastion collapses on the plain, entombing many of the host in the work of their own hate.

But it is more than the collapse of a wall, for when the bastion fails a wind erupts from within, a wind of such force all the catapults and bitter siege engines are shattered where they stand. None but Kyto and the Lord are able to hold their stance as all others are blown flat to the ground. The Espers vault upward in expectation, but Lady Luna holds her place beside Kyto, and though she and he are bound now in their valor and nobility, they have not a moment to share a word nor glance, for the tremors of ill portent shake the very earth beneath Kyto's feet.

Revealed in the rubble of the bastion is a brilliant light, white but with shifting tones, a twisting dance of ivory hues. At its core stands a solitary figure, gleaming silver sword in hand, ruby eyes alight with distemper, platinum hair an undulating corona, tapering white veils a shifting sphere of gossamer about her. It is none other than She of the Thousand Fold Gossamer Veils.

She has heeded the call she has so long sought to avoid. The full radiance of her presence is as nothing that the world has seen. Even the Espers, even Lady Luna in her twilight luminescence, appear as nothing but twinkling stars in comparison. Such is her brilliance that the host cannot bear her sight. Even as they cringe, cower, and hide, their very eyes boil and bubble from their sockets before their innards roast and burst within their bodies.

Yet Kyto is spared such a fate, for loyal Lady Luna protects him in her own shifting veils in return for his having saved her. From behind her guard he witnesses what no living thing of the world has yet witnessed. In the clash of the Lord and She of the Thousand Fold Gossamer Veils, all the elements are set upon each other and the firmament of the world screams in tortured protest. The battle they fight is not one of hate, but one more against themselves than against each other.

The time has come, the moment encircles them, and they can avoid each other no longer. For all they have wrought they have no wish to destroy that which they created in their love for each other in the Time Before Time. And that which they created is the world and its countless living things in all their coupled and contrary complexities. It is the source of the ironic curse laid upon She of the Veils and the Lord by their Master. For in the Time Before Time it was the Master's desire to craft a world, with He and She as servants in its making but, in their desire, they had foregone the decree laid upon them, and so the world lacked the perfection of its original intent, but perhaps was all the more vital for the intricacies of their differing natures.

But such notions were lost memories, bitter and entombed within He and She, and yet smoldering within them to drive their ruinous confrontation. Such as the brightest candle burns all the faster, so too their clash cannot long endure, for the full vent of their powers would break the world they so treasure, and so, too, they know this, and find their end in the only way they know, in the only way that is left at conquest's end, and that is to dispel their lives for the sake of what has so troubled and consumed them with longing.

Kyto sees little of it, for She of the Veils streaks toward the Lord with otherworldly speed, and he spreads his arms defenseless to accept her, yet calls out upon the roiling clouds to summon many bolts of lightning upon him, and so, too, upon her. Even so, she does not yield. There they meet upon the bastions' ruins, and there her sword impales his heart, and there his lightning enmeshes them both to consume her with him.

Beside the Sea of Senility the world cracks, and the Three Kingdoms of the mortal world are shorn free to at last find their own fate, and the now orphaned ground of the ethereal realm disintegrates beneath Kyto's feet. He tosses aside his sword to accept his end, glad for what he has done in his last moments, but he is stunned to find Lady Luna before him, about him, surrounding him with her many shifting veils, and she smiles upon him, and takes his hands, and her grip is both warm and cold. Though the crumbling of the firmament is a deafening roar, his fear fades as he meets her unearthly gaze. She lifts him skyward, and the Sea of Senility speeds beneath with its lazy swells of forgetfulness, and the Tundra's Tongues sap him not.

His armor is shed and lost, his memory dims, his vision fades, and then there is only the enchanting presence of fair Lady Luna and soon nothing but the endless blue gaze of her sapphire eyes. Then the change comes, and nothing is known to him as he has known it to be, but she speaks his name with the whispers of the Four Winds, and the world and its woes are forgotten.

***

What then is the nature of these careless whispers of loss and futility, that all must be divided against itself, and that the world must know no peace, but that mortal men must feel at odds with their mortality, and not know their place and call until some last desperate moment, and live among the bitter echoes of regret for so much of wearying Time's span allotted to them, and compel the greater mysteries that linger into the age of the world to hide themselves, trade off their glory, barter their pride, their majesty, so that restless mortality may find its own way, and cause those such as I, Lady Io of the Espers, to forfeit our path to that of dreams and passing fancy?

Kyto stands among the grove of cherry trees, their blossoms floating about him on the warm spring breeze. He looks to his hand, his boy-sized hand, and wonders at the longing in his heart, for he feels as if he has stirred from some terrible dream and he trembles at the ghost of its passing. But then the breeze blows again and the cherry blossoms rustle in the air. It comes as a voice to him, and he knows peace within his heart, and solace in the world, and wonder for the many living things.

Laughing, he spreads his arms, and runs between the trees, flying on murmuring winds among shifting blossom clouds beneath a sapphire blue sky.

Turn the Wheel

"Is this thing recordin'? I've been savin' up to tell this for a long while, so now that I got myself up to it, I only want to take one round at it. Anyway, here it is.

"It was a day that started like any other. It was Summer time up in the hills where we lived, and I'd spend my time ridin' my dirt bike in the woods. I miss those times, ridin' alone with the wind on my arms, some mud on my goggles, my ears ringin' with the popcorn-whine of the bike's two-cycle engine. Usually those times was good times, bein' out on my own with nobody yellin' at me, but the particular day of this tellin' it wasn't so good. I was standin' on the foot pegs of my bike, ridin' the way I always did. My ridin' friends, they thought I was kind of crazy ridin' like that all the time, because my butt hardly ever touched the seat. Really, though, it was one of those little half-lies, of which there was many. Most times, it just hurt too much to sit on the seat.

"My Ma caught me that mornin', caught me sleepin' after Pa went off to the bike shop. She come in my little room and like usual she started swingin', ambushin' me before I woke up. It was always that first shot that stung the most, and she always made a point of plantin' it right on my ass, so none other would know she done it. I got wise to her though, usually makin' sure I was up and out of there before she rose from her whiskey coma to take out another day of misery on me. But, the night before, me and my friends stole a few cases of beer and got awful piss-drunk, so she was hot-mad because I come home late and didn't have none for her. So it was a double beatin', the usual for bein' on the planet, and the other for bein' a selfish drunk. She broke it on me, the plastic bat she'd found in the trash. No bother to her. She'd find another, like she always done before. She'd taken a likin' to them bats, that's for sure. See, those bats got this seam where they put the two halves of the mould together, and if you open it up some with a knife, when you hit a body with it, well, it just burns hot, like lightnin'.

"So like usual, by the time she was done and left me pretty much a mess she gone and flopped back in bed and I got the hell out. And that's why I was ridin' up there in them hills, only stoppin' when I had to steal some gas that afternoon before makin' my way back, knowin' my Pa would be comin' home. Ma knew better than to be takin' hand with me under his watch.

"Pa, you see, he'd been 'round the rough track, and come back a different man. He gone to jail for stealin' some snowmobiles while Ma was pregnant with me, so he wasn't there whiles I was little. Before he come home there was word goin' 'round that he killed a man in prison.

Got away with it, too, they said, 'cause there was a riot or somethin' goin' on. I first met him when I was still a boy. I came home from school one day and there's this man sittin' on the step of our trailer, and he says he's my Pa. And the thing about my Pa, since I didn't know him before, is that knowin' him as he was then, he has this thing of puttin' different ideas together in strange ways, like connectin' stuff that don't get connected. 'Juxtaposition,' he used to say, when he was workin' on some of them foreign bikes—but then again, he used to mumble to himself a lot.

"Anyhow, that day I first met him I come home from school and there he was sittin' on the step. He stuck out his hand to shake, which I liked 'cause it made me feel like a man, and he told me he was my Pa, and he done some wrong things, and he gone round the wheel the hard way, but he'd found the Lord before he come back to me, and he was goin' to see to his best to keep me from makin' another turn of the wheel like he'd done. I don't know, it made no sense to me, but at least he was there, and I thought it would make life, as it was, better.

"So anyway, on the day of this recollection I come ridin' back to our trailer out of the woods and there's my Pa sittin' on the step of the trailer, just like he done that day I first met him. And he was havin' a smoke, which was odd, 'cause he said it was bad to smoke. The door was open behind him, swingin' on a broken spring, creakin' away, which was out of sorts, 'cause it was the only sound, and it wasn't ever quiet like that in the afternoon, at least not with Ma 'round. So it was in a careful way that I rolled up to the house. I kept my distance some, but Pa waved me over and patted his hand on the step next to him. So I sat, because I knew better than to say no to Pa when he seemed in one of those quiet moods. And the minute I sat, I knew somethin' was really off, 'cause he lit a smoke and gave it to me. I thought it was a trick of some kind, 'cause he'd beat me before for catchin' me with smokes.

"'It's all right, boy,' he said. 'You go ahead.'

"So I took it, and we smoked a while, but my heart was poundin', 'cause I knew somethin' was up and near the end of the smokes, that's when he told me, with his eyes lookin' out over the trees, and what he said then, I'll never forget.

"'Son, when I met your Ma I was six years old, just like she. And I thought that first time I saw her that she was the prettiest little thing put on this Earth. She had this hair, like angel hair, almost white, she was so blond, and it was in a long braid, and she had this beautiful smile. I came to think that smile was for me, 'cause she always laughed at the stupid things I done.' Then he ground out the smoke under his foot and looked right at me … through me, you could almost say. 'Life put her to the test, son,' he went on, 'and part of that was my misguided ways when I was young and wicked. So I'm sorry for what she done over the years, but you're free now, and I want you to know none of it's yours for the blamin'. But she was your Ma, even for all she done. So you remember her just as I told, 'cause she was a lost girl, and the sadness got the best of her.' He opened his hands in front of him, like he was offerin' somethin', but then he lit another round of smokes for us, and he went, 'Now you can go in if you want, but I don't want any questions 'bout it. You can take a look, but then you go back and wheel 'round the wood chipper so I can take care of it all.'

"That's about the time I understood. I went in, and it looked like a tornado come right through there, tearin' it all up inside. Not that any of the three of us was much on housekeepin', but it was like somethin' exploded in there. I found her back by the kitchen, under a pile of cans and pots that had tumbled out of the pantry. There was just this mess, and her bare feet stickin' out, and by the way they was, I could tell she was face down under all that.

"Pa often said he had violence in him. He said it was like some thing we pass on, like blue eyes. But he told me once there was two kinds of people with violence: ones like him that are just lost in it and don't know better, and then there was the other kind, the ones who were just plain dangerous. He said to me sometimes that Ma had become one of those, that the drink had put a madness in her that stole her soul and sent it away somewhere. Standin' there lookin' down on her, I believed him, 'cause for some reason, in that moment, I knew I had no memory, not one, of her with a smile on her face.

"I remember not thinkin' or feelin' too much. I was just sort of numb, I guess. I didn't give a thought as to what made it happen. I guess seein' her there took away any need to know what made him do it. I always thought one of us was gonna end up face down one day, the way things was in that house, but seein' it, it was like bein' free and not free at the same time, like floatin' under water, that moment right before you run out of breath, when you're still okay, but you know you're just hangin' on.

"So I started movin' like I was told. I went out back and brought the chipper 'round and left it there. The chickens was struttin' 'round the coop like usual. I don't know why that sight stuck on me. Pa got up and told me I best be gettin' on, and not to come back 'til later. He said it was his to clean up, and he didn't want me takin' any hand in it, except to stay quiet 'bout it, 'cause it was just 'bout us and our concern and none other. I got on my bike then and went off, up into the hills, and I couldn't hear the chipper runnin' over the popcorn-whine of my bike, and I didn't miss it none.

"Up those hills I rode. I don't know, but lookin' back on it now, I don't remember what I was thinkin', all I remember was wantin' to get away. And that's where the other half of my life came in, the half Ma and Pa knew nothin' 'bout, that I kept as my own. You see, there was this program at the high school, kind of like this charity thing from the families that had somethin', to make themselves feel good for helpin' people like me who were livin' on nothin' up in the hills. So I got picked as one of their charity cases earlier that spring. The girl that was doin' my outreach, she said she picked me 'cause my Pa been in jail and 'cause of the rumors floatin' 'round 'bout what my Ma done while he was sent up.

"Truth is, I signed up 'cause all those girls runnin' that charity were pretty, even though some of 'em were up-tight church types. But the girl who got me, she was real pretty, and to boot she wasn't one of them Bible-thumpers, and once we got to talkin' she said I had a real nice smile. Thinkin' back on it now, I bet that's why she picked me. Her name was Lucy Sue Everly. That first day I met her I took her initials and just called her Elsee, and she smiled real bright at that.

"Anyhow, we got right friendly as school ended, and sure, even though she was a senior and bound off to college in the fall, and kind of popular, she always found some room in her time to talk with me if I came by her house. Her family had some money. They had a house, all brick, with air condition, and with a pool and big yard. The hills ran along behind their yard, so if I wanted, I could come up real quiet by rollin' down the hill to the back of the house and then roll away just as quiet down the side slope of their land to disappear back into the hills. Her dad was some professor at the state college and her mom was some kind of special kid's doctor. They were both real nice to me, kind of those high-minded liberal types, so they were okay with me bein' there to see their daughter now and again, long as I behaved on my best and brightest. My world didn't cross with theirs anyhow, so they wouldn't know nothin' 'bout my lesser moments.

"Well, it was gettin' on evenin' by that point, so I rolled down into their yard and as luck would have it, her parents was out. I walked right up to Elsee's window, bein' the house was like a big long ranch, and knocked on her window so as not to scare her too much. She was sittin' at her desk typin' somethin' on her computer. When I knocked she jumped a bit, but when she turned and saw me she smiled, pretty as can be. So after beatin' the trail dust off my shorts and shirt I came in the window like usual, but she went and got me a towel so I could wipe down my arms and legs and face. Normally talkin' with her was real free and easy 'cause she always had a way of makin' things seem not so bad and makin' me think I could do somethin' with myself other than scroungin' for a life, like most people I knew. It was nice and all, but it was like a dream 'cause she didn't know nothin' of what was goin' on for real since I made a point of never once tellin' her. Comin' to see her, that was my escape time. I guess that's what brought me there that day.

"She started talkin', bright like usual, but I didn't say anythin' back and so she knew somethin' was up. And I don't know when it happened, but next I know I was curled up like a baby by the side of her bed, against the wall, with my knees pulled up to my chest. I wasn't cryin', 'cause I stopped cryin' long ago. Elsee came over to me. I think she didn't know what to do, but then she sat down next to me and put her arms 'round me and held me. For some reason, even with all that stuff I'd just rode away from, I got this warm feelin' in my chest, and it was like I was bare before her, just me, and not all that vile stuff back in my life, just a kid lost and lonely. All the things in my head that I'd built up 'round her, well, they all became real, so she was like some angel come to me, and she was all mine. I loved her so much right then, and she was so beautiful that I think now it couldn't have gone any other way. The happenin' of it, it's like a blur now, bein' that I was just a kid, but I think that was part of it, 'cause even though we were right there in her room findin' the mysteries that exist between men and women, it was real innocent, like child-innocent, if that makes any sense.

"After, we was layin' in her bed, and I was starin' at her as she lay there with her head back on her pillow, her eyes closed, this lazy smile on her lips, and all that chestnut hair of hers spillin' like waves across her pillow. We had the sheets pulled up, way up to our chins, like we was hidin' or somethin', and that's when things started to change in me. Like I said, I was just lookin' at her as she was layin' there next to me. I could hear the crickets makin' their racket as the sun was settin', and this *thing* woke up in me, and I wasn't there with Elsee anymore, and this beautiful thing we just had, it fell apart. I remembered what I'd said to her when she held me on the floor, these half-lies that I was goin' to miss her, that she was the only good thing in my life, that I loved her, and I started thinkin' that I'd played her, played her the way people play in gettin' other people, the way they *pay* for gettin' other people, and it's just this cheap dirty thing between people.

"You know, I have these memories in my head, things stuffed way deep down, and they came floodin' back on me then, these pictures of my Ma when I was a little kid, when Pa was still in jail. I'd see myself peekin' out of my room 'cause of all the gruntin' I hear, and I just see her bent over the dinin' table, and men—different men, different times, but somehow all the same—behind her, some lookin' angry, some lookin' mean, but all of them lookin' like they're runnin' some tough race, like they bein' chased by some demon. And some of them, they push her face down hard on the table, they pull her hair tight, they call her all sorts of vile things and I guess it's like they got to demean and degrade her 'cause they know they're givin' in to the filth they got inside themselves. It's all hate and anger and corrupt and when it's over and it's just us again she pushes my colorin' books aside and tells me to sit at that same table. Then she counts up some money, or looks at me with those glazed, hard eyes of hers and tells me not to worry, 'cause there's gonna be electric, or food, or television again tomorrow.

"And somehow, someway, but anyhow kind of sudden, I was lookin' through those memories at Elsee, and that *thing* stirrin' in me, it grew by leaps. It had some kind of voice in me, kind of low and slithery—like a snake, I guess—and it told me I should do to her like those men done to my Ma, give her somethin' else to add to that snotty little smirk on those lips of hers. Maybe she'd even like it, me puttin' the force on her, puttin' the *violence* on her, callin' her all sorts of ugly things, 'cause in the middle of that nightmare runnin' in my head I thought again how we ended up there in her bed, of those things I said, and they got all twisted in what I'd seen my Pa done and how it got that way. I thought maybe Elsee saw me less like some pity case, that she'd drew me in her arms so some night when she was fat and fifty and lookin' at her borin' husband she'd satisfy herself knowin' there was some stain of me still in her, from the little walk she took with her dirty boy from the other side of the tracks.

"I rolled away, 'cause I was feelin' bad lookin' at her right then, but then other things came to me, like the spring-fresh smell of her flowery quilt and sheets, the white walls of her room, the shelves of trophies over her desk, her cheerleader uniform hangin' behind her door—all those things of a shiny life I had no part in, that I had to hide away from in this horrible thing that had come into my life, that was eruptin' in my life as my Pa worked away on cleanin' things up.

"But cleanin' what up? There were stains all over the world that day, all the ones you can't ever see under the sun, but blot out the light in your eyes. And I knew I had to go, 'cause that *thing* growin' in me was *the violence,* come to visit me, sprung up from its roots buried in me. I had to go, I had to stop it. I knew, I knew from tip to toes if I stayed I was goin' to hurt Elsee, and there'd be no comin' 'round from that, just like there was no comin' back for Ma.

"I got up and got dressed. She sat up and looked at me, wonderin' where I was goin', but I gave another half-lie and told her my Pa needed me for somethin'. And before I bailed out her window I turned 'round and took my last look at her, and she was kneelin' up on her bed, holdin' the sheet over her chest, 'cause she was a respectable girl. She smiled on me, that beautiful smile of hers between those waves of hair fallin' to her shoulders. So I waved and lit out of there. Got on my bike and tore up into the hills.

"Now this next part here I never told, not to no one. You see, the thing is, I didn't go home. Least not straightaway.

"No, it took some ridin', and I had to get my courage up to do it, but the more I rode, the more I tried to hide from it all, the more I knew I had to do it, 'cause the more I knew it was what my Pa was expectin', what he'd planned from the get go, when he told me to leave him to do the cleanin'. So instead of goin' home I went toward town. Outside the bar where Ma used to wait tables I knew there was a pay phone. And my heart hurt so bad it felt like it was breakin' 'cause I knew what I was 'bout to do. You know, even though we was poor, and I got a beatin' more times than I could count, the only good memory I got was me and Pa fixin' up my bike. He'd pulled it from the junk pile and gave it to me one Christmas. But I put that feelin' away. I put a rag over the phone and I lowered my voice and then I done it. I told the state troopers what Pa done to Ma, clean and simple.

"Then I hung up the phone and the shakes that came on me were like nothin' I'd ever known, worse than not havin' proper heat in the winter. I had to stop ridin' and somewhere out in those hills, lost in those trees, I cried, I screamed, I puked with the mess of it all, 'cause I knew what was goin' down, and how Pa had made it all be the way it was gonna be. And, even though he took his hand to me on occasion, I finally understood him, understood his way of lookin' at violence and how this had to go, how this had to end.

"By the time I got to the trailer it was over. The troopers told me he'd come out the door blazin' away with the shotgun so they did what they had no choice but to do, and they put him down. One of them was firin' wild, though, and blew off the latch on the chicken coop, so all them birds had come runnin' out flappin' their wings in a panic in the headlights of the cars. By the time the troopers got everythin' squared up there were these white feathers spread all over the ground with my Pa layin' there dead in the middle of it all. They found the chipper behind the house, soaked from bein' washed off, but sittin' in a big red puddle. The story made some news, but most folks waved it off, figurin' it was one of them crazy hill-people stories.

"Well, I got shipped off to the next town over where one of my Pa's cousins took me in. And things got better. That family done right by me, and done the best they could for me. I was a handful for them to deal with, what with me smokin' and tearin' off on my bike to get piss-drunk with my friends. Elsee went off to college at the end of the summer, and I never did see her again.

"Anyhow, that's it. Now it's all there, not just what was in the files and so forth, so you might know a little bit more why I'm comin' to the sessions. I got a wife, I got a boy, and I got to do right by them, but sometimes *it* comes up on me, and my temper gets white hot and the violence stirs up those knots deep inside me. When that happens I think of Ma and I think of what Pa done, what he said, and I think of Elsee, and the way it all come together that summer day.

"So that's when I pray it'll be all right, and thank Pa for makin' me as free as he could, so that maybe I could go 'round in some better way, and I'd have my own chance to pass the Test."

Beheld

In the Beginning, the Deity pondered.

***

It was not like the random thought of a man, but in some ways it was indeed like that of a man, in such a way that a man could understand the Deity. For It was the Deity, and It was boundless and, in the beginning, It was a curious thing, for It knew not of Itself. It was more like a man who first falls asleep and begins to dream, for though he dreams and the dream exists within itself, it is nevertheless master of the vessel in which it unknowingly resides. Yet, it knows not how that vessel functions, and what laws it must obey. So it was with the Deity, for though It was aware of Itself, It was not yet conscious unto Itself, and the universe, which was Its vessel, was an unknown thing.

So it was, and the Deity considered this, and though Its thoughts were as yet without shape, there was one thought that gained shape of its own as a question. It resonated at the Deity's core, and so became seamless with the Deity, and remained open, as endless as the Deity Itself.

This fundamental question was simplicity incarnate, and though there was yet no notion of language, it nevertheless awoke within the Deity, and the question was this: *Why?*

***

The universe, for all its complexity, is akin to a song.

Such was the way the Deity became aware of Itself and illuminated a momentous deduction: all which was in existence had not existed before. Being the Deity, It knew all, and so knew with certainty of Itself, but not of that beyond Itself. And in that pondering It began to associate those parts of Itself that were It but not recognized as such. Like a sighted man who has lived his life in total darkness, not understanding what sight is until he first sees light and perceives a timeless but unrealized reality around him, so it was with the Deity as Its pondering took new forms and reached new extents and became fully conscious of the universe that was its body.

In this way the Deity became aware of all the mysterious laws and mechanisms of the universe, like a man waking to the function of every cell and synapse within him. It was perhaps a strange moment in the universe, for the Deity not only became aware of all the laws of how Its vessel functioned, not only gained innate and instantaneous understanding of the firmament of Its vessel, but heard the living echo that was the remnant of Its creation.

That sound was the low, undulating whoosh of cosmic radiation, a haunting melody that for eternity would knit the universe together to form the Deity's vessel. And It thought of this melody as a song and so became aware of rhythm. With rhythm, the Deity in Its vastness considered the alternating nature of rhythm. It was the property of change, of things that were, then were not, and then were again, so that the Deity perceived singular images of Itself and the changes between them. It then brought temporal order to those images, and so brought order as well to the universe.

By such work the Deity implemented Time.

***

Time was a plaything, and even though it was of the Deity's creation and so part of the Deity, in the vastness of the Deity it was meaningless.

In the evasive slipstream of the Deity's complex consciousness, It became aware of something It had not considered before in the creation of Time. It went back to Its thought of time, of things that were and then were not and then were again, and translated them to three interconnected states: that which was known, that which is known, and something mysterious—that which is yet to be.

The Deity decided to look upon these three unruly siblings as Past, Present, and Future. The Past was predictable, and ordered, and the Deity thought little of it, for the Past was obedient and dutiful in its predictability. Once something went to it, the Past changed to accept it and put it to rest. The Present was curious and embodied many things that the Deity prized within Itself, for the Present was at once all knowing and yet all learning, and the energy of its endless curiosity was a gift that the Deity bestowed upon it, so that it, like the Deity, might embrace the vessel of the universe, and not become mute like the Past.

And then there was the Future, the capricious offspring of the Deity that embodied a part of Itself always new and uncreated in any possession of the Present. In the energy of Its pondering the Deity came to understand that It only existed as there was yet some other manifestation of the universe for It to absorb. The moment Its pondering ceased, the vessel would go dark for It would then preclude the necessity of Its own existence and vanish with the universe as if neither had existed.

It remembered the fundamental question of *why* and knew the first reason for the question's existence.

In the greater unknown of those ruminations, the Deity knew not what was to come of Its own thoughts which lay beyond the mechanistic doldrums of Its vassal vessel universe. Within was something the Deity came to call Uncertainty, and Uncertainty was the wild spirit that kept the Future darting about the universe to set the Deity upon new paths to explore. For the Deity knew not where Its thoughts might wander, even as It was driven with inexorable momentum to evolve new thoughts to necessitate Its existence. So the Deity came to understand that with the creation of Time It saved Itself, for without Time, the Deity's considerations might lock in repetitive loops and erode the fundamental question.

Time continued, the Future came in its endless forms and, with the servitude of Past and the endless curiosity of Present, the ages of the universe took shape.

***

The Deity, though, was restless.

It thought often of the song of the universe and sought to weave other things into the song, for the song was the metronome of Time. As such, it kept check on the unruly siblings of Past, Present, and Future. It seemed only natural, and right, to set all things the Deity created within the universe to follow the song. This greater melody It then knew as the Song and, after much thought, the Deity renamed it Nature.

Then came a great blossoming as the Deity explored the wondrous couplings of the physical universe on all levels of scale, and the myriad forms of Its contemplations illustrated every reality within the universe. Countless incarnations of the Song came about in Nature, spawning life in the diurnal variations and separate circadian cycles of countless orbiting bodies. It was an exquisite dance of particles, atoms, molecules; of planets, stars, solar systems; of galaxies and super clusters. All were set in motion and balanced within Nature, kept in harmony with the Song made possible by Time. They could move and alternate and be things in one moment that they were not in the previous moment and yet be something else in the wondrous unknown of the Future.

Oceans took their tides, trees grew through their seasons, and leaves gained their color as they wavered in the rustling winds of change.

And yet, the Deity remained restless.

It questioned Itself for many ages, puzzled that despite all It had wrought through the creation of Time and the birth of Nature that the universe was as yet sterile with predictability. The prospect left Future dejected, and with its gloom, the Deity at once understood what Nature lacked: an unbridled element of change, an element that could, like the

Deity, summon thought.

And the first thought would be none other than the fundamental question.

***

Long was the matter contemplated by the Deity. It looked deep within to fashion an image akin to Its nature, but different as well.

There were many incarnations that passed through the Deity's considerations and, since what It willed was what would be, there were many new things within Nature. Each of them was distinct, imperfect in the same way that their individual considerations were imperfect as small domains within the continuum of the Deity's thought. And when restless Future stirred at these new awakenings, it also sensed the perfect imperfection and imperfect perfection of what the Deity wrought.

The Future understood the Deity could not recreate Itself, for the Future knew as well that in the creation of Time there was always some part of the Deity that yet lay undiscovered. Any image the Deity might create of Itself was imperfect by default, for the creation of the image would in turn introduce a new and unknown existence. So it was, and so the fundamental question was once again affirmed as salvation.

But the Deity spent little energy on such riddles, for It sealed away such thoughts in the abyss of incongruence. Instead, It flowed with the Song, watched Its creations, and though it may have lasted a moment—or perhaps a millennia—in the end, life breathed anew in all the creations in their strange and sundry surroundings. Each was fashioned from its environment, patterned for its environment, part of its environment for the sake of harmony within Nature to avoid discord with the Song.

For the Deity, creation was imbued with patience. It was not an instantaneous thing, nor a miraculous thing; rather, it was the culmination of plans long in the making, careful in the making, to abide by the fundamental mechanisms embedded in the firmament of the vassal vessel universe. Just as a man grows a beard and, though he may wonder what his body has created, it was nevertheless created by the laws of his body's function; so, too, was the making of the Deity's creations.

With many different eyes those creations looked up and a new thing was revealed within the universe. For among Its many creations the Deity let play a new song born of the fundamental question, and it was called free will.

***

Ages passed and the Deity watched.

In the endless perception of Its omniscience, the Deity did not fail to sense the chorus of thoughts that rose up in the many developing minds of its creations, a blaring cacophony over the peaceful undulations of the Song. So the Deity considered new things, and this time the Present stirred, for the Deity sensed curious intellects among some of Its creations reminiscent of Its own curiosity and was most pleased. The Deity reached out to them in their many places, across disparate times, for each of Its creations progressed in their own fashion, not yet understanding their perfect imperfection. The Deity, then, was revealed to them in many shapes and words, and Its nature was probed with a curiosity much like Its own so that the universe was alive with thought.

But, beneath such curiosity, there lurked a darker aspect of free will. It was the raucous discord of anarchy and the destructive rebellions and revolts of those who embraced its hollow lure. Because of their choice, they knew not from what they turned, and knew not the torment and turmoil that unknowingly spurred their actions and inclinations. Yet, after much time, the Deity decided the matter was as It decided it should be in the beginning of Its creation, for the intricacy of the Deity's thoughts was impossible to plumb and none could fathom such subtleties without the Song in the conscious mind.

So it was, and so it continued, and Time wore on and the Deity thought of other things, things beyond the understanding of Its creations, and they felt lost, victims of an ambivalent universe, adrift in a careless void. They were unaware of what surrounded them, and saw not as the Deity, for part of their imperfect perfection was yet to emerge from the veils of discovery.

Time was meant to be their mentor, not their trap. In their restlessness they looked to the stars above their worlds and, upon perceiving the vassal vessel universe, their minds grew so that they began to ponder greater things.

***

For many generations the Deity observed with passing interest what Its creations fashioned from the elements of the universe, for to create was innate to the Deity and to It the elements were as the cells of a man's body. The Deity manipulated them with both perfect understanding and perfect ignorance, for it was without effort that the Deity built things from the vassal vessel universe.

What the Deity noticed was the development of Its many creations and how their minds changed with what they learned from their handiwork; how it made them look deeper into the workings of the universe to fashion ever more fantastic devices. For the Deity, these were taken as compliments, for It was satisfied with Its creations and took pleasure to see them move about the universe with ever increasing freedom, ever nearing some vague semblance of the Deity's own awareness.

Across the void the creations met one another, and though there were often generations of terror and titanic struggles, in the end the Song was not to be denied and the harmony of the universe won out. In this fashion the many disparate creations came to be one and, in the vast understanding of their own natures, they embarked upon a new course for they perceived a mystery at the center of their existence: they were many imperfect parts of a greater whole, yet perfectly imperfect, for they could merge in seamless, and long unexpected, ways.

And so the great merging began. For generations it persisted, until the many creations of the Deity became as one kind and they were humbled, for though in this form their power to probe and affect the universe was without precedent, they perceived that they were as yet dwarfed in their existence. Although the universe brimmed with life and intelligence from the perspective of the Deity, to Its now unified creations, the universe remained a dark, cold place of impenetrable distances.

But the Deity's subjects did not despair and did not lose their way. Rather, they took heart, for in their humble wisdom and their hard-learned harmony with Nature, they at last began to perceive that which bound them from their beginnings and brought them to their Oneness. They detected the Song and mastered free will. Discordance left them, and the Oneness were at peace.

In that time a miraculous thing happened, or so it would be termed, for the Oneness understood a miracle was only the remote emergence of infinitesimal probability. They took heed, and perceived a great portent, an unresolved uncertainty fulfilled. It came as one of their own, a creature of such intelligence and understanding of their own intricate and vast knowledge that, to it, all was second nature. The Deity stirred and was pleased as It had not been before and looking upon this creature, termed it the Likeness, for the Deity saw within it much of what It treasured within Itself.

Then the Oneness gathered their collective guile and, with their perception of the Song almost in full, it was the Likeness who emerged as the final piece of an impenetrable puzzle. For though they dared not deceive themselves in their wise humility to think they could wield the power of the universe as their own, they nevertheless sought the connection they believed would come with such power. It was not to wield their might, but to unveil the mystery behind it, and perceive the

Deity on Its own terms.

They hesitated in fear of this audacious thought and instead referred to Its omniscience as the Wellspring, and pondered It without relent as they sought an answer to the primordial questions of awareness. Foremost among them was to discern the reason for their existence and to answer the fundamental question in full.

Then the Oneness, in their span of years almost free of the mortality so long restraining their ancestors, and under the guidance of the Likeness, finished their work. It was as something such as they would make, and so not something the Deity would create, for they were not yet even a single facet of the Deity. They called their creation nothing more than the Machine, for they wished to pay homage to the elaborate and perfect working of the universe. Although they could manipulate the universe, and thought of it as the vassal vessel, they knew they were still bound by its laws of Nature as defined by the Wellspring and so treated it with reverence.

The moment came and, with great celebration and many thanks, the Machine was brought to bear. It harnessed the power of stars, lit the darkness, and glowed with a life seemingly all its own. Its energy was something yet to be witnessed in the universe and so became something new within the pondering of the Deity. Then the Machine had a wondrous effect: it caused the Deity to take note. Time was subdued, and the siblings of Past, Present, and Future felt joined in a way they had not felt since the time of their creation and division. To the Machine the Likeness departed and within it, the Likeness retired, and there it remained for what would have been many cycles of the ancients.

With great patience the Oneness waited for they knew the working of the mind of the Likeness was more evolved than any of their minds alone or in combination. They hoped the revelation of the Likeness would be something new within the universe, something to answer their greatest questions and, perhaps, the fundamental question, guarded since free will first awakened their conscious thoughts. So they waited, and they were confident that their patience would not be in vain for they believed in the rightness of their humility, the purity of their respect, and the truth of the path they had chosen.

Time passed and, without warning, the light of the Machine faded. The Oneness knew the meditation of the Likeness was at last done and they gathered in great anticipation.

Then it was that the Likeness emerged from the Machine and spoke words that erupted in the Deity's consciousness at the same moment. "I have looked unto the Wellspring and beheld nothing but the endless mystery of that with which I came, for I am."

Then the Deity thought in a way It had not thought before, for It at last plumbed the depths of Its own nature, and in that moment became something yet again new, for the Deity then knew Itself as It had not known Itself before. It and the Likeness had become One, and so both the Deity and the Oneness became the One, and the One then knew the purpose to Existence as if It had posed the query to Itself within Its own thoughts, for the fundamental question was at last answered. Just as a man's perception of himself is forever altered the first time he sees his reflection and his countenance is revealed in absolute form, rather than subjective perception, so, too, with the Deity. Yet Its awareness spanned time and space and so the shift in the work of the Machine and the meditation of the Likeness and the glimmer of the One was momentous.

But the transformation was not without its demand. Time evaporated. The siblings Past, Present and Future went senile. The vassal vessel universe was created anew and all things were not quite as they had been before.

When it was done, the Deity awoke to Itself once again and thought returned. Nevertheless, it was a singular moment, and so the Deity was alone, and being alone, the Deity did what was within Its nature.

In this new Beginning, the Deity pondered.

Titalis

The Tragedy of Eurimedon

PROLOGUE

Behold, upon the fertile plain a once great city and its high walls of crafted stone. Proud it remains in its state of ruin as a regal ghost of mighty ambitions, and yet, like apparitions who lack corporeal form or substance, this broken realm, too, is a hollow shadow of the foundation over which it was built. Mighty was its reign upon the lands and long its reach—too long, perhaps, for its firmament to sustain. But such considerations are hindsight judgments; whispers on the trailing winds of Fortune's mocking little laugh and do not serve justice to those whose memories haunt the moonlit lanes.

Like all tales of lost glory, there is more than what the ruins suggest, and yet not so, for if the tales of men hold one untiring truth, it is that people destroy themselves from within.

Such is the tale of this city, a place once known as white-walled Eurimedon.

ACT I

It was a glorious sunrise, and Mylo crossed his arms on the crenellated precipice of the city's walls as he gazed to the horizon. He scratched his beard and frowned at the little cough in his throat before taking a swig of ale from the goat skin dangling at his shoulder. He turned when he heard a similar cough behind him and stepped from the wall to look down from the battlements. He stood for a moment, chuckling, until his cough returned. He took his long spear from the rack beside him and leaned his old body against its sturdy length as he watched his brother shuffling up the ramp toward him. Mylo cleared his throat and spat to his side. "Ah, so he nears, so he nears! Look at you, my aged brother. I see you can still wake with the dawn."

Pylo glanced up at his twin, annoyed at once, even as he used his spear for a walking staff more than anything else. "Ah, yes, so I near, so I near, brother Mylo. Do not grade me, you creaking elder, unless you forget it was you who fell first from our mother."

Mylo grinned. "First to cry, you walking waste, but roaring last if I have my way."

Pylo pointed as his shoulders sagged with the last length of the ramp. "Roar if you will, but know this—from the morning bed I will be the one who springs last." He stopped before Mylo, exchanging a glare until he smiled and clasped his brother in a tight embrace. "There now, brother, let me have at that ale," he said, reaching for the skin slung from Mylo's shoulder.

Mylo raised the skin's sling over his leather helm and handed it to his brother. He patted Pylo on the shoulder as he led him over to the edge of the wall, leaving his spear in the rack. "It is a good thing, is it not, that we still share such humor, two old dogs as we? Lucky we are to still walk these walls as guards. Better for us, now, to stand at this height than to stand as we did in our youth on the field before this gate."

Pylo gulped some ale before raising the skin in toast. "Blood letting is for those who never fear theirs shall one day run dry. Honor to them, glorious fools," he said with a belch.

Mylo laughed as he leaned on the wall. "Good brother. I think your blood shall not run dry no matter how tired your arms, so long as your humor keeps it warm."

Pylo took another swig of ale, closing his eyes as he let the brew roll down his throat. He shook his head as he capped the skin. He handed it off to Mylo, but his gaze lingered on the distant horizon. "Listen to you, you lamenting goat. Did we not, in our days, beat back the barbarous Totuks? Did we not, in our last active days, join brave Titalis in his war to bleed Totuk ambition white?"

Mylo sighed as he nodded. "Aye, good days those were, and good service we paid fair Eurimedon for the glory she has given two dogs such as we." He slung his skin but, glancing at it, decided to take a gulp for himself before capping it. He wiped his mouth on the back of his hand and looked to the horizon, following his brother's gaze. His eyebrows sank until he rested a hand on his brother's back. "Tell me, did you hear the good word that came last eve?"

Pylo nodded. "Aye, hear it I did, and grateful I am. The winds blow, brother, they blow strong upon us weathered stones no matter how we resist its call to change." His eyes narrowed, but then he slapped his thick hands on the battlement and let out a loud laugh. "But grand news it is, a great telling of grand victory and pillage for noble Titalis—honor escorts him home, and speeds his march."

Mylo stared into the distance and shook his head. "I see nothing but night's dusky retreat beneath the horizon."

Pylo grabbed his shoulder cowl and shook him. "Look, look you milk-eyed donkey," he said, pointing to the distance. "Do you see there, the rising dust, the gleaming helms, and the snapping pennants of our many men-at-arms returned to us at last? See there, what the wise men say we shall soon know. The Totuk storm has passed and the dawn of Eurimedon will be a new light upon the world. See there, Titalis approaches now, ten years of struggle and strife endured, through which trial only he could deliver us."

Mylo stared, blinking beneath the bushy gray mass of his eyebrows. "My eyes see not what you say, but in my heart I will believe it to be so. For too long have we yearned for days of peace so that we may lay our bodies down among song and plenty, rather than blood and misery. Fade we will, dear Pylo, but not until our worries are done." He turned to his brother, thumping his fists on Pylo's shoulders before stepping to the edge of the wall and cupping his hands to his mouth.

"Rejoice," he bellowed with all his strength. "Guards, to the gate, Titalis returns!"

***

Within the wide enclosure of Eurimedon's walls resided many homes, markets, and the palaces of the city's highest citizens. Long years of war with bands of Totuk savages had left the crafty citizens of Eurimedon with little choice but to expand their defenses as much as they could, encircling all but their farm and graze lands. Down into the ground they had burrowed, loosing quarries of sturdy stone for the walls as they founded their fortified city atop an underground stream. It was to this stream that they had dug so it could fill the city's cisterns in times of siege. The far enclosure of the walls overlooked a cliff where the river dropped in a foaming cascade from the mesa upon which sat the city and its fields.

The city was planned on the same sense of order the people of Eurimedon held as their pride and so the streets were arrayed like the spokes of a mighty wagon wheel with the hub of the wheel the wide city center. To the east of the center, and overlooking its spacious square, rose the high columns of palaces with their sequestered gardens consuming the space between the square and the far wall nestled at the mesa's edge.

To the square marched the host of Eurimedon, much to the applause of the citizens, to whom many of the city's fighting men were long missed brothers, sons, husbands, and fathers. Discipline, and the pride of their victory, held the men in check, for they knew after ten years of war and marching they only need hold for a short measure among the comfort and bounty of their own people, before at last finding their long sought refuge in the homes they missed beneath so many star filled nights.

Marching at their lead was Titalis, unmistakable in his height, even as he carried his crested helm in the fold of his arm. Though his jaw was wide and square and his eyes resided under a forehead reminiscent of the city's walls, the look of his gaze was kind, and his smile, though proud, was welcoming. To either side of him strode his captains, foremost of them keen-eyed Capestes, the royal heir to the city, and stout Eikoptas, a commoner, but held most in trust by his lord, Titalis.

Titalis raised his arm as the host filed in full to the center of the square, surrounded by the cheering citizens. He turned as he stepped free to stand on his own, waving the crowd to silence, before he looked ahead to the gathering that approached. At their lead was none other than he who carried the burden of Eurimedon upon his brow, proud King Teleimon, his might swathed in flowing purple robes to set him apart from the white robes of his attendants. To him Titalis paced, and to him, and to no other, after ten years of war and conquest, Titalis at last settled upon his knee, set his helmet and sword on the ground to either side, and bowed his head.

The crowd stilled. As one, the host let out a single shout of address.

King Teleimon looked across the host, drinking in the site of the city's strength for several moments before he was able to smile in acceptance of the reality before him. He rapped his staff on the white paving stones of the square only to lean against its length as he extended an open hand to Titalis. "And what say you, Lord Titalis?"

Titalis took a breath, but kept his head down and remained on his knee. "Noble King Teleimon, honorable father-in-law, gentle sovereign who took me as an abandoned child, you who raised me as one of your own, to wed to your own, to be kin to he who will be king in his time, heart and spirit of white-walled Eurimedon, it is for you that we return, bearing good tidings."

Teleimon took a step, but his hand tightened on his staff. "Hesitate no longer, my champion. Tell us, do you bring a settlement from King Totuk?"

Titalis raised his head to meet his king's gaze. "Hard fought and hard pressed were we, my king, yet, indeed, we have wrested a long awaited victory." He opened his hands to either side as he gathered his breath. "With the plans of your brilliant son, Prince Capestes, with the lashing tongue of good Captain Eikoptas, and with this sword I bear, with these three—allies invincible before all foes—I fought in your grace's name before Totuk hordes. Their numberless savages we broke and their king himself cowered beneath my blade." He took up his sword and stood to his intimidating height. "With his own lips King Totuk offered peace, peace long and lasting, and with it a promise that never again in our lives shall we see armed Totuk bands camped in malicious embassy before our gate."

Teleimon raised his arms, holding his staff high to silence the city as it threatened to break out in deafening celebration. "Ah, my ears hear, but my heart trembles. So many of our sons have gone to Death's cold bed, so many of these days I have spent in mourning that I fear my senses, once so acute, have been dulled. Tell me, do I dream?" He opened his hands to either side of Titalis. "Tell me, my son, my prince; tell me, faithful servant, my faithful captain, does Titalis speak in the true world of day, or does night mock me in sound sleep with dreams of unrivaled hope?"

Capestes stepped forward, clapping a hand on Titalis' shoulder. "You hear true, my father, it is Titalis who speaks, and know that it is he who breathed life to my stratagems."

Eikoptas glanced at Capestes before mirroring him, stepping forward and clapping a hand on Titalis' other shoulder. "Know that you hear true, my king, and that it was he, Titalis, who led our men in noble fury."

Teleimon raised his arms so that the bright light of day lit the gold eagle atop his staff. "Blessed is this day, and all to follow. But tell me, my great champion, what is it you took from savage King Totuk to bind tight his word?"

Capestes smiled, but Titalis sheathed his sword and gave Capestes a glare. Titalis turned to the host, beckoning to their gathered mass. He waited until several of the men stepped aside. Between them came two men-at-arms, leading a slender figure concealed beneath a long blue robe.

Titalis looked back to his king as Capestes and Eikoptas backed off a step to make way for the men-at-arms. "My lord, if you will, I will produce before you a prize beyond measure of wealth or realm, a bond of peace stronger than stone itself, an oath in flesh from King Totuk, a pledge that fair Eurimedon no longer live in fear." He glanced over his shoulder. "Guards, bring her forth."

The men-at-arms stopped beside Titalis, parting to either side to reveal the slender figure behind them. They each took a piece of robe and gave a sharp pull. The robe parted to reveal itself as two robes and, beneath the covering lengths, there stood a tall woman. Her black hair hung loose in a wavy mane down the length of her back, her body wrapped in bleached hides secured with lacings along her sides, her feet protected in fitted boots that rose to her knees. Her gaze manifested within a set of piercing eyes that bore an almond taper, residing above lips that would have been full, were they not pressed tight.

A simple iron circlet adorned her head.

Titalis gazed at her for a moment before looking back to his king. "Behold, my lord, Princess Totuk, She of the Plains."

The citizens stilled, their eyes widening as they stared in disbelief at that single woman, the only one of her kind to ever stand within white-walled Eurimedon.

Teleimon, too, seemed struck by her presence, his arms sinking to his sides as he studied her, his gaze sweeping over her from head to toe. He stepped forward, a cautious step, but then he took two more steps, putting himself an arm's length from Titalis. "Ah, I see, I see, and yet I wonder just what this is, this most curious creature I see before me. Ten years have I watched your Totuk men before our gates in all manner of barbarous garb, but never was there a figure of grace among them. Yet here I witness living proof of culture well founded, and a surprise it is, to me."

He stood straight, staring into her eyes until her gaze sank. He rapped his staff on the ground. "Princess, witness before your eyes the high court and airy lanes of white-walled Eurimedon, home of the stout defense upon which your nation broke. I, King Teleimon of Eurimedon, welcome you to our home and to the fold of our humility. And know, Princess, that it is from this abode, from these people who now take you as sister, that was born the plague of your people's warlike ambitions — my brilliant Titalis, sacker of your realm — lest you forget your proper station among us.

"But now, no more talk of war, or strife, but only of celebration." He raised his staff, looking over his people. "Eurimedon, rejoice!"

Capestes and Eikoptas waved off the host. At last, they broke rank, and opened their lines to welcome their families. The tumult of cheers and cries of joy drowned all sense of order or restraint. Among such celebration an insulated privacy remained around the lords of Eurimedon, ensured by the slow circling of Teleimon's attendants. As for the king, he could not help but continue his study of She of the Plains, her every detail consumed by his dissecting gaze until he sought to confirm her substance by summoning the courage to reach out with his staff and give her shoulder a gentle prod.

Her eyes flashed with indignation, but Titalis stepped before her, resting a hand on his king's staff. "My lord, she is but a woman, a defenseless supplicant among us. There is no need to fear her."

Teleimon raised an eyebrow as he glanced at Titalis, but then withdrew his staff and tipped his chin. "True, but still, I would keep a wary watch upon her. Totuk cunning is something that has cut us far too often over the wearying years. Fetching a creature as she may be, my champion, do not forget she is spawned from the bosom of Totuk fury, their proud king."

She of the Plains trembled before clenching her fists at her sides. "King Teleimon, what are these things you say? You lay a public address of honor upon me, but niceties escape your inner humor, and so I shall mix similar falsehoods with you. I hear nothing but arrogant words from an arrogant man, and I tell you now it was my choice to die rather than come here a prisoner to Eurimedon's vanity, but the choice was not mine to make. No, king, kin, and brethren of the Totuk nation decreed my sacrifice to pacify bloody Titalis, this rueful bane upon Totuk strength. Lecture me not on place and humility, Lord of Eurimedon, for it is I who should lecture you. I who by force abandoned both birthright and namesake to live among my sworn enemies."

King Teleimon succumbed to a low laugh, goaded by the chuckling of his attendants. He opened a hand to the city about him as he regarded She of the Plains with an uplifted eyebrow. "Ah, so she speaks, and bravely, too. Totuk women, it seems, are no less fierce in words than are Totuk men at war. In measure of sympathy, though, I shall warn you once, Princess. Strange, foreign, and royal you may be, but resident and subject of this city you have now become and your place you best remember. You shall guard your words with me, lady, and display me a lord's due respect."

She of the Plains clenched her jaw in fury, defiant under Teleimon's glare, but it was Titalis who once more stepped between them, smiling with good cheer as he opened his hands to lord and lady. "Hold, hold, good people, let not the old strife ruin this day. Accord yourselves as strangers first met, and make allowances as your courtesies advise. To one, and all, I shall tell this once, of burdens and labors ten years endured. In both field and forest we grappled with Totuk, if not with blade than with hand and tooth. Such was the savage spite with which we fought, and many a good man, both Eurimedon and Totuk, met his dying day. A thousand lives my hand alone surely doomed to death, a hundred Totuk champions I felled, my very body soaked in their lives' blood. I beg both of you a warrior's virtue: a proud honor it is to die in war justly closed, but sad disgrace it is when violent death is repaid with treaties ripped by hasty words. Soon, too soon, I would forfeit the life of these limbs than live knowing I lost men for nothing but hot pride."

Capestes stepped up to the other side of the exchange, clasping Titalis' hand in sign of agreement. "Father, I beg you, heed this plea of Titalis while I offer a wanting solution of wisdom. We have here a princess proud but of a shrew's disposition, ignorant in our ways of a woman's proper place, and so, in extent, blameless in her boldness. I ask a moment's patience for her demeanor, and a further moment of consideration. Perhaps marriage to a good Eurimedon man shall break her wild horse's fury and let her emerge from her Totuk cocoon to be a proper lady of court."

She of the Plains drew in a breath, her lips parting, but a wary glare from Titalis stilled her words. She held his gaze for a moment, hesitating until he tipped his head for her to calm, and so she did.

The exchange did not miss Teleimon's perception, and her consent to Titalis' unspoken warning rallied the king's better spirits. He turned to his son with an appreciative smile. "Ah, fair Capestes, your long lost mother's temperance rings true in you. I shall entertain this thought of yours, and make it so."

He tapped his staff on the paving stones and looked to She of the Plains. "A match of suitors we shall have, and we shall have it this very evening to dispense with this matter. A celebration of peace and marriage we shall entertain, even though in my wisdom I know such things mingle little in the privacy of home," he said with a glint in his eye, and waited for the laughter of his attendants. He clapped his hands. "Yes, indeed, indeed, I venture to say that such a union will breed grounds urging for disunion, but a union there shall be." He patted Capestes and Titalis on the shoulder before turning to his attendants. "So it will pass, my good men. To every man-at-arms, citizen, and lord of Eurimedon let the word be passed, that tonight the revelry shall be multiplied in two, for a war's end, and a marriage made."

Titalis and Capestes stepped back as the king's attendants led She of the Plains away in Teleimon's wake. Champion and prince exchanged a glance and a sigh of relief, but Capestes spoke first. "Well said, my friend, well said."

Titalis laughed as he nodded. "Aye, and well met, Prince Capestes, well met." He opened a hand as if he wished to say more, but several of the king's attendants came to him and escorted him to follow in the king's train.

Alone among the revelry, Capestes stood his ground, resting a hand on the pommel of his sword until he noticed Eikoptas. His fellow captain also stood alone among the crowd, but his gaze was hard upon She of the Plains as the royal party led her away. The corner of Capestes' mouth rose in a crooked grin before he raised a hand and called to Eikoptas. "My fellow, my dear fellow," he said with a laugh as Eikoptas neared. "And why is it that you look so glum among such merriment?"

Eikoptas stopped beside Capestes, shaking his head before looking to the prince. "Ah, noble son, you know what it is that bothers me so."

Capestes grabbed Eikoptas by the shoulders and gave him a good shake. "You old war dog, does the unseen wound still bite deep within you?"

Eikoptas let his head hang. "It would not be the first that you have endured my confession, but know this, Prince, that among home and hearth the wound bites all the deeper when from it I thought to find refuge. Never in my life or marches long and far did a beauty such as hers, so raw and vibrant, catch my hungry gaze. Of Totuk blood she may be, but my warrior's tastes are unrefined. Rather than see her head as some hollowed trophy raised on a spear, I dream to see it smiling back at me from my bed, master to a willing body of my possession."

Capestes looked about before putting an arm around Eikoptas' shoulders to keep him close so that none could hear their words. "Is this madness I hear from one whose wits are as cold as the steel he bears? What mischief is this I tolerated during our march that it still lies within you, dormant no more among the safety of our white walls? Tell me I have lost my wits along with my hearing; tell me this parade is no charade of folly. Dirty-handed, low-brow Eikoptas, dare you tell me you still wish to hold her hand in love, to claim her with no star-crossed intention as a wife under Eurimedeon law?"

Eikoptas frowned before he spat on the ground. "Love? Love, you say? Love is the play of the highborn. I am but a common man, as you know, dirty-handed and low-brow as you say, and yet it is something I bear with no remorse or guilt for I know my station and have made of it what I can. No fortune of good birth such as yours has graced me, and no birth of good fortune such as Titalis knows has graced me, but in boredom of long march I have devised a final plan I find most cunning. Society's badge of grace is what I hope to receive. Foreign this Princess Totuk may be, but royalty she remains and, in union, I, too, shall become so. Call me mad, but I will suffer the stable-life no longer, and after ten years' trial the bright life of gardens and sweet fruits I seek for the days that remain to me."

"Then to you, good Eikoptas, I have words upon which you can act."

Eikoptas looked to him. "To what plan do you now allude?"

Capestes raised his eyebrows. "Not one of craft or guile, but only one of chance and the moment, partnered under the open mantle of the unexpected. Did you not see the daggers between my father and She of the Plains?"

"Aye, and sharp they were, but I heard not what words fended their stabbing points."

"Then know this, my fellow captain, that she whom you seek tested my father's wrath and was saved only by Titalis' steady demeanor and my own words of inspiration. Wild and unruly she is, and so she must be broken. Harsh is the horse master's whip, but more subtle, and so more effective, is a husband's guiding hand."

Eikoptas' eyes lit. "She is to be wed?"

Capestes tapped a finger on Eikoptas' chest plate. "Aye, upon my counsel to my father, she is to be wed in a contest of suitors this very eve."

Eikoptas stepped back, clasping Capestes' hands before bowing his head. "My fellow captain, my good prince, I am in debt to you. Now, if you forgive me, I must go and wash."

They each thumped a fist to their chest in salute before Eikoptas marched off through the crowd.

Capestes stood still, breathing in the fresh morning air. He let his head roll back, and his eyelids glowed yellow when he closed them beneath the bright sun cresting the clear sky.

***

The afternoon seeped by and though the city was busy with the night's many coming celebrations, the royal palace busied itself with preparations of its own for the suitors' contest. Capestes secluded himself from such commotion, instead taking his leave to his private rooms and the tending of his private servants. They bathed him, massaged his sore muscles with luxuriant oils, and then he bathed again while his mistress, Lissandra, brought him a succulent meal of smoked meats and fresh fruits.

He asked her to stay as he ate and talked with her of his time away and how it was that she had entertained herself in his long absence. It was no secret between them that he was testing her. After the third cup of wine brought a warming blush to his face, he was satisfied that she had remained true to him and did not stray to another man's touch in his absence. It was less a fear of his retribution than an acknowledgement of love, for they both knew if he doubted her he wouldn't hesitate to turn her over to the stable hands and reduce her to a hay girl, a play thing for the rougher men of the city. Eurimedon's walls were white, but Capestes was wise in deeper things and it was such wisdom that he held over his mistress. She, in turn, basked in this power she knew he was willing to not only taste, but also indulge, where so many other lords pretended such extents did not exist.

She poured him more wine as he rested a hand on her knee. Her fragrant skin was soft and warm. He looked into her eyes as he slid his hand up the length of her thigh. She held his gaze, rolling her shoulders back as her tunic slid across his forearm. She smiled, and shrugged off her robe. She settled in the water with him, holding the cup to his lips so he could drink. "My lord is as I remember him," she whispered. "It is a good thing to see you so."

He held the wine on his tongue as he drew her close to kiss her. The sweetness mingled between them, buoyed by the heat of the alcohol. He cupped his hands in the bath before raising them to let the warm water run over her. Her eyes slid shut as he smoothed back her hair, framing her face with the glistening length of her brown locks. "The roots in me, they never change," he said under his breath. "Through many nights, many nights indeed, I dreamed of this moment."

She grinned as she draped her arms over his shoulders and held him firm between her thighs. "Long I waited for your return, my prince, and held close the wise lesson you left me."

He pressed his fingers against the small of her back as he stared into her eyes. "And which lesson might that be?"

She mirrored his knowing smile. "That the wine held at arm's length is all the sweeter when at last it meets the tongue, my patient one."

"See, Lissandra, why I favor you so? Wiser you are than twenty of my father's clucking lords." He pulled her tight against him so that not even the water lingered between them. If his father was near, he would have laughed at the old man for all the prattling maidens his father asked him to court. He knew a hot flame tempered a keen blade, and he believed his blade to be most sharp, nimble, gleaming, and yet concealed in its shadowy play. It was not something the airy-minded women of his father's court could comprehend. Lissandra, a commoner, understood this inner nature of his, understood the lurking malevolence within him and embraced it, embraced it with the hunger of one who has known hardship and was willing to face the price ambition demanded.

His gaze bored into her eyes. He knew what set her blood ablaze and knew it burned unspoken between them. Nevertheless, deluded by his long held lust, he let the words seep from his mouth. "Stay true to me, and queen you shall be."

He found her lips as he clutched the length of her hair in a tight grasp and welcomed the press of her fingers into his shoulders. The heat of day beat down upon them and warmed their blood all the more.

The fruit, forgotten beside them, shriveled under the sun's merciless rays.

***

Adrift in the lingering rapture of Lissandra's charms and comfortable in the return of his old ways, Capestes took it upon himself to wander the private gardens that linked the palaces. Clothed in a simple white tunic, he grinned as he let his afternoon dalliance replay and plucked an apple from one of the ornamental garden trees. He rubbed it on his tunic, sank his teeth through its skin, and closed his eyes as he moaned in delight.

On he wandered until he climbed several steps to enter a courtyard of luxuriant grass framed by trimmed hedges and blooming flowers. He paced about, enjoying the apple, letting his thoughts run until he took one last bite and tossed the core under one of the hedges. Clasping his hands behind his back, he glanced over his shoulders before clearing his throat. He had to focus his plans, he knew, and the tutors and orators from his youth had hammered into him that such processes were best done in open voice, where one's ears could serve as the first, and perhaps most influential, of critics and censors. There were many things for him to consider, many things that troubled him, and they all lurked beneath his impenetrable facade of complacent ease. He looked up, unable to check himself any longer.

"So, tell me, you gods who mock mortal trials, what measure of joy do you draw in witness while in your grasp we suffer our ends? Is free choice the cruelest of your many jests upon us? For I challenge, in my brazen spirit, to define what is free, and what destined, for so much in life is decided before life, with ancestry set before first breath can be breathed, entitlements granted before we learn to speak, and good fortune of loving parents beyond our infant's query. See me here, before you, a prince by your will, a man blessed with such treasures as may exist. Born to a good father? Indeed. Born to title and inheritance? Indeed, but a vacant, burning desire exists in my heart, that the ancestry which I had not petitioned will likewise be denied without petition. My mother was untimely taken; my father selfish in his warlike pursuit, indeed—and of my title and inheritance?

"Yes, I fear this last gem I possess sits jeopardized. Ten years I watched, helpless, as the threat grew. Tormented have I been, for the threat resides so perilously near to all I treasure. By the name of Titalis is this threat known, a worthless orphan until blessed with my father's regal charity. Now I, a prince, have to share my only bounty in life, while a common bred ox revels in the gratuity of extended birthright? I suffer slight upon tireless slight; I, a clear-minded hereditary high born, displaced by a strong armed babe. Now, upon victorious return from war, who is it that shall draw reward from father's burdened brow? I, flesh and blood, successor and son? No, I fear all glory shall pass to Titalis. His hacking arms, strong though they may be, would have fought in futile hope had it not been for my stratagems. Yet the greater claim in this city goes to he who holds the mightiest sword, not the sharpest mind. So, before king and city he draws the favor, while I must stand to his side, subordinate, mere captain, equal of stable-bred Eikoptas, diminished to the role of petty collaborator.

"So it is my thoughts circle back, yes, so it is. I did not choose this unwitting rivalry, this device of my father's unintended creation. I fear high-viewed Titalis shall one day be king, chosen in my father's latent pride over me, his own seed. A harsher wound it is than twenty Totuk spears. Yet my defense is up to my will alone, so that which I had not the power to create I must devise upon my own to destroy."

He froze, his ears perked at the call of a herald's voice.

"Prince Capestes?"

He frowned, debating with himself before letting go a sigh. "I stand in the Reflecting Garden." As he stood, awaiting the untimely interruption, his thoughts churned within him once more. "Ah, and who is this I am to receive? Could it be that good fortune will bring me Eikoptas, this ally to make and break?"

He turned, and rejoiced, for it saved him the labor of feigning his greeting. "Ah, my good fellow, Captain Eikoptas. What brings you?"

Eikoptas strode toward him with a determined energy to his gait and stopped to bow his head in respect before speaking. "My prince, I hoped to try your patience for some well tendered advice. It is for the suitors' challenge that I seek your aid."

Capestes threw his shoulders back so that he looked down on Eikoptas' stout stature. "How now, Eikoptas, you bid me for favor? Did you and I not stand shoulder beside shoulder, fight blade beside blade, never wavering before dreadful Totuk onslaught? Indeed, my steadfast companion, we are brothers under war's red banner, and my aid you need not beseech, for it is always yours."

Eikoptas rested a hand on Capestes' shoulder. "Aye, and so I would return to you though my plate offers so much less. True it is what you say, that many a day we fought beneath foreign skies, our bodies war-wearied and wounded dearly, yet on we fought, laboring in vain, it seemed, to keep pace with Titalis' murderous fury."

Capestes sighed. "A great warrior he is, to that I shall testify."

Eikoptas gave him a curious look. "Testify? How say you?"

Capestes shrugged. "How say I? Young, passionate Eikoptas, I venture that your lust has ruined your ears. I believe I said, 'I shall not lie.'"

Eikoptas hesitated before nodding. "As you say, yet I believe my senses have not failed me."

Capestes let out a little laugh. "Poor Eikoptas, your blameless brutishness unseats your better judgment and wisdom. Have not emotions unseated sense in history? I would that they could, and sometimes should, for a hot, heavy heart can turn a mind to wood. Now, if you find it within your addled lust, tell me what you seek, if you must."

Eikoptas' shoulders sank as he shook his head at Capestes' word play. "Oh, if only my tongue could pose such verse of lyrical whimsy. I fear my years of military pursuit have dulled any gentler nature I possess."

Capestes' eyes narrowed in thought. "And still you insist upon this foolish pursuit, this hapless quest to secure She of the Plains as bride?"

Eikoptas stiffened. "Prince you may be, but mock me no longer, friend."

Capestes smiled to disarm his fellow captain. "Oh, it is not a mock but a gauge, a gauge rather than a gouge, a search for your inner heart's resolution, a mere test to see how stout your determination."

Eikoptas clenched his fists before his chest. "I tell you, I am determined."

Capestes opened a hand. "Then, may I pose a consideration?"

Eikoptas eased somewhat. "Consider you may, but do not jest."

Capestes held his smile, but held up a finger to signal a work of his wit as he patted Eikoptas' shoulder. "My good man, a jest is just if your ambition is lust, for in this endeavor resolution is a must." He laughed, and was happy to see Eikoptas calm and laugh with him. "Eikoptas, you say you seek a marriage on high, and so through wedlock bond gain what you lack in birth, seeking through will alone to correct Fortune's shortcomings. It is a query familiar to me, but, despite similarities, I must sincerely ask, why not a fair Eurimedeon maid for this task?"

Eikoptas bobbed his head to either side. "Ah, a point well made. My goals are not of circumstance, but my aspirations are wholly of that nature. You and I, royal and common, through military suffering leveled as one, though in our haughty community's eyes you remain lord, and I a swaggering thug. So, how, I ask of you, could a fair maid be worthy if her gaze was forced so low?"

Capestes let out a long, sympathetic sigh. "Yes, yes, so it is when we find no happiness in our soul, that we cling to the clowning of another's jocularity. So it remains that you seek a wife where none would be. Always, it seems that a man's nature in the world of trials is to seek without what he lacks within."

Eikoptas shook his head, stepping away from Capestes. Possessed by his anxiety, he started pacing, making rapid little courses before his prince. "I must have her," he said, glancing at Capestes, but continuing his pacing. "On fields of strife and suffering I walked as a captain of men, both liked and respected, yet in these times of peace I become pride's tortured prisoner. Is this the folly of men-at-arms, my friend? Am I to fight for king, state, and honor, but in the end find nothing for my own self? Ah, Capestes, it is not vanity that spurs me, but rather a worry that in age I shall be my only companion, a neglected elder upon the street with no title, my service held with the same senile contempt as the work of last season's sturdy mule. It is in this vein that I beg your help. Aid me in this cause, gracious Capestes, so that I do not diminish, and become a forgotten man."

Capestes tipped his head back, scrutinizing Eikoptas. "And help you I will, if you answer me this. You seek a custom unprecedented within our walls. Disagreement may arise, and a match ensue, you understand. The matter will become the judgment of the Peoples' Voice, a title championed by none other than your dear friend, Titalis. Would you risk the work of his hands to be beaten blue by he whom you call friend?"

Eikoptas stopped short. "Ah, cruel life. I cannot defeat him in contest of arms, and I know he, in his steadfast allegiance, will swallow his friendship to me and do what the rites demand of him."

Capestes stepped toward Eikoptas. "Perhaps you need not desist so quickly, my fellow."

Eikoptas' eyebrows drooped low. "What is it you see? Is there yet hope in my cause?"

Capestes let his smile resume its place. "Indeed, and victory as well." He pointed to Eikoptas' waist. "Show me, what is this folded in your belt?"

Eikoptas blinked before looking down. He pulled a cloth from his belt and let its length sliver free from his grasp to reveal a violet cape. "It is a possession most dear to me," he said, looking back to Capestes. "It came my way when we crossed those far Totuk lands. Strange men we encountered one day when I rode ahead of the host, and I traded it for a simple wine sack. I have never known a cloth of such nature as this. Light as the breeze it is, yet solid as something of much heavier weight with a sheen the likes of which my eyes have never beheld. I was told it is the work of insects. Despite its rarity, I would offer it as a gift to She of the Plains, if Fortune were to present such an opportunity."

Capestes took the violet robe from Eikoptas. He held it up to the sun before pulling its length through his other hand, his gaze returning to Eikoptas as he felt the smooth run of the cape across his palm. "Ah, Eikoptas, silk this is called, a material both supple and strong, much like your Princess Totuk in character. True it is that it comes from mouths of the meek. Crafted by caterpillars, the wise say, so, from the tongues of reviled creatures there emerges a work most inspired. As such it shall be fitting coming from you."

Eikoptas tore the cape from Capestes grasp. His face burned red. "Enough with your insults! I will suffer them in public where I have no recourse, but not in the privacy of a garden where I come to you as friend and fellow."

Capestes held up his hands and bowed his head. "My apologies. I meant no harm, but rather to illustrate a point. I offer that perhaps you can match Titalis where he is weak and use your voice to best the Peoples' Voice. I will devise it to be that you confront him in a contest of wits, and so, through clever words, find your favorable marriage, and silence your fears of a life dwindling and meek."

Eikoptas folded the cape, his jaw muscles clenching and releasing in cycles of thought. He frowned as he tucked the cape in his belt, but then nodded, and looked back to Capestes. "Aye, I see the wisdom in your mind's work, but plans conceived must be executed, else they are wasted effort. No fool am I, but I possess no gilded tongue such as yours and in a contest of refinement I will still fail before Titalis. Commoner he may be, an orphan by birth, but he was afforded a king's rearing."

Capestes smiled. "Would you think I had it in my mind to cast you as a naked babe before a lion? No, my friend, I would do no such thing. Get you now to my royal tutors and scribes, inquire of them in my name's sake and ask of them a quick education in rhymes and riddles. Listen to them with keen ears and this match you need not fear."

Eikoptas took a deep breath. He looked to Capestes, sank to his knee, and took Capestes' hand. "Kind prince, to your debt I shall be held. Dignified I may soon be, but, even so, your faithful servant I shall ever remain."

Capestes looked down on Eikoptas. "Ah, good man, you forget that oaths should never be made before their just dues are realized. Patience, you see, is a far more penetrating temper than hot haste." He grinned as he pulled Eikoptas to his feet. "Off with you now, my fellow, time's pursuit you must chase, if these things we plan are to pass."

Eikoptas thumped a fist to his chest, gave Capestes a quick bow, and hurried off.

Capestes watched his fellow captain depart before cupping his hands behind his back and returning to the audience of his private thoughts. "Ah, plans, intrigues, plots, contrivances, all complexities that stem from Fortune's simplicities. See her, trickster that she is, this creature we call Fortune, once cruel to me, now in faith offering me a channel of hope. In due course hapless Eikoptas shall be a slave to me, bound in his ignorant ambitions, an unwitting tool for employ in finality against dim-witted Titalis. And with he of the strong arms and the slow mind dispensed, so, too, then all threat to inheritance will be past and forgotten. Through my will I shall have the crown and prove my worth beneath its circlet in a way no birthright could attest."

He stopped and looked up to the sun. "Aye, through my will I shall have the crown, and, if need be, I will destroy them all to make it so."

***

Across the expanse of the gardens, yet under the same sun, Titalis, too, found himself pacing, rapping a fist into his open hand as his meal sat forgotten on the ledge of a reflecting pool.

A woman came and sat by the pool, a woman of surpassing beauty. She was Deiphos, sister to Prince Capestes, daughter to the Lord of Eurimedon, King Teleimon himself. A slender silver circlet adorned her head, the flowing length of her golden hair held in check by translucent wraps of green linen. Several sprigs of fragrant white flowers were tucked in the length of her wavy locks. Her eyes, bright and blue as the cloudless sky above them, watched her husband. But for all the rapture held in the beauty of her countenance, there lurked signs of unease about her eyes and the corners of her mouth, where her soft lips hung somewhat in dismay.

"My love, tell me what it is that troubles you so?"

Titalis stopped his pacing, but kept his back to her. He closed his eyes, his imagination painting a likeness of her by the pool in his mind's eye. His yearning perfected the image, only to double her allure when he drew her flawless reflection on the pool's surface. He struggled to swallow. He found himself cut down, ridiculed as he stood in the shadow of his own name, rather than the man he knew himself to be when he looked into the pool. He drew a breath, rallied his nerve, and turned to face his wife.

To hold his ground, and not cave to his base desire to take her in his arms, was a struggle more fearsome than any hornet's nest of Totuk spears he had faced.

"What is it that troubles me?" He thumped his fist in his palm once more. "Aye, troubled I am, and doubly so to have to bring the thoughts I bear to life with my voice on this day of all days. My precious Deiphos, ten years I labored in the wilds of Totuk lands with every victory hollowed without your watching eyes, and every night under the open stars a torture of isolation." Caught in his passion, he stepped to her, and when he next spoke, his voice trembled in his throat. "But none of this is in contest to my disappointment this day, when upon my return I find not you, but only the ghost of your absence."

Deiphos stood, and the hurt in her gaze was plain to the eye. "Husband, do you dismiss my love with such callous, careless words? Whom better than I, daughter to king, sister to steadfast prince at your side, to know the burdens you bore? You suffered separation, as did I." She went to him, taking his hands to hold his attention. "In my hapless, brooding lethargy my maids induced me to flee the city. To the far meadows we resided day after longing day, keeping white-walled Eurimedon out of my body's eye, but you, my husband, never once was removed from the teary sight of my heart. Too late last eve did we receive word of your return. Two steeds I rode down in my haste, and nearly a third, but I had no more to waste. I paused only on return to wash for you, hoping to greet you as a sight of unblemished virtue."

He drew in a breath, shaking his head for a moment before embracing her, clutching her to his chest as he pressed his lips to her forehead. "Ah, my faithful one, forgive me. The years have eroded my patient temper. I meant you no accusation or disrespect. Many nights have my mind and heart wrestled in conflict, one each day telling me to stay for king and kin while the other begged to fly to you. For guilt and honor I pursued wearying war—in honor for the preservation of Eurimedon, in guilt for the many fallen brethren of our ranks, who, like me, risked a grieving widow as their soul's trophy."

Deiphos tipped her head back. "But you are here, now, before me, and should put such fears to rest. If it is guilt that plagues you, then know that you have my ear, and let your troubles pass. Immortalize your lost fellows by telling me their stories so that you no longer serve as their lone host."

He kissed her again, cradling her face in his hands. "Aye, if you wish it, I shall tell you all, yet I would ask one return for the stories I forfeit. If I relate these tales to you, you must in turn pass them to the city, for it is to those who are lost from us that the victor's glory should go. Champion I may be, yet breathing I remain, while others in selfless sacrifice surrendered their lives. I had to care for myself, you see, for without my walking form the host would have been lost. Already I fear faithful Eikoptas may feel slighted, and Capestes as well. I never once doubted their labors, for without them there would be no success to toast. I dread your father will not see their just reward and see only the racing chariot, rather than the yoke and rope that let it fly."

Deiphos tipped her head as she rested a finger over his lips. "Noble Titalis, do away with these concerns. Hear me now, and mark the words spoken from she who loves you most and knows you best, from the inside of the heart that beats within you. Displace not your worth; incriminate not your actions of restraint, for I know you as a living tribute to all the good of men. Destroyer of hosts you may be, but your orphan's humility you hold close, a secret and sacred shield within you to the sweet deceptions of power and glory."

He laid a hand over hers. He looked down, noting how her delicate, thin fingers nestled between his calloused, powerful hands. He closed his eyes before resting his forehead against hers. "My sweet Deiphos, if I had returned defeated and bloody, the dead host a burden upon my bent back, if I had but glimpsed you once before I fell, I would still count myself victor."

She rested against him, turning her face into the seclusion of his neck. "Speak no more of such things and forget for a moment your faithful men. The night's festivities draw near with a steady pace and time closes upon us. Let the duties fall to others, and to us, let us retire to our privacy, and put our longing sentiment to rest."

He stared into her eyes. His heart stilled for a moment, but resumed with a thunderous beat. He could smell the fragrant meadows on her, and his eyelids drooped shut as he found her lips.

ACT II

King Teleimon walked the length of his throne room ignoring the attendants and servants busying themselves for the evening's celebration. His gaze lingered on the throne, a wide chair of gilded oak set atop several steps of polished stone adorned with arrangements of fresh wild flowers picked from the distant meadows. His feet moved, the rap of his staff serving as a steady metronome to his thoughts as he neared the throne. He stopped before the first step, his eyes narrowing as he looked up to the royal chair—his chair—his mind's eye recalling distant memories when he stood in the same spot as a boy, imagining himself king in his father's stead. So many years removed from those recollections and simplistic and idealistic notions, he felt his shoulders sink under an unseen weight.

He was loath to consider himself an aged man; indeed, he had stood shoulder to shoulder with Titalis before the city when the Totuks in their brazen savagery had assaulted the white walls in open siege. In those days his beard was a rich brown, like the oak of his chair. After, when Titalis and Capestes launched their brave plan to depart the city with a mighty host to take the war direct to the Totuks, his beard had grayed and then whitened like the wintry peaks of the distant mountains. His heart had hardened in resistance to the ever-present Totuk threat, something he had lived with all his days, while the only soothing dream he knew was the elusive prospect of the Totuks subdued in defeat and their dark threat lifted.

Yet, like so many dreams, inhabiting the moment of his dream's fruition left him detached from the solace he sought for so long and, in its stead, he found a new set of worries. Lowering his head, he took the crown in hand, leaning against his staff as he studied the gleaming prize.

"Ah, look at you, cold, wearisome circlet of gold, you allow the bodies of men the pleasures of gods, but burden my brow with unseemly weight. Many times have I forgotten that you, as symbol, and not I as man, hold charge over lords and commoners from the greatest champion to the lowliest stable hand. Faceless diadem, forget me not when I pass. Like the proud lineage before me I must leave this world, but you shall remain and find life anew, drawing your vitality from the brow of another. Know this, though, that I still breathe, my heart beats true, and heartless you may be, but my head you shall call home for some days to come, lest you forget he who has served you for so long. Now, resume your seat and comfort an old man."

He put the crown on his head, closing his eyes as he drew a deep breath. He stood straight, his hand tightening on his staff. "Oh, listen to me, lost in trifling thoughts and minor annoyances, though, I must admit

I find them pleasant company in their own way. For ten years have I clenched my teeth over hard war and now, on the very day of claimed victory, I feel only loss. The dreadful question calls its due at long last, a horrible choice clutches my throat, for its demand must be answered — who shall it be to succeed me?"

He stared at the throne, only to frown as he scratched his beard.

"Aye, true it is that noble Capestes is mine own born son and, tried and true the birthright custom is, yet in generations past the tradition has been flouted to produce reigns long and prosperous. The crown belongs with he who holds the city's honor, but, more so, to he who holds the love of his people. Capestes, my son, you return in shadow. Pale you are beside he I took in, valiant Titalis, he who holds the eyes of the people, and their love. Rightly so, with his acts saving us from despair. But where is he, this son of mine, while the palace toils for celebration? Yes, the court calls, but instead he spends his lust with sultry-eyed Lissandra — alluring stable-stock that she is — rather than secluding himself in rightful privacy with a noble wife.

"Aye, aye, indeed it is as I see it, and so it must be. Titalis has been forged true in the kiln of men. I know he would still bow even if Capestes stood over him as king. There is no treachery in his nature and perhaps having been born with nothing, he embraces the city that has embraced him, unlike my son, who has known only the contempt afforded by privilege and luxury. Yes, yes, it must be, I must have known it to be the path to follow when I wedded Titalis to sweet Deiphos, my precious daughter."

He let his breath go and nodded to himself. "So it must be, so it must be. I trust in your wisdom, my son, but alas, not as king. For you, proud Capestes, I know not what else to say. A subordinate you will remain, for as king you shall never play."

He turned at the sound of horns echoing in the palace antechamber. He rapped his staff on the floor, a sharp sound to stiffen his back and raise his head high. His chin tipped up as attendants scrambled about in a last mad dash, lighting the torches along the many columns lining the chamber. The procession of lords and ladies entered the room, the women dressed in their very best, the men concealing their grappling cloths beneath rich capes clasped at their sides. Minstrels came with them, blowing soothing melodies on their pipes. Lesser servants scurried among the crowd and stooped to escape gazing eyes as they brought out plates of delicacies to adorn the tables along with countless pitchers of wine.

King Teleimon looked with pride upon the best of the city, watching them as they fanned out to take their places at the tables. Titalis and Deiphos took their place to his left, while Capestes strode to his right, taking position just behind his shoulder. Unlike the suitors, he wore his formal tunic and left his cape open to show to all that he would forfeit the suitors' challenge. Teleimon frowned at yet another pass of his son to secure legitimacy, though he sensed beneath this latest insult perhaps a dawning taste of humility, declining the challenge so as not to revel in the wisdom of his own counsel. Teleimon was about to test this supposition when the palace horns issued their rallying call and summoned his attention back to the room before him.

He waited for an attendant to announce him before stepping forward to speak. "Lords and ladies of Eurimedon, many days it has taken to whiten this beard of mine, but never in the counting days of that process has so noble an array of suitors taken presence in Eurimedeon court. Let us not forget the pretext of an occasion such as this. It comes on word of victory and let that serve as the main fulfillment among such fine food and drink." He smiled, and raised a finger. "And among our revelry, let us not forget that which we use to signify our glorious day. For, among all our effort and victory, we come in good hearted contest to a suitors' challenge for the hand of our fallen enemy's princess, She of the Plains. Now, then, bring her forth, let the time for words pass and let the match begin."

He rapped his staff on the floor before turning to take the steps to his throne. He settled with a sigh, but held his head high, looking over the suitors as they departed their tables, left their capes, and took their positions in pairs upon the open floor. He glanced to Capestes, who bowed his head and opened a hand to the far side of the room where two men-at-arms stood with Princess Totuk, dressed now in proper Eurimedeon fashion, rather than her heathen bleached hides. Satisfied, Teleimon rested his staff against his shoulder, opening his hands to the suitors before clapping for them to begin.

In successive rounds they grappled, contesting each other in grasp and check, each seeking to strike the other off balance and so send an opponent to the floor in victorious claim for that round. Those cast down stood, bowed to king and victor, and received celebratory toasts of wine between rounds so that no honor escaped its proper due. Through the rounds, Titalis remained at his station with Deiphos, for, as Peoples' Voice, he would not have to match, unless King Teleimon deemed it so. Capestes paced in the narrow space between the throne and the table of Titalis, exchanging shouts and claps congratulating certain close contests or a well executed move. Teleimon noted his son's spirits were high, even in Lissandra's absence. Due to her stable-stock lineage, she fell under the court ban and so held no privilege to be present.

The rounds reached their conclusion as darkness settled outside the room. The final round found Eikoptas and one other suitor on their feet.

They stood before the throne and bowed in respect, holding until Teleimon addressed them.

"Ah, strong limbed Eikoptas, Captain of the Guard, you show your skills well."

Eikoptas replied with another bow. "My lord, in contests of honor and grace my strength will always keep apace, and so it has this eve, in contest fair."

Teleimon smiled upon him before looking to the other suitor. "And who might you be, young man?"

The suitor stood straight. "My lord, I am known by the name Akketor, and, indeed, I am but a young lord, yet versed I am in the royal arts. I am known among the royal trainers for my skill with the sword, and I am known with equal regard among the court orators for my grace in song, dance, and recital. I say such things not in boast, my king, but rather to attest that there can not be a more fitting bride for my noble soul than a princess."

Eikoptas' eyes narrowed, but he refused to cast even a single glance at Akketor. "My lord, I ask that you call the match anew so that I may dash this boastful whelp's pride and teach him one last lesson he has yet to learn."

Akketor shifted on his feet as he looked over at the dense, hard musculature of Eikoptas' war-bred frame. He swallowed and looked to the throne. "My lord, I respect this honored man-at-arms, but would sooner yield my life than be surpassed by common birth."

Eikoptas turned, but held his silence as Teleimon raised a hand, his gaze flashing on Akketor. "Arrogant youth, be watchful of your words. High bloodlines do not imply nobility without proper dose of humility. Remember, it is with ease that the high can look down upon the low, but ease is not the course of wisdom, rather it is the drunken delirium of ignorance." He clapped his hands. "Now, enough talk, let this be decided. Have at it, and may Fortune smile upon he who is true at heart."

Eikoptas spun on Akketor, his eyes burning as his gaze swept past She of the Plains. He dodged Akketor's advance and, for no reason but to teach him a lesson, threw a vicious punch that crashed into Akketor's temple. The young man staggered several steps, raising a hand to his head, but shook off the blow. It was a moment too late, as Eikoptas was upon him, grabbing him by the shoulders. Eikoptas sank to lower his body, bent his knees, and heaved with all this strength as he turned at the waist, tossing Akketor past him. Akketor crashed to the floor, blood spurting from his slender nose as his face took the brunt of his body's impact on the paving stones. Eikoptas raised his hands but, to his surprise, and against all custom, Akketor refused to announce his yielding call. Instead, he planted his hands on the floor, pushing up on trembling arms as blood dripped from his nose.

"I shall not forfeit," he said, spitting a wad of blood on the floor. He turned his head to look at Teleimon. "My lord, I beg you, another chance?"

Eikoptas said nothing. Instead, he walked past Akketor, out of the young man's sight.

Teleimon gave Akketor a quizzical glance. "And why should I give you such opportunity?"

Akketor blinked to focus his eyes. "I ask it of you to maintain the nobility of this court."

Capestes stopped his pacing, tipping his chin up as he cupped his hands behind his back. He leaned to his side, toward his father's ear. "My king—"

Teleimon shook his head. "You would place your pride as the sole defense of Eurimedon's glory? Foolish man," he said, and nodded to Eikoptas.

Akketor turned his head in surprise, but Eikoptas seized him by the hair, jerked his head back, and then dropped his weight to slam Akketor's face against the pavers. Capestes pressed his lips together at the loud, sickening crack of Akketor's head on the floor. Teleimon leaned forward in his chair as Eikoptas stepped back. Akketor laid still, his senses dashed on the floor with the blood of his pride.

Titalis put down his cup of wine, looking with some surprise at Eikoptas before looking to Teleimon.

Teleimon clapped his hands. "And so, as we see, the false of heart fall at the feet of those who are true. Well fought, Eikoptas," he added, opening his hands to Eikoptas as several attendants carried Akketor away.

Eikoptas waited to bow until Akketor was gone. "My king, I have bested the suitors, and won the challenge. I petition your grace for the lady's hand and ask your mercy for my effort, that you do not elect to invoke the Peoples' Voice."

Teleimon eased back in his throne. "So I would have it, courageous Eikoptas, and so, too, I hear your plea, but, as we have just seen of fool-hearted Akketor, it is best we adhere to our customary ways and follow our codes as we must. The tradition shall stand, and the suitors' challenge will reach its proper conclusion. Our laws require the consult of the Peoples' Voice, and the will of the Peoples' Voice met in agreement by I who am king. Only then, my good captain, shall you have she for whom you have fought so bravely."

The audience turned to Titalis as he stood, but he kept his cape clasped. He bowed to Eikoptas to congratulate him, though his gaze lingered on the small pool of blood left by Akketor's shattered face. He took a breath and looked to Teleimon. "If your lord pleases, I wish not to pursue this contest. I, as Peoples' Voice, seek to invoke my right. I nod to a fair victory, and a contest well fought, with honor and skill, and yield to my companion, good Captain Eikoptas. So, if you will, I would have the bond go forth."

Teleimon gazed on Eikoptas before looking across the room to She of the Plains, who stood brooding in dutiful silence between the men-at-arms. He shifted on his throne, debating with himself, his lips parting and closing as his thoughts vacillated on the matter.

Capestes stepped forward to whisper in his father's ear. "A moment, if you will, my king. Perhaps a continued test of brawn serves us ill. None here of sound judgment would dare dispute Titalis' skill. Rather than turn his war-bred camaraderie with Eikoptas to biased physical conflict, perhaps in its stead we may entertain a peaceful challenge—a challenge of words. A suitors' challenge for a Totuk bride is a new day for us, and so, perhaps in turn we should meet a new day for the resolution of the challenge. Now, I leave it to your judgment to weigh this condition."

Teleimon pulled at his beard as he considered his son's words. "Yes, I see your point, and I agree that all holds true, these things you say. No, I would not pit the right hand against the left, and such it would be, to pit captain against champion, and have a friendship unnecessarily tested." He nodded, taking a breath as he looked back to Eikoptas. "Honorable Eikoptas, you shall have the go, but not as you know. A contest of a riddling sort I order to pass. He who can not guess shall be considered in the loss, and to the cunning wit I may give my nod."

Capestes smiled. "Come now, Eikoptas, enlighten us with a hidden nimble talent, if you can."

Teleimon opened his hand. "Yes, have the first go, Eikoptas, and speak."

Titalis eased, and let loose a good-natured laugh. "Aye, I shall entertain such a match." He opened his hands. "Begin, Eikoptas, if you will."

The guests rose up with various calls for Eikoptas to speak, but Deiphos leaned toward her husband, laying a hand on his forearm to secure his attention. "Ah me, my proud hearted husband, have your endless victories made you forgetful? An unmatched fighting spirit you possess, but, by your own admission, your wit in words is a factor not ready for testing."

Titalis turned to her, his lips parting until the room fell silent.

Eikoptas stood with a hand raised, nodding to himself as he gathered his thoughts. He clasped his hands behind his back and lifted his chin as he took a breath and turned to Titalis. "Titalis, my good friend, to you I shall pose a question of sorts, and please wait 'til I finish for your retorts—the answer I defy you to supply, unless you feel good to answer, and then, be not shy."

Capestes smiled, but his eyes narrowed. A surpassing fast learner Eikoptas was, more so than Capestes had expected, and he warned himself to be wary, lest the tool cut the hand of he who puts it to use.

Eikoptas, though, rallied with the applause he received for his opening discourse. He turned on his feet, pacing along the length of the guests' tables. "Now listen, listen all, as I tell you this, that I am only a beast and so bails of hay serve as my daily feast. A large, lumbering frame of a body I command, but I plant my gray feet at the dictate of delicacy's demand. My face is a riddle wrapped in skin, for two ears I have, each flopping like a fish fin. In similar fashion, I own no ordinary nose, but rather one like a snake, tough as a leather hose. From this appendage fantastic echoes a noise rather bombastic, and, flanking this appendage, yet betwixt my ears, I carry on my head two sprouting white spears. When I move the ground will rumble and shake, for in travel with my fellows a mighty herd we shall make."

He stopped, turning to direct himself to Titalis. "Now, I vouchsafe this creature exists. If not, then my suitor's challenge desists. Tell me, Titalis, what say you am I?"

Titalis looked about, swallowing as the attention of the room focused upon him. "Indeed," he whispered, "what to say?"

Capestes watched Titalis, counting the mounting moments until he leaned toward his father once more. "Oh, my king, methinks the champion thwarted," he said with a chuckle.

Teleimon turned, distemper clear in his eyes. "What is this you have done?" he hissed. "Why have I listened to you? Think you that I shall sit here and suffer my champion deposed, knowing such cost was inflicted for no more than the prize of a Totuk bride? No, no I say, for this contest I have lost my taste." He slapped a hand on the arm of his throne and looked to Titalis. "Keen perceiving Titalis, my champion as Peoples' Voice, what say you?"

Capestes raised an eyebrow. "Indeed, Titalis, what say you?"

Deiphos looked to her husband. "My love, what say you?"

Eikoptas stood his ground, though his fingers twitched in the ball of his clasped hands. "Good Titalis, I await your answer."

Titalis looked about, blinking in confusion until his teeth gnashed between his tight lips. He clenched his fists and rapped them on the table. "What say I? What say I? I say nothing more than this riddle is a ruse that does not amuse. See now, tricks of verse are not beyond me, but it is unfair to expect me to see the figment of another mind's eye."

Eikoptas fell back a step in surprise. "Do you stab me with unjust accusation?"

Teleimon looked between the two men before rapping his staff. "Hold, hold! Morality stems from bold facts. If this thing which Eikoptas riddles in rhyme exists, then yes, you are morally sanctified, but exist not, and a foul deceiver you be, and in contempt of this challenge you shall be found."

Titalis, his face red, glanced at his king before pointing to Eikoptas. "I challenge that no such creature to which you allude exists in these lands, and if I am wrong, I demand you prove it so."

Eikoptas fell back another step, his gaze darting between champion and king before he opened his hands to Teleimon. "My lord, I need protest this shift and sway. To the statutes I have conformed and yet I am to be wronged to preserve fragile pride?"

Titalis' eyes bulged. "Fragile? Foul friend, how dare you speak so? Ten years you could not match my fury in war, only now to call me fragile? I shall show you fragile." He turned to his king. "My lord, I rescind my blessing. I call for a match."

Deiphos grabbed Titalis' arm and hissed in his ear. "What is this you commit, what vexing nature do you court in this hot tempered moment? What source, this rage bursting forth? Has glory for your strength so taken you that one reminder of mortal imperfection beguiles you?"

Titalis pulled his arm free, lashing her with a burning gaze. "What knowledge of a warrior's hard earned honor does your gender-granted domesticity dare presume?"

Deiphos blinked, stunned, and withdrew her calming touch.

Lost in his pride, Titalis jabbed a finger at Eikoptas. "Answer your own riddle, duplicitous Eikoptas."

Eikoptas set his jaw.

Capestes caught his gaze, and tipped his head.

Eikoptas took a breath and refused to relent. "Answer I shall, in wrongful need of defense. The creature I riddle is living and true. Men of the distant wilds term it an olifant."

Teleimon hesitated, but then let out a long breath. "Olifant? Aye, truly this word does exist, and so, by nature, no word can exist without a thing. Thereby the logic follows, and so it is as it is claimed."

Eikoptas gave a quick bow. "Then, my king, I petition the victor's nod."

Titalis stepped toward his king. "My lord, it was my contention that this rhyming riddle described no such creature within our lands. I hold that this is true, and so, the nod should be mine."

Eikoptas' lips parted, but he found himself with nothing to say.

Capestes frowned in thought. "Oh, a quandary this is."

Titalis took a step toward Eikoptas, his fists still clenched, his eyes red with blind rage. "My lord, I ask your ruling," he said, his gaze locked on Eikoptas.

Teleimon sat still, but then raised his hands to still the room. "A moment, a moment, good lords and ladies, so that I may contemplate." He debated with himself, pulling at his beard, until he felt compelled to look to his son and summon him to his side. "My son, what shall I do? I would give the nod not to diminish good Eikoptas, but to diminish Titalis is a price I shall not bear, even were it done in falsehood to a challenge won."

Capestes' eyes narrowed as he laid a hand on his father's shoulder. "Dear father, I fear your eyes fail to see the problem. I advise that for Titalis you should hold no concern, for there is a greater evil here that seeks to harm you."

Teleimon shifted in his chair. "What is it you speak of? It was through your cunning this situation created, two friends turned, right against the left, so the poisoning damage done. With friendship lost only the question remains. Titalis was sorely tested, and the Peoples' Voice left silenced. There is no place left for my yea or nay and, legates aside, I feel I am inclined to give the suitor the nod."

Capestes shook his head. "I will not dispute what you say, but consult your vision for your nod's repercussion. A commoner lifted to nobility is ground for discussion, but nobility of Totuk nature is insidious. For more than ten years they worked to be rid of us, and now you would grant their princess a seat near to us?"

Teleimon frowned. "My son, you must lay your hostility aside. She is a woman, not an armed host in rank. The enemy is vanquished and peace upon us. We need not consider her person a threat."

Capestes tightened his hold on his father's shoulder. "If you shall not consider my word veiled, then allow me to illustrate a case before you. There are flowers that bloom in peaceful beauty enticing, then bear fruit of inbred poison. Nod to this mixing marital bond and you will stamp legitimacy upon Totuk blood. A child she may bear, supple and dear. Down time's stream a hidden threat will draw near; Totuk blood well bread and diffused, and one day a true Eurimedeon king refused as the crown passes to one of Totuk blood infused. To this man of slowly crept Totuk descent the lineage would then pass so that the enemy we defeated in hard battle would, in the end, sit to rule noble Eurimedeon lords like cattle. This, dear father, is the lurking threat I propose. Act now; this marital bond I urge you to quickly dispose."

Eikoptas stepped forward. "My lord, shall I have my just nod?"

Capestes stepped back, his chin sinking to his chest.

Teleimon sucked in a breath as his son's words went to work on him, rousing his temper to likewise rouse him from his seat. He stood, and rapped his staff once more before pointing to Eikoptas. "Impatient man, you shall have a nod."

Eikoptas' face lit. "Then, I will have the princess' hand in marriage?"

Teleimon pointed to his side. "If you can defeat Titalis in match."

Capestes raised his head and stepped forward. "The king has said his favor, Eikoptas. His opinion and mind are his, and not mine to waver."

Teleimon nodded. "Come now, the match, the match without delay."

Titalis thumped a fist to his chest. "Indeed, my king."

Deiphos reached for him, ignoring her place to speak out. "My husband, I pray you, ignore this hostility, and upon your friend do not pounce."

Her voice was lost, though, as the nobles of the room rose in a chorus of shouts for the match to ensue. Deiphos sank to her seat as her husband tore his cape from his body and marched toward Eikoptas. Capestes stepped back once more, though he glanced to She of the Plains to note the bewildered look on her face.

Teleimon stepped down from his throne. "Quick tongued Eikoptas, I give you one chance to desist. For you this storm has brought its course. If you defer, then you shall never pass to marriage's altar, no matter the hand you seek to bind to your own, whether it be lofty lady or stable wench."

Eikoptas looked about the room, shaking his head. "Aye, I see the course has been laid to force of arms, and none else, this contest betrayed." He set his jaw and drew in a breath to address the audience. "I shall fight, and may the gods favor the just."

No sooner did he speak than Titalis charged him in full force of his fury. Eikoptas dodged him, stepping aside, and almost caught his friend in his mad dash. Titalis was too fast and too strong for Eikoptas to restrain. He broke the lock Eikoptas sought to execute. He made several advances, all of which Eikoptas evaded, much to Titalis' rage and the rising jeers of the watching noble folk. Eikoptas retreated three steps, keeping his space, but then held his ground, his gaze taking in the room as his ears were swamped with the derision heaped upon him. He looked to his friend, his lord, transformed to a raging monster of misguided pride, and knew there was no choice in the matter.

He fixed a final, longing gaze upon She of the Plains before turning to Titalis. "Do as you must, my friend."

Titalis bore down on Eikoptas. When his strength met no resistance in Eikoptas, he held, and blinked in confusion. It was too late to back off and too late to see where his hot temper had led him. The moment had a momentum of its own, a temper of its own, and so it kindled his rage anew, not for shame, not for Eurimedon, not for long cast fears of insidious Totuk lineage, but for what he realized he had to do, and for the simple, stark reality that he had no choice in the matter.

He shook Eikoptas in his grasp. "Forgive," he said, but his plea was lost in the deafening cheers about him and, with nothing else to do, he heaved and threw Eikoptas down, at the last moment realizing he cast his friend into the lingering puddle of Akketor's blood.

He stood over Eikoptas, watching as Eikoptas rolled on his side, and glared down at him. The room went silent about them. As Peoples' Voice, he knew he had to issue a proclamation. Desperate for any words, he looked down, holding until he stood up straight and let his hands dangle at his sides.

"Of your quizzing tongue I shall hear no more," he said. "Be as I, and accept Fortune's granted station. As captain you have honor, lust not for more. Now rise, Eikoptas, stand before me and let the conflict pass and be done so that, as gentleman, we can forget this fetching sport."

Eikoptas pushed himself up, but remained kneeling. "Fetching?" he said with a bitter laugh. "Easy to say, when it is you who still stands."

Teleimon rapped his staff. "The suitor lies deposed and so the matter is decided. The Peoples' Voice has won and so I shall have my say. No Totuk shall join our nobles in my life's span, and no barbarous blood of theirs shall enter our proud ancestral lines. In defense of pure and proud Eurimedon I shall issue this final passing judgment: this marital bond shall go to none of our men, and to ensure it so, this Totuk witch will be banished to the harlots' den. Let her virtue be reduced to shame beyond pardon so any lord whom her charm seduces will be reviled as society's vandal."

Eikoptas jumped to his feet, his jaw dropping. He turned to see She of the Plains numb with horror until the men-at-arms seized her. She struggled with a cry, but stood no chance against their strength as they dragged her from the room. Eikoptas opened his hands at his sides as he turned to the throne. "My king, my kind sovereign, I beg you not to do this. Must my failure condemn her to a fate of surpassing cruelty?"

Teleimon took his staff in both hands and jabbed its butt into Eikoptas' chest, driving him back. "Dare you question me, brazen commoner? Were it not for your service such words would be your last before I ordered your head duly parted from your neck. This proposal, entertained but once, has bred dishonor for all of us, all of us high lords of white-walled Eurimedon. Praise Titalis for saving the sanctity of our ways.

"Now one, now all, forget this moment, and pursue proper festivity to the city square. Heralds, blow your horns, minstrels, sing your songs of our ancestors' glory, and in victory, let us toast all days to come."

Eikoptas ignored the crowd as he sank to his knees. He looked into his hands, those that Eurimedeon philosophy taught as the makers of a man's destiny, and clenched them to fists. So it was that he sat until the empty silence of the room penetrated his senses, and he threw his head back to the unseen stars above him.

"Ah, low wretch of common blood that I am, with hope and reputation lost, my deeds ignored, and a long wrought friendship in tatters. I, who no Totuk spear could kill, this day cut down by mine own brethren in the worst of betrayals. Most penetrating is the unseen blade, and deepest indeed it cuts." He let his head hang only to see the silk cape tucked in his belt. He pulled its length free, staring into its violet depths. "And worse yet, injury upon injury, a woman foreign but innocent discarded to the worst sentence of defilement, reduced to an object to be ravished in unspoken dungeons of this white-walled city, while victory banners of honor are raised high."

He ground his teeth, wrapping his fists in the cape before jerking it tight to test its strength. "Hear me now, you despicable gods of Eurimedeon temples. This night has created debts of bitter lament, and old sacraments eviscerated of their proper aim, so that all the good for which I fought in heart and soul lies revealed as black deceit and vengeful spite. To this, at cost of life, limb, blood, and the heart which drives the red river of my fury, I now swear—exact your price upon us, and I shall see it paid."

***

Capestes walked between the shadows of his palace, grateful his servants had retired for the night. Several candles flickered in the darkness, doing little to dispel the quiet loneliness of the empty rooms. He came to his garden and lingered behind a pillar as he took a moment to drink in the view before him.

Lissandra sat on the ledge of the bath bobbing her feet in the warm water as she hummed a soft tune. She had an elbow propped on her knee, and her chin rested in her hand. She held a goblet of wine in her other hand, forgotten, it seemed, as she cradled it in her lap. Her face glowed under the moonlight, her eyes held upward so that her gaze drifted among the stars. Her hair hung loose, its dark length nestling her slender neck in seductive shadow before cascading down her back.

He felt his heart quicken, but he calmed himself, his desire checked by the bitter ache that welled up within him. It pained him that the city's customs forced her to remain hidden, when he knew she could outshine any of the vacuous noblewomen who held place in the court. It hardened his resolve, narrowing his eyes with the glare of his ambition.

He took a breath and whispered her name so as not to startle her.

She straightened, her chin rising from her hand. Her gaze softened when she watched him step from the shadows. "My love," she said, reaching toward him with an open hand. "I still hear the music of the celebration and yet you return. Did the challenge fail your expectations?"

He walked to her, taking her hand as he looked down to her eyes. "On the contrary, all is as I wish it to be." He smiled, hesitating a moment as he considered divulging his plans to her, but he decided it was best to protect her with his silence and shield her with ignorance of his schemes. He left the celebration only after satisfying himself that he had indeed met his ends. His father, once again lost in the delusion of the court's praise, would hear nothing of the wrong done to Eikoptas. Titalis, ever dutiful, spoke no criticism or remorse for the outcome of the challenge. Deiphos, for her matter, took effort to speak to her father and met nothing but rebuke for questioning his decision to condemn She of the Plains to mortal shame.

"Prince?" Lissandra squeezed his hand. "It seems you dream with your waking eyes."

Capestes shook his head before smiling once more. "No, though I must admit, I feel my dreams within my grasp, elusive as they are. I have done my work well and have sundered my fellows much in the way the whispering winds part thoughtless blades of meadow grass. In that parting gap I shall find my way. It is only a little farther now that I must go to see it so. When my plot is done, it will be too late for any of them to stop me. Too proud they are to dispel my way with open reconciliation between them, and too loyal are they to criticize my means afterward."

She kissed his hand. "Clever you are, in more ways than I can guess. There are chambers within your heart locked to everyone around you, even to me, for I know your spirit is an elusive creature. Never have I asked you to reveal to me more than you wish, and never will I pretend to know all your considerations. Nevertheless, I beg you to take caution."

"Caution?" He turned his hand to cup her chin. "Ah, my lovely one, I know no other way." He drew her up so that he could kiss her and pulled her into his embrace. "Yes, I know no other way, if only my patience can hold out to the last. The prize is so close, and its lure quickens my desire like a feather brushing my thigh. All that I desire, and all that I desire to give you, hang like ripened fruit before me."

She put her hands on his chest and rested her head on his shoulder, turning her face into his neck. "I know you wish to make me queen, and I must confess I yearn to stand above those who have looked down on me in their misplaced arrogance. But it is a little thing to gain, my prince, for the risk you tempt."

He leaned back so that he could look into her eyes. "Lissandra, many treasures there are within these walls, but none to me as great as you. I wish to see you shine with as much hunger as I wish to seat the crown upon my head. Our stations of birth seek to keep us apart, but I will employ mine to undo yours, and so we shall have our mutual way."

She grinned. "Must you always seek to turn the rules against themselves?"

He rolled his eyes. "The work of rules is most curious when they are pushed before a mirror. Witness the example embodied by good Titalis." He grinned. "Perhaps, when all is done, my queen, I shall order the noblewomen to address you as Ardnassil."

She laughed at the reversal of her name and shook her head before kissing him.

He held her close, sliding his fingers into her hair to keep her lips to his. Often, during the long march home, he watched the way the wind played with the long locks of She of the Plains and knew the more bestial recesses of his soul desired her with less noble intent than foolish Eikoptas. He could have taken her, if he had decided to do so, but he defied the decadent temptation and its lure of false, facile pleasure.

Holding Lissandra, feeling the warmth of her breath, the beat of her heart through her chest, he at last applauded his restraint. Lissandra was his, and he would suffer nothing less than the ruination of Titalis to secure the crown. He had to be king so that Lissandra could be queen at his side.

Until then, he knew his ambition would know no rest.

**

At the far side of the city there ran a street where the walls were perched on the edge of a cliff, and the subterranean stream that served the city's water stores cascaded from the ground in a foaming torrent. Once a scenic overlook carved from the cliff face, it became a favored target for Totuk archers during the dark times of the city's encirclement. Afterward, it fell into disrepair and became a pathway to the caves of ill repute beneath the city. With its glory gone, it gained another purpose, serving as the last walk for those of the city condemned to death. They would be tossed from the height and find whatever mercy the gods might grant them in the long plunge to the waters below.

Two men-at-arms led Princess Totuk, against her will, along the street toward the unspoken, candle lit corners of the city's underworld. Her gaze swept over the cascading water that plummeted like a silvery curtain past the street to where it bore into the cliff face. She knew not what manner of vile inhumanity awaited her, but simple instinct told her that her fate was better left to a quick plummet to the waters far below, rather than the certain nightmare of endless shame under the king's decree of banishment.

As a final escape, she considered to tempt the wrath of the men-at-arms and entice them to slay her. She stiffened her legs and twisted, managing to wrestle free of their grasp before they were ready to meet her defiance. Rather than run, though, she stood up straight, proud in what she believed her last moments in the realm of the living. "Why, why must I be condemned to this miserable fate? What wrong have I done?"

The men-at-arms pulled their swords. One of them stepped toward her. "Be silent, witch, else I shall take your tongue and feed it to the palace dogs."

She spat on the ground at his feet. "You brutes, both of you, you stand like two spotted mirrors of your people. Is it ever enough for Eurimedon? You have slaughtered our embassies of good faith, destroyed our sturdy men of battle, kidnapped a virginal princess as hostage, and now you heap evil upon evil, my body not only abducted as peace token, but discarded to a fate of perpetual shame. If there is but one measure of decency in either of you, you would kill me, rather than make me a whore."

The man-at-arms closer to her kept his sword and gaze on her, but turned his head somewhat to his mate. "What say you, Tychus, should we listen to any more of her witching tongue?"

She clenched her fists. "I am no witch! Enough with your insults and base superstition, you block-headed thug."

Tychus put a hand on the man-at-arms holding the sword. "Take ease, Porto, take ease," he said, but then turned his attention back to She of the Plains. "You best heed his advice, fallen woman, and still your tongue, else suffer repercussions."

Porto's scowl eroded to a leering glare as he tapped the tip of his sword against the princess' cheek. "Aye, true you speak, good fellow. The city revels, and no shrieking protest would they hear."

"Well put," Tychus said, nodding as he put his blade back to its scabbard. He let go of the pommel, grinning at the sound of the blade slithering home under its own weight. He stepped forward, patting Porto's chest as he glanced at the walls above to see that they were empty. "Indeed, well put. Why should all else revel while we walk this dark street doing the city's desperate duty? Why not take our leave now, here, and have the first touch, rather than the last? None will take note, and none will care, among the craven denizens of the underworld."

Porto looked to him.

Tychus smiled. "Virgin fields hold the most luscious treats."

She of the Plains paled at their threat and fell back several steps under the glare of the men-at-arms. She turned to run, but no sooner did her feet slip on the wet street than the rough hands of Porto and Tychus were upon her. They wrestled against her flailing limbs until they slammed her against the hard stone of the cliff face, knocking the wind from her. Porto, the rougher of the two, took delight in grabbing a fist-full of her hair to pin her head against the cold rock while Tychus seemed to delight in the horror lighting her gaze. He worked his finger under the clasp holding her robe, but froze at the sound of a footfall. He exchanged a glance with Porto. They shared the better thought, stepped back, and resumed their hold of her arms as they waited to see who intruded upon the abandoned street.

Eikoptas stepped from the mist that was drifting through the air as he crossed under the waterfall, only for his eyes to narrow when he found the three before him. "Good eve, my men of the Guard. Hold, if you will."

Porto and Tychus bowed, but Tychus spoke. "As you would, Eikoptas. May I remind our good captain that we act under the king's order?"

Eikoptas tipped his head in acknowledgment. "I come not to refute my lord's order, but only to ask a moment of time to speak with this lady. A parting farewell I wish to offer her, so, if you can entertain your captain's pride, and afford me my privacy," he said, waving them away.

Tychus took a breath. He glanced up and noted Mylo and Pylo on the wall above them. He softened his stance and opened his hand. "As you would, Captain," he said, and put out his arm to push back Porto as he retreated to the shadows.

She of the Plains put her hands to her face, but checked her tears. She stepped to the stone balustrade, peering over its edge to the precipitous drop of the waterfall to the unseen waters below. She clutched at her cloak before turning on Eikoptas. "So, you come to me once again, Eikoptas? Must I bear your sight in this last moment before my shame? I caught your watching eyes upon me many a day during the march to Eurimedon. I have not forgotten the nights you brought me dinner and sat as guardian over me. You always offered proper accord to a woman by protecting me and I view you as a man of honor. Do you wish now to throw that away and seize by force that which by your maddening customs you failed to secure?"

Eikoptas' head hung. "I shall not defend myself to this accusation, baseless as it is. I sought only a moment to confess before you the unwitting part I played in your humiliation. For aristocratic title I sought your hand, but I have been entranced by your beauty and spirit as well, and these two, braided about my heart like a noose, now mark the measure of my failure."

She of the Plains stepped back from the balustrade, her eyes narrowing on Eikoptas. "Proud man, if it is forgiveness you seek, then a scolding I will give. For all white-walled Eurimedon's claims of honor, truth, and fealty, I see nothing but corruption, greed, and treachery. Perhaps there is hope for you, Eikoptas, as you come to me to repent, but I must tell you, doubtful I am. We Totuks may seem simple and strange, but such festering debasements as have been levied upon me would never transpire within our realm."

Eikoptas let his breath go. "Princess, to these scorching ranks I will offer no retort. Know this, that this heart within me that no Totuk spear could harm has been branded with your words." He ground his teeth, but then shook his head and pulled the violet cape from his belt. "Fair princess, this gift I hoped to give you in marital bond, though now, in banishment, I know not what use it shall serve you. As a trifle, keep it, so that in shame you live not alone."

Above them and unseen, Mylo and Pylo looked to each other. Mylo shrugged as he took the stopper from his ale skin. "Quite strange to bestow a precious item on a lady lost."

Pylo shook his head as he took the skin from his brother's hands. "Blind hearted brother, do you fail to see this as well? His intentions lie in symbols."

Mylo frowned. "Aye, and so a husband I never was. Look, now, she takes the gift."

She of the Plains studied the cape and its violet luster before looking back to Eikoptas. "I shall keep this, good man, if none else than in memory of a life that was, but think not that this excuses you in the eyes of the gods for my plight."

Eikoptas stepped to her. "Lady, you miss my intent." He pushed his cape aside to rest a hand on his sword. "Plots I have conceived," he whispered to her, "and they dangle but by a slender thread. Others have plunged from this ledge by criminal sentence of our lords, but not all have perished. The height is great, but the water below deep and the carrying current strong. Long limbed you are and possessed by supple strength. Survive the fall, make the swim, and your freedom from this cursed place you shall have."

She glanced over the balustrade. "If you take faith in this plan, then join me."

His face fell. "Aye, if only it could be so, but I must remain and meet my other ends. Take your leave, but thank me not, for the burden of your matter still rests upon me." He looked over her shoulder. "Ah, they come." He peered up to the stars for guidance, only to find Mylo and Pylo on the wall. Cursing his luck, he waved them off, fighting to check his hand when he heard a scuffle behind him. He turned to see Tychus and Porto seize She of the Plains, wrenching her arms against her shoulders to still her struggle.

Eikoptas' hand closed about his sword. He moved, but he was too late. The men-at-arms were down the street, dragging her away. The violet cape dangled over her shoulders. "Is there no mercy for my plans?" he said under his breath. "One last chance, and now it, too, lies in ruin."

He looked down at his sword. His cape slid over his arm, concealing his weapon, and his intent.

The sound of footfalls caught his attention. He looked past his shoulder and fell back a step in surprise.

Capestes strode toward him, hands clasped behind his back, chin tipped up in his usual manner of self-satisfaction. "Ah, Eikoptas, so it is as I thought, that I would find you trailing in the wake of She of the Plains." He stopped beside Eikoptas, only to rest a hand on his fellow's shoulder. "So, indeed, the challenge did not go as we sought to make it, but do not despair, good friend. I believe I have found an out if you care to hear more of my advice."

Eikoptas closed his eyes for a moment before looking back to his prince. "Carry on, Capestes. My ears shall listen, though my heart no longer cares for my fate."

Capestes waved off his gloom. "Speak not with such undeserved sadness. I have devised a way to prevent dishonorable doom. With an argument both wise and foolproof you shall debate before my father and a great reversal you will create. Now, our honor may rest in Titalis' strong hands — this orphan who has displaced all others in the eyes of our people — but a noble wife you may still secure, despite my father's decree. Note well, though, that it will weigh heavily upon Titalis, this friend who in his heat forgot friendship, and spared no hesitation to dishonor and shame you."

Eikoptas' head hung. "Darker and darker grows the noble light in this city."

Capestes shook his friend's shoulder. "My stubborn captain, lose not your resolution. Listen with care while a scenario I describe. It is you who sought a princess for noble bond, thereby to raise you equal to a noble peer, yet the court rose up in jeer. Now, here comes the catch and the bait, at the cost of Titalis you need no longer wait, for our empty-headed brawling champion came not from a noble womb, yet in time he secured a wife like a queen. In this dwells your claim to redeem, and hear now the master stroke of my scheme.

"Petition the king once more for a noble wife, but know that in hot distemper he shall shun you at once. Then, and only then, remind him of Titalis and Deiphos. Yes, Deiphos, my sister, Princess of Eurimedon, wed to an orphaned babe by my father's decree and approval, from her shall stem your open lane. If so can be done for Titalis, than surely you, valued Captain of the Guards should be of equal, least not of all for a lesser princess, She of the Plains. And, if not, then no other logic follows but to disband Titalis and Deiphos, for in legalities fairness is not always the rule as what holds for one must for all sometimes disappoint. Remember, at the last, to me as a faithful servant you swore. Revoke your oath, and know that between us there shall be war."

Eikoptas shrugged off Capestes' hand and stepped away from him. "My prince, what is this you demand of me, this mad deceit that you cloak in disarming rhymes?"

Capestes smiled as he opened a hand. "Forgive the rushing babble of my tongue. I shall slow and simplify, my friend. It is none but you that Titalis has humiliated; it is none other than your bond petition repudiated. Know this, that the odds I have considered and find it more in favor that by example of Titalis and Deiphos my father will have no choice but heed your argument. Yet, should he choose the contrary, then avenged you shall be for your humiliation at Titalis' hands by his receipt of an equaling end—his bond with Deiphos broken."

Eikoptas took several steps before turning on Capestes. "What is this madness that has consumed you? My ears fail to believe what they hear, and my eyes swear they must be fooled, for I see the likes and hear the voice of good Capestes, yet the intent revealed to me is petty and vile."

Capestes' smile fell. "Insult me as your thanks for all I risk for you?"

Eikoptas clenched a fist. "And to what gain? My humiliation? A woman's despicable shame? Titalis and Deiphos disgraced? A king humiliated by portent of recanted will? I have suffered enough with your plans and will endure no more."

Capestes' face flushed. He stepped toward Eikoptas, unable to contain himself. "Dare you test my patience? You know not what storm you unleash upon yourself! Dare you insult me when I offer you untold opportunities?"

"I see no opportunity in your rhyming poison, only ruin and a private agenda lurking secret within you. Bring your storm upon me; I shall weather what I can, for I know suffering, unlike you. Though I have been sorely stung by Titalis, my champion he remains, and my loyalty to him I shall not discard. But you, ignoble prince, I perceive that all your bile boils for none but Titalis, and it is to him that your stabbing tongue aims."

Capestes bared his teeth. "You swore an oath to me."

Eikoptas waved it off. "Indeed, but in humiliation's wake have I learned many things, and a greater eye has opened within me. Rot filled prince, false intentioned oaths hold no more weight with me. Common born and beneath you I may seem, but in humanities my heart beats leagues above you. I see now that you sought to pit me against Titalis. I shall confess this treachery. Upon these knees I will plead forgiveness, and with Titalis let go any error so that friendship can stand restored, no matter the wrong that left it broken."

He jabbed a finger at Capestes. "Look now. With the passing of each word of mine, your secret nature spills from you like ink. Your eyes twitch with hate, your hands clench with jealousy, while tension knots your brow. That is it, I must presume, my gut tells me now that you feared the crown would go to one other than you—to Titalis? Traitor, I shall tell this, too, to Titalis and King Teleimon, so all may know what falseness came so near to the throne. Farewell, you rabid dog, I have none else to do with you, and if my head be taken, it shall fall with righteous blood."

Capestes' eyes went red with rage. His lips parted, but his wits failed him, his pride imploding upon his discipline. He lunged, drawing a knife with the quickness of his hand, but Eikoptas' hand whipped free of his cloak, his sword flashing under the starlight. Its tip found its mark before Capestes could strike, tearing through his innards and life with equal ease. Eikoptas stepped back, grabbing Capestes' hand as the dagger fell, and tugged his sword free. Capestes staggered, his life's blood pouring from the gaping wound in his belly, before he slumped against the cliff face.

Eikoptas looked to his sword, his eyes wide on the running blood of his prince.

Capestes' knees shook, and then buckled. He slid down the wall to slump on the street. He coughed, blood spurting from his wound into a dark puddle. He looked down at his reflection in the red water, his arms trembling against his mortality. "What torture is this?" he said under his breath, drooling blood from his lips. "The tool turned against the master, a game of Fortune's mark that left me no recourse, here to die in my own pooling blood, betrayed by my own hasty discourse." He chuckled as he realized his dying rhyme, his gaze sliding toward Eikoptas. His eyes darkened, and, with a defiant shout, he flopped dead on his side.

Eikoptas stood, frozen, unsure what to do. "Ah, what is this, what madness is this? Desperate act, entwining treachery, snaring webs, to what hopeless pit have I fallen? Treachery to secure a proper place for myself and murder to deny treachery? To what justice does Fortune lend her conscience?"

A hail made him spin on his feet, only to see the men-at-arms returning, hurrying down the length of the street. Porto led the way, Tychus lagging behind as he dragged She of the Plains by the arm. Porto picked up his pace when he saw the blood on Eikoptas' blade, but he was yet to make out Capestes, slumped in shadow.

Eikoptas turned toward them, his sword kept ready.

Porto came to a halt. "My captain, we heard a shout, and feared you a victim of some villain upon this street." He looked to the slumped body against the wall, his eyes going wide before he looked in shock upon Eikoptas. "Gods, what evil is at work here?"

Tychus came beside Porto, but shoved She of the Plains to the ground when he made out Capestes. He pointed to Eikoptas. "Treacherous man, you have killed the prince!"

Eikoptas held his ground as Porto and Tychus drew their swords. "Good men, I beg you listen, the prince came upon me in surprise. I had no witting part in this violence."

Tychus shook his head and cupped a hand to his mouth as he bellowed to the walls above. "Guards, sentries, men-at-arms, the prince is slain."

Eikoptas ground his teeth. Fortune had cast a web about him and he saw no other way but to act. He rushed the guards, ducking under the wild swing of Porto's blade. He spun, whipping around his extended arm, his whistling blade almost cutting Porto in two. Blood and entrails erupted from the gaping wound, but Eikoptas rolled aside, evading a downward slash of Tychus' blade. Tychus turned, thrusting, but Eikoptas parried the blow as he rose to his feet. He grabbed Tychus' outstretched arm with his free hand and swung his sword around to hack Tychus' arm free above the elbow. Tychus' gaped, but the expression froze on his face when Eikoptas swung his arm back the other way, decapitating Tychus in one clean stroke. Tychus' body dropped to the street as his head rolled away. Blood pumped from the stump of his neck in a running red puddle.

Eikoptas held his sword ready, his gaze sweeping down either side of the street before he looked to She of the Plains, cowering on the ground. "Lady, rise."

She hesitated, her gaze fixed on the blood dripping from his sword. "My lord, what wildness has seized you?"

He took her hand and pulled her to her feet. "Time is wasting and vigilance soon upon us. You need know only this; a whispering plot was hatched within this diseased city. Upon the unwitting forehead of our champion all our fates have turned and all we know is ruptured. I beg you this one opportunity to listen to me and hear this phrase I speak to you here: to your foreign face and exotic nature I was drawn, but through lesson of the unjust wrongs heaped upon you I have come to see all I thought I believed in a new light. For this, among all else, I tell you now that I love you, one who in name I was sworn to detest."

She stared at him, unsure what to think. "You lords of Eurimedon, you possess hearts full of chaos."

He took her hand and led her to the balustrade. "Quick, my love, flee this place, take your flight upon Fortune's buoying draft and make your way from here before this second opportunity is lost. For me, I must remain, and make sure as best I can that all else remains with the peace of our people, though my will begs I take the plunge with you. Now, go, be free of Eurimedon, and may the rushing waters cleanse your memory of our atrocities."

He spun, hearing the clang of armor and boots from the walls above. He looked to her one last time, caressing her cheek before stepping back to wipe his sword clean on Porto's cape. He blew her a kiss and ran down the street, disappearing in the shadows.

She of the Plains watched him go until she stood alone among the dead bodies. She turned on her feet, unsure what to do, but the clamor atop the wall grew in volume and she knew her moments were wasting around her. "Fortune, I beg your mercy," she whispered, drawing back to the cliff face. She took a deep breath, and then charged, taking the balustrade like a horse, and its ledge as a saddle she sought to mount on the fly. Her legs served her well but, at the last moment, the violet cape snagged on one of the swords left on the street and unfurled from her shoulders as she disappeared among the cascading waters.

Above the bloodied bodies, atop the wall, Mylo came to a halt, gazing below until his eyes focused. "The prince," he called to anyone who could hear. "The prince is slain!"

Pylo came beside him, heaving with the exertion of his charge. He grabbed his brother's shoulder and pointed to the violet cape draped over the balustrade. "Ah, behold. Silent witness in testimony to murderous acts. See, Eikoptas' cape given to Princess Totuk, there snared in guilt upon hasty escape."

Mylo clenched his teeth but looked to his side and bowed. "Brother, the king, the king approaches."

Pylo watched as King Teleimon hurried along the length of the wall with Titalis and many men-at-arms in their wake. Before the king peered over the wall, Pylo stepped before him and sank to his knee. "My king, I beg you, let me tell what my brother saw from the wall so that there is no false witness. Eikoptas came upon Porto and Tychus as they escorted Princess Totuk to the sentence you levied upon her. We saw him give the cape below to her, and then they parted company, she in the company of Porto and Tychus, who lie murdered below. We know not where Eikoptas is, but we vouch he parted and we saw no more of him. Guiltless, he is."

King Teleimon pushed Pylo aside to peer over the wall. He stared, but then let out a shriek of grief when a guard below bellowed that it was indeed Capestes sprawled among the dead. "Ah, what treachery is this, what injury to long sought peace? For a Totuk witch must we lose my only son? A thousand tears of grief shall not wash the sin of his spilled blood, spilled by the work of Totuk witchcraft."

Titalis embraced his king, holding the old man's weeping rage until he noticed Eikoptas running toward them from the other end of the wall. He stepped from his king, though he kept a hand on his back and pointed to Eikoptas. "Eikoptas, tell us, what did you see?"

Eikoptas came to a halt. "My king, my champion, I know only what I tell you now. I followed She of the Plains and, indeed, I gave her the gift of my silk cape, but then I parted, and left that dark street to find my bed. Along the way I met Capestes, and, when I inquired as to why he walked such a street at night, he said that he, too, had parting words he wished to levy upon Princess Totuk and that he wished to go alone. Heeding his wish—though I curse myself now for the turn of it—I let him go, and carried on my way."

Titalis frowned, but turned to his king, and raised a fist to the men-at-arms around them. "My lord, here lies our noble kin murdered, by what dark work of a Totuk sorceress I dare not imagine, after she came on words of peace from the Totuk nation. I say for this outrage that the peace rests dead with Capestes. What say you, Eikoptas?"

Eikoptas looked about, unnerved as the men-at-arms rose up in cries for war and blood. "I say nothing," he heard himself mutter, and happy he was that it was night, so that the sun could not illuminate the pallor of his fallacies. "I know only what I see, despicable acts beyond erasure." He stepped forward, resting a hand on Titalis' arm. "Good friend, to you I have been unworthy, in ways time will not permit me to explain, but know this, if war is to resume its way upon us, your faithful ally I remain, and I hold no blemish between us."

Titalis clapped his hand on Eikoptas' shoulder. "Aye, good friend, faithful Eikoptas, it is I who should offer the treaty, for rage clouded my mind, but not my heart. Know this now, that my friend you shall always be, and the best to have at my side." He clenched his fist and thumped it on his friend's shoulder before turning to the gathering host about them. "Is there none who sees this act, this murderous crime, committed before us? If so, let his name be reviled, for a crime indeed was committed in the bosom of our white-walled city, upon the son of our king, under the banner of peace. Rather than meet treachery with a whimper, we shall meet it with war. To war I call, war to erase every last Totuk from the lands of the living."

King Teleimon gathered himself and turned, holding his staff high. "Indeed, to war, to war, to merciless war. Slaughter them all, every last man, woman and child, except their king, whose head I seek upon a stake, and his witching daughter, his vile princess. I want her brought to me alive, untouched. Raise her up upon a stake we shall, and burn her alive atop the walls so that her last agonizing sight is her nation destroyed."

ACT III

Amid the flurry of activity surrounding Capestes' death and the gathering of Eurimedon's might, Lissandra stalked her prince's private chambers, her heart darkened, her future extinguished. She kept to herself, hiding when some attendant or other came to the chambers for fear that King Teleimon would cast her out in some lingering disdain for his son's attachment to her, but such was not the case.

Only one man of the court came to call upon her, none other than Titalis himself. When she heard him within her prince's antechamber, she hid herself, fearful she might betray some lingering schism of her prince for the blameless champion of Eurimedon, and so instructed her fellow servants not to betray her hidden scrutiny. She watched as he strode into the palace, gird in armor for the rallying of Eurimedon's host, until he stood still, calling for her.

He turned to one of the women of the palace. "Tell me, where is Lissandra? Has she fled?"

The woman bowed. "I know not where she is, my lord. I have not seen her this day."

Titalis frowned. "Leave me," he said, and waited for the women to depart. Alone in the palace, he rested his hand on his sword and shook his head. "Lissandra, if you hide yourself for fear of me, then fear not. I do not come to banish you. Much I know of what you meant to Prince Capestes and the place you held within his heart. I know, too, the dilemma you may fear, for it is one close to me. We cling to a narrow thread, we common born who mingle in the court. I have asked the king to give you refuge in my house, but he refused my petition, for wrath has filled his heart. Duty-bound I am, and can offer you no more than an early warning, a plea to flee. I know it is little aid, and I ask your forgiveness, but it is the best I can do in remembrance of my fallen fellow."

He stood for a moment, shifting on his feet. "If you hear me, I wish you well," he said, and departed.

She trembled at his words, fearing the worst and, though she continued to cower in the palace through the night, no royal attendant came to evict her. Whether it was some hidden mercy from the king, or more that he forgot a creature as meek as her in the greater considerations erupting within the city, she could not be sure, but she was unwilling to test one certainty or the other. If she was wrong, she knew what awaited her, and she would rather leap the falls as Princess

Totuk had than abase herself to the touch of some rough stable hand. No, Capestes may have been firm with her during his more heightened impulses of lust, but he never hurt her, or, at least had not hurt her more than she was willing to entertain in the darker measure of her inner passions.

It was such thoughts that at last moved her, not for desire of his intimacy, but rather for the nagging void of his absence. There was a shadow over her, born of her stark realization and conviction that she could find no other mate so suitable, or no lord with whom she could fittingly match. There may have been a streak in Capestes' blood that ran black as pitch, but she understood him, and he her, so that their bond was something surpassing the shallow arranged marriages of so many other lords. He was true to her, and she to him, even though by his birth not a word would have seeped from anyone's lips had he entertained the company of others, as was the standard and secret custom of the court's lords and ladies. Except Titalis, true hearted Titalis, who cast no stray glance from precious Deiphos, a loyalty she returned in kind over all the years of her lord's absence.

Wrapped in a black cape, Lissandra strode from the chambers into the garden, standing beside the pool where she knew her prince's embrace, so strong and vital in such recent time. The sensual rapture of the memory overwhelmed her and drove the wetness from her eyes. "Ah, but what am I to do, what plan shall I make?" she whispered to the stars above her, an empty plea to the deaf ears of the pitiless gods, until her mind sparked with dawning hope. "Yes, yes, there it is, a life of chastity, but a life within these walls nonetheless if I can beg the mercy of sweet Deiphos and find comfort within the kindness of her heart. The king in his wrath might refuse his champion to harbor me, but I think he would not refuse his only daughter and only remaining child. To her I shall repair and seek my ends."

By cover of darkness she eluded the sight of the palace guards to enter the hallowed chambers of the court, a place that she, given her low birth, had no right to enter, even on the arm of her prince. Silent in her leather sandals, her mane of brown hair and black cape allowing her to seep like oil from shadow to shadow, she at last penetrated the throne room itself to find Capestes put out in state before the royal dais. Clutching the cape about her face to hide the pallor of her desperate grief, she dared not test her luck by stepping out from the walls into the amber glow of the vigil candles. She held still, her lips pressed tight to hold within the sorrow that sought to burst from the prison of her reservations, and gazed from the anonymity of darkness to the stilled countenance of her prince.

The sound of footsteps caught her ear and she pressed her shoulders to the wall in fear, but her eyes were keen in the dark and she gazed toward the entrance of the room. There she spied none other than the princess herself, Deiphos, as she waved off her attendants to walk alone in the court, stopping only when she stood beside the adorned mortuary table of her brother.

Deiphos put her hands to her cheeks, shaking her head as she gazed down on Capestes. "Ah, fair brother, like you my tears are lost, orphans to this cold reality that now snares us in its pitiless web. What are we to do, for all our bluster, for all our rage and grief, for our woes born of betrayal? Titalis, my husband, may be our heart, but with you in your funeral shroud sleeps our cunning, my wily brother. If I could, know that I would drain my heart and with its stormy flood bring warmth to your limbs and raise you up anew. Though you dwelled in the shadow of Titalis, never did I note a shade of envy upon you. You and I, our father's children, were both displaced in his eyes by Titalis, but for me it is a different course than you, son to the crown, yet you accepted your place as Fortune cast it and took Titalis as brother as much as I took him as husband."

She let out a long breath, her shoulders sagging as her hands sank to rest on Capestes' chest. "In this eternal sleep of yours I hope you find whatever solitude it was you sought in the recesses of your heart, even as your crafty tongue is forced to rest from its labors. Often it was you were hard at work with the tasks of our father and so I had not the opportunity to see your full spirit and all its glittering facets. If I hold a greater woe for your passing, it is that I failed to know you full in life. But, know this brother, I have decided upon an oath, and to your empty vessel I now speak its truth so that it may fill this lifeless void and the gods bring it to you, wherever it is you now reside in those places shut out from the sight of the living. Titalis has tasked me to scribe the tales of war with Totuk and the deeds of our fallen men, but none shall I utter this day, or any other, until I see your death avenged. In life we may have been distant in the roles which we lived, but in death I shall serve you true."

Lissandra watched, breathless, as Deiphos' words thundered through her soul. Her hands trembled, for she saw in Deiphos that for which she had hoped, and yet, something more. "Yes," she whispered to herself, "a protector, safe harbor for me, but something more as well, an instrument for me to use, to use in Capestes' namesake, and so he shall live on." Rallying her nerve, she took a breath, and prepared to reveal herself until a guard stepped into the room.

Deiphos turned, her eyes lit with sudden distemper. "I asked not to be disturbed."

The guard bowed. "Your forgiveness, Princess, but Captain Eikoptas presents. I thought it best to ask if you wish his company before letting him pass. Shall I detain him, or allow him entry?"

Deiphos turned away, staring into the shadows where Lissandra lurked, though the distant cast of her gaze showed no recognition of what the shadows held. "Only now he comes to mourn?" she said under her breath, her gaze darting to her brother. "True, I have seen his strange manner these times since the murder. A known and trusted man he is, befriended to both brother and husband, but a fancy he held for this Totuk witch upon whose point Capestes died. Is there some truth he hides, brother, something in death's silence you have no breath to speak?"

"My lady?"

Deiphos turned to the guard. "Good sir, allow him in, but tell him not of my presence, and play none the wiser to my whereabouts."

The guard bowed once more. "As you wish, my lady."

Deiphos shifted, looking about the court but, to Lissandra's surprise, she bolted toward the very spot where Lissandra lurked. She seized the princess in the shadows, clamping a hand over her mouth to silence her cry before whispering in her ear. "Princess, fear not, it is I, Lissandra."

Deiphos turned her face, staring in horror at Lissandra. "Hiding are you, to spy on my mourning and breach this most private of moments?"

Lissandra held Deiphos fast. "No, my princess, I beg your mercy. As you know, I am banned from this chamber by my low birth, even for mourning. Forbidden am I to shed my tears upon he whom I loved and share with him those last little parting tokens of mine. Forgive me my brazen entry, but no longer could I suffer to stay away. I thought to have but a glimpse of fair Capestes from these shadows and in silence wish him to sleep well. Know this, I swear it, that I arrived as you came to this shadow. The sanctity of your sibling's grief rests between you, your brother, and the gods."

Deiphos eased. "Then you best go, before you are seen. Eikoptas nears."

"Yes, I should go, but you saw me not, and neither shall he. I heard only what you said last, your utterance that some dawning suspicion of this man wakes within you. Know now that such distrust dawns in me as well. The day of the suitors' challenge he came to your brother and they spoke at length. As to what, I know not, for Capestes had not the time to tell me, but I suspect it might now be revealed, when this man thinks he has the favor of solitude."

Deiphos nodded. "Then we shall listen together and, if need be, bear communal witness." She sucked in a breath at the clank of armor. "Silence now, he comes."

Lissandra kept Deiphos in her embrace, but peered over her shoulder, her cheek pressed against the cheek of her princess so together their eyes could bear four-fold truth between them. She could feel the anxious pound of Deiphos' heart, resounding through her slender frame into Lissandra's chest and warming her blood with the certainty of a newfound ally.

None the wiser, Eikoptas walked into the court, his breastplate, greaves, and helm gleaming with the candlelight. He hesitated several paces from Capestes, but then removed his helm, and fixed a hard glare on the corpse before him. He took another step, then two, his lips pressed in a tight line as he fought against himself to lay a hand on Capestes' shoulder. "So, here it is you rest," he said, the strained words passing from his lips like muzzled dogs held fast by taut leashes. "Prince you were, but not of men, only of schemes. Aye, I no longer fear to say it aloud for the gods to hear as they already know this belief within my heart. In my guilt I feared you might arise as an avenging ghost, cast out by the spirits of the Otherworld to sate your thirst upon my doom, but it seems they have taken you to their bosom and hold you fast in their embrace.

"Strange comfort to me, this rest of yours, for now your disease rests upon me. Look out from whatever abode holds your spirit—or should I say look up, you feverish deceiver—and behold the resurgent mass of Totuk wrath. For two days their strength has gathered, spied from the walls by faithful Mylo and Pylo, whose dim wits have at last united to one vigilant eye. You may not care, you who died assaulting me until I stilled you with my own blade, pressed and pushed to unsavory ends by your will. But I tell you now, dead prince, an act such as that you sought to force upon me has washed all our mutual guilt blameless in my heart."

Lissandra exchanged a glance with Deiphos, the princess' eyes burning with rage over Eikoptas' admission. She strained to burst from Lissandra's grasp, but Lissandra held her fast and resumed the clamp of her hand over the princess' mouth for fear her soft lips would part and let her voice fly.

Eikoptas shook his head as he stared down at Capestes. "I sought no ill with you, prince, and I would let it all pass and put it to Time's senility, but the matter has raced beyond my grasp, and I know not how to reign in so many wild furies. For all your black bile, we need you, need you now in this war, in our desperate need. Titalis lacks the wit, and I the authority, to drive the men in proper fashion in this newfound conflict. Not only your poisoned blood rests upon the blade you gave me no choice but to turn within you, but the blood of Eurimedon."

"See him," Lissandra whispered into Deiphos' ear. "Vile traitor. I know what my lady seeks. Know now that I would give my life to her, and join her brother, to make it so."

Eikoptas settled his helm on his head, his lips falling in a frown. "To the task I go, Capestes, but I think I shall meet you again soon enough. King you sought to be, and soon you shall be of all of us, your servants in death." He thumped his fist to his chest in salute and, with a final glance to the unseen stars above, left the court.

The moment he left, Deiphos found the strength to break free of Lissandra, only to spin and grab her shoulders. "Lady, lady, dear Lissandra, do you hear this—deception, betrayal, murder, murder? Foul hearted pig he is, this common born wretch Eikoptas. Hear me, hear me now, this eve I swear an oath and let the gods mark it as so. Life for life, pain for pain—so the low to the high, than the high to the low. Upon my pledge this fool shall meet his doom, not upon my father's decree, but upon my action in honor to my fallen brother, that Eikoptas knows in afterlife that it was a familial hand that served his death. Not even to my husband shall I entrust this act, for he still considers this traitor a friend— more so with my brother lost, cruel irony—and never would he raise his hand against Eikoptas after shaming him at the suitors' challenge. Ah, how I regret my words to stop him that night. Now, how am I, a lady, to strike down this man? Tell me, Lissandra, know you of some agent, some device, to make it so?"

Lissandra let herself pale. "My lady, do you ask me to raise my hand to a man of Eurimedon, one to whom I am still beneath by custom?"

Deiphos pressed her against the wall. "I ask it, I ask it! Fear not, good Lissandra, for your safety. I will take you, and my eternal favor you will have for your help in this despicable matter. My handmaid you shall be, you shall live as a sister to me, and never have fear of the outside world, nor suffer the prospect of some filthy herdsman's hands upon your fair frame. Now, will you be true to me?"

Lissandra let her tears run. "Yes, yes, my lady, for love of your brother, I shall."

Deiphos eased her grip of Lissandra's shoulders, smiling upon her before kissing both her cheeks. "Ah, such a burden I place upon you, poor one, orphan to Fortune's decrees. Such I would never dream to ask you if my husband had but two wits beyond the valor and truth of his heart. Mighty as those are, in guile and subtlety he is lost, still an orphan in the woods for he sees only the good of those around him and will hear nothing of foul ambitions, or acts of wanting retribution, when some sense of justice stands abashed of their demands."

Lissandra's eyes widened. "My lady, an option I have for you."

Deiphos squeezed Lissandra's shoulders once more. "Tell!"

Lissandra nodded. "From my youth I know my way about the distant fields and meadows, lands you traversed in your longing for your lord, when the men were yet to return."

Deiphos blinked. "Yes, I know of what you speak. A catalog I kept of those meadows, of what to pick for seasonings and what to leave in place. Learned am I in the knowledge of herbs and mushrooms and see of what you hint. Though I know little of swordplay other than a playful thrust and parry, I will arm myself in ways no man of war would suspect. Ah, Fortune, I see your hand at work in this matter, of disparate things now shown to be joined, twisted about each other like hair in a braid. I must ride, yes, in haste I must ride, to the meadows and back this very night and a deadly potion I shall concoct, one to match the poison of traitorous Eikoptas' black heart."

Lissandra clutched Deiphos' hands. "Let me ride with you, my princess. There is a stable-man I know whose gaze has tracked me, though I never suffered his touch. With a sweet word I will secure our mounts so that none in the palace need know of our flight. Not even your husband, busy with rallying the men-at-arms, will be left any wiser to that which we pursue."

Deiphos kissed her cheeks once more and released her. She watched Lissandra step away before returning to her brother. She kissed his cold forehead as she pressed a finger to his lips. "Patience, patience, dear brother. You must sleep in torment, but not for much longer, no, not much longer. Soon you shall possess the soul of Eikoptas, and the endless suffering of his spirit can then serve as your eternal pastime. Now, I must go, I must fly, gather my poisons, and cook them within my urn before Totuk in marching haste closes us in line from the meadows."

Lissandra lingered by the wall, but Deiphos returned to her, took her hand, and led her away. Lissandra cast a longing, sorrowful gaze as she passed Capestes and, even though Deiphos had her back to Lissandra, it seemed she sensed that gaze and stopped her flight. She turned to Lissandra and laid her hands on Lissandra's cheeks. "Go, sweet woman, and have your moment with him, as it should be, in all fairness to the loyalty you held for him, and the affection you held for each other, so that he may hear your voice one last time."

Lissandra sniffed and kissed Deiphos' hands. "You are too kind, my princess." She turned, wiped her eyes, and went to Capestes. She hovered over him, tracing his countenance with a gentle finger before leaning over to put her lips to his ear. "I hope it pleases you, my love, the little I learned of your ways, and that I put it to use."

She stood straight, kissed her fingertips, and pressed them to Capestes' lips.

They felt warm to her, even in death.

***

The gates of Eurimedon ground open, hauled with humming ropes over a series of pulleys by two teams of sturdy mules. A phalanx of men, huddled behind their shields, spears held level in rigid defense, marched forth until they filled the gap of the gates. Above them, along the white walls of the city, more men-at-arms flanked a small party. Foremost among them was King Teleimon, flanked by Titalis and Eikoptas, with Mylo and Pylo behind them, signaling to the mule teams.

A small Totuk party waited on the plains before the gate, their horses sniffing the green turf as the riders dismounted. An ambassador, clad in hides died a rich blue, strode forth, opening a hand to the walls as he removed his helm. Two Totuk warriors trailed behind him, one a large fellow, the other slight in comparison, but both wrapped in black riding cloaks, their eyes the only visible aspects of their faces.

The ambassador gave a ceremonious bow, an exaggerated gesture to reinforce the idea of his presence as a speaker, and not a man of war. He had no intention to return home on his back, pierced by a score of arrows. He coughed, somewhat unnerved by that image, but rallied his nerves and stood up straight to meet King Teleimon's gaze. He took a deep breath, and loosed his voice.

"Warriors, kinfolk, elders of Eurimedon, hear me now as I convey these words to you, on order of my lord, King Totuk. 'Many stones it takes to build a house, yet, of them all, the starter stone alone is key. Likewise, in peace, the stones take on the likeness of longevity, and a treaty justly secured likened to the starter stone. I, King Totuk, declare that Eurimedon has cracked such a stone, pulling down years of hopeful peace in their arrogance.' So speaks King Totuk."

King Teleimon shifted on his feet, glancing at Titalis and Eikoptas before tapping his staff. "Ambassador, test not my mercy, else your people once again strain the tradition of safe passage granted to messengers. Hear me, you brazen savage, as I say this once, and never again. Pack your lord's windy threats within your rough shawl and let them carry you homeward. If talk of stones interests your king, then tell him of a funerary slab, the one upon which my son lies in traitorous death. It is this stone that crushes our sad house of peace, and nothing else. For this, Totuk is to bear the sin, and the peace dashed. Convey this message, ambassador, and beg mercy when your day comes, for I shall unleash a slaughter upon you the likes of which neither man nor god has ever had the pain to witness."

The slight warrior behind the ambassador shook his head. "Brave words, coming from atop so high a wall."

King Teleimon's face flushed red, but Titalis rested a hand on his arm to give him pause. Titalis pointed to the slight warrior, but kept his gaze on the ambassador. "Man of words, you best council your king to rethink his message and intent. If he has none else than high-pitched boy warriors to cast down our mighty hosts, he best reconsider, and remember the horror I brought upon his people, and what I have done to the best of your kind, laying them low to eternal slumber, so that they trod the fields of battle no more in flesh, but only in memory."

King Teleimon failed to hold his anger, pulling his arm from Titalis' restraining hand. "Enough! You Totuk savages, we are in the right, for we have suffered the wrong. My noble son lies murdered at Totuk hands, the second best of our kind laid low, victim to the cowardice of witching designs, rather than bare-faced honorable contest."

The slight warrior let out a loud laugh. "See the mighty man atop the wall—yet he says that by a lady did his proud son fall?"

The ambassador turned, clenching his fist to the slight warrior. "Enough," he hissed, "or else the trap springs premature." He turned to the wall and cleared his throat. "King Teleimon, know this, that even though my lord would eagerly claim credit for your prince's demise, in his death we took no part. It is you, and your kind, who hold the blame; it is you, and your kind, who have instigated our nation with the shameful burdens you heaped upon our lady, even as she went to you under a treaty's vow of safe-keeping."

King Teleimon pointed his staff at the ambassador. "And tell your lord in counter that it was he who made a mockery of the treaty's safe-keeping. A princess we were to collect and hold as testament to peace, but we did not receive an innocent noblewoman. No, a sorceress we received instead, beguiling our good men's sense with her harlotry while she claimed false chastity."

The ambassador drew back a step. "Grave are your words, King Teleimon, but relay them I shall."

Teleimon waved him off. "Away, away you maggot, before I order you slaughtered. I shall converse no more with you or any other black-tongued attendants of your lord. If it is battle your lord seeks, tell him that it awaits him here, and that our swords, spears, and arrows still hunger for Totuk blood."

The slight warrior stepped forward, standing even with the ambassador, and tore free the black riding cloak. A mane of dark hair fell about the warrior's shoulders, revealing Princess Totuk, She of the Plains, her eyes burning with wrath. "Harsh king, you shall receive that for which you beg, and regret it for all your remaining days. I, whom you condemned with lies and unspeakable shame, have returned to you with a nation enraged."

Archers atop the wall scrambled to the forefront, knocking their arrows for a fatal flurry, but Titalis and Eikoptas stilled them with anxious waves.

"Yes, remember at least the custom of peaceful embassy," She of the

Plains called up to them. "As for you, foolish king, lord of ignorant fear, if indeed you believe I am a witch, would I not have thwarted the judgment you laid upon me?"

Teleimon stuck out his hand. "I shall not speak with you, heathen, yet I marvel at your bravery, so distant from us. I will tell you this: although I decreed that you burn as unholy, my mind seeks a new course. I will take your head, set it upon a silver plate at the foot of my son's funerary table and watch two stable rats pluck out your tongue and devour its wretched morsel so that your cunning is nothing more than the stench of their waste."

The ambassador waved his party back. "Lord of Eurimedon, I will convey your words of hate." He set his helm upon his head and turned a sharp glare to She of the Plains. "My lady, speak no more, I beg you."

She of the Plains was enraged, though, and refused to suffer a word unmet. "In passing I have one thought left to offer, clay-boned king. Know this, that I possess a keen eye of both mind and spirit so that I have peered within your Eurimedeon hearts. In horror have I seen the darkest depths of false nobility, yet in a man or two a treasured soul remains, revealed in acts both selfless and honorable. Bravery indeed I witnessed from such a rare find, bravery to stab injustice rather than blindly obey and grace enough afterward to regret ill-forced actions. If such hidden treasure still remains among you, then I offer one last chance to steal away, steal away from the self-inflicted doom of your people, and know that the grace of my hand and heart will protect you among the Totuk people. For your favor you shall have due renown, and no ill intent levied upon you."

King Teleimon held his staff high. "Foolish witch, your sight is blinded by hate. We stand as one, and none care for your lies, or deceitful efforts to erode our solidarity."

She of the Plains laughed. "Then be resolute, for the horrible clash nears, and you know not what wrath you have stirred. And to you, King Teleimon, be wary of threats that rebound."

The handful of warriors in the Totuk party raised their fists with a shout, rallying around their princess. Together, the party mounted their steeds and departed at a full gallop, with She of the Plains shaking a spear over her head as she glanced back at the city.

Atop the wall, the men-at-arms looked to their king, their captain, and their champion.

Titalis stepped beside his adoptive father, speaking to him so that none could hear. "My lord, I beg you to find some calm in your heart. Spite not the nature of She of the Plains, for that is part of her black art and so allows her hexing ways to rob you of your best sense."

Teleimon ground his teeth, in no mood for thoughtful counsel.

"Back," he hissed, his eyes lit with fury, "back from me, and back from matters of state, you orphan." He spun to his other side, pointing his staff at Eikoptas. "See, Captain, the vile nature of this sorceress you sought to take in marriage? See from what depths of despair my wisdom saved you? Never again protest my judgment. To this witch you gave a prized possession and she repays it by bloodying my life's dearest possession. A thread of silk for thread of lineage, an unfair trade, and something you could not expect to understand. Kneel before me, kneel so that her slander flies over your head and thank me for your perceptions cleared."

Eikoptas' eyes fixed on the end of the staff, gleaming beneath the sun, until he met his lord's stormy gaze. Despite the staff and crown, Eikoptas stood fast, and would not take his knee. "My lord, understand me, it is not your honor I flout, nor your due respect, but I shall never sink upon theses knees until this terrible conflict has met its ends."

Teleimon stared at Eikoptas, his eyes widening until he waved a hand over the men-at-arms around him. "All of you, all men of Eurimedon, do you see this honorable man, courageous Eikoptas? Is there no greater virtue in time of war than such a man, he who seeks no end but his enemy's blood?" He took his staff in both hands and raised it high above his head. "Let this staff rally your hearts and its shining head be that of Eurimedon's heart. To arms, to war, to victory!"

A flurry of shouts rose up, swords and spears shaking in lifted arms as the host of Eurimedon cheered to resume the field and seek vengeance for their prince and the honor of Eurimedon. The host's rising fury buffeted Eikoptas until he let out a harsh shout to still the men. King Teleimon turned on him, ready to strike him with his staff for restraining Eurimedeon wrath, but Eikoptas spoke, and held the attention of all around him.

"Men, men of Eurimedon, listen to me, a word from your friend and fellow. I, Eikoptas, Captain of the Guard, I who take your discipline as my charge, say a warning to you now, one to hold dear. From the lips of crafty Princess Totuk have you heard the words of cunning and seeds of treachery she seeks to lay within your hearts. She begs you to contemplate, yes, to contemplate your allegiance, to forget your homes and the homes of your good neighbors. I give you this to consider: rally your will, and do so publicly, for among blades of deep rooted grass no sickly weed shall find purchase and all shall bow together with the blowing winds of Fortune's breath. Now, to your lord's bidding."

The host doubled the fury of their shouts, rallying around their king as Teleimon strode from the walls, down the ramp toward the city square. Eikoptas leaned against the wall, watching them go, until Titalis came beside him, startling him with a clap of his hand on Eikoptas' shoulder.

"Ah, steadfast friend," Titalis said with a smile, "ever your words bolster us and keep us strong in our focus."

Eikoptas looked to his champion. "I would do what Fortune bids," he said, not sure what else to say. "But thorny conflict is no easy path to follow, for no matter the strength and loudness of rallying words, its barbs always snag some tender part."

Titalis nodded. "Aye, that it does, but victory shall be ours. We have felled the best of their host and left their numbers in a sorry state. Boys and old men we shall meet and send them running with a simple draw of the sword."

Eikoptas opened a hand to the city. "Such was my intent in stirring the hearts of our host. If we make a fierce show, perhaps King Totuk will see the futility of his wrath and a new peace can be found without the spilling of any more needless blood."

Titalis smiled. "Well said, well said. Fear not, good fellow, for we shall march home once more, and this time with no doubt to what we have won."

Eikoptas bowed as Titalis left him. He lingered by the wall, lost among the shouts for Totuk blood until he had no choice but to turn away. He rested his hands on the wall and gazed out to the horizon, across the vast distance. Somewhere, She of the Plains rode, and he closed his eyes to imagine her hair trailing in the wind, her eyes narrowed against the setting sun even as it lit her skin in golden tones.

He let out a sigh. "Ah, me," he said under his breath, "to what ends shall I direct myself?"

Mylo clapped his shoulder, startling him. "My captain, what is it that bothers you?"

Pylo reached over to take the ale skin from his brother's shoulder. "Indeed, in bravery and war-lust we doubt you not, but best watch yourself, else some other foolish goat accuses you of hollow speeches."

Eikoptas shook his head. "Good brothers, I see that nothing escapes your vigilant gazes, whether it is sight of scene or soul. The concern you see upon me, and the weight you spy upon my shoulders, I shall not hide from you. It is the field I study and from the lay of the land, I hope to discern some past method of Capestes to employ, and summon a ghost of his wits."

Mylo lifted his ale skin after Pylo took a swig. "A gut of ale and you will see all the ghosts you desire," he said with a laugh.

Eikoptas laughed with them, but waved off an offer of the ale. "And a good night of revelry would serve me well, but I must keep my wits sound. Now, if you would, I seek a moment alone, so that my thoughts may condense their wisdom."

Mylo bowed. "As you say, Captain," he said, giving Pylo a shove.

Eikoptas watched them go. Alone atop the wall, he looked back to the distance, and rubbed his face. "As I say, as I say, so what is it that I say? I say I see green fields this day, but tomorrow I see nothing, my gaze clouded by the evils of circumstance. I wish my heart could be like those of my fellows, their hollowed chambers lacking any steadying weight and so swayed this way and that by the sweet, weightless powder of confectioned words. Ah, but for me, my heart wavers not a hair and rests upon a heap of guilt within me. Love and justice pull me toward a forbidden desire, but honor and birth whip me to march with king and countrymen. Thought and emotion, they wrestle within a man's will to wear the crown of resolution, yet to these very contrary calls my resolution becomes like a leper. Broken and diseased are my standards and guides for in every nature of green fields known between men and gods I have grown to be the weed eternal."

He dropped his hands and took a breath. He looked to the fields, and his heart stilled in his chest.

The black cloak that had disguised She of the Plains remained, tumbling across the green turf with the waning winds.

***

Dawn lit the next day, and a glimmering band of rosy light backlit Eurimedon. The city's mighty host rested far ahead of the gates in a war camp, awaiting the day's show of arms. White tents wavered in the morning breeze, their various banners rising in the mounting currents to snap to, unfurling the color standards of the host's phalanxes. Sentries stood their guard, but they leaned on their spears as they fought not to fall over in sleep, their helms hiding their drooping eyes.

Titalis looked over the sentries as he emerged from his tent. He gazed at the darkened horizon toward the unseen lands of the Totuk nation. He looked over his shoulder toward the dawn, his eyes narrowing against the growing light. "So, I see a blood red sun rises this morning, a fitting stain of light for those who must die this day. My gentler spirit tastes lament, but my sympathy lies in slumber, restless though its sleep may be, knowing that the act of war is one of killing and full of destructive hate. In the heat of battle, blades are pulled and hearts concealed, though in the aftermath blades are put away, and hearts revealed. Glory or mourning, the difference sometimes escapes me, for in these pursuits I know there is always loss, such great loss."

He pulled his sword, studying it until he slapped his palm against the flat of the blade, and listened to the tempered metal's resonant hum. "Aye, sing your song of death, you who serves me so well. In the onward count of days I hope to give you rest, and when my count runs its due course and the last grain of sand slips from my inverted glass into mortality's pit, I wish that you lay rusted and dull, so that I know I went in peace, rather than violence. This vision is a prayer for me, for within my orphan's heart there beats a fearful doubt that with Capestes lost a royal burden shall be heaped upon me, and so these shoulders of mine shall know no rest. Yes, to wild war I have been pushed and its call I have met to my best. Its glory I have taken in full, but as reward I seek a quiet age of peace. A mocking shadow of my deeds I might become, but a life of rest, with wife, and a child or two, would be more than enough to satisfy this man. But, with Capestes gone, now the king shall pass to me that which Capestes desired so deeply, the crown of Eurimedon."

He closed his eyes and lifted his face to the sky. "Gods, know my heart, and hear these hushed words as the truth within me. I am but an ox, strong and simple, proud in my humility, possessed by a sense of justice, yet hot-tempered, my only request a direction to follow, and a yoke to till said path. Such things as ambitions, plots, and schemes are nothing but vague mysteries, distasteful delusions of those men too complex to accept their proper stations. My humility seeks only three merits in life, that of family, friend, and honor. These three, and none else, are the wealth of men."

He took a breath, holding it before letting it go. "Yet, for all those dear things within me, I must confess that in the hidden parts of my heart I do desire the gold circlet of Eurimedon. Thankful I am for the graces afforded me by my adoptive father, but in them even I can see the hypocrisies surrounding my life and the strife they can cause. If it were to be mine to decide, if I could but fasten the yoke of the crown atop my head for only one day, I would set those wrongs right. The cruel dictate of lineage I would depose so that no man would know a station other than the one he creates for himself, by effort of his will. No man would suffer disgrace as I was forced to inflict on poor Eikoptas for his ambition to secure noble station through marriage, for under my rule men and women would have their free choice in a mate, such as I enjoy with Deiphos. Poor Lissandra, the love of Capestes' inner heart, could sit with him in open court, rather than suffer banishment for no other reason that she was born on hay, in a stall, rather than on linen in a noble bedchamber.

"Yes, such things I would set right. Tough labor it would be, but it has been my life to suffer selfless labor, and when my eyes close for the last, I could know those pure labors came with no cost in blood or mourning misery, but were met only with relief, and rightful joy.

"Ah, if only it could be so. It seems war and its cold doom are indeed simpler things."

He opened his eyes to the brightening sky. He waited several moments, hoping for some sign or whisper of portent, but he heard nothing, and saw no clouds from which to divine some shape. Frowning, he looked down to his sword, turning his hand to let it catch the light of day before he slid it back into its scabbard. He clapped his hands, squeezing them so that the muscles of his arms began to bulge. He looked back to the horizon, away from the dawn, to the coming darkness of Totuk war.

Three scouts emerged from the darkened horizon, their horses trotting beneath them. Eikoptas held the center. He rode up to Titalis, waving off the other two men before dismounting. "A fair dawn greets us," he said, pointing behind Titalis.

Titalis held his gaze on his friend. "That it does. News from your scouting?"

Eikoptas let his breath go. "The Totuk nation comes in full force. I fear any hopes of a bloodless day have fled." He tipped his chin toward Titalis' sword. "I see you keep your blade at the ready. Do you hunger for their blood?"

Titalis looked at his blade. "I wish more so."

Eikoptas' eyes went wide as he stepped toward Titalis. "Smother your words," he hissed, so that the sentries would not hear. "What brings this from you, this hesitation?"

Titalis shook his head. "It is not fear that stills my appetite, but the heavy hand of Fortune that presses me, my good friend. The Totuk nation comes this day in final contest so that the fates of our two peoples are to be decided over a single woman's honor. If such a struggle is to go our way, then those wrongs, too, shall pass, but a greater worry concerns me. With our good prince gone to mortal sleep, who will bear the crown?"

Eikoptas opened his hands. "It should be none other than you. For faith of heart, for purity, it can only be you. You answer every call of Eurimedon, yet ask nothing for yourself."

"Ah, but I pale before such portent," Titalis said, and let his gaze bore into Eikoptas. "This task is not mine to bear. Know now, there are things I would do, wrongs I would right, but they are dreams and will be nothing more than that elusive ether which whispers to our sleeping mind. Such is what my heart tells me and I fear how that path shall be made."

Eikoptas put his arm around Titalis' shoulders and led him several steps away, pointing to the horizon as if he was discussing his scouting. "My lord Titalis, no more of such talk," he whispered. "Old wisdom has measures of tried dictates and I would remind you of one. In battle fight your foes singly; so, too, in your mind do not let your woes ally." He patted Titalis' shoulder. "Come, the field and deployments we shall observe and some crafty stratagem we must deduce."

Titalis looked into the distance. "Capestes' work this is, that calls to us now."

Eikoptas turned to him. "The wind caught your words. What says my lord?"

Titalis let out a sigh. "Oh, none else but selfish yearns, Eikoptas. Had not Fortune seen to Capestes' death, then no battle would be fought this day. Had not Fortune seen to Capestes' death, then with plots and plans would we fight. Had not Fortune seen to Capestes' death, then the crown would still have a royal head to find its rest. Selfish though it may be, I fail to disavow the course of a simple thought, that in death Capestes does us all a great disservice." He looked to Eikoptas. "Now, a moment, so that I may think and perhaps gain some plan of my own."

Eikoptas watched as Titalis strode off. Standing alone, he looked away from Titalis to glance over his shoulder toward the camp of Eurimedon's host. He looked back to Titalis and the shame welled up within him. "Ah, a thousand curses upon my head," he whispered to himself. "Fortune strikes another stinging slap, as he whom the treacherous prince sought to destroy desires the company of said deceiver. I wish a numbing stupor upon my tongue for these pains of hypocrisy cripple my inhibition to shout forth the rotten prince's ambitions. How I wish release from so many stained moments. All that remains to me is to serve my champion well and seek refuge in this last honest thing within me."

He took off his helm and walked to Titalis' tent. There was a small table outside with several spears and Titalis' helm. Eikoptas set his helm next to that of Titalis, took a spear, and hurried off to join his friend.

Unknown to either, a set of eyes had kept careful study of them and waited to observe a precious opportunity for the mind they served, and they served none other than the mind of Deiphos. She moved among the camp in the guise of a man-at-arms and so escaped notice among the host. She had heard of the deception of She of the Plains, how this wily Totuk woman had approached the city in the guise of a warrior, her nature unknown beside the Totuk ambassador until in her brazenness she could no longer bear to hide her countenance. Deiphos had no intention to follow such a foolish extent of the deception, but she had every intention to remain hidden and, when the moment of conflict came, to hide altogether and so escape the risk of clashing arms and armor. No, she came to the camp for her own reasons and with her came faithful Lissandra, dressed as a simple servant girl, so that she, too, could move about the camp without note thereby doubling the vigilance of Deiphos' gaze.

Deiphos moved, walking toward the table of helms with one hand on a spear, using it as a staff much in the way of the sentries, as her other hand trembled within her cloak, clutching the product of her labor. "The moment presents itself," she whispered, the rush of retribution failing to restrain her tongue. "The scoundrel talks with my husband and so affords me the matter of his undoing. A poison potion for his helm so that when upon his head in protection it sits, his undoing it will affect as it soaks into his cursed scalp. So he will drop and none the wiser to how his fate was crafted."

Her hand emerged from the cloak and she popped the cork from a small flask with a flick of her thumb. She pressed her lips together, keeping a watchful gaze on Eikoptas and her husband as drops of the syrupy poison fell into Eikoptas' helm. "There, let it sit in silent hate until through his body and to his heart it can permeate."

Lissandra came around the tent. "My lady, I have secured two steeds. We must fly and abandon this deception."

Deiphos turned on her. "No, I must see it to the last, I must see the helm upon his head and know the work is done."

Lissandra grabbed Deiphos' hand but froze when horns sounded out from the camp. "My lady, the camp rallies. We must go or else be caught in the maelstrom."

Deiphos sucked in a nervous breath and yielded but, at the camp's sudden commotion, she bucked in fear. Not knowing what else to do, she pushed Lissandra away and dropped to the ground, drawing the loose flap of the tent over her body to hide. She lifted the flap to call to Lissandra, but she saw a man-at-arms grab Lissandra's arm and shove her, shouting in rebuke that she had no place in the camp and should depart with the other servant women to the city. Lissandra glanced toward Deiphos, but the man shoved her once more, threatening her with a raised arm as he shouted orders to the host.

With a great clamor of arms, the mighty host of Eurimedon formed its strength, arrayed in fierce phalanxes before the camp. Eikoptas leapt atop his mount and rode off to issue the battle orders, first to his right, then, speeding past, to his left, all the time waving his sword in the air so that its blade caught the light of day. Titalis, too, drew a mount, and from the saddle surveyed the battle, shouting out to orderlies so that they could relay his instructions to the phalanxes. The purple banner of Eurimedon was raised high behind Titalis, and Deiphos trembled with the earth beneath her as fleet hooves of the mounted Eurimedeon knights charged at full gallop from the rear of the camp, their lance points decorated with purple pennants in honor to their city.

A steady beat of heavy thuds sounded from the distance. It was the call of Totuk war drums reverberating across the fields to keep Totuk warriors in line. Deiphos cringed at the sound, but still she hid, unsure how to secure her escape. She was desperate to flee, yet she was stung by morbid curiosity and fascination for the battle, to see her husband in his glory send many Totuk savages to their deaths. She turned where she lay, lifting the inner edge of the white tent canvas to peer inside. Finding it empty, she crawled in from under the canvas and, maintaining the guise of a man-at-arms, she hid her slender frame beside the tent's flap so that she could gaze upon the battle and yet remain unseen.

She looked out upon the field, across its slow rise to the horizon, to see past her city's host and witness the Totuk force in marching advance. Eikoptas came back to Titalis and the two men exchanged a quick talk before they separated and rode forth, shouting for the host to advance in full. The flanks of the host split off, marching double quick to encircle the nearing Totuks. Missiles took flight from the Totuk lines, goblets of smoking oil that crashed upon the field and cast a pall so that nothing but sound carried forth from the clash, the horrible sound of shouts and screams as men tore the life from each other and the green field became stained red with their blood.

So it raged, and it seemed endless as much as it seemed a heartbeat, for Deiphos longed to see her husband once more and thereby know when he emerged from the blinding smoke that he was still of sound body. Soon enough the moment came and he returned with Eikoptas at his side with their swords red and dripping, nevertheless cheering each other. They dismounted, embraced, and Deiphos grew certain that victory was at hand by their demeanor.

"The day is ours, the day is ours," Titalis shouted to the messengers of the camp. "Send word, fly as fast you can, let our captains know on the flanks that they are to rush in their advance and seal off this Totuk horde so that we may slaughter them to the last."

The messengers mounted, but Eikoptas pointed to them in turn. "Tell them both, our captains Deimas and Martres, indeed to spur their advance, but warn them against the distant woods to either side of us, lest they fall victim to some Totuk ambush and be delayed in skirmish. Go now, tell them."

Titalis turned to Eikoptas and clapped his hands on his friend's shoulders. "Ah, ever cautious you are, but not in need this day. See you, how they flounder before us?"

Eikoptas pointed toward the battle. "Aye, see it I did, when we rode forth even without helms to partake of the battle. But still they stand and stubborn is their fight, more stubborn than any sound mind could perceive given their disposition before us."

Titalis laughed. "Fear not, good fellow. The day is ours and tonight we dine in victory. See now, word comes from messengers."

Two men rode toward them, one from either side of the battle, the nostrils of their mounts flared with exertion. The men dismounted, bowed to Titalis, and let go the reigns so they could get fresh steeds.

Eikoptas opened his hands to them. "Speak now, what news have you?"

The first messenger pointed to his side. "My Captain, upon the left savage Totuk breaks and to the high hills we are in pursuit of their desperate flight. Our lord Deimas has driven us hard for victory's sake, stopping only to keep our line in order while before us Totuk fell back in sad retreat."

The second messenger pointed to the opposite side. "My Captain, upon the right we fair just as well, driving yelping Totuk forces all the way to the deep woods. Eager Martres slowed us only to pass a stream, yet he still leads our men forward."

Eikoptas shook a fist to both men. "Now go, with all speed, and let your captains know again not to pursue Totuk warriors to the woods but to hold in the meadow so that no waiting evil can spring upon our men. Take the word and let them know all goes well in the center."

The messengers thumped their fists to their chests in salute, mounted new steeds, and thundered off to their charges. Eikoptas glanced to Titalis, but found him looking up to the rising smoke from the Totuk missiles.

"Ah, curse this smog," Titalis said with a wave of his hand. "A foul odor it brings from the oil it burns. It clouds witness of this day so that our king upon the wall sees little of what we accomplish in his name."

Eikoptas looked back to the city. "He shall know it well enough when the day is done."

ACT IV

The battle raged throughout the day and Deiphos hid within the tent, listening to the messengers as they came and went. Men rode to the city to convey the good tidings of the battle and men returned with orders from the king that Titalis was to hold at the camp and not risk himself in this last Totuk defeat. It was news that soothed the heart of Deiphos, but it left Titalis pacing in frustration for he wished to be at the front, as was his way, hacking through his enemies with his men. In prior days, Capestes lingered at camp and managed the orders.

To her disappointment, the safety of her husband also meant the safety of he whom she wished to destroy, Eikoptas, for her husband kept his traitorous friend at his side, letting his counsel steer the battle. Their helms sat neglected on the table outside the tent and the work of her poison sat dormant, still awaiting its victim.

She considered abandoning her disguise and revealing herself to her husband. Yes, it seemed a brilliant plan, to surprise him so, and then ask good Eikoptas to escort her back to the city. Titalis would admonish her for taking such risk, but she would accept his wrath, for she would understood its source, the deep love he held for her. From that he would unwittingly seal his friend's fate, asking him to take Deiphos, to arm himself, and ride with her. Then the poison would meet the wretch and, when he dropped dead from his saddle returning to the camp, none would know the cause, other than to blame it upon a failure of his heart, as can happen to the elderly, the stressed, or those ill in body or spirit.

"So fitting, in every way I know," she whispered to herself and made her mind.

She put her hands to her helm and was set to cast it aside when a party emerged from the smoke toward the camp, headed by several Eurimedeon men-at-arms shouting with glee to Titalis. They possessed a chain of Totuk prisoners, among them the Totuk ambassador, the proud man who had spoke before Eurimedon the day before. The men-at-arms forced the Totuk warriors to their knees, striking several of them across their heads with the flats of swords when the Totuks refused to obey. When the savages went still, one of the men-at-arms stepped forward and bowed to Titalis.

Titalis took a bite from the apple he held in his hand as he looked over the prisoners. "And what is this I see?" he said to them, pacing down their line until he stood before the ambassador. "Ah, behold, the proud head of Totuk messengers, a man who brought many threats to us over the years, now left in submission." He turned to the man-at-arms. "Tell me, how is it you came upon this prize?"

The man-at-arms tipped his head. "In defense this party held when we came upon them between two Totuk bands, but their numbers failed them. Stubborn to these last few they were until in careful contest we were able to strike their weapons from them and secure this prize for you."

Titalis smiled upon the prisoners. "Good man, remove their helms."

The man-at-arms moved, but the ambassador's voice burst from his lips. "Hard-hearted Titalis, I beg your mercy. In all your days of war upon us, a reputation of grace always went in escort with you. I beg this of you now as well, that you not humiliate these poor youths who are the last of our strength, by casting their helms from their heads."

Titalis tossed his apple aside and pointed at the ambassador. "Ten years you taunted us in war and, before that, five years you brought siege upon siege to our very walls, and now you ask my mercy, with my prince slain? In gentler times such a petition I might have entertained, but now when you come upon us once more, I wonder if you would grant the same mercy were our fortunes reversed."

The man-at-arms opened his hands. "My lord, shall I remove their helms?"

Titalis nodded. "Proceed man, cast them down."

Eikoptas stepped forward, putting out a hand to halt the man-at-arms. "Titalis, my good friend, I ask you, must we do this? We know from our time in this battle that the Totuks come at us with boys, barely men who have yet to shave, and so, too, these warriors, from their slight stature. Is this what we will hold as our honor, which not only this day we had by demand to kill youths, but by choice humiliate them as well and dash our own honor with theirs?"

The ambassador wept. "Honorable Titalis, I beg you, heed your captain's counsel."

Titalis hesitated, but then shook his head. "No, such mercies I can no longer entertain. You heard the king's decree, Eikoptas, as well as I, that there is to be no more space for mercy or halting hand this day." He waved on the man-at-arms. "Proceed with their helms."

The ambassador cried out. "From these knees, I beg you."

Titalis drew his sword and put its point toward the ambassador's heart. "Make no mistake to mock me with your humility, emissary. The choice is not mine to make. Off with their helms and then off with their heads if they have no wisdom to share of Totuk battle plans."

The man-at-arms went down the line of prisoners slapping their helms from their heads to reveal fresh-faced youths with tears of shame upon their cheeks. At the last, though, the man-at-arms recoiled and all fell silent in wonder.

The man-at-arms pulled his sword. "My lord, the Totuk witch."

She of the Plains threw her head back, her hair coming loose and falling past her shoulders. She looked about with cool defiance before spitting on the ground before her.

The ambassador let his head hang. "My lady, to what madness did you submit?"

The men-at-arms found their wits and shouted their insults.

Deiphos stared in wonder, but her gaze snapped toward Eikoptas to watch him wilt where he stood, his face filled with horror.

"Take her head," one of the men-at-arms cried out.

Eikoptas sprang forward, his sword flying from its scabbard as he took his ground before She of the Plains. "Back from her, back, you wolves. Is this your nobility, to gloat over a noblewoman taken prisoner? Honor turns its face from those who spit on the weak."

Titalis put out his hands, stepping forward to still the confrontation. "Men-at-arms, my good captain, all, hold. Indeed, Princess Totuk finds herself our prisoner once more, but this day she shall have no favor and doom closes upon her." He turned his sword from the ambassador to She of the Plains but she did not flinch before him. "Lady, you know in our long homeward march I gave you due respect and held you in my protection, but for your sake the peace we all sought was dashed. By your making or not is not mine to judge, for judgment has been passed upon you and its measure I will fill, as is my duty."

She of the Plains looked to the sword of Titalis before meeting his gaze. "Do with me what you will, but know this, proud champion, not all is as you think it to be, and from my Totuk lips you will hear truths that reflect upon your decision and may find purchase upon some private grace within you. I believe your heart beats strong beneath the Eurimedeon rot under which you reside."

Eikoptas shifted on his feet. He took a deep breath and moved forward, tapping the flat of his blade against the blade of Titalis to draw it away from She of the Plains.

Titalis blinked in surprise, but he looked to his friend. "Eikoptas, what madness is this you hatch upon us? You know full well our king's decree."

Eikoptas waved off the men-at-arms and grabbed Titalis' arm. "Dear friend, I must ask your ear, and beg you listen to words in concert with Princess Totuk, bearing witness to sharp words argued true in support of one another. A case exists here of which you are unaware, an underlying bitter root beneath all that has entwined us. For all the ruin it will cast upon me, I can suffer its burden no longer, and dread its weight levied upon a guiltless party as I stand silent."

Titalis fell back a step. "No, my ears fail me, my senses betray me. Do I hear you true? Is this what you claim, that you are in league with Totuk cunning?"

Deiphos grew tense, eager for her husband to strike.

Eikoptas lowered his sword. "My lord, spare her, disregard the suspicions against her for she is blameless, a mere victim in a terrible circumstance none sought to embrace."

Deiphos clutched the tent canvas in her hands. "Yes, that's it," she whispered. "Speak your treachery, meet your death on my husband's blade and here I shall watch, an angry lady avenged of her brother's death with no stain upon my hands."

Titalis shifted on his feet, looking between Eikoptas and She of the Plains.

His hand tightened upon his sword until his knuckles blanched.

Deiphos sucked in a breath.

Titalis turned to Eikoptas.

She of the Plains stuck out her hands. "Wait, Titalis, wait. And you, noble hearted Eikoptas, why did you not heed my warning? Be silent, and save yourself at this last moment. Let not your love destroy your good sense, for this loss is no longer yours to suffer. I made my decision to be here, in defiance of my father's order."

Eikoptas held his ground, keeping himself between her and Titalis. "No, too long now have I stood by while this net constricts us, but I will not die a coward under the harsh light of truth. By my warrior's oaths I shall not stand by to see a lady sacrificed or take the burden of my guilt." He turned to Titalis and put his sword out to his side so that he held no defense. "Titalis, about you many plots turned, but know now that it was my hands that were blood stained."

Titalis fell back a step. "What's this, what's this? Do you speak of unspeakable treachery? I pray you, tell me now that she conjures about you, that she witches your tongue to this evil and this very moment I shall strike her cursed head from her shoulders rather than hear your good name muddied."

Eikoptas shook his sword. "Ah, a thousand curses of black art I would pray over the miserable truth, but this lady I will not let pass undefended. My lord, my friend, I call upon your mercy to pity a man victimized by his own misguided ambitions; betrayed, it would seem, by the very grip of his loyalty to you."

The ambassador crawled forward on his knees. "Titalis, you must listen."

Titalis turned. He stared at the ambassador a moment before plunging his sword into the man's chest. "My patience is spent on you, deceiver. Riddled I may be, but I will not suffer the orders of a Totuk cur." He yanked his blade free and kicked the ambassador onto his back before spinning on Eikoptas, blade on the ready. Blood dripped from its point. "Now, let nothing else interfere in this vile proceeding. Confess before me, Eikoptas, mince not another word, spout not another circling story, but reveal your crime before me so that I may hear it from your lips even as I suspect its nature in my heart."

Eikoptas glanced at the ambassador and the blood gurgling from his chest before looking back to Titalis. "Then hear me, and know it as truth. It was Capestes who lurked behind the suitors' challenge. That ignoble prince sought to split us in violence, for his jealousy stole his wits, jealousy for you, for he feared the crown would go to you. Destroy you, yes, that was his aim, and I his weapon to yield, all so that the crown could rest upon his head. His pride could not suffer his birthright lost to an orphan, but when his secrets spilled to me in a fit of black conspiracy, I threatened to tell all in truth to you and our king, regardless of its reflection upon me. He came at me in rage and his life was dashed in the struggle so that upon my hands his treacherous blood rests."

Titalis shifted, baring his teeth as he shook his sword in Eikoptas' face. "You make my life weary with such words, Eikoptas. For all your claims, it seems to me you know nothing of loyalty. If you did, then that night of Capestes' death you would have joined him rather than condemn so many to the ruin of battle in your weak-hearted deceit."

Eikoptas shook his head. "Have you not heard what I said? Do you fail to mark my words and fail to believe them when they offer me nothing but loss?"

Titalis rapped the tip of his sword to Eikoptas' breastplate. "Aye, I have, but in my heart there rages a deadly tempest. You speak of loyalty and heavy crimes that you bear in your heart, but all I see are base words, deadly lies. Look around you. Do you not see peace aflame and nations engaged in deadly war, but in all you held your tongue and put all these who die today in balance to your own shame? This you call an exercise of loyalty? Tell me of your loyalty and I shall tell you of your dire delusion, for this war was started by your hands. Tell me of your loyalty, and I shall tell you of my loyalty, the loyalty of Titalis. My heart tells me to set this Totuk lady free, for it seems she is a sorceress in rumor only, but I must obey the cruel decree of my king for that bond is all I have to claim on this earth and in this life. Loyalty wavers not to personal convenience, but asks one to be selfless to higher callings. A curse upon you, Eikoptas, that you took all our fates upon you. What concern is king and crown when you feel it best with your secrets to rule over us? Perhaps tomorrow you risk our lives to cover some new murderous deception that you suddenly deem worthy during sleepless night? You are a detestable traitor to me and your name a curse. This day you shall have your marriage with your Totuk witch and consummate it with both your deaths."

Eikoptas looked in disbelief upon his friend. "Listen to your rage, and know it even now as the insidious work of Capestes' poison."

Titalis shouted for his helm, rapping the tip of his sword once more against Eikoptas' breastplate. "I will offer you this one last favor, only in debt to the man I used to know, and once called friend. Raise your sword and have your last defense for I will not slay you like some Totuk savage, but rather let you stand your ground against me so that Fortune can be blameless in your death."

Eikoptas let his arm sink to his side. "I will not raise my blade to you."

She of the Plains grabbed Eikoptas' wrist. "Do not let your blood spill in vain."

Titalis turned on her. "Silence, you foul-tongued witch. My friend you have cursed to his destruction, but I will not extend any more courtesy to you. The king's decree I hasten upon you so that I suffer your voice no more." He pointed to the men-at-arms. "Take her now, take her from me and do not return until you bear her lying head in a sack. Fetch my helm."

The men-at-arms seized her, Titalis stilling Eikoptas with a flash of his blade to rest it at Eikoptas' throat. She of the Plains struggled against the men-at-arms, but they overpowered her with ease and hoisted her to her feet.

"Take her," Titalis ordered, his gaze locked on Eikoptas.

She of the Plains spat at one of the men-at-arms, distracting him enough so that she could wrestle one arm free to point at Titalis. "Foolish Titalis, let your teeth gnash in tired frustration like the rocks within your head. Know this before you seal my doom, that your white-walled Eurimedon perishes this day by Totuk hands. In one night the rot of your city accomplished what all the years of war failed to do. Upon my escape, and the news I brought of the shame your people intended for me, all the Totuk chiefs rallied to my father's call so that you face not only my father's people, but all the Totuks, in numbers indescribable, closing about you in murderous ambush even as we speak."

Titalis shouted to the men-at-arms. "Her head, her head before I take yours as well."

Eikoptas watched her go as the men-at-arms dragged her behind the tent. "My friend, if she speaks true, we must desist and attend to the host, we—"

Titalis seized his helmet from the man-at-arms at his side, settled it on his head and with a mighty shout, swung his sword in rage. Eikoptas dodged back, almost losing his bare head in the swing, but he met Titalis' attacks, refusing to offer any of his own in return. The men-at-arms watched, bewildered, as their champion and captain clashed while the rage of battle sounded out around them. Deiphos cringed in her hiding place in the tent, remembering the horrible beating Eikoptas had put on Akketor, but then she steadied herself when in turn she remembered the ease with which her husband subdued Eikoptas.

Titalis swung, opening a gash on Eikoptas' leg. Eikoptas staggered but caught his footing before Titalis' next attack. Titalis lunged, looking to drive his blade through Eikoptas' gut, but Eikoptas spun to the side, whipping his sword around. The flat of the blade struck clean to Titalis' head and the champion almost fell under the horrible clang of blade to helm.

Deiphos shrieked. She clamped her hand over her mouth, worried that she had betrayed herself, but she heard another shriek, followed by two angry shouts. Eikoptas turned at the sudden outbreak, only to see She of the Plains run out from behind the tent, a slender blade in her hand, its point bloodied. One of the men-at-arms chased after her, but the second man limped out from behind the tent, blood streaming from his thigh. He grabbed a spear from the table, planted his feet, and cast. It flew true, and the heavy point found its home, tearing through her innards until its bloody point burst from her chest. Her legs gave out beneath her and she toppled to the ground.

Eikoptas froze in horror.

Titalis grabbed at his tattered helm and tore it from his head.

The man-at-arms chasing She of the Plains raised his sword high and swung as he came upon her prone form. Her head popped loose, rolling across the green grass as blood spurted from the stump of her neck.

Titalis called Eikoptas by name. When Eikoptas spun, Titalis drove his arm out and his blade tore through Eikoptas' throat, such that blood gushed from his mouth. His body went limp, the sword falling from his hand as he dropped to his knees. His head all but severed, he looked up the length of the blade into the rage clouding his friend's eyes. His hands twitched, blood bubbled from his lips, but his eyes welled up, and so all the elements within him seeped forth in death. Titalis planted a boot on Eikoptas' chest and yanked his blade free, watching as Eikoptas sank away, his blank eyes full upon the sky.

Deiphos stepped into the open, her mouth agape at the scene before her. "Ah, the deed is done, the wretch has died among his lies, but yet the battle rages on. Gods, what are we to do?"

Titalis drew himself up, backing away from Eikoptas. He turned to the Totuk prisoners still on their knees and with an angry shout waved for them to run. The men-at-arms stood, befuddled by what they had witnessed, as the Totuk youths scattered toward the blinding smoke rolling over the camp. The heavy sound of Totuk marching drums came to them and Deiphos recoiled, fearing a sudden truth to the last claim of She of the Plains.

Titalis wiped his face, throwing his sword to the ground as he shifted on his feet. "Black day, black day, where is victory among such sorrow?"

Two messengers charged from the smoke, their horses rearing to a sudden halt at the messengers' sight of Eikoptas slain and She of the Plains without her head, a spear protruding from her back. They dismounted, mumbling in confusion, until Titalis turned on them. "What word do you bring? Speak."

One of the messengers swallowed, blinking at the thud of a Totuk drum. "My lord, I bring desperate news from the left. Fortified, we were in stout line at the base of the distant hills and above us we thought Totuk held trapped from the battle until with a roar they charged forth, their strength replenished anew. Where we had fought one, we fought two, and soon where we fought two, we found ourselves fighting ten. Outnumbered and surrounded we were and brave Deimas fought until

Totuk spears ripped his life away. With his dying words he ordered to hold against Totuk onslaught and bring last word to you that the left is lost and the flank defenseless."

The second messenger listened in horror, shrinking against his horse at the nearing pound of drums and the fevered screams of the battle in the blinding smoke. "My lord, so it is the same on the right. Brave Martres led us across a stream to hem the Totuk savages in the dense wood, but no sooner did we believe them caged in those thickets than the woods themselves erupted with unseen Totuk hordes. Where we fought one and two, we also were soon faced with ten or more in raging ambush, and not the boys we had fought before, but full grown Totuks in colored hides we have never before seen, from nations we never knew. Martres held us fast until a sword pierced his gut and dying on that blade he shouted to hold off the ambush as we could, and send word that the right was lost and the flank defenseless."

Titalis looked to the messengers. "The left lost, the right lost, and the center pushing upon us. She spoke the truth, and I, in my rage, too foolish to heed her words, even if they were spoken in last hope of salvation for fate-crossed Eikoptas. Now, what to do, what to do, other than make hasty flight toward the city?"

A final messenger rode from the smoke, slumped over the neck of his mount with three arrows in his back. Titalis seized the reigns, grabbing the man's shoulder as blood dribbled from his mouth. "My lord, the center is lost. They come at us with numbers innumerable, like locusts upon the plain, devouring everything before them. Fly, fly, you must fly," he said with his final breath and, loose with death, he slid from the saddle to land in a heap at Titalis' feet.

Deiphos backed into the tent, clutching her hands to her chest. Her gaze swept over the white canvas enclosing her, paltry substitute for the white walls of the city. "What is this, what horrible work is this that Fortune spits upon us? Is it true what Capestes planned and have the gods now decreed we are all to perish for these sins?"

Titalis' voice came to her from outside the tent. "Messengers, hear me now, go to any men of the host you can find and order them to make the city with all haste. I shall stand this ground and cause the delay so that they may find their way in safety and keep the city safe. Now, question not my sacrifice, but do this thing I bid, else all will be lost. You there, you by the tent, my helm is broken. Fetch me that of Eikoptas so that I may face the Totuks in full gear and exact of them what I can."

Deiphos blinked, frozen until the words of her husband pierced the veil of her horror to stir her limbs. She threw off her helm and burst from the tent, her hand outstretched, only to see her husband settle Eikoptas' helm upon his head before turning to her in surprise. She froze, her breath lost, her heart stilled, as the vessel of Eikoptas' destruction enclosed her husband's head. She fell back a step, and then two, until she lost her footing and sank to the ground, staring at her love, mute with his surprise. "My husband, my beloved, what is this, what is this tragedy? No, wake me from this nightmare; snatch me from this cruel turn."

Titalis blinked several times. "Tell me, is this my wife I see, my lovely Deiphos here among this horror?"

Deiphos ran to him, sinking to her knees as she grabbed his wrists. "My husband, I beg you, forgive me, forgive me the wrong I have done you." She wept, her tears running down her cheeks to sink among the blood soaked grass. "Gods, do you laugh at us now from your cold palace above as we succumb to defeat wrought by our own hands?"

Titalis swayed, blinking again. "What is this, what is this strange thing at work upon me that I see you through a white fog and your sweet voice is but a whisper in my ears? My hand I can not feel, but I know it holds my blade, and despite the fog that shrouds my senses, I swear that this is my wife submissive before me, rather than home among our white-walled city, safe from this fatal place."

Deiphos rested her head against his thigh. "You hear true, my lord, it is your wife and I have come to you and will not leave your side."

Titalis looked up as several men-at-arms ran from the smoke behind him only to see them felled by javelins and arrows. Screams surrounded them as the smoke pressed forth and the heavy thud of Totuk marching drums sounded across the field. He looked down to Deiphos and caressed her cheek with his blood soaked hand. "Deiphos, indeed it is you, here in this place. I fear Eikoptas struck me harder than I thought and some evil is at work upon me, sapping my life as I stand here, so that all seeps through my senses like a dream, a dream from which I fail to wake, and fear I will never wake. Tell me, why are you here when in safety within the city you could hold your refuge?"

Deiphos stood and kissed him. "Dear husband, hate me not for what plot I sought to follow. I wished to right a horrible wrong, the same wrong for which you struck down Eikoptas. A poison I concocted to serve as silent assassin and within his helm I poured its fluid, but now upon your head it sits in circumstance I never foresaw, so that it is I, your wife, who has sealed your doom."

Titalis swayed, steadied only by Deiphos' grip of his shoulders. "Aye, so it seems, yes, so it seems that I am condemned to death. You seek my pardon, but I hold you blameless, for I feared this day to be my last and in shadow of deceptions revealed, and lies uprooting all I know, I think it the better that I know no tomorrow. Cry not, sweet one, for I see no pain and no wrong in what you have done, but see only comfort now, for the poison numbs me, and so the piercing blades will not fill me with their pitiless agony. I would tell you to fly, but there is no escape now, not for me, you, nor Eurimedon, so stay, and we shall die together and wander those distant fields of which we dreamed, where we may know a time less bitter than the poison you have crafted."

Deiphos shook her head. "No, my love, we must make our haste and pray that in this rolling smoke we can find our way. Now, if we go, I may find a remedy, and—"

Titalis rested a finger over her lips. "You sing a soothing hope, but hollow it is, and its echo rings in your tears. See, my world has gone mad and all I have known has already died this day. I will depart, for the world and I have grown estranged, through no fault, I think, of my own. Now, forgive me this last thing I do, for like all other foul acts this day, I am but a mule obeying the whip of some careless master."

"My lord?" Deiphos said, but then she convulsed against him with a cough. She looked down to find his sword thrust within her and her blood running down its naked length to drip from her husband's hand. She looked to him, but found no breath to speak.

He kissed her and sank to his knees to rest her upon the ground. "I will not suffer them to defile you. I would rather have your blood upon me than know any hand but mine ever touched your beauty. On this day, even love is death. Now, let me go, and do what I must, so that I can join you."

She reached up to wipe the wetness from his eyes. She held her hand to his cheek, but her breath seeped from her as her skin paled. Her fingers slid from his face as her hand dropped to her chest, and her eyes slid shut. There she died, Princess Deiphos of Eurimedon, beloved of Titalis, and he put his lips to hers one last time before whispering a final farewell in her ear.

Totuk war shouts sounded from the smoke as it shrouded the camp. Titalis held, but then he trembled and, though his limbs grew heavy and his blood slithered through his veins like pitch, he forced his body to a stance. The whites of his eyes boiled red and his lips turned an unsavory black from the poison, but his rage burned within him.

He turned to the charging Totuks, took up a great ox-hide shield, raised his sword, and let out a roar like no other man of war would ever bellow and, for a moment, his fury drowned the din around him. Then he charged and he met the Totuk horde alone. Nothing could slow him, not the Totuk arrows as they bounced from his shield, not their javelins whistling past as he dodged them in his nimble grace. When he met their line he threw the shield like a mighty discus and its spinning mass careened through the crowded Totuks, shattering heads along the way. He took his sword in both hands and hewed in half the first Totuk he met. He swung in his fury, lopping off limbs and heads of any who neared him until the warriors gave way for a thundering mass of mounted Totuk spearmen. He roared once more, held his ground, and the red fire of his eyes panicked the first steeds nearing him so that he slaughtered mounts and riders as one.

Their numbers were vast, though, and he a lone champion. The first rank of mounted men crashed dead around him, but the spears of the following rank dropped level in charge and held true. No one of them could claim his death for it took many to still his murderous sword. Such was the number of piercing points and hacking blades it took to at last silence him that the Totuks thought they had discovered some last hardy phalanx, only to find that it was one man, one man alone, the champion Titalis, the great warrior of white-walled Eurimedon.

So came his death, and never again was a man of such valor seen in that age.

***

King Teleimon stood atop the wall between Mylo and Pylo, clutching his staff as he strained to see some news of the battle below, covered as it was by the wide bank of smoke set forth by the Totuks. It enveloped the camp of the host and still no messengers came from that gray shroud, but ever louder grew the screams and crash of arms until there was nothing to hear but the steady pound of Totuk drums.

Teleimon fell back a step, his lips quivering, even as Mylo and Pylo held their ground. He knew not what to say, knew not how to voice his grief, knew not how to deny what he realized had come for him—the end of his reign, and the fall of his proud city.

Mylo and Pylo gasped as they looked about the fields before the city as the smoke yielded its blinding screen. Thousands of Totuks came into view, charging toward the city, shouting their victorious rage.

Mylo turned to the king. "My lord, what shall we do?"

Pylo paled. "What to do? There is nothing left to do. All of the host's strength left for battle and now we have no defense but you and me, two hobbled gray goats." He looked to the king. "My lord, if you wish it, we two will take a stand and offer a final defense."

Teleimon fell back another step. He looked to his staff before letting it clatter at his feet. He shuffled away toward the ramp and waved a hand at the brothers. "Open the gate and give no defense. Lay down your arms, and heed me no more, for my days are done."

ACT V

Panic filled the city, driven by so many years of Totuk war, but the fears of the Eurimedeon people were both less and more than the reality they received. They feared they all would be put to the blade and the city made home to a vast stack of corpses. But this was not to pass. Rather, they were to suffer the terms the Totuks had enforced on other nations, as well as among their own, in times of their own strife. Through such revelations the people learned how vast an enemy they had incited and how little they knew of what wrath they had tempted when their king sought to defile She of the Plains.

Any homes of the city that could burn went to the torch, the people left to run in fear until herded by Totuk warriors to behold the fate of the Eurimedeon nobles. Among the smoldering ruin surrounding the great city square, the noblewomen came forth to stand in line, only to be divided as spoils among the many Totuk chiefs who had joined King Totuk in battle. The women cried in protest, but the Totuk chiefs made public claim that, unlike the rough handling of She of the Plains, the noblewomen of Eurimedon would receive safe passage among their newfound homes. To their husbands, the noblemen of Eurimedon, the Totuks worked a terrible revenge. In remembrance of She of the Plains, the Totuks dragged the noblemen to the top of the wall, where it overlooked the falls cascading to the great depths below, and cast them over one by one. Fickle Fortune levied her judgment on them each in turn, but never again after that precipitous fall did anyone see or hear of those men, for it seemed the river was careless to their fate.

Most pathetic was the doom of Akketor, he whom Eikoptas had defeated at the suitors' challenge. Too vain was Akketor to show himself and his bruised countenance among the men of the host, where was his rightful place, after the night of the challenge. He had avoided the battle by hiding in the city as a servant woman, concealing his broken face beneath a long shawl. So he skulked about, only to be apprehended in a failed attempt to evade the city's fate. He received rough treatment for defying the orders of the Totuks but, when they discovered his true nature, the Totuk warriors decided to mock him for his cowardice. They tied the shawl around his neck and stripped him naked, then tied the loose end of the shawl to a saddle. In such fashion they dragged him to the wall and the people of Eurimedon pelted him with dung from Totuk horses as he wailed for mercy. Atop the wall, he made one last attempt for his life, shuffling on his knees from one Totuk warrior to another until a lingering nobleman of Eurimedon throttled him, choking the life from him, to spare the city the disgrace of his behavior. For this act of rightful pride the Totuks decided not to cast that one nobleman from the wall, instead, affording him a quick end with a spear thrust to the heart.

In the court, Totuk warriors gathered the remaining servant women while Teleimon's attendants lost their heads in prompt order. As with the noblemen of Eurimedon, the decapitated bodies of the attendants were tossed from the wall. With this done, the servant women were made to stand in line and, like the noblewomen they once served, they were divided among the chieftains to add to their spoils.

Lissandra was among them, but King Totuk spied her from the rest of the lot. Beholding the fiery spirit lurking within her eyes that none other than Capestes had previously discerned, he went to her, and bid her step forward so that he could see her loveliness in full. He offered his hand and she sank to one knee, meeting his gaze as she kissed his palm. Then he claimed her as his own, and took her. Before he escorted her from the court, she glanced over her shoulder to Teleimon and showed him a smile, but for what, he did not know.

Deposed, Teleimon nevertheless sat upon his throne. He had no choice, as there the Totuks bound him. King Totuk himself hammered shut a crude iron collar about Teleimon's neck. A heavy chain was fitted to the collar with its opposite end attached to a large iron eye hammered into the floor. The court was to be his prison and from there he could not stray. He would have to depend on the mercy of others to feed him and, if they chose, take away his waste, so that he need not wallow among his feces like some rabid dog. The brothers Mylo and Pylo, faithful to their old allegiance, two men once mighty in war, took this task, and abased themselves to the work of dung shovels.

From his prison, Teleimon heard the loud boom of the city's gates crashing down and the deep thuds reverberating through the ground as the Totuks did what they could to demolish the city's battlements. At the last, with so many of the city's people driven off in fear, its noblemen cast to their deaths, its women both royal and common taken as prizes for Totuk chiefs, its defenses left broken and useless, King Totuk came to Teleimon with Lissandra at his side. He strode across the court to Teleimon and pointed before him for Teleimon to meet him. Teleimon shuffled from his throne, his heavy chain clanking down the steps behind him, and stood before King Totuk.

Not a word passed between those two men, for the pain and enmity that loomed over them was too great for them to find any fitting words. King Totuk slapped Teleimon once, a single strike for the death of his daughter, She of the Plains. Then he took the last thing left to Teleimon: the crown, the precious gold circlet of Eurimedon. He stepped back and, calling Lissandra to him, set the crown atop the gathered mass of her hair. He kissed her forehead, declaring her queen above all his other queens, so that she would be a woman without parallel among his nation.

She sank to her knee and kissed his hands, but then he raised her.

"Never again shall you kneel to men," King Totuk declared, "and free you are from the ways of this place that refused you to grieve for a man you loved, for no other reason than station of your birth."

She made her last bow to him, then turned and walked to Teleimon. She looked over his haggard face, his broken gaze, and his filthy robes. "Lofty Teleimon, I need not address you by title, nor suffer in subservience to you anymore. Know this, proud man, that although this is not as I would have planned it, I still stand satisfied, for I at last possess that which you deemed I should never know in marriage to your son. I loved him, I peered in his heart and loved him as no other could, and yet you would not suffer me as his wife, for no other reason than lack of noble title. So now, after many tragic twists and turns, here I stand. Know me, Teleimon, as I am now from these days forward, and obey this decree I lay upon you, stable-beast that you now are. Take your knee, address me as Ardnassil, and give me my due."

He hesitated, but then he sank down. He cleared his throat as his eyes slid shut. His face bunched up, but the tears nevertheless seeped from the corners of his eyes, falling from him like clods of mud as they cleared tracks of filth from his cheeks. He trembled, but then let his head hang, his shoulders sagging to leave his hands limp at his sides.

He found his voice and it came as a weak rasp. "Queen Ardnassil," he said and slumped forward, groveling in shame.

Satisfied, she turned, and took her king's arm. She departed without another word and let the apathy of silence serve as her final condemnation.

King Totuk took her upon his horse, as was the custom among his people, and she clasped her hands around him. He let his mount move at a patient trot, his guarding warriors around him. Onto the field they went where the people of the city still labored to bury the tangled corpses strewn across the grass, staining it rust red with their rotting blood. Black carrion birds circled overhead and their harsh squawks marred the peaceful blue sky.

They came upon the remains of the camp, with its tents trampled flat, the sheets of white canvas tangled and tattered with muddy boot prints and sprays of crusted blood. King Totuk brought his mount to a halt, patting its neck before turning to regard Lissandra. "It is a horrible sight, is it not?"

She turned her face into his shoulder, revolted by the stench of death, and nodded.

He patted her hands as they flattened against him, clinging to his frame. "Such waste, such folly, it sickens me that it had to be so."

She looked to the sadness of his face. "Have they found your daughter?"

He frowned. "Among all this violence, among the smoke and mad rush, many were trampled into the earth and their likenesses lost from recognition." He sighed. "It is a lesson of Fortune, such a sight, that for all claims of high and low, of just and unjust, of love and hate, that our mortal vessels are indeed fragile. Mere pots are we, delicate clay pots within which the gods choose to light the fleeting fire of life."

"I shall plant a garden for She of the Plains so that she may be remembered in times of fragrant blooms."

He reached back to stroke her cheek, studying her unblinking gaze before resting his hand on his leg. "Is there some man among this waste that you wish to have found and given proper honors?"

"None, my lord."

He raised an eyebrow. "None? Not even Titalis, the great champion of your city, should his remains be found?"

She looked across the vast carpet of corpses. "He was not a close companion. I knew little of him other than what my reckless prince would tell me."

Curious, King Totuk tipped his head. "And what did this man, your prince, tell you?"

Lissandra sighed as she thought of her days with Capestes and the things he whispered to her when life was different. "He told me of the purity of Titalis' heart and the smallness of his thoughts. Though the mind of Titalis was a simple thing, it remained a difficult thing to fathom. Bound he was by unwavering devotion and loyalty, at once proud and selfless in his servitude. Never was it his to question what was asked of him, and such conviction was his greatest strength, and so its blindness his greatest fault. Even so, he seemed a creature other than a mortal man, an ideal to fill a dream, an impossible ideal, and perhaps best kept as such so that the dream's allure would not suffer the blemish of human imperfection. Like the cup of wine held at arm's length for which one longs to taste, knowing the taste will be all the sweeter for the long wait, perhaps it is best never to taste it, so that its conception remains pure."

King Totuk smiled. "Your wisdom does not disappoint me, my lovely one. Despite what my daughter recounted, I believe this prince taught you well."

She shook her head. "I am but a common woman, and claim nothing more."

"So, too, was the claim of Titalis, that he was a common man, and nothing more." He looked to her. "Nevertheless, he was a great man, this champion of your city. Odd it is that one so low could rise so high under the dictates leveled upon your people. Perhaps you should make record of his story, and his fate, so that it may serve lesson to others, and grant him the immortality of myth and legend."

She sighed. "Perhaps. I know, in the least, how my view would suffuse those things of him I did not know and so make him more complete in the telling."

King Totuk bowed his head. "Best it is, then, that you give him some due."

Lissandra drew a breath. "If you allow me, then one tear I will shed in remembrance for him, a single beam of light among the dark corruption that swallowed Eurimedon."

She wiped her eye and looked to the tear hanging from her fingertip. Crystal clear it was, but when she peered into it, the world was distorted through its clinging sphere. It held her gaze for several moments and then she snapped her hand out to cast the tear upon the dead. She turned her face into the king's neck and squeezed him in her arms. "Now, let us go, my kind man, and leave this sorrow behind."

He looked across the carnage. "Rest well, troubled ones," he whispered.

He spurred his horse.

So it was that they left the silent dead, and ruined Eurimedon, to the shadows of sunset.

Sing, muses, of our gathered sorrow,
tell us of our foolish pursuits on this earth
and that which robs all good from tomorrow—
tell us of hollow Temptation's bitter worth.
Time draws close now, our last light grows dim,
and all that was once fair is now left to fade;
for, if nothing else, in war we were grim,
only to see bright hope lost to dark shade.
Dispirited, yet haunted, we walk fate's shore,
knowing past glory, now lost, shall be never more.

***

In elder days how trumpets would shout
and fields of bounty adorned the wide land—
in honest labor the people were humble and stout
yet proud enough, and not hesitant to stand.
In those the seeds of our hardy souls were set
and despite some dark winters long and cold,
resolute we were, and the hardships were surely met,
while in snow laden nights proud tales were told.
In those cold idle times certain ideals grew—
20   perhaps it was Winter's solitude to blame—
but one Spring more than seeds sprang anew
and the ideals could no longer be kept tame.
In those days a summoning call went out,
from fields, hills, forests and streams it took hold;
all the elders gathered then from far and about
and between them the ideals hatched ripe and bold.
And in that meeting it was promptly decided,
announced shortly after the dinner bell's last ring,
that our lands and people were soon to be united
30   and as one the elders serve beneath a crowned king.

***

That day was decreed ever after as the Springtide,
celebrated in innocence by all in their dearest finery,
but hidden beneath grew threat with cheer, side by side,
and hearts darkened despite the warm flow of the winery.

Words were whispered in the deepening quiet of night;
some elders debated the kingship as a burden unneeded
while others said the glory of our future was in sight,
and yet others sighed that yea or nay, caution was unheeded.
By dawn the pendulum had swung tirelessly to and fro,
40   a kingship realized was to some elders power at hand,
and so the wheels were in motion at rosy light's first glow —
among the elders certain few drew their companions into a band.
Outside the high stone arches of the lofty communal hall
the Springtide celebration rejoiced in kingship promises untold
and soon enough the creeping mutters spread from stall to stall:
before the day was out the name of the king would unfold.
The gathered crowd celebrated with an uplifted toast
and all cried at once the good news should double the feast,
yet in our carelessness we became an unwitting host
50   to that in the hall, Greed's entrance as a skulking beast.
As the elders continued their cunning crafts debated
no one noticed the symbol of the day's sun waning
while within the hall any steadying voice was quickly berated
and when rising ire was heard suspicion was clearly gaining.
Yet it is said that all good sense was not that day lost,
for a few elders stood fast and would not be swayed,
they saw to glimmering greed our future quietly tossed
and as such terms of resistance could no longer be delayed.
So ended the second day, and still no king to crown
60   but the king, though unnamed, in spirit had come to be
and while each elder parted that eve with a frown
what tumult the next day would bring none could see.
For that horrible night the moon was washed red,
a tradition among us long held came to naught
for with the dawn several elders were found dead —
on the point of a treacherous knife the crown was bought.
Sorrow seized us and overwhelmed all sense that dawn;
such was the whetted point of that hidden murderous plan
that before startled eyes the last debate would be withdrawn —
70   there would be no more talk, for there was anger in each man.
Then stood forth the wise elder Glima, the last lonely level head,
and he thought then and there to make a final stubborn stand,
but about him he found his like minded fellow elders lay dead,
and only that, it is said, stayed the vengeance of his hand.
With a final warning of dark portent he abandoned the elders —
he and his sturdy folk, the Glimoiki, to the hills retreated —
sad irony, that his passing words no one now remembers.

"For through the acts of his seed all hope will be defeated,"
ran the rash words of the starry-eyed elder Caron's retort,
80   and to Glima's back he threw the burden of murder's accusation—
such was Caron's way, that any truth by need he would distort—
and so the debate went not by fact but by false reputation.
In that time no one knew the way of wily Caron's deceit
and so none looked to the elder to see him as a coiled serpent;
even though the crime of murder and more he would repeat,
from his lips he would never utter a single word of repent.
Dismay then took the day, never before were we divided,
but upon this as well Caron fell like a bridge over a chasm,
"Be wary, be wise," he advised, "for at once it must be decided,"
90   and with that he earned the crown among the elders' moral spasm.
"Glima shall not rest," he warned, "he will put us to harsh tests,
and though we have yet no crown cast, we best each find a sword,
follow me and I promise time later for the making of gold circlets,
but first we none can rest until Glima's head is nailed to a board!"
To newfound King Caron's call rose an angered warrior's cry,
for all wisdom was lost, passion tempted by quick distrust,
none thought how with war our bounty we might swiftly belie
for all hesitation was trampled in the fury of black war lust.

***

Under the long hot summer sun the smiths eagerly forged
100   while Caron forbade any talk to the Glimoiki, even a barter,
and despite the weekly swelling of his armory engorged
during sleepless nights he would tirelessly plan all the harder.
It is said as well that wary and wise Glima did not rest content,
rather in his dreams the conflict with wily Caron loomed;
in those dark visions perhaps he heard whispers of lament
for the Glimoiki increasingly sensed that they were doomed.
Nevertheless they only had to peer down to Caron's growing walls
to know for sure the crown's hateful breach would not quietly desist;
Glima too saw this and quietly reinforced his mountain halls,
110   for though he sensed ill comings, Caron he would bitterly resist.
"I am in the right," Glima would utter over his smith's hammer,
"and our values I would not abandon for any crown of gold,

for even as I see in tomorrow's thickening mist war's clamor,
the memory of lies and murdered friends can not be sold."
So too Caron would stand upon his latest grounds fortified
and with his hard dark eyes to the snowy mountains staring
knew he had to pursue Glima's fault as he had falsely testified,
rather than reveal his own crime and face his subjects' glaring.
Then as Autumn grew near the crushing pressure began to break;

120   angered glares focused on Reddening Mount and its bare turf
       slope,
       and beneath many heavy marching boots the leaf dappled earth
       did shake
       as Caron and Glima each summoned their forces with victorious
       hope.

***

No one remembers if Glima or Caron chose that fateful day,
or if both Glimoiki and Caronite each blindly chose to a man
that for once no steadying word their rash anger could sway,
nevertheless, over the turf Glima and Caron each enacted their
plan.
Despite the cold air the blood of the men began to slowly boil;
as if in heavenly shame gray clouds gathered and no sun shone,
swords were drawn and spears leveled in levy to war's toil,

130   from Distrust's sour distemper the hate had now fully grown.
       Glima and Caron each then ordered their gleaming ranks in line,
       innocent of pain and sorrow the men stared over blades and
       spears
       as each felt his last hesitation dispel as a slight shiver of the spine,
       and then there was nothing left of Peace's hand-halting fears.
       At Caron's signal his guards let their bright trumpets sing
       and in that moment of the noon hour bloody horror loomed;
       the Glimoiki faltered as the trumpets made each helm ring,
       but then the roll of Glima's drums between the hills boomed.
       It was Caron who sent the violent order first,

140   his men charged out to slake their blood thirst,
       forever then was the peace of Springtide forgotten,
       like an overripe fruit fallen lost and rotten.
       Up the hard turf the Caronites grew near
       and with their numbers victory seemed clear.
       Too late Caron saw the mistake of the mad dash—
       by Glima the slope narrowed, choking the clash;
       and the mass of his men would serve no gain—

in those narrows his advantage would not remain.
Then Caron's fear doubled as the Glimoiki parted,
150   only to reveal boulders they had wearily carted—
at Glima's sudden shout the carts were tipped
and through the Caronites careening boulders ripped.
With the Caronites panicked and seeming broken
Glima believed that evened then was the battle's token
and with another shout set the Glimoiki loose,
certain now he held the Caronites in a noose.
But to both the great elders' shocked surprise
they learned in war best laid plans are lies,
for when the lines crashed with savage cries
160   they saw that win or lose many a man still dies.
All of the day the battle bitterly raged,
both sides fighting like wolves strongly caged,
yet in the midst of that wild bloody slaughter
neither army could issue the decisive order.
Then as one Glima and Caron each took to horse
and through the tangled mass charged on course,
for each was maddened to see a final end
when it was clear neither army would bend.
In the midst of battle weary they shouted clearly,
170   each the other for resistance to be taxed dearly.
At their sight the armies swelled to a thunderhead
and ever faster filled the dark halls of the dead,
for where Glima and Caron met at long last
the fury was such no other could stand fast.
Their blades crashed in a shimmer of sparks,
but in their attacks neither could find their marks,
and as they shouted with their boastful pride
they knew as well neither could run nor hide.
Only when their swords shattered did they part,
180   each claiming the other had lost his heart,
and riding then to their points of command
they finally saw the day's bloody demand,
for that evening strewn across the Reddening Mount
the best of our kind lay dead beyond mournful count.
The crimson evening light fell on the cursed scene and caused a hush
as in that moment hope was lost for what each side felt they had fought,
both armed forces seeing that the other they had utterly failed to crush,

so that it was only empty futility they had with so many lives bought.

It is said that of them all only Caron still held bloody sword in hand,

190   for many saw Glima pale and sicken on his horse plodding the dust

before he looked across to Caron with a glare none could understand

and cursed him with the disgusted shout, "Look upon this you must!"

To this Caron stubbornly stared and offered no verbal reply,

rather he cast off his helm to let the evening light reveal

that which the gruesome battle, though even, had failed to deny:

a secretly crafted circlet of gold to be his royal crowned seal.

And with that, there crept upon the pitiless earth a heavy sense of dread,

as all eyes roamed the countless tangled bodies on the hard rough turf

knowing that without victory both sides would soon add to the dead,

200   for all left breathing under war's red banner were likened to a humble serf.

***

Neither Glima nor Caron would retreat on that following dark night,

as safely encamped both felt the inescapable pull of war's bloody claws,

and decided in their sleepless pacing a truce must be brought to sight

even though pride and anger left them with tightly clenched jaws.

Anxiety won out over slumber for each man before that dawn,

both Glimoiki and Caronite finding no valorous rage in their gut

when upon the first gray glow of day they looked with faces drawn

across the wreckage of death before them that had filled Sorrow's glut.

But stubborn Caron decided he would not suffer his army to mutiny,

210   rather he raised them harshly and ordered them to line in the soft rain,

for he felt by blade or word he could satisfy the needs of his

destiny,
and rid the future of a crown disputed and with it uncertainty's
stain.
With the ordering of the Caronites below Glima left his morning
fire
and ordered the Glimoiki into a battle line cold, wet and weary;
even though the first day's losses had left him in a situation dire,
his pride still held and pushed him through a contest that cost
dearly.
Then to his surprise Caron rode forth with a scribe, two utterly
alone,
only to hold where yesterday he and Glima had bitterly fought;
it was Glima then who felt the frost thaw from his every bone
220 as he perceived that perhaps with parley a decision could be
bought.
Down the slope Caron and his scribe waited among the battle's
waste,
patiently the newly crowned king surveyed Glima's darting
glance
knowing that his now bloodless plan was conceived with ruinous
haste,
and yet with its despicable route there may reside a successful
chance.
As for Glima, he spoke not even to his most trusted gathered kin,
for a distemper had seized him as he perceived some newfound
plot
and with a snort refused to barter Caron's suspected wages of sin,
until his kin rebuked Glima's righteous ilk as the source of his rot.
"You must speak with him," urged Glima's kin, "for he knows,
230 as well as all our gathered men in this morning of dreadful rain,
that another long day's burden of wearisome war's brutal blows
shall rip out the heart of the Glimoiki and let run their blood's
stain."
And then a fit seized Glima as he stared on his kin most curious
while he urged his horse away from the army he had created;
his eyes darted from his kin to Caron until he grew furious
and finally sighed, "I am caught between hammer and anvil
mated."
Down the slope of the bloodied wet turf the two elders' parties
met
where Caron sat expressionless on his steed and patiently waited,
only to be greeted by Glima's sour scowl of fast nearing regret,
240 certain that by the crown a still deeper moral debt would be

created.
Caron nodded to Glima and ran a finger along that golden crown—
a cunning move, done to rouse Glima's heat and usurp his sense:
"Honorable Glima," he began, "both our people have won renown,
yet at the cost of so many laid low this conflict we must dispense."
To this Glima held in silence and would not divulge any thought
until Caron sighed, "We both know we must end these bloody ways,
for our people will have no share of bounty until peace is bought,
and in its dear embrace leave our future kin to find brighter days."
But there Glima was again tempted bitterly by his tumultuous pride

250 and let lay bare the Springtide murder of his fellows in accusation—
"I shall not insult the wrongful dead by letting their abuser hide,
and I shall not suffer the ranking of any more false reputation!"
So impassioned was Glima he noticed not as his kin withdrew
first one step, then two, all to Caron's barely restrained delight,
until Glima turned to see that from behind a deeper threat grew
and hurled his curse to them that they only secured their plight.
The kinsmen undermined Glima as they demanded he seek amends,
only to leave Glima stranded before Caron's growing royal bluster:
"So it is no longer upon my terms the peace undeniably now depends,"

260 Glima scolded, "yet you know not what Caron's desire will muster."
Then Caron came forward and advised Glima to listen for his people's sake—
"See now, we must find a way for lasting peace our future to enmesh,
and a process, a measure, to be conceived that no one man can break—
it is from this," he added with lowered voice, "our peace must be in flesh."
Perhaps Glima then perceived what his kin did not see of Caron's mind,
for as he recoiled in shock his kin held and from Caron drew a

smile:
"You see, honorable Glima, your hate and pride you must leave behind,"
and with those words Caron knew Glima's kin he could beguile.
"I shall hesitate no more and disclose a plan in which our descent joins,
270   for in such wasteful manner as ugly war there will never end the strife,
rather the only lasting ties that bind are the human roots of our loins—
I propose we each to make a child—each to lay with the other's wife.
Yes Glima, I knew I would see in your eyes that you would not agree,
but by now you know as well it is too late for you the crown to contest,
for if you did your Glimoiki shall surely then perish by your decree—
as you know I can summon ever greater forces at my behest.
Even were you this moment in rage to sever my crowned head
a decision upon you to take the crown or fight another is forced—
you are wise enough to see that the crown's symbol rules in our stead,
280   and, until our breach mended, from the crown's power you are divorced.
Surely I see you receive my simple words with contempt and disgust,
but if we a son and a daughter were to make and then royally wed,
the breach would be closed forever and certainly see this you must:
both Glimoiki and Caronite will be gloried from that matrimonial bed.
Now consider this dearly, both you, Glima, and your trusted close kin,
for I know a deep consideration of this for honorable Glima is a must,
but I clearly promise you this—I care not how offensive this plan's sin,
and if you reject it I shall grind your every weeping child into the dust."
Perhaps that moment Glima alone saw the dark pools behind Caron's eyes,

290   for only he spoke a rebuke and over his kinsmen voiced his objection,
"I say these words heavily, Caron, that these terms I deeply despise,
and I would say further any true hearted man would agree in rejection."
To this Caron showed no waver or discomfort, only a calm blink,
as he opened one hand at the Glimoiki in their gathering bleak:
"You are a blind fool, Glima, if from this offer of mine you shrink;
only look to your own kinsman for their validation of what I speak."
"Glima, you must accept this," one of the kinsmen then decreed,
"you see yourself only bloodshed lies aside from this offer sordid;"
"You shall each and all deservingly be cut down like a weed!"

300   Glima cried angrily, but to Caron he glared and viciously retorted:
"I see through you now like cold water to its darkest muddy deep,
and know this, lowly king—I know my own will you wish to break,
but rather I offer you this and advise that what you hear you keep—
I would sooner die than for you my own bastard child make."
At this Caron's hard eyes flashed beneath his circlet of gold,
and such was the horror of empowered rage within his glare
that Glima thought twice of the lives he had unwittingly sold,
while in disgraceful cowardice his kinsmen refused Caron's stare.
Yet to them no further word from Caron's set lips was uttered,

310   for he spurred his horse toward the Glimoiki and rode to their line;
with no fear his eyes fell upon them as their courage stuttered,
only for him to smile and offer, "Peacefully, gentlemen, let us dine."
With that he turned and to the waiting Caronites quickly rode,
raising his fist with the cry, "Peace, men! Peace has been made!
Now let us join and bury hate with our dead deep in earth's abode
and dream ahead to remember that this day to war we farewell bade!"
A cheer rose up then that shook the mount and its bloodied ground,
but the route of King Caron's cunning was not yet wholly done,
for as he rode by Glima flushed with his victory newly found

320   he said simply, "Put your protests away, Glima, for I have won."
But the outrage within Glima's heart only grew out of bounds:
"Know this, Caron, I will not abide unless from me my seed cut,
and even so, know that tonight during your ceremonial rounds
that my own wife I would sooner kill than have her be your slut!"
And with that Glima rode off to his cold mountain hall in a fury
to leave Caron pondering who of the kinsmen he could royally
bribe,
until the kinsmen with parting word and bow told him not to
worry—
only for Caron to note to his scribe that such kinsmen should
have died.

***

Yet when Glima riding came to his mountain hall of wintry
height
330   he found his lonely return met with neither a question nor a
glance,
for many of his people had watched the battle's wasting of their
might
and now knew that through dark war there stood neither hope
nor chance.
It too is said that a mournful change came over stout Glima that
day,
for when Medra, his wife, emerged from their hall in joyful
greeting,
Glima met her not but sat upon his horse and kept himself at bay,
refusing in guilt both to Medra and himself their love in meeting.
So he sat, until dismounting he walked silently by her in his
gloom,
and Medra following sought to ease his brow creased and
troubled:
"For with your wife's gentle hand forget war and its hard doom,"
340   she begged of Glima and smiled as her warming efforts doubled.
But looking upon the wife he deeply treasured only sickened him
more
and from his tight lips he resentfully spat Caron's despicable
terms,
revealing to his wife the betrayal of the kinsmen he unwittingly
bore,
and how rather than meet Caron's will he would rot with the
worms.

"For it is upon our every joy a stabbing pain he wishes to inflict,"
Glima growled, but to Medra that day the cooler wisdom went—
"No, Glima, from the greater need your pride you must dissect,
or would you rather all the Glimoiki children's lives be spent?
If one dark night of shameful lust is the only price we need pay,
350   then I say it is but a little price and one well within the long cost,
for what place in memory's forgetful years will rank one dark day
compared to all the innocent lives otherwise to be bitterly lost?
If no one else matters over your pride think then of your own son,
and know finally in truth as I tell you now that he is sickly
weak—
would you have then in the absence of any warring victory won
your boy reduced by vengeful Caron to a beggar blind and meek?
And I tell you that in this light I do not feel utter shame in this,
for we all have seen the sorrow now of wasteful war and death,
and unlike you as a wife I know that not all our duty is bliss—
360   yet the stain will fade with peace found on a child's breath."
But Glima turned upon his wife, lost in his stormy black mood—
"Think me a fool, wife, that I have not perceived these things?
Even though you sway me I see evil in this royal bastard brood,
and, rather than peace, only sorrow this cursed plan surely
brings."
They then fell silent, wanting nothing more of the poisoned talk,
and hearing the heraldry of the kinsmen in their horses' clatter,
hand in hand about the hall they took their last intimate walk,
knowing that by morning there would be no escaping the matter.

***

And so came the next dawn, and with it the harsh fateful day,
370   for at first light anxious Caron sent a party for the exchange,
none the wiser that Medra eased the making of his plan's way
by riding out before dawn's light across the mountain range.
There under night's starlit dome the two wives' paths crossed,
and none can say if between them came any word or glance,
while Glima unsuspecting in wine-laden sleep turned and tossed,
for Medra saw it better his hot pride not to once again chance.
As for Glima he woke to the sound of his child's stuttering cry,
and listening to the calming efforts of Medra's sister brought
tears,
when in the wake of her gentle singing voice he could no longer
deny
380   that his first and only born would never see youth's vibrant years.

So he slowly rose to don the thick pelt of his white winter fur
and, emerging from the archway of his hall into the morning's
glow,
his eyes fell on Caron's wife Aerin framed in a snow-laden blur,
only for him to be struck at once by the sharp arrow of Desire's
bow.
For known to none, hidden even from Glima's beloved wife,
was that in his youth Glima once met Aerin upon a green field
in that forgotten peaceful time before the gold crown and its
strife,
and between them came a sudden love wanting to be sealed.
In that time to Caron it was already arranged that she be wedded,
390   and even though rumors of her luminous beauty crossed the land
her wary father kept her guarded safe so not to be untimely
bedded,
for then in shame she would never hold a proper husband's hand.
But though her fairness remained unblemished by the long years,
her heart within slowly changed and became a thing icy cold
as over the lonely winters Caron's neglect dried out her tender
tears,
and transformed her to a likeness of Caron as his way took hold.
None of this poor Glima could see as she greeted him by name,
for his memories of that distant time left him suddenly blind,
yet he perceived his slip of judgment and sensed the vile game,
400   and this use of Aerin he judged of Caron a deceit most unkind.
As for Aerin the sight of Glima transfixed there in his white pelt
was as a man cruelly entombed in the mystery of his memory,
and though deep inside her a softer stirring she may have felt,
upon the deafened ears of her heart fell that sentimental reverie.
And in that moment Glima knew his destruction was complete,
for in sleepless nights to Aerin's field of old did he often return—
despite his love for Medra he sensed harsh Temptation's defeat,
and for his unchecked passion knew he would eternally burn.
Though in that moment it seemed best his own life to take,
410   he turned to see Medra's sister with his beloved son crying
and knew there was no decision for him, only his spirit to break,
to satisfy Caron's way and leave his every last goodness dying.
There in Glima's hall to Aerin a greeting the kinsmen blurted,
only for Glima to break the courtesies like a rock cast in a pool
by claiming in quiet defiance that the kinsmen best be alerted,
unless they too like Glima be used as Caron's devious tool.
As for Caron he gazed into that very same dawn and waited,
and while he was certain Aerin's work would be well ended

he knew that his trap for kind Medra must be subtly baited,
420   for to secure a way with her he knew upon her passion depended.
And to this end in his cunning way his plans were carefully set:
unlike Glima, who unsuspecting met Caron's plan of wives in trade,
Caron saw this as his resolution when crown and conflict first met,
so his thoughts close guarded had exercised their intent deeply laid.
How he smiled then when he saw Medra wide-eyed before his gate,
looking upon a rich city of Caron's dreams both wondrous and fair,
finding familiarity only in the stone communal hall of Springtide late,
resting at the city's center where a tower was met by a winding stair.
Caron rode to meet her and behind him his gathered guards grew—
430   dressed they were in bright flowing tunics of green and white,
with white flags on their raised spears snapping when the wind blew,
all in hope to diminish any fondness in Medra for her memory's sight.
When Caron patiently trotted to her with his open hand extended
she blushed in shame, but nevertheless before him she still held fast,
as her shame was that such a city might see its high days ended,
for if its foundations were to endure, so too the king must last.
But despite all his guile, it was Caron who in the moment mistook,
and with a courteous bow asked Medra not so quickly to despair—
rather, he asked she come to the wondrous city for just one look,
440   and, even if she were only a little pleased, then to his tower repair.
To Medra came then the wisdom of simple sight in her quiet reply:
"Caron who would be king, in this city I see the fruit of your intent,
but even were this city to spread to the heights that the eagles fly,
still the crown's hollow, hungry circlet would drive your discontent."
Yet to this wily Caron held his peace and to Medra evenly

retorted,
"Then I shall only say this once: a lesson of soil, Man, and power —
for all other things and thoughts distract and serve a reality distorted —
that we are our own judge, not some gods in their heavenly tower."
And so the sharp and stubborn exchange ensued between those two,

450 but in the end it was King Caron who had the better of the debate,
as Medra found herself at last in his tower with naught else to do,
for once she accepted his company she felt the cold hand of Fate.
From the balcony of Caron's tower that night Medra stood staring,
and to the distant mountains she lifted her voice in mournful song,
driven by sentiment for the high mountains' rosy dawn light glaring,
only to leave Caron listening as for her desire he began to long.
Her effort was not lost in the depths of the lonely darkening night,
for perhaps the pitiless gods woke and yet pitied her love's lament
to let her gentle song echo as an ally for Glima in his own plight,

460 and so, in war against Aerin's allure, to Glima's heart her voice went.

***

Unseen, then, came a hold to Temptation's cold meddling grip;
the wayward seductions ceased in their insidious ebb and flow,
and a threat whispered caused Caron's plans to suddenly slip
when a long-silent secret rose anew as a dangerous foe.
The rumor came first to Glima's own windy mountain halls,
and, though wary of what he heard, Glima welcomed a respite,
for in the mountain passes animals were taken from their stalls,
and the staunch Glimoiki tasted the dawning of an old fight.
To Aerin it was no secret why Glima hastily rode away,

470 and despite the tremors of fear beneath her angelic grace
she put away what she had once heard Caron timidly say
as she looked beyond to see a new seduction come in place.
For the threat was as Glima and all the elders had known,
that beyond the mountains in the forgotten world without

many generations ago dark seeds of doom had been sown
among the tribes beyond the snowy mountains' redoubt.
The lost truth hidden with the elders had reared its head,
for though none could recall through all the forgotten ages,
it was we who came of the Outlands and seized this homestead,
480   and of its dwellers of old they were driven out in wooden stages.
But of those we forced out the insult was not to be easily forgot;
our fields of green they lost to have in their stead hostile plains,
and so the bitterness held fast as we enjoyed the far better lot,
yet they unlike us held their slow revenge with patient pains.
While we comfortably prospered on our rich bountiful yield
those we displaced would regularly test the hard mountain ways,
ever searching for a pass unwittingly left opportunely unsealed
and by force of arms take back their prized loss of ancient days.
In those times to the hardy Glimoiki was charged the defense,
490   and for several ages the Outlander clashes were bloody fierce,
until their pace changed to leave them as a rumor to dispense,
as in Glima's time the high passes they did not try to pierce.
Yet Glima in his wisdom did not fail to preserve a stubborn
patrol,
even as the threat dwindled to a few farm animals to quietly take,
Glima intended never to abandon the passes without deadly toll,
for he ever envisaged a bloody Outlander storm soon to break.
It was from this concern that he failed on the Reddening Mount—
refusing to void his responsibility to the mountain boundary line,
he could only face Caron with a sharply diminished army count,
500   and so, with divided defense, elusive victory he could not design.
With such haunting thoughts Glima rode to the mountain ways,
and finding several bands of hardy Glimoiki armed for a fight
he easily forgot sultry Aerin and Temptation's long trying days
to join his clamoring people in their quick but violent delight.
Casting then their fear and caution not too lightly aside
they followed Glima as he hastened to the nearest way,
using the paths of old so the Outlanders could not hide
until at the last they were betrayed by a donkey's bray.
Then Glima fell upon the Outlanders with a furious shout,
510   so horrible was his assault that he seemed some warrior of old,
and with the Glimoiki rallied in rage the battle became a rout
until one Outlander pressed forward, a man both huge and bold.
There Glima's slaughtering madness was stopped in its tracks;
as his sword rang against that wild Outlander's ox hide shield
he knew he had met a foe that could equal even his attacks,
and despite another perilous slash the Outlander would not yield.

A mighty exchange of hack and stab erupted between the two
until Glima cried out that he would take the savage's head,
only to find in a blur of snowy wind that the man withdrew
520   leaving Glima alone with the man's mocking laugh instead.
Then in the sudden quiet Glima stood with a furrowed brow,
for though the Glimoiki took heart in the fallen savages bested
and Glima's pride unwilling this small victory to disavow,
he perceived from this one brazen man that he had been tested.
And as he stood with this unsettling development to ponder
the mocking voice of that savage echoed in the cold air—
"Prepare, prepare, soon in harshness you too will wander;
prepare, prepare, under the name of Borogos you shall despair!"
Now during that stark contest of the cold mountain height
530   Aerin paced her rooms deeply imbued with Caron's thought,
so that from the victorious purge of sudden Outlander blight
she could more easily secure the child she eagerly sought.
As mysterious night came she set her crafty wheels in motion,
having ordered a celebration in the halls with wine and dance,
she concocted a delirious atmosphere as her seductive potion
and grew full sure she would be the victor in rosy romance.
Beneath twinkling starlight Glima returned to his stone hall
still flushed with the violent battle's heedless red rush,
until he noticed the sound of song while in his horse's stall
540   and quickly joined his people with wine's sultry blush.
There is a reason that night sees a man's darker impulse—
and it was to this that stalking Aerin planned regress,
for as ignoble deeds are met by the sun with repulse,
so too Aerin clothed herself in a shimmering black dress.
In the deepest night the celebration began to slowly wane,
and lost in the quick ebb and sway of rich red drink
Glima sought solace from talk of battle and bruising pain,
so to his bedchamber he went with little power to think.
But there in the lonely dark depths of his drunken daze
550   he came upon lovely Aerin by the window in quiet song
and usurped by delusion he saw not through the wine's haze,
and embraced Aerin as the wife he had missed for so long.
Yet no darkness could hide the sins of men from moral sight,
for as Glima mindlessly spent his passion and pride to dust
the mountain wolves howled through the rest of the night
and echoed down the Reddening Mount to wake Caron's lust.
He rose from his bed then like the hungry craven undead
and stiffly paced to his high window to look out east,
until with the nervous thrill of destiny he shook with dread

560   deciding at last he would abruptly listen to his inner beast.
      In the still of his tower he ascended to Medra's room,
      only to find her startled from the howls and slowly waking
      to find a man before her unlike any gentlemanly groom,
      for lost in his self-drawn rage King Caron stood shaking.
      "It is done, it is done," wide-eyed Caron spoke with a hiss,
      "for tonight all things pass that were and become anew,
      so too for you, fair Medra, the end of courtship's bliss—
      best now to bend and yield, for I wish not to hurt you."
      Hearing the baying of the wolves Medra turned and wept,
570   for she knew all choice and chance were now spent,
      and closing her wet eyes against the shame she kept
      swore that from this sin the world would never repent.
      And with the dawn was felt no warmth in rosy light,
      as sleepless Medra was left by skulking Caron in her bed,
      she wished upon herself that all fertility be met with blight,
      that from poison seed all life should be quickly shed.
      But she knew not that cruel Fate had seized the reins
      and decided her silent wish would not unheeded fall,
      for ruthless Temptation would keep Its ill gotten gains
580   by sending greedy dark Death silently to Glima's halls.
      When the Lord of the Glimoiki rose from his leaden slumber
      he at first knew not why Aerin stood by with a wide smile,
      until in the clearing of his daze he saw his lusty blunder
      and saw in Aerin's eyes the depth of her merciless guile.
      Yet he left her untouched as he was silenced by his pride
      and to his servants' dismay walked about as if blind—
      but soon he understood that from his sin he could not hide,
      even as his wayward conscience set his teeth to guiltily grind.
      It was then by chance he found Medra's sister sadly weeping
590   and remembered how every morning his sickly son had cried,
      but as she neared like a ghost he felt a nightmare creeping,
      only to hear proof that in the darkest night his son had died.
      Amid the sudden chill of those words hesitantly spoken
      Glima sank to the deepest depths of Sorrow's black sea,
      and seeing the cruel levy of newfound life's bartered token
      swayed as if he were an old, leaf-shorn and vine-choked tree.

                              ***

      In the weeks that followed any doubts faded to clear certainty,
      for there was no hiding the fast take of wily Fertility's roots
      as both Medra and Aerin met the swell of their pending

maternity—
600   so too these tidings were crossed on swift messenger's boots.
For Caron and Aerin they both smiled at their plan well set,
but despite how Medra had spoke to Glima of duty and its place
there was no happiness for them as Caron and his queen had met,
rather the Lord of the Glimoiki and his Lady felt stung by disgrace.
And while the thick wintry snows melted in an early spring thaw,
Glima's kin saw in their lord a depression that would not fail,
for the sickly son he had lost left a void that continued to grow,
even as the kin sought with soft words his sorrow to derail.
Yet in that time of the mountains' fragrant Springtide bloom
610   Aerin would sit quietly by her window and patiently sow,
watching the look of Glima's eyes swell to that of cruel doom
until she let him feel the small child inside her kick and grow.
"A pity this is," he said to her one day with a slow thought,
"that this guiltless, unknowing child which I prefer to cherish
bears the unseen blemish of the sin from which it was brought,
and yet for it to be alive so much else in me has had to perish."
But Aerin replied with a query to the source of his torment:
"Good lord, what is it you make with such sorrowful chatter?
Ever I see you suffering in self-sentenced torturous lament;
620   better for you it is to look ahead and see happiness in this matter."
And to this Glima found himself with nothing left to say,
only serving to hasten Aerin to seek the aid of his kin—
too willing were they to serve her and keep their lord at bay
by enticing him with Outlander threat and a defense to begin.
Yet the rumor of their hasty lie swiftly shadowed the sky
so that Caron too took to raising his armed warriors' might,
only to return the surprise of a late summer Outlander war cry
with both Glimoiki and Caronites rallied for the fight.
What began as another small Outlander mountain raid
630   quickly roused the watchful Glimoiki into a vengeful tempest
to grapple with the Outlanders tighter than hair in a braid,
and in the middle of that bloodshed fought Glima without rest.
For Borogos he eagerly shouted,
and a duel no one soon doubted,
but among the red snow and gore
Borogos he could find no more.
In the fury of that sudden war
were wrought great deeds of lore,
for at noontime's solar height
640   a shout arose of sudden fright

as Borogos wearing a bear's hide
came forth with a furious stride,
and behind him many men to battle
intent to slaughter Glimoiki like cattle.
But in that hour of great need
Glima charged with his steed,
and hacking through the fray
sought Borogos to cruelly slay.
Yet those two would not meet,
650 for the battle tide caught their feet,
and hemmed by the mad fight
barely kept each other in sight.
Still the dead piled about those two—
how many, nobody ever surely knew—
for though Glima stood stubbornly fast
the wearying Glimoiki could not last:
when the Outlanders stood in full rank
the tired Glimoiki fighting spirit sank.
Only then did Glima look left and right
660 to see Outlander waves fill his sight,
and there in the evening twilight
thought he would perish in that fight.
But little did Glima or Borogos know
that messengers quickly crossed the snow,
whipped to speed at Aerin's behest
to summon the Caronites to the bloody test.
Hidden on high Caron had waited,
watching the battle sorely debated,
for he saw neither ally nor foe below,
670 but rather two threats bound in tow.
Patience was always his better thought,
for though victory he certainly sought,
something greater he began to taste
as through careless war's endless waste
his mindless foes would mutually diminish
before the bloody battle he sought to finish.
Only when he thought the Glimoiki would fall
did his rallying horns finally send their call.
The Outlanders turned with one horrified stare
680 to behold the charging Caronites' armored glare:
with their green and white banners streaming
Caron's knights rushed forward screaming.
Through the Outlander lines they crashed,

and Borogos then left with savage hopes dashed —
with a last vengeful roar he turned and fled,
taking his panicked few who were not dead.
Then it was King Caron who was astounded,
for though the Glimoiki had been surrounded,
twenty times their small number they had bested —
690   and that when they were not well rested.
Among his mounted knights Caron then rode satisfied and nodded —
from neither Outlander nor Glimoiki would he feel any more threat:
while Glima and his last men to their homes wearily plodded
Caron saw only his careful plans in constructive complement set.
For in his hidden heart he saw that with all his foes' strength spent,
that in his tower he would keep Aerin's bastard and his child
and care not to what places the low Outlander savages went,
or if the remnants of the Glimoiki joined them in the wild.
High in his tower he knew those children he could safely raise,
700   free of troublesome Glima and any boastful moral threat,
so that in all the land he and his kin would meet praise,
from green field sunrise to the furthest mountain sunset.
And so it may have been if upon us Fortune had smiled —
but not all comes to pass as we sometimes wish it would —
even Caron, for all his schemes, by Desire would be beguiled,
for not all turned out quite as simply as he thought it should.
While Caron went home with his knights in victorious celebration,
in the barren mountain heights there was no joyful digression
as the Glimoiki were one and all overcome with lamentation,
710   burying their countless war dead in a slow funerary procession.
And as Caron's people filled their city with song and dance
with his gleaming armored knights raising their banners in pride,
lonely and desperate Medra forswore her last suicide chance
and accepted the child within from which she could not hide.
For in those grisly and haughty tales of bloody Outlander defeat
she discerned the horrendous losses of her sturdy Glimoiki kin,
and guessed that their measure of death was of Caron's deceit —
to be repaid by her child as a new Glimoiki strength to begin.
So, fleeing the celebration to the tower's height she went,
720   until at last from her balcony she looked upon the moon's face,
and then to the dispassionate gods her every thought bent
in her last wish for indifferent immortality's merciful grace.

Up went her words to the black ocean of star-filled heaven,
and upon some sleepless, wistful god's ear they surely fell,
for that night against us new schemes the gods began to leaven,
sending swift Fertility for maternity's quickening to tell.
None knew what stirred in the liquid tides of fickle Fate,
or what lay ahead from the pain of mothers' membranes torn,
for our future rests in the hands of wily immortals who create,
730   leaving us none the wiser about any who are innocently born.
At the morning's first faint reach of bright-eyed, golden Dawn
from Aerin and Glima there was revealed a daughter created—
named Aerina for the warm spring breeze at her first breath
drawn—
and Glima's kin rejoiced as with a queen strife was now abated.
But to Glima he saw suspicion in the child's striking beauty,
for with her birth Caron's way was now upon them sealed,
and despite himself he heard the call of no fatherly duty
and knew the undoing of his hereditary title had been revealed.
No sooner was Aerina born than a messenger was quickly sent;
740   across the high mountains with Aerina's tidings he passed,
through the low paths and down the Reddening Mount he went,
until in late afternoon to King Caron's tower he came at last.
Within that stony height all was anxious and busily astir—
storm clouds gathered about the city on a cold rush of air
as Caron paced his chambers waiting with time a mocking blur,
while above him Medra writhed in agony upon her bed bare.
At the day's last hour her worrisome child came out—
our world that babe had unwittingly come to join—
signaled to all in the tower by Medra's wailing shout,
750   summoning Caron himself to behold the fruit of his loin.
Medra opened her eyes to the late storm's lightning glare,
eager to see her child now that pregnancy's wait was gone,
hopeful to receive a son in response to her desperate prayer,
and then grimly rejoiced by naming her infant boy Typhon.
But Caron was most displeased upon entering her room,
for to him the name he heard proclaimed was a vile curse—
"By naming this boy as you did you have sealed his premature
doom,
for aside from his namesake mountain-storm there are fates
worse!"
Then seizing his son by the feet he lifted him high,
760   and in a fit of black rage was ready his brains to dash,
yet he was stilled neither by child's squeal nor Medra's cry,
but by the sudden roar of wind and the storm's crash.

With a gasp he turned and held his son to his chest,
and though he claimed no faith in gods or pitiless Fate,
he decided it suddenly wiser their wrath not to unduly test,
nor by newborn blood spilled invite upon himself their hate.
Then he looked down on his son with renewed clarity
and whispered as his harsh countenance began to soften:
"Know this, my son, no matter the crown or pride's depravity,
770   that you are Caron's stock even if they call you Typhon often.
Upon you and within you there will be no Glimoiki taint,
and if you feel within you your namesake storm's wintry howl,
know that my blood beats in your heart without restraint,
so rebuke your vindictive mother's black hate with a scowl."
Then with a silent wave he emptied the dimly lit room
and turning on Medra with Typhon held to his chest
reminded her that even though Glima was once her groom
it was upon Caron's lineage Typhon's future would rest.
At dawn once again swift messengers were outward sent,
780   up the slopes they charged and into the mountains' embrace,
to Glima's stone carved hall their fleet intentions were bent
until they divulged their tidings to the Glimoiki lord's blank face.
And though Glima's kin at once rejoiced for the news,
Glima faded back in the finality of his moral defeat,
for then he knew his wife had been paid to Caron's dues,
leaving the downfall of their marriage's sanctity complete.
That day no weary messenger would meet rest at hand,
for Caron sent tidings of mutual birthright celebration,
and to his city summoned all the elders of our land
790   to bow to peace and the royal crown's final vindication.
All through that day Caron's city bustled with commotion
as he waited in his tower for his tired messengers to return,
expecting certain news of every elder's heart-sworn devotion
until he sought his room before the last evening light's burn.
And when all else in the dark rooms of the airy castle slept
Caron ceased his pacing and seized his son to swear an oath—
to his high balcony with long shadow in tow he slowly crept
as he considered himself and his crown, and a promise to both.
"Ah, pity you, you poor, helpless creature of mine," he sighed,
800   and was yet unaware that in the shadows quiet Medra hid,
"love you I would, but to the crown then I will have lied,
for all that I have done and have yet to do is for regal bid."
And while Medra watched as Caron held the sleeping child,
fear and pity grew upon her at this man she saw as a slave,
for though she felt in him unchecked greed grown wild,

she knew ambition's endless appetite would dig his grave.
So too Caron's counterpart could find no restful sleep;
no, the Lord of the Glimoiki in his halls wandered aimless,
trying to discern some holy pledge he could quietly keep
810   to dispel any curse about these two children blameless.
And when Glima at last fell to his relentless guilt's despair,
he stalked about his bed and lovely Aerin peacefully sleeping
only to look down upon his newborn child so wondrously fair
and leave his hall to the cold dark night bitterly weeping.
"For it is a cruel thing you have done, you gods on high,"
he cried to the black sky's dome as he cared for himself no more,
"to curse my sin on the breath of this innocent child's sigh!"
and with that he rode off, never again to be part of men's lore.

**

820   Onward trampled the restless fleet feet of Time,
and so the slow count of days ceded to years tallied,
one upon the other with seasons in four step rhyme,
until beneath the crown all our people were rallied.
But not all was met with such senile peace and joy,
for of the mountains none envied the Glimoiki's lot,
as with Glima gone and the death of his only boy
the Glimoiki could only look to the son Medra begot.
To Glima's false kin the festering blame finally went,
for even as Aerina's birthright embers continued to burn
830   it was clear that to Caron both Aerin and child would be sent,
and, as for Medra, Caron would never willingly let her return.
Then it was that the hardiest of our kind were broken,
and surely to this Caron must have gratefully sighed,
seeing the Glimoiki splintered without a word spoken
just by the ongoing lineage of their lord's blood untied.
Yet, as the gentle years passed and sturdy Typhon grew,
Caron saw a warning in the way the Glimoiki were sundered
and sensed whispers of a sneaking suspicion he not as yet knew,
nagging him in restless sleep that somehow he had blundered.
840   So it came to pass that in the eighteenth prosperous year
the power and glory Caron had sought now became a cage,
and he set his eyes on those about him with suspicious fear
until he tasted the bile of his self-spawned paranoid rage.
Within that high stone tower all was joy to our blind eyes,
yet ever deeper each year the vile poison's roots crept,
ever thinning that skin of the tower's innocent guise

left to conceal the old temptations so tenuously kept.
For if black suspicion had clouded Caron's probing eye,
it only deepened the divisions he had unwittingly created;
850   even had he not failed those subtle undercurrents to spy,
there was little that would have left those tides abated.
When in darkest night he then pondered his emotions' brood,
from within him something of his taut suspicions changed and grew,
so that as he sat and schemed and pondered a new wanton mood
he felt the roots of his melancholy distill to a potent, decadent brew.
Of this maddening liquor he then so gladly and steadily drank
until his very innards putrefied in the toxin of that heady potion;
none the wiser, it was the return of his own sins that he should thank
as he set about the worst of his crimes that he would set in motion.
850   For this thing that had woke within and seized him was black lust,
a voice that slithered through all his better senses like silent thunder
and ground his reservations of careful consideration to wistful dust—
all from the shaming of Medra and his will's usurpation by that blunder.
With each passing day his skulking stare grew sharp and bright,
so that at the dinner celebrations no self-serving praise would he utter,
yet careful enough he still could be not to let his hidden desire see light,
as even for him the new compulsion he courted drew him to shudder.
He became a man possessed by this darkening stain of unholy desire—
even to his wife it reached as their marital bond he wished recanted,
860   yet ever by anyone remotely queried his outrage betrayed him as liar,
for it was to his wife's daughter, lovely Aerina, that he became enchanted.
The crown he would stubbornly keep and forego the promise of any heir,
as in his selfish heart he now desired to make young Aerina his

wife,

and, for his son, sturdy Typhon, his sight the king could no longer bear,

but then schemed to destroy him through devious ingenuity of strife.

***

Now, of noble Typhon and lovely Aerina some things must be revealed:

unknowingly ensnared were they as their menacing sovereign schemed,

while their place and sway in the court was not to be concealed,

for as both the king's heirs they were free to do as they deemed.

870   It was said of bright Aerina that of all she was surpassing fair,

that none after could match her in the beauty of her features—

even her mother, Aerin, who would regard her with a jealous glare—

but it was Aerina's way that such notions were for unworthy creatures.

For within her the heart of her mighty father beat strong and true,

and just as hardy Glima would not suffer any petty, taxing rivalry,

so too Aerina would look away from her envious mother as she grew,

and found her desire drawn more to the intentions of noble chivalry.

The gods had willed it so that within Aerina her natures intertwined,

and through the hidden contest of her parents' very different ways

880   there came an outcome perhaps not even Wisdom had divined,

and was yet to be revealed in youth's quickly flowering days.

For more to noble Typhon as they matured her eyes were drawn,

and so it seemed all proceeded as the crown had originally depended,

until Caron sipped that potion of his heart to let a new plan dawn

that strove to shatter the very bond he had shamelessly intended.

Through those tangling bitter knots growing in Caron's dark mind

Typhon all too soon and unseen in this evil tragedy was mired,

for to him never would he yet believe there was treachery to find,

as all that he had been promised was not all that he desired.

890 No, for within Typhon the struggle between his natures was a riot,
less resembling either of his parents in his steadily growing might
until his prowess would accept no bonds nor stay obediently quiet,
instead giving rise to a man grim with noble passion and eager to fight.
To him Medra had whispered tales in the secrecy of the quiet night,
telling him of his name and waking within him crafty Glimoiki intuition,
so that only thoughts of wintry mountain heights gave him delight,
and left brooding melancholy over the burden of the crown's tradition.
So it came to be those first signs grew under Caron's own roof,
unseen they went as the skulking, crafty harbingers of our plight,
900 so that amid the very halls of our brightest all so selfishly aloof
they could bring upon us endless misery and calamity without respite.
For all too often great plans of men meet the mocking laugh of Mortality,
that hunchbacked spirit of the gods sent to keep our aspirations at bay
through the unraveling of grand ideas by the harsh demands of reality,
so allowing the gods on high to maintain on us their immortal sway.
And so it was set upon us that for all Caron's twisted intentions
that he finally gazed upon Typhon and Aerina not as his goal fulfilled
but as threats whispering to him from the shadows of his suspicions
to convince him the only rule and future was to be what he willed.
910 Age it was that drove Caron to partner his greed and black lust,
to believe that without an heir the gods could not will him to die,
leaving his hate full focused on Typhon like a storm's raging gust
that scatters Truth's fallen leaves to make all promises one dark lie.
"Death to all except precious Aerina, who will be mine,"
Caron concluded one night as reason failed him at last,
"and immortality to he who cuts the ancestral line!"

he claimed to the ghostly moonlight that silvery Luna cast.

***

Perhaps this dark bestial oath stirred the gods in their lofty tower—
then again, perhaps they were moved by ambition gone awry—
920 nevertheless, they cast their eyes upon us, pawns of their power,
to see if Fate's serpentine ways King Caron could yet defy.
For surely in their penetrating and timeless heavenly gaze
the turmoil of Caron's stained heart could not long be hid,
and awoke the bitter oaths of old of our lost innocent days
before blameless Typhon and Aerina came as Caron's regal bid.
Deep, then, rang the passions around these two Caron had created,
and the echoes soon beat near in wily Suspicion's pointed ears
to set this most elusive of godly messengers to work unabated
in making real the slithering shapes of King Caron's fears.
930 Upon leathery wings Suspicion descended one moonless night
and, transforming to shapeless shadow, into Medra's ear spoke,
summoning from long slumber her ire to set the wrongs right,
such that in the silent black night she bolted and suddenly woke.
"Tonight, tonight, upon this night the time has finally crept,"
she whispered earnestly to the dark with her keen eyes wide,
"tonight, tonight, this last night for all my tears bitterly wept!"
she swore and remembered her vengeful prayers denied.
Yet more clever was she, Lady Medra of the mountain kin,
than any in Caron's tower had ever thought to give her due,
940 for all Glimoiki knew that against the mountains none can win,
but to get their ends some other crafty means they must woo.
So to brooding Typhon her son this time she did not appeal,
rather with Glimoiki cunning she sought the indirect course,
and to Aerina tales of mighty Glima's deeds she began to reveal
as she pursued her newfound purpose without halting remorse.
For Aerina, Medra's mountain tales took purchase and whispered their call
as each passing day Medra upon Aerina ever so patiently worked her way,
and within Aerina grew vibrant visions of Glima before his untimely fall,
and ever more distant from Caron grew Glima's child Aerina each day.
950 Not that all such subtle things missed their signs and failed to be

noted:

for there were two eyes, cold and blue, yet not so readily deceived,

that jealously regarded the sway of one upon which they had once doted,

and so Aerin decided the match for her child's influence would be received.

Yet her sudden advance upon her bright daughter was met with repulse,

as Aerina looked upon the icy mother from whom she was estranged

and felt the pull of Suspicion's hand to question her mother's impulse

at the overtures that seemed so conspicuously and hastily arranged.

There came a melding of wits then that even Fate could not perceive,

for these three ladies did not sink into predictable venomous strife

960   as they surmised whom it was that they together ought to deceive:

their king, now the target of three—daughter, concubine, and wife.

And so they spun their three-way plan as the yearly Springtide neared,

all the while unseen by King Caron as his own schemes steadily grew,

for he, like those three, dwelled on him that to the people was endeared—

noble Typhon, who yet felt that to himself the elders ever nearer drew.

And at that yearly feast where we once gathered in peace and joy,

echoes of the bloody past came upon us once again with insidious portent,

ignored by Caron as he played with our fate like a lone child with a toy,

until the hardy but forgotten Glimoiki came with a tale of pitiful lament.

970   They told of fearsome Borogos returned with his wild Outlander tribes,

how he battered mercilessly at the craggy border like the ocean tide,

offering respite only at the greedy penalty of ever growing bribes,

even as he threatened to pour into our ripe fields green and wide.
To this threat Typhon took note and ordered the knights to muster,
and drawing his sword pointed to the mountains cold and white:
"I will not suffer abuse by this wild man and his empty bluster,"
he declared, "and we will put these Outlander savages to flight!"
But unseen to all was the motivation of young Typhon's heart,
that which was held secret despite the schemes about this prince,

980 and had it been known it would have torn Caron's court apart
to leave our black hearted king in leprous remorse to wince.
One night before that fateful Springtide to Aerina it was revealed—
summoned in premonition, it seemed, by this dire Glimoiki tale—
that Typhon would will a future other than that Caron thought sealed,
and so threaten Caron's dearly purchased regal plans to utterly fail.
For, proud though Typhon was, his wishes he never debated,
knowing full well the folly of Caron's kinder will to entreat;
rather the wiser to follow Medra and hold passions within unabated
until in full maturation their final energy would accept no retreat.

990 So it was that Typhon followed Aerina from the tower one star laden night,
knowing that when Caron's ambitions ranted she would wax reclusive,
and flee the stony tower alone mounted on a swift steed's nimble flight
to enter the city's adjoining woods where she could be stubbornly elusive.
But in the wisdom of tracking and pursuit to Typhon none could compare,
and so he came upon her alone in a meadow beneath night's black dome—
the very same where long ago Glima had found young Aerin in despair—
and beseeched lovely Aerina to linger before returning to their home.
"What troubles my prince, that he thinks from him I would surely flee?"
Aerina wondered, even there wary of lecherous Caron's inescapable jealousy,

1000 to which Typhon knelt and whispered, "Surely, you know what it

must be,
that I wish to give voice to things our king would surely consider heresy."
And taking his hand Aerina looked upon him and bid him to rise,
sensing that a moment had come to greater fulfill the three-way plan:
"Our lives have been found upon despicable crimes and poisonous lies,"
she said, "any more left to say can trace blame to only one crowned man."
Then Typhon set his teeth in sudden passion and glanced up to the night:
"Know what I tell you now as the dearest hidden truth of my soul,
that within I care not for king, nor crown, nor any royal birthright,
that I would rather have them all drown in some dark abyssal hole.

1010   Away from all this—crown, elders and Outlanders—I would swiftly ride,
and, passing over the distant wastes, press my way to the rocky shore—
all this, only if you and your love I could have with me at my side—
and to the depths of the gods' senile sea send the crown to pass from lore.
There is no redemption for the blood and guilt forged in the crown,
no salvation or pardon for the pitiful plight of our high Glimoiki kin;
no, for there to be promise for our kind, the crown must be cast down,
for none can escape merciless Justice in Its determined trial of sin.
I see we two as the future, but a future to restore the just past,
for within us Medra has stirred the pride of our Glimoiki heritage—

1020   from that strength recalled within is where our future must be cast,
so that we can be delivered from the curse of Caron's named lineage.
For though he is my father I never once looked upon him as such,
no, for I never saw else but distrust and greed behind his dark eyes—

I need only to remember how he made my mother suffer his touch
to recall that he has lately surrounded me with murderous spies.
And this other thing I tell with the certainty that the sun will rise,
that in his abominable vanity he now believes he needs no heir,
that he can cheat inescapable Death if his own son prematurely dies,
and supplant his own progeny by marrying his adoptive daughter fair.
1030   Now in this moment do not pretend that this lust you have not seen,
for I have learned through the hunt the certain look of cornered fear,
and such I see in you when you sense the king's wayward gaze unclean
as he seeks to pitilessly pierce you like an arrow into a helpless deer.
So tell me now if you agree, and a moment of chance I shall seek,
wherein this vile man and his cursed crown I shall both destroy;
but I will tell you as well, if against me you unwittingly speak,
then, against us, devastating retribution Caron will certainly employ.
Be wary, my love, but know that to you in the end I pledge to be wed,
not to satisfy any plan, but only for the goodness I see in your heart;
1040   even if Caron, or Outlander hate, or unseen scheme should leave me dead,
raise your voice in song, and even the Underworld shall not keep us apart.
These grim things I tell you now as my promise and solemn pledge,
and all that I ask in returned faith is that to me you remain ever true,
and before Caron's relentless pursuit that you neither waver nor hedge,
for in the end upon my bitter blade his waited justice will come due."
To his oaths luminous Aerina laid a trembling hand upon his chest,
and in hushed words gave voice to emotions long kept securely gated:
"Noble Typhon, you need speak no more of what we know to be

best,
rather know that as prince or exile, my love will never suffer abated.

1050   Upon us I feel the gods have levied Fate's hand to weave a design—

trapped then we may be, yet I see from it a fleeting sweet deliverance,

that it is this very threat that for each other causes us to immortally pine,

and, among our kind, in time our love will have eternal remembrance.

'For none like us have ever lived,' so in the court we so often hear said,

and though within us there is no purchase of vanity such as with our king,

it yet seems only as natural as the seasons that we are fated to be wed—

so let Fate's circuitous turn of destiny take us and serve as matrimonial ring.

And this I promise to you, that such oaths you have taken I now gladly return—

my love I give to you, and we as one beneath the heavens shall not be broken,

1060   even if to hold your hand I must surrender to Death's kiln my heart to burn,

gladly I would pay it, for in relation to love, is life naught but a fleeting token?"

Then, by exchanging these oaths of love and the overthrow of Caron's deceit,

free at last they reveled without care beneath the glittering stars of night,

until in the still seclusion of that twilight meadow their desire could meet,

and, for a time, they knew happiness away from demanding Fate's sight.

But when all these things the gods saw they gave only a tired lazy sigh,

until Fate became aware and hissed a harsh rebuke on the cool breeze:

"Is this not the way of mortals, to see deliverance only before they must die,

for if not, what need have they for we gods and our impenetrable mysteries?"

***

1070   So the die was cast, and to us all the world seemed wondrous and
fair,

but not so in the mountains high where the Outlanders tirelessly
raged,

where for our aspirations and our high schemes Borogos had no
care,

as he knew for not much longer could the Glimoiki keep him
caged.

It was in those grim days that upon each mountain he took he lit
a fire,

fueled in the cold by that which burns longest, the hapless and
lost dead,

and so their stench rose with the black smoke in each such
Glimoiki pyre

to set the disparate hearts of our people alight with both rage and
dread.

In King Caron's tower he brought the elders from Springtide to
hold court,

but, in his twisted way, it was an act to merely blind their slow
suspicion,

1080   for from his scouts in the mountains he had received a detailed
report

and counseled his war captains for armed parties of knights to
commission.

Despite the evils ever gnawing at the firmament of Caron's crafty
wits,

he yet grew all the wiser in the careful conception of a veiled
scheme;

like the starving beast that ever more readily sniffs out the last
edible bits,

so his faculties smoldered then to allow him to do whatever he
may deem.

But there too blindness can lay, and with it sly Fate's cruelest
humor,

that the desires of the scheme strangle the voice of the greater
goal,

to let the lurking dangers bloat and grow, hidden like a violet
tumor,

and cast the greater goal like a storm-tossed ship upon a jagged
shoal.

1090   In all these ways the many paths of Caron's closed mind were bent,

so that rather than thoughts of Borogos, Outlander, and mortal threat,

his greater cares were not concerned as to where those threats went,

but instead only how to secure his immortality and Aerina without regret.

Now in that moment he perceived Borogos and the Outlanders as a tool,

one to use as he had in the past to leave his rivals and foes alike gutted;

so it was he sought to play Typhon and the elders together as the fool,

and once done have the door wide to leave his lust in Aerina rutted.

Ever suspicious of all those that to the court seemed to be held dear,

he withdrew any notion of his decree on the threat of an Outlander fight,

1100   and decided only to his wife, Aerin, in secret to give a deceitful hint clear:

that he would let Typhon take the lead, and champion the Glimoiki plight.

Yet unwise Aerin did exactly as cunning Caron had deviously intended,

and that was to Medra to whisper how upon Typhon treachery grew nigh,

and that, if upon him their entire three-way plan now tenuously depended,

that from the tower he and the elders must without hesitation hastily fly.

So the warning passed from Aerin to Medra, and then to Aerina's lips,

to send Typhon with one small party of knights ready upon their mounts—

then the gods wept at last, for disaster is the sweetest wine one eagerly sips—

and off he rode with a trusted band of knights as prey for Borogos to pounce.

1110   But for all talk of Outlander threat, little safety there was in Caron's tower,

for the king waited ever so calmly with fiendish patience to vent his rage,

berating Typhon as coward and deserter until all sought some corner to cower,

leaving him to exercise his bloody malice on the three now trapped in his cage.

To Medra first he came with eyes flashing a madness of red anger and guilt:

"Curse on you, Glimoiki witch," he seethed, "for the traitor you conceived!

Now in our time of great need he betrays all that I have so carefully built,

no doubt guided by you and the poisoned suckling of your breast he received!"

But then rage met rage, for in Medra her long hidden Glimoiki fury took voice,

and she rebuked Caron, sensing the nearness of her mortality's emancipation:

1120 "Cursed man, now pay your debts, for in you lies the source of Typhon's choice,

seeded that stormy night when I suffered beneath you my body's desecration.

To the windy mountain hall of Glima I told him to ever so hastily remove,

and there to hide among my kin until this Outlander threat has finally passed—

a choice all the more bitter to you, for of his survival you will not approve—

especially if it be you and not he that before Borogos is then untimely lost!"

Then Caron stood transfixed in the unseen reality of his scheme's fruition

before he silently closed the door to Medra's room and her life as well,

but he held, and in cruel mercy offered her a final, false hearted petition:

"Your life spared, if you tell me from whose lips the threat to Typhon fell."

1130 Yet Medra turned away, refusing to the last to be used as Caron's tool,

and from her sleeve plunged into her tender belly a hidden slender knife

to pierce her vital innards, and so she sank into her own body's bloody pool—

but as she lay in the moonlight she smiled, at last free from her life's strife.

"Go then, foul woman, and know soon you will meet your bitter offspring,"

Caron seethed, but stood over her until she sighed her last long breath,

lingering so that he knew to some last tenuous thread of life she did not cling,

for no reason but to excuse himself from any crooked blame in her death.

Nevertheless, he bowed his crowned head as he stood over Glima's widow,

curious as to his continued pause in the dark mystery of that deep night

1140   before passing into the halls like a gold circlet above stalking shadow,

to send even the lesser many-legged creatures of the tower scurrying in fright.

In such a way he came upon his waiting wife clothed in mortuary black,

and for a moment he was stilled again, struck by her now frigid beauty,

as she leveled upon him an incendiary gaze that did not waver nor slack,

for she knew now that it was he who bore no loyalty to any oath's duty.

"Many years you sat alone at night rather than heed the soft call of Desire,"

she hissed, "yet never once until you demanded it of me did I ever stray,

and then only under your persuasion that it was what our future would require,

but now against your adoptive daughter you fail to keep incestuous lust at bay!

1150   I know that this night it is my wretched life you have finally come to take—

if so, then know that I have made my peace and your way I will not resist,

for I seek to hurt you, and the last sprout of remorse within you I wish to break,

and if to your own inner hell I can so send you, to that I will gladly assist."

So went the vein of her defiance, but from Caron garnered no further rage,

and with his hands about her ivory throat her soul's strands he began to tear

as he felt in the darkness the misty gray glow of the gods' cruel theatric stage:

"My wife, you never once knew what burdens I would so willingly bear."

When it was done, to the cold stone floor he let his wife carelessly drop;

there he stared out her window to the funerary pyres of the mountain peaks

1160   and felt no fear, seeing his wife cut down as one more stalk of an adversarial crop,

the bitter harvest sown of greed and deceit that fickle Fate ever so warily speaks.

Then he trembled as his heart stopped before resuming like a crash of thunder,

to realize in the madness of his spousal slaughter that he had been caught blind,

only too late now to see how Medra and Aerin had induced his fool's blunder

to give young Aerina time to evade his craven trap and deceive him in kind.

For bursting into her room he ruefully discovered she was not to be found,

and summarily to the tower brought her servants all trembling with dread

until the tower he sealed to let fly a murderous frenzy without merciful bound,

and to the last pursued them until that tower was littered with the bloody dead.

1170   Not until day's stark first light from that dreadful carnage did he finally emerge,

and ordered the tower locked until with Aerina he would triumphantly return—

to this false claim, he ordered all his gleaming knights upon him to converge—

while he schemed to imprison Aerina with the tower's dead and let them all burn.

Such was the mad fury that had unseated the sanity of our once cunning king,

that when a remaining elder advised less haste in this sudden armed campaign

Caron seemed to ignore him, and ordered his war captains about him in a ring,
so that they might witness Caron as he beheaded that wise elder with disdain.
"We have sat too long content and secure in our strong-walled city of stone!"
Caron cried out and caught the sun's golden gleam as he raised his sword high,

1180 "Now, with me ride to war, and crush every savage Outlander body and bone,
until they all, and their beastly master Borogos, on the cold mountains die!"
Then as one the might of our rallied armed host let out a terrible shout,
so that we in the city and far fields felt our victory was already cast,
and watching that charge of our embodied fury we knew no doubt,
and rejoiced as the mountains echoed our trumpets' communal blast.

***

Quickened then was the tremulous passing of our diminishing days,
as in the way a diseased man with his last breaths feels all the lighter,
so too we flew headlong and pursued without care our various daily ways,
only believing every next dawn our fortunes would shine all the brighter.

1190 Perhaps it was as well for Typhon and Aerina in the cold mountains high
in those days, ever moving from mountain hall to well hidden snowy height,
in hope careless of the twin threats of King Caron and Borogos that drew nigh,
but nevertheless bringing to them what remained of hardy Glimoiki armed might.
And so it was the long held defensive passes were left without watchful eyes
as King Caron pressed into the high mountains with ever more vigorous raids

to unwittingly unleash the beast who all agreed they could utterly despise—

for Borogos had returned, wearing bear hides, and eagle's claws in his braids.

Like a storm the Outlander fury surged into the unguarded passes of old,

like the raging sea that reverses the proper flow of flooding rivers and streams,

1200 so came the Outlanders and Borogos to reap bloody vengeance of depths untold,

and of the remaining Glimoiki folk they crushed their lives in horrified screams.

But such a massacre could not long continue among the Glimoiki and be unmet,

for those few who survived ran and were caught by Caron and Typhon in turn

so that these two both gathered their armed host to wager war's brutal bet,

each then vowing that upon a pike they would set Borogos' head to burn.

Yet the Outlander chief held a far greater horde than had ever been seen,

and, familiar with the mountains after the counting years of bloody strife,

set his various warrior bands about the peaks in a way that was most keen

as he sought a crafty victory, like the way an unworthy man courts a wife.

1210 Would it have been different had the gods not sat in their tower to laugh,

while Fate pursued the completion of her intricately conceived and silken design,

but rather if just one god had taken a stand and with the rap of a heavenly staff

decided not to abandon us, and left not our doom for vindictive Fate to malign?

No, for so many oaths had been bitterly cast in the lonely confessional of night

that even the gods in their lofty palaces resting besotted, ambivalent and content

could not have denied the convoluted stirring of Temptation and Fate to set right

all those sins that had been committed with no thought to their levy of lament.

Perhaps they gathered in audience to witness our tragedy in its final spasm,

much as the puppeteer looks upon his stringed servants with masterly arrogance,

1220 so those gods looked down over their food and wine to one mountain chasm

where subtle designs converged upon us to leave us without a second chance.

In the late afternoon Borogos received word and began to draw in his noose,

for his wily Outlander scouts had hid in many shadows cold, dark and deep,

so that as Caron and Typhon refused to let their own pursuits run loose

their movements came back to Borogos as his own deadly secret to keep.

And deadly it was as the red sun painted the snow with portent of slaughter

as Borogos let loose an eagle, the winged signal for his trap to finally spring,

when rumor came that not only hardy Typhon , but as well old Glima's daughter

neared; that eve every god's aid they needed if to frail life they intended to cling.

1230 For it was cruel Borogos' intent to defeat his foes one after another in turn,

much as he had learned at the hands of Caron in his last disastrous defeat,

that a stubborn old log cleaved in two is all the easier and faster to burn;

so he sought to reveal his plan and at last make his brutal ambition complete.

Ever faster flew the shuttle of restless Fate's tapestry to summon our doom,

and so like a swift sailed ship or diving hawk with an unknown broken wing

never seeing how quickly the jagged shoal or rough ground can so greedily loom,

we like they pursued our course blind to what the next moment could bring.

Into the depths of a wide mountain valley wise Typhon sent a small band,

and how alone their footprints seemed in that expanse of untouched snow,

1240   when the hellish cries of Outlanders ripped from their throats across the land

to leave Typhon's little circle of startled men seemingly with no place to go.

Hardy to the last, those few Glimoiki were, and stubbornly held their place

even as the heights darkened with the downward rush of an Outlander deluge,

for in the noble warrior's sturdy heart beats the truth that war has no grace,

and from its brutality only the weak of hand or heart foolishly seek refuge.

Yet watching from the valley's lower mouth was Typhon with his men,

and further away Aerina as well, skillfully trained in the art of the bow,

waiting for Typhon's word to pull arrow from quiver and loose right then,

so on that final day from the Outlanders the Underworld's toll would first grow.

1250   But when noble Typhon and his men raised their swords and began to charge,

summoning to them the forward band standing now ever so perilously alone,

Typhon noted with horror how the Outlander horde continued to rapidly enlarge

until their dark mass swelled and pressed around him like muscle about a bone.

And though the hunt they had pursued now threatened to end in checkmate,

Aerina let her stinging arrows fly without sign of any worry or mortal care,

rallying the Glimoiki around her to follow suit and not let their courage abate

as they sent a storm of missiles that impaled any Outlander flesh left bare.

Yet, even under the mounting carnage by so few Glimoiki quickly wrought,

Borogos roared for his hordes to continue their charge and offer no retreat,

1260   for he knew that from the Glimoiki no easy victory could ever be

bought,
but rather the only answer was to inflict a slaughter unsparingly
complete.
But such was the utter devastation of the bitter Glimoiki arrows at
first
that the Outlander rush broke and stumbled over its own
mounting dead
to leave the first to engage the Glimoiki like a mist to a man dying
of thirst,
so quickly consumed were they, that the Outlanders were filled
with dread.
Typhon then united two of his three-part Glimoiki host,
and such a feat was no light thing to casually boast,
as with Borogos' roar the Outlanders kept to their pace
and pursued Typhon in a most deadly and tiring foot race.
1270   Yet here too the Glimoiki seemed to enjoy Luck's sway,
as in regrouping with Acrina Typhon had the battle his way,
but seeing the Outlander hordes close a circle complete
Typhon knew this day could well bring his final defeat.
But in the clash of arms there was no more time to think
as the battle had stepped off from Fate's merciless brink,
even as the Glimoiki fought with a rage of godly power,
startling the immortals high in their heavenly tower.
For it seemed that in every blade a Glimoiki could wield
came the strength to hack through helm and sturdy shield,
1280   so quickly through Outlander bodies did they cleave
that those wild savages found it difficult to believe.
Even when some great one among them issued a roar
and stormed in like some mad, ravenous boar,
quick Aerina took aim and let a merciless shaft fly
to drop that great man with an arrow through his eye.
And wherever the Outlanders threatened to open a gap
Typhon emerged with the fury of a thunderclap,
such was the gluttony of his murderous red blade
that foes toppled before him like wheat cut in a glade;
1290   such were the growing piles of tangled Outlander dead
that the Glimoiki found themselves in a fortress of dread.
The slaughter only doubled to its own merciless decree,
collecting its victims like so much careless autumn debris,
as the Glimoiki drew rank ever more to their cause devout,
fighting tirelessly from the horror of their bloody redoubt.
Once more wild Borogos saw his vast numbers of no use,
as upon the tight Glimoiki he could rein only limited abuse

and suffered still the blight of Aerina's feathered curse,
her unfailing accuracy making the suffering all the worse.

1300   But as Fate adorns her halls with gleaming mirrors so that history must repeat,
like the cold images of Fate reflected between those panes with untiring repetition,
so as well her designs for us work their way until her heavenly pattern is complete,
and as to those of us caught in those threads, no kind ear awaits mercy's petition.
In this way it was that King Caron came upon the heights of the valley unseen—
or so he believed, refusing the wariness of his scouts in that unknown wintry height—
and looked down upon that maelstrom with a vision of Outlander victory to glean
if only they could destroy those two that had emerged upon them as a pivotal blight.
For Caron's keen gaze failed not to discern where the battle's balance rested
as he watched another mighty Outlander chief fall stone dead with a pierced eye,

1310   for if Aerina was subdued and Typhon dead, only Borogos remained to be bested,
and such a path to glory King Caron's ambition convinced him to recklessly spy.
But no sooner had he ordered his gleaming line of armored knights into the battle
than Borogos set loose that harbinger of ruin, the hoarse squawking black crow,
to summon a second surge of Outlanders to fence Caron's knights like cattle—
and then to the Underworld did the sad march of the fallen ever faster grow.
For a moment King Caron shuddered in the temptation of a victory obtained,
as his widening eyes swept over the converging storm of wild Outlander might
that stymied his knights' charge and from Borogos left them sorely detained,
to leave Caron's golden crown glittering like a lost star in the eve's long light.

1320   For Borogos could no longer contain his own fury and loosed a

booming cry
that through the wide valley's length relentlessly and
thunderously boomed,
so that his fearsome towering might none there could ever claim
to deny
and say that about this Outlander chief nothing but cowering
terror loomed.
For Borogos in his might hefted and threw a massive gray stone
and the Glimoiki warrior it hit was left with no unbroken bone;
such was the berserker rage of Borogos now run without reign
it seemed that day no challenger would he be able to claim.
But opposite the battle from Borogos came a dire challenge
indeed
as Caron led his knights onward, each like a demon on his steed,

1330   to stubbornly smash their way free of the rough Outlander
surprise
and turn the ambush's tide to run them down to their demise.
So it was Caron wrested the advantage and reformed his line,
but still that day knew that Glimoiki help he could not decline.
With a wave of his sword he led his stalwart knights gleaming,
and stampeding forward they roared beneath banners streaming
until Outlanders before them fled, no matter how stubborn or
stout,
to shake their entire host with creeping dread and ruinous doubt.
Yet Borogos that day would not dare suffer a debilitating defeat
nor accept any hesitation or return of stark humiliating retreat;

1340   rather he seized from a nearby warrior a long and heavy spear
and raising it high waited until he had a casting sight clear.
Then with all his brutish strength he let that spear fly,
and yet holding true it toppled King Caron with a cry,
for it was his speeding mount that the shaft had impaled,
and with Caron thrown down his charge was quickly derailed.
There where he rolled to a halt the Outlanders quickly flew
only to once again learn where the king's reputation grew:
for even alone he fought like some tireless champion of old
and upon that field there seemed none more brutal or bold.

1350   But to their lone king the knights in haste emerged to rally
and upon the Outlanders inflicted a new slaughter beyond tally;
yet following the lesson of Borogos' spear the Outlanders held to,
and any shaft they possessed to a knight's mount they threw.
Like crows they converged on any unhorsed and fallen knight
to overwhelm him with their relentless, numberless might,
until some Outlander with the wicked swing of a battle axe

dashed the knight's blood to leave him dead in his tracks.

Steadily then the deadly battle ensued until all in that valley were enraged,

whether it be Glimoiki, Caronite or Outlander no quarter was there to offer

1360   as these three hosts ripped and tore each other like wild-eyed beasts caged,

all the time their deaths clinking like bloody coins into Fate's cold coffer.

But in the midst of that battle bitter came something without a single hint,

stirring Fate from her idle observance of her pitiless and tightening design:

a development that went unseen until upon a wayward blade there was a glint

to reveal he that within this doom Fate had neglected to utterly entwine.

For it was none other than mighty Glima who had come to join the fray,

the lost Lord of the Glimoiki returned in rage as a prophesy of doom

to summon the meek living ever faster as inescapable Death's prey,

so that over us Fate's deepening shadow could threateningly loom.

1370   But it was to Fate in particular that this development sorely stung,

for among her mirrors and tapestries of destiny's intricate design

there was no thread or weave upon which Glima's return could be hung,

and so his every action seething Fate hastily busied herself to malign.

Yet, stayed were her hands in the ruthless working of her bitter craft,

for the gods took quick delight at the surprise of this unexpected turn,

and soothed Fate with the dispatch of Death and his three-pronged shaft

under the promise that by night her cold demands he would surely earn.

So it was, and better sense could not cause Glima's steaming rage to abate

as his noble heart thundered with the charge of his heavy-hoofed steed,

1380 for within him all voices of guilt, shame, and regret had lost their debate
to the savage call of haughty retribution's vindictive and bloody greed.
And as he neared his burning eyes fixed on those two he hoped to save—
Typhon and Aerina, their likeness brought to him etched atop a ram's skull
by she who was shortly after abducted in Outlander raids and taken as slave,
Medra's sister, whose faultless loyalty Glima now rode to repay in full.
None more than Borogos fought to disavow the sight of Glima nearing,
for to Borogos any rumors of Glima from Glimoiki captives were refused;
mocking the mighty Outlander as he beheld Glima felling a bloody clearing
only to haunt Borogos with memories of Glimoiki prisoners cruelly abused.

1390 But for all in that moment such concerns were not regarded
nor their memories given any due measure of purchase or pain,
for in that cataclysmic spasm of violence sanity was discarded
to more freely fill sullen Fate's cup with blood's wine-red slain.
Among heroic lore sturdy Glima's advance was a testament of valor,
unstoppable in his righteous rage through Outlander lines dashed,
leaving many a mighty savage chief emptied to death's gray pallor
until against Borogos himself this legendary charge of Glima crashed.
For Borogos had turned from his threat to the struggling Glimoiki ring,
and charged its batter and end to a bloodthirsty Outlander war-chief,

1400 while he sought to engage the blade of none other than Caron the king
to leave him slain and depose his stubborn knights with bitter grief.
Powered then by will of cruelty not to give any hard fought ground,
Borogos felled Glima's charging steed by cast of his last long

spear
to bring down the roaring Lord of the Glimoiki with a horrible
sound,
and for his return hopefully inflict upon him a price violently
dear.
Then how all those fearsome men were tested,
as champions none would suffer to be bested,
and so these three came at each other without rest,
all for the sake of fickle Glory's behest.

1410   And seeing them Typhon's fury erupted
as he rallied Glimoiki defense corrupted;
while Aerina loosed from her bow a piercing flurry,
quickly to the looming clash Typhon sought to hurry.
For to him was known the likeness of Glima's face,
described to him by Medra in tales of Glimoiki grace,
so that if the old lord one day sought to return
his identity need not be a wanting thing to learn.
Upon standing, to wild Borogos Glima at once turned,
and in both their eyes pitiless rage hotly burned,

1420   but even though Borogos made the first attack,
Glima met him in kind and turned him back.
And so these two met like warring titans of old,
none other could claim a deadly contest so bold —
yet it was such a claim that drew he who waited,
once again perceiving opportunity's trap well baited.
For rather than call his gathering knights to steadily draw
Caron instead stabbed out like some penetrating claw,
and hacking his way through Outlander lines tangled
felt his deliverance and destiny ahead enticingly dangled.

1430   He cared not then to whom his deadly surprise went,
for through the din he saw those two wounded and bent,
but for old memory's sake upon Glima he first neared,
and with one last Outlander felled the way was cleared.
Without a sound treacherous Caron lunged and stabbed
while Glima and Borogos grappled, sword hands grabbed.
Into Glima the pitiless blade plunged just above his hip
and tore through until Borogos as well felt the sharp tip.
Glima screamed as from his belly his life's blood erupted —
unstrung, he fell away, his life's strength utterly corrupted —

1440   only for King Caron with a heave to pull his sword free
and glare down on the Lord of the Glimoiki with glee.
But such a vile murder did not escape completely unseen,
and, though some distance away, the facts Typhon did glean,

for with wild Borogos staggering and clearly weakened
the guilt upon wily King Caron's brow only deepened.
But mighty Borogos shrugged off his wounds and rallied,
and with savage intent sought to increase the dead tallied.
For through war's filth he perceived the bright crown of gold,
and lusted it as a trophy in his old age to proudly hold.

1450　But treachery met treachery then in black-hearted kind,
for in that moment a wise plan came to Typhon's mind —
breaking free of the battle near Caron, "Father!" he cried —
bitter irony that by paternal call was the reason Caron died.
For Borogos then swung his blade with a mighty slash,
and unseen it hacked into Caron's shoulder with a crash.
Through bone and lung and dark heart it pitilessly tore
to leave Caron collapsed in mortality's gore.
No sooner had these two deaths transpired,
than old Fate ever more hastily conspired,

1460　and fueled by pitiless Death's bountiful yield,
desired that no life should know Mercy's shield.
Despite the felling of Glima and King Caron, Typhon knew his foe,
and hastily sought to depose him who had wrought so much woe,
for Typhon believed with Borogos dead surely the battle must end,
as Outlanders were not keen to war without a chief their will to bend.
But with Caron bested it was the crown wild Borogos wished to take,
and in that moment so tempted was he that his warrior's sense did break —
to his outstretched hand the cold blade of Typhon's sword duly leapt
so that not only the crown but Borogos' hand Caron in cold death kept.

1470　Yet ever more than just a hand from the Outlander chief did raging Typhon demand,
for in this brutal exercise of justice upon Borogos no final mercy could he describe,
and so with dawning futility Borogos bellowed for his chiefs to aid in a final stand,
as if in bloody defiance to entreat cold Fate, and her black enmity somehow bribe.
But so entwined then was he in Fate's design that to him was

turned a closed ear,
to leave him staggering before Typhon with his own ambitions
suddenly dashed,
and left unstrung his bestial Outlander resolve with a debilitating
realization clear:
that alike under both Typhon and inescapable Fate's wrath he
was to be smashed.
And so the death of Borogos came ever so quickly under the
waning light of dusk:
that Typhon thrusting drove his blade straight through Borogos'
snarling face,
1480   to obliterate the Outlander's feared countenance and fell him like
a dried husk;
there Typhon let him slump dead between Caron and Glima as
his resting place.
Yet to weary but triumphant Typhon came a swiftly
disheartening dismay,
as he like all others began to recognize the empty glory of mighty
men felled,
and with grim fury saw that these great deaths upon the battle
held no sway,
so that, like the greedy rushing tide, Death's appetite had not
been dispelled.
No, rather it was that pitiless Fate now sought to settle all the
gods' scores,
for in our tragic fall so many vows and sins alike had unwittingly
been fused
that to leave any measure forgotten would leave the gods feeling
as whores,
and anger further all those divine forces whose subtle energies we
had abused.
1490   Though we lowly mortals wish in our power the course of the
world to steer,
we attribute what we both dispense and suffer to the gods in their
lofty tower,
and so create the spell of Fate upon mortals and gods alike by the
gods' fear:
for if we were to have our way, then upon us the gods would lose
their power.
So under this threat Death, at Fate's call, whipped the slaughter
double time
to levy upon us the judgment of the gods in reaping faultless
Typhon's life,

and so etch upon us the message that we all must suffer the guilt of any crime

that threatens the world with such endless bounds of war's murderous strife.

Such was the debate among the untouched gods in their cloud-dappled tower,

and, bothered to miss a beat of the folly that Fate wrought, they halted Time,

1500   stilling his tireless turning of the wheels of existence in their heavenly power

before loosing him and looking back to our own woeful fate mired in grime.

There they beheld Typhon fighting as if the war weary world was about to end,

ripping the lives from the Outlander hordes as for the crown they made a rush,

only to meet the darting death of the blade of he alone who refused to bend,

even as the press of the endless Outlander mass threatened his will to crush.

And there to him he sought the last hardy knights to gather for a final stand,

hoping by such to create for Aerina and the last Glimoiki a chance to retreat,

yet he knew as well the knights would rally to none other than royal command,

forcing upon him a final desperate plan of failing hope to grudgingly entreat.

1510   Then in eve's fading light from Caron's brow the golden crown he duly seized,

and raising his head high let the sun's long rays upon him enticingly dance—

but unknown to all was that Glima lived, and, witnessing the crown he wheezed;

ire stirred his limbs in death's daze as his vengeance perceived a last chance.

For though he lay wounded mortally, his soul clung to a last fleeting flicker

to be sure in stubborn revenge that to devouring Death Caron went first,

and so, enlivened by the sight of the crown rising his heart pounded quicker

as his hand closed on his sword to at last quell tireless

retribution's bloody thirst.
But to this threat unseen with back turned Typhon stood unknowingly blind,
his wits bent upon the sudden surge of Outlanders to depose the crown's might—

1520   such was their rage that a new thought of tragic irony took form within his mind—
that despite his broken vow to avoid the crown he still would not live the night.
Even as the last scattered knights were felled he stubbornly held for his final stand,
swearing that for Aerina's sake the entire Outlander army he would alone fight;
he shouted with doom until a bolt of agony broke him and numbed his hand,
so that dropping his sword he looked down to behold his call of Death's blight.
From his belly his life's energy steamed where a bloody blade had erupted,
and staggering on his feet he turned to find Fate-cursed Glima slumped dead,
the price of Typhon's broken vow—the crown to disavow—paid in life corrupted,
so that sinking to his knees his once stormy strength he knew from him had fled.

1530   Then it was with despair that Typhon looked across the Outlanders as a storm tide,
for such it was that they became in their black-armored boiling berserker rage
that his spirit believed from this tempest Aerina could neither escape nor hide,
so to grasp a hope for her he sought to make himself the focus of their rampage.
In death he saw redemption in the burden of the royal crown's deceptive gleam,
and its chorus of multiplying sins ever increasing within its band he denied—
for with Aerina saved, his bargained soul the gods could do what they may deem,
so seizing the crown and with fading breath to the heavens then he defiantly cried:
"Never again, you gods on high, shall one be cursed with this crown of doom—

to your heavenly tower and its darkest dungeon imprison this careless curse
1540   so that none like I ever again be played the hapless fool as Fate's groom—
take it now as I cast it high before Death sucks my soul into his black purse!"
With those words he cast the crown high beneath the echo of his oath sworn,
and like a star it rose for Aerina to see from the valley's darkening gloom
for her to shudder, as with his cry she knew from him his soul had been shorn
to let Fate banish her and the last Glimoiki to an inescapable Outlander doom.
But then, with Typhon lost, the gods finally surmised in full Fate's tapestry cruel,
and hearing the echo of his last oath honored it with their own heavenly reply,
for Fate to spin in rage as before her they stood unified to contest her in duel,
so that she skulked away as their crackling bolt blasted the crown from the sky.
1550   "Let them stir and sob, these infantile deities, in their selfish fit of pointless pity,"
Fate muttered in her mirrored hall knowing the gods wished such an ending be cast,
"for capricious as you fools may be no one escapes the Underworld's silent city,
and no matter your flights of regret none of you can reshape the woven past."
But Fate herself was moved in reflecting on she who was separated from he,
and so looked from her loom to the wintry heights and the battle in its final throes
to the lonely sight of desperate Aerina, her eyes devouring an end that would be
at the hands of angry savages who would heap defilement upon her mounting woes.
Then it was that Aerina lowered her gaze from the last felled Glimoiki to shiver,
for before her was the sudden and swift end all Caronites had inwardly feared,
1560   and looking away from bloody war she trembled to see but one

arrow in her quiver,

stunning her to the bitterness of life's vitality soon to be lost in death that neared.

But in that last moment the oath she held with her lost love whispered throughout

to let her perceive a way to seek an end at least of choice and honor on that day—

with a beat of her heart and drop of a tear it solidified until resolute, without doubt

that the divinities in ageless times ago must have willed it to pass in such a way.

And then to lonely Aerina went the course of her own legend's divination

as she raised her voice in a slow song of sorrow so immaculately pure

that upon any heart which still beat with desire it wrought utter ruination,

such that in her presence and beneath her song no will could long endure.

1570   Nor was it heard in that valley alone, for her voice defied any celestial bound

to ripple on eternity's waters, so that even Time slowed his faultless pace,

until it echoed through the silent Underworld and pacified its guardian hound

to rouse Typhon's spirit from death and fly unseen past that guardian's face.

To the sky above the valley his will soared to fulfill that solemn lovers' vow,

that between Typhon and Aerina was spoken one night seemingly so long ago—

a memory buoyed by heavenly messengers who acquiesced with a silent bow,

and let their woe seep to the valley below where their wept tears fell as snow.

When Aerina's song was done, to the heavens she let her last bitter arrow fly,

in the hope that at some mercy her tender heart the returning tip could pierce

1580   to free her from this bleak world of melancholy and grief with a silent cry,

unblemished in her slender grace by the ravishing of any Outlander fierce.

Yet it was no god, but Typhon himself who took that last arrow in
its flight
and, reaching down, held Aerina's hand in the fold of his
unearthly apparition,
so that he embraced her to the last, and she felt no pain in
mortality's plight,
to desert the Outlander horde in a final act of Fate's ordained
contrition.

***

So it was our sins were paid by Typhon and Aerina on that
wintry height,
but such was yet to be known as we waited about the Springtide
hall
for some news of our knights and king engaged in the desperate
fight,
and in its outcome what shade of future would upon us
inevitably fall.
1590   But no tidings came, for on the field of battle only Outlanders
remained,
as with our heroes every knight and Glimoiki were sprawled cold
and dead,
lost among war's indignant passion between the desperate cries
of the maimed,
inciting the anxious, vengeful Outlanders to flee that scene of
disgusting dread.
As one they moved, without Borogos or any other chief to order
them still,
for, in their eyes, with Typhon and Aerina lost by other than their
own hands
their embittered rage was left unmet, and so ever more the
desperate to fill,
until without need of any chief they charged forth in their wild
warrior bands.
And so the lonely valley was left in the unearthly silence of so
many spent lives,
a lost place left to the frozen dead, haunted by the unheard hiss of
Fate's loom
1600   to whisper a soon coming day ripped by the wailing of so many
widowed wives,
while buried in the mountains' snowy blanket their men would
find their tomb.

But of all these things we as yet in ignorant bliss knew naught,
and so we waited within our walls for an uneasy day and night,
until with messengers riding out in rising trepidation we were caught—
but when they too failed to return our mood turned to chilling fright.
So it was that cold day our treasured customs made a departure swift,
for aside from tower and crown we had lived lives of surpassing ease—
shelter, food, drink, and the three-fold security they imply are a gift,
and soon forgotten until in need Nature's harsh laws we must appease.

1610 For in those years with Caron as our gold-crowned stubborn king
we in our daily ways knew or cared little for distant Outlander strife;
rather, we about our evening table ate in plenty within our walled ring
never believing in the law of opposites, that Peace belongs to War as wife.
But such was the nature of that wild bond that we suffered its divorce,
for too many of us, senile with content, lived that dreamy life of denial
all too unaware that upon us Fate's design would still fall without remorse
to leave those who would suffer tragedy's disillusion to face a harsh trial.
Yet some few of us stirred that anxious night for lost scouts yet unheard,
and grabbing what we could in the darkness from the city stole away,

1620 haunted by a vulture, that harbinger of Underworld thirst formed like a bird,
and doubled our pace for fear that upon our resolve dalliance would hold sway.
Better it was that from the doomed city we wary few had so hastily evacuated,
for that dawn down the Reddening Mount the Outlanders in fury quickly spilled—
if only so many of our brave kind had not in old upon the Mount been devastated,

perhaps the Underworld's stores of broken Outlander men we could have filled.

Not so, not so, and what of our naked city and its terrible fall shall not be told,

for none were left to take up the hungry bladed sword and the bitter pointed spear,

other than weeping round-faced boys and their hobbled grandsires weak and old,

to stand hapless and hopeless in pathetic rank upon the wall and shake with fear.

1630 Such then as a boulder rests upon a shore and to the rallying waves thinks little,

but under repeated blows its defense fails to the obliteration it thought slept,

until with one last thundering roar that boulder reveals its eroded nature brittle;

so too fell our city, as in our old undue confidence ruin ever so stealthily crept.

The sturdy walls, left without defense, the Outlanders quickly breached,

only to pour in like the relentless surging tide and explode in a vengeful riot

so vile and merciless that to the gods even unruly Death for peace beseeched,

until with lightning to set a pillaging blaze our screams the gods sought to quiet.

Among our flaming city's funerary pyre Caron's stone tower stood to the last,

bolstered by his corrupted ghost in a final futile act of defiance's temptation,

1640 but in the roaring hellish heat the well-set stubborn bricks lost their sturdy cast,

and the tower duly collapsed into itself, roaring in a plume of utter ruination.

***

Such then came the pitiful end of all that we had hoped to achieve,

leaving those scattered bands of us who yet lived to ever further flee

until in a barren cold place we were forced to finally settle and grieve,

for we had found our eternal exile beside the threatening black
sea.
And so, here we find a sad plight from those passed gloried
times,
where for our sins dwindling generations scrape up the moral
cost—
yet in the cold of night we huddle not under the burden of crimes
but rather in memory of Typhon and Aerina, our heroes untimely
lost.
So, muses, sing the sad course of our tale,
revive our noble dreams for the young to know,
let not our old gilded memories fade and pale,
and, among our ghosts, find a new hope to sow.

Tumbleweed

—or—

An Ode to a Well Endowed Gunslinger

Now, I remember when I was just a little fella',
like that lawman before me I'll be a story tella'.
Seems like only yesterday I done got caught
walkin' out the store with somethin' I ain't bought—
I remember the sheriff's greasy hand grabbin' my arm,
and how I done looked up in wide-eyed alarm.
"Set down, boy," that fat lawman said—
you know, he was quite overfed,
but in stories he was well read.
"You listen carefully to the law this time,
'cause I'm gonna tell you the bad life of crime."
So's I sat myself down and started listenin',
but I'd rather been in the jailhouse pissin'.
But this here is the story Lawman Bob told me,
so listen good, else its lesson might get lonely.

Hmm hmm hmmm, hmm hmm hmmm
Lawman Bob, he's a slob
tells a story, full of glory.

"In our little town of Tumbleweed
there once occurred a horrible deed;
listen here whiles I tell it to you,
I'm a lawman son, straight true blue.
My tale might be unsavory sleazy
but on this Sunday morn hot and breezy
if your childhood morality is clingin'
get runnin' while the church bell's ringin'.
Now just hold on one second more,
'cause I needs to reload my chaw."

Hmm hmm hmmm, hmm hmm hmmm

Then he slurped and burped and spit—*thweep*—
"Got you 'tween the eyes, you varmint snake creep!"

Hmm hmm hmmm, hmm hmm hmmm.

"I say, open those big ole ears boy,
this here tale ain't no childhood toy.
Now it all began out in the desert waste,
where for hard livin' it gives you a taste.
There was a clan of dumb ass Cajuns,
took a likin' to huntin' them Injuns,
and they was all mean, every last one.
But none done rivaled their youngest son,
born so ugly he brought tears to his momma,
for simple snorin' he shot his sister Donna,
then his ma went hollerin' to the boy's daddy
but that crazy old coot was drunk and crabby.
Now, that pig-nosed boy, his name was Ted,
and when he come to town we was full of dread.
He carried on him a big pistol named Cracker,
the first painted harlot he met he sacked her,
and cussin' over a two bit charge he whacked her.
She went a'cryin' in her best dress to Lawman Jed,
but Two Bit Ted went and shot him in the head.
Now we thought our little town would go unruly,
but you see those lowbrow ladies loved Ted truly.
People said he walked funny from ridin' horse,
but we all knew the unspoken truth, of course—
Two Bit Ted was damn ugly and scraggly lean,
but he possessed something mighty between;
just nod your head if you know what I mean.
Even whiles Ted took to loathsome drink
and like a cowpuck he'd sometimes stink,
still the mayor's wife herself asked him to dance
just so she'd feel that danglin' snake in his pants.
Soon all the town ladies offered their romance,
and us poor little cowboys didn't stand a chance.
In short time we all grew vengeful lusty,
but in gunslingin' we were none too trusty,
so to Ted we sent good ole Preacher Bill,
but I guess that man lost the high Lord's will.
Next time we saw him he was drunk and lewd,
before God he gave a sermon bare skin nude—
man that Two Bit Ted sure was shrewd.
How our poor Preacher Bill became unsightly
as he took to parading with harlots lightly,

all while Ted laughed in the house of ill repute
knowin' we was too chicken to shoot."

Hmm hmm hmmm, hmm hmm hmmm
Two Bit Ted, had balls o'lead
so he said, born in a pig shed.

"Now we was real close to despair,
even our horses started lookin' fair,
but when we was about to give up hope
in come to town some dandy Yankee dope.
At once we took to callin' him Wild Eye Willy—
he had one eye straight, the other went hilly-nilly.
He claimed he was some sort of book-smart teacher—
don't rightly know, he saw nothin' with our preacher—
wed he was to a rich old maid and leeched'er.
I tell you that boy was wise in the ways of man,
why he done showed in our town I can't understan',
I don't reckon now if he was crazy or brave,
but the boy certainly carried on like a knave.
Now even though his eyes was crooked
we took his hand and eagerly shook it,
he said he appreciated havin' new friends
but we told him on a favor that all depends.
Not knowin' Two Bit Ted he done took the deal,
and before he knew it he became a lawman for real."

Hmm hmm hmmm, hmm hmm hmmm
Wild Eye Willy, his eyes a-silly,
he was dumb, sucked his thumb.

"With those eyes rollin' crazy
Willy set off without bein' lazy.
He strolled right on over to Ted's bordello,
where on the porch Ted was drunk and mellow.
'Now you listen here,' Willy declared,
but with threats Ted weren't scared.
No sooner did Willy's first words fly
then Cracker fired with Ted's grin sly.
After that Willy had no pride to lose,
'cause he done pissed in his shoes.
But to Two Bit Ted's dreadful surprise
his booze-glazed eyes were tellin' him lies—

where there was one, he done seen two.
With a spit and growl his flatulence blew —
'Come back at noon, ye cowardly skunk,'
Ted cried, 'and try me when I ain't drunk!'
A-feared of his life Willy ran with legs loose,
he moved faster than crap through a goose,
and gave Two Bit Ted a real good hoot,
but Willy was stubborn like stank in a boot.
He wasn't givin' up yet,
he told us not to fret,
he'd devise a revenge well planned,
but who he was lookin' at I'll be damned."

Hmm hmm hmmm, hmm hmm hmmm
Done in rhyme, tales take time
Lawman Bob, what a job.

"Now as night drew on Willy changed his socks
while in Ted's house the ladies lifted their frocks.
Willy came up before that house of ill repute
and pistol in hand he started his dispute.
'Two Bit Ted's a girl!' he bravely mocked,
then out Ted came, with whiskey crocked.
He fetched his gun belt and a bottle of gin,
the rest of him was shameless naked pigskin.
He looked at Willy and dropped his booze —
that varmint, he reckoned he couldn't lose.
'Yer goin' to hell,' Ted swore and spat,
'I'm a gonna kill ye, an' that's that.'
Now Wild Eye Willy proved he weren't no rat,
'cause he done stood tall and replied to Ted's chat.
'Humor the brevity of my discourse,
it is time for you, Ted, to hit the road.
Your privies are like those of a horse,
but your behavior is akin to a toad.'
So listen to me when I tell y'all
Ted weren't lookin' for just no brawl,
he honestly looked to kill our Willy,
but Wild Eye knew booze makes men silly.
Ted's hand darted for his trusty Cracker
but instead he grabbed his fat tally-whacker,
and here comes the twist to this yarn —
Wild Eye couldn't hit the side of a barn.

He sent all his bullets a flyin'
and people all over started dyin'.
For his wicked ways one caught Preacher Bill—
he done died emptying himself from his still.
Out the window came his loaded chamber pot,
when it hit Ted it split his head like a fruit gone rot.
Nasty old Two Bit Ted had finally bit the dust,
holdin' tight in his hand his partner in lust.
Then Wild Eye Willy retired from law in fame,
but in the end I guess it's all a downright shame.
You see, each of us who took from Ted a pretty dame
all soon heard in the dark, 'Oh dear, you're so lame.'

Hmm hmm hmmm, hmm hmm hmmm
Two Bit Ted, now he's dead
this tale's done, hope ye had fun.

Dissociated

Four stories are laid out in neat stacks across a counter top, their white paper contrasting with the dark blue surface. Before them stands a man lost in confusion, perplexed as he stares at the four stacks. After some time he decides it's the last stack in particular that holds his attention but, when he reads the words on the first page, he comes to the unsettling conclusion, and the absurd certainty, that the story before him is *this* story. Somehow, in some way, in some impossible conundrum of time, creativity and illusory reality, this story exists before him, written and complete, before he himself has fully conceived it. He is yet to write it, yet it's already written, written with an ending, but that ending is yet to occur; the idea's primal form coalesces in his head, yet it's already complete, and the tale and meaning of its creation locked in the writing.

He scratches his head.

"Four more?"

He looks up from the stories to the woman sitting on the other side of the counter.

"Well, aren't you the creative machine." A grin pulls at her lips at the faint echo of her sarcasm. She stirs her tea, her gaze rising from the stories. "Can I take these?"

He blinks, rubbing his forehead as he looks across the stacks. "All but this last one."

"Still a work in progress?"

He tips his head. "Ah, yes, still a work in progress."

She gives him a nod. "Okay."

***

He stares at the front door to his house. The counter with the stories is to his left. There are two new tales next to the one he can't figure. He compels himself to lift the first page, his unease such that he has to look at what's written. Sure enough, he reads this, concerning his staring at his front door with two new stories completed, and reads that he read it—it's an imploding case of infinite regression that's almost coma inducing. On cue, her voice comes to him and she says what she said before in that story, which is really this story. In both cases he swoons with the dizziness of it all.

"Two more," she says. "Where do you get the time?"

"I haven't slept." He looks to her and asks what he knows he has already asked. "Where do you come from?"

She looks up and taps her spoon on the rim of her mug. "What kind of question is that?"

He points to the door and looks back to her. "Where do you come from?"

She shrugs, a sober expression in her eyes. "I've always been here. You know that."

He stares at her. To him, the cryptic simplicity of her answer is no answer at all. He rubs his forehead and looks back to the door.

Sitting there, she opens a hand to the door. "I think you need some fresh air and the warmth of the sun on your body. Why don't you go outside?"

"I don't know," he says with a sigh, but then his fists clench because he knows the answer. He can read it in this story, right after this next sentence. He forces himself to swallow, and when he finds his voice, it comes as a whisper. "I'm afraid to go out there."

"Why?"

He thinks for a moment. He hasn't read that far ahead. "I, I really don't know." He frowns as he waits for the rest of his thought. "Right, that's it. I'm afraid of getting lost." In the absence of a response from her, he turns to see her reading through one of the new stories. "Do you like it?"

She nods as she continues to read. "This hits a little close to home, don't you think?"

He fidgets in a fit of self-consciousness before answering. "Just another tale of madness and mayhem, of love and loss." He shifts on his feet, a nervous laugh bubbling from him.

"Oh, come on now," she says through a pleasant smile, seeing through his dodge. "There's more than that."

"Well, they say you should write what you know, right?"

"Now there's a loaded statement." She looks up, studying him for a moment before looking into the dark depths of her tea. "You should stop hiding."

He opens his mouth, but he has no reply.

"So this other story, you're still working on it?"

His gaze falls to the neat little stack as he scratches his forehead. "I'm not at peace with it yet. You know I can't let them go until I'm at peace with what's in them."

She nods, but her gaze is on the story, this story's title. Reading any more will summon a caustic rebuke, his typical reaction to those who pry into his unfinished work. She looks back to him. "So, it's called 'Dissociated'. Hitting even closer to home with this one?"

"I don't know. I'm not settled on the title."

She opens her hands. "I think it has potential. Run with it."

He looks back to the door.

***

He leans on the counter top, setting a new stack on its dark surface. He glances at this story, still sitting in the same spot. He can't resist the temptation to read farther. It festers within him just the same as it fosters his growing anxiety but, whenever it waxes he worries that he'll read this and find that the story has, with an ominous undertone, come to a sudden stop.

But it hasn't stopped, and it isn't quite finished.

Then a thought occurs to him — more a notion of curiosity — that gives him pause. Perhaps his stories and his creative impulse are the workings of some vast, complicated mechanism within him, and hitting the keys that type his words are nothing more than variables of an intricate lock working through its secret combination. He wonders what it might reveal, what the end effect of it might be, when that last variable — that last word — answers its summons and finishes the puzzle. It would explain the lock tumbler-like click of his keyboard as he types.

He stares at the title of this story and lets his breath go.

"I'm very confused. And I think I'm a little crazy, too."

***

The new story sits untouched beneath her gaze. "Can I take it?"

He blinks and looks to her. "What?"

She pats a hand on the story. "Are you done with it?"

"Oh, sure, yes." He glances to the door before looking back to her. "Can I ask you something?"

She opens her hands. "You can ask me anything. You know that."

"Where do you take my stories?"

She smiles and points to the door. "I take them out there."

"So, you're like a courier?"

She holds her smile, but there's a quizzical look in her eyes. "Well, somebody has to take them out there or they'd just pile up in here. We couldn't have that, right?"

He frowns. "No, that would be disastrous."

She tips her head. "You know, you should try going out there yourself. You never know what might happen."

He fixes a sharp glare on her. "That's exactly why I don't go out there, because I don't know what might happen." He falls silent, but reconsiders. "Sometimes, though, I really want to go out. I want to be out; I don't want to have to wait for you. These things the stories say, I just want to say them myself. I have a voice, you know, and I'm tired of hiding it. Actually, to tell you the truth, I wouldn't mind giving it away so that I can have some peace and quiet. You know it never stops, these things in my head. They never leave me alone."

She shrugs. "Some day they might."

"What? Don't ever say that."

A notion of surprise at his outburst passes over her gaze. "It was your idea, not mine."

He opened his hands. "Don't you see? Wherever these things come from, that's a part of me. Whatever drives that, I don't know what it is, and I'm not always happy with it. I want to be left alone sometimes, I want peace from it sometimes, I want things to be quiet in my head sometimes, but at the same time in all those times, it's an integral part of me, and I'm afraid what I would, or wouldn't be, without it." He shakes his head as he rubs his face. "Would I still be me?"

She puts her elbow on the counter top and rests her chin in her hand. "Oh, I don't think you'll ever have to worry about that."

"How? How do you know that?"

"Simple. If you stop, then I won't have to come here anymore because I won't have anything to take out there," she says, pointing to the door again. "And that, you see, is simply not the way it was meant to be. We were meant to have these little meetings of the minds, and I was meant to take your stories out there. It's the natural order, the systemic process of things, like the turning of gears."

"Don't patronize me."

"I'm just trying to get through to you. Consider this. If this little routine we have came to a stop, what would we do with ourselves?"

His mouth opens, but then he frowns. "I don't have an answer to that."

***

At last the time arrives when his anxiety wins out.

He moves to the counter and stares at this story. Nothing new has come to him, so no other story has been added to the counter. It makes for a lonely moment because he wants to talk to someone, but there's only one person he speaks to, and the hungry void of her absence is overwhelming. He enjoys her company, even if it relies solely on the sporadic production of his creativity to churn out new stories. He looks to the door, debating with himself.

In the end, he looks down at this story. He flips the papers over before flipping the last page back to read the ending. His face falls.

"In the end, I just had to know," he reads aloud as the thought occurs to him.

He puts the paper down. He walks to the door. He thinks of the title, and it starts to make sense. He can feel it, can feel the sense of peace growing within him. It's time to go, time to let it go. He hesitates before opening the door.

He peers out. It takes a few moments, but then he understands the timing of the story, why it was written when it was, why it is being written, why he will soon write it again, why he must, and why its circuitous nature forms a timeless singularity.

"In the end, everything has to come back together."

So he departs, and rejoins the depths of his self.

About the Author

Roland Allnach, after working twenty years on the night shift in a hospital, has witnessed life from a slightly different angle. He has been working to develop his writing career, drawing creatively from literary classics, history, and mythology. His short stories, one of which was nominated for the Pushcart Prize, have appeared in many publications. His first anthology, 'Remnant', blending science fiction and speculative fiction, saw publication in 2010. 'Remnant' was followed in 2012 by 'Oddities & Entities', a collection spanning horror, supernatural, paranormal, and speculative genres. Both books have received unanimous critical praise and have been honored with a combined total of twelve national book awards, including honors from National Indie Excellence, Foreword Reviews, and Readers Favorite. 'Prism' marks Roland's third stand alone publication.

When not immersed in his imagination, Roland can be found at his website, rolandallnach.com, along with a wealth of information about his stories and experiences as an author. Writing aside, his joy in life is the time he spends with his family.

ALL THINGS THAT MATTER PRESS, INC.

FOR MORE INFORMATION ON TITLES AVAILABLE FROM
ALL THINGS THAT MATTER PRESS, GO TO
http://allthingsthatmatterpress.com
or contact us at
allthingsthatmatterpress@gmail.com

Made in the USA
Charleston, SC
21 July 2014